DIANA FINLEY was born and grew up in Germany, where her father was a British Army officer. After a move to London, at eighteen, Diana spent a year living with nomadic people in the remote Pamir mountains of Afghanistan – an experience about which she wrote several stories and accounts. These helped secure her first job, as a copywriter and then as writer and editor of children's informa-tion books for Macdonald Educational Publishers.

A move to North East England meant changing direction. Diana took a degree in Speech and Psychology, and worked for many years as a Specialist in Autism, publishing a professional book on that subject. In 2011 she completed an MA in Creative Writing with distinction at Newcastle University. In 2014 her debut novel, *The Loneliness of Survival*, a moving family saga, was published. It is now published by HQ Digital, HarperCollins, under the title *Beyond the Storm*, as is her second novel, *Finding Lucy*. *The Lost Twin* is her third book.

The Lost Twin

DIANA FINLEY

ONE PLACE. MANY STORIES

HQ
An imprint of HarperCollins*Publishers* Ltd
1 London Bridge Street
London SE1 9GF

This paperback edition 2018

First published in Great Britain by
HQ, an imprint of HarperCollins*Publishers* Ltd 2020

Copyright © Diana Finley 2020

Diana Finley asserts the moral right to be
identified as the author of this work.
A catalogue record for this book is
available from the British Library.

ISBN: 9780008331078

MIX
Paper from
responsible sources
FSC™ C007454

This book is produced from independently certified FSC™ paper
to ensure responsible forest management.

*For my wonderful family, especially Terence,
who encouraged and supported me through
all the ups and downs.*

Chapter 1

1970

Marie

'Push, girl! Push!' Sister Bernadette growls like an angry bear, gripping my left leg so tightly her bony fingers press painfully into my thigh. It feels as though I'm being tortured. What am I doing here? I want my ma. How could this possibly be happening? God, how I want my mother. What would she say to this …? What would she say to *me*? No, maybe I don't want my mother.

'Oh, oh, you're hurtin' me, Sister,' I can't help gasping with the pain.

'Don't make such a fuss, girl! Whose fault is it you're in this mess – you tell me that, you little whoor?'

I turn my head to the right, away from the furious hostility of Sister Bernadette, to look at Sister Aileen's face. It's a gentler, kinder face – a soft, rosy-cheeked face. Right now I feel in great need of kindness.

'Sure now, you're nearly there, Marie,' Sister Aileen says quietly.

1

'Just a few more good pushes, girl, when the contractions come, and it'll all be done, thank the Lord.'

I try to focus on the woman's face, her smile, her soft brown eyes, gentle as a fawn's. But the pain is fair tearing me apart and I can't concentrate on anything. Another contraction grips my whole body like a vice. I let out a long, agonised scream. I can't help it. The sound of it fills the room, echoing as though the very walls are screaming back at me.

'Ahhhhh! It's killin' me! Sisters, can you not give us something to take the pain away? Oh God, oh God, oh God!'

I arch my back and try to lift the great swell of my belly off the bed. Sister Bernadette's furious face, all screwed up in anger, descends on me. She yanks my leg fiercely up and back.

'You stop that, you wicked girl! Taking the Lord's name in vain! The pain's your punishment for what you've done – and fair punishment it is too, to be sure. There's nothing will take that pain away, Marie Tully. Likely you'll have it for the rest of your life, and rightly so. You deserve it.'

As Sister Bernadette bends close and hisses those words at me, tiny drops of her spit strike my face like vicious little bullets. The look she gives me is one of total disgust, and her grip on my thigh tightens further still.

'Now, open your legs and push the poor little bastard out! You were happy enough to open them to get it *in* there.'

Sister Aileen tuts softly. She wipes my face with a flannel and gently pushes the damp hair back from my forehead. Then she moves down the bed to examine me, peering under the sheets.

'Nearly there now, Marie – I can see babby's head! Ooh, here it comes now … yes, the head's nearly out … just another push, dear … yes, oh yes … here it is!'

I feel an intense burning sensation and a primaeval scream bursts out of me. A moment later a shudder goes through my whole body, and then … a sudden feeling of great release.

Slowly, slowly, the pain subsides. Sister Aileen is gently easing the baby out. It slithers onto the waiting towel like a slippery, wet fish, with no effort on my part.

'It's a boy! You have a beautiful little son, Marie!' exclaims Sister Aileen, smiling broadly.

'Hmmph! I don't know about *beautiful*,' says Sister Bernadette with a scowl. 'He looks scrawny as a rabbit, considering the girl's been the size of a battleship these last weeks!'

She takes the baby roughly and rubs him with the towel. He splutters, sneezes and then finally gives a thin wail that brings tears to my eyes.

'Oh, he's crying! Oh poor little baby. Be gentle with him, Sister, please. Oh please pass him to me! Just let me hold him.'

I try to reach for him, but just then my entire body is consumed by a further spasm of pain.

'Aaah, no more! Please make it stop, Sister. I can't stand no more!'

Sister Aileen lifts the sheet again. Her soft hands gently feel all over my swollen abdomen. 'My, but there's another one coming! It's no wonder you were so big, Marie – you're after having *twins*, girl!'

'*Twins* …?!' Sister Bernadette huffs and tuts, her brow furrowed with disapproval, as if producing *two* illegitimate babies is twice the sin of one.

Thank the Lord, the second baby is born much more quickly than the first. A few more contractions and it's out.

'Another boy,' Sister Bernadette announces. 'Even skinnier than the first one. Get the girl cleaned up now, Sister Aileen, and then put the infants to the breast. There'll be no milk yet of course, but let them suck anyway. Get them used to it. They'll need feeding up, and we'll not waste good bought, powdered milk on them, not if it can be helped. Sure, we'll need to get them looking a deal bonnier if anyone's going to want to adopt them!'

Sister Bernadette stomps out of the birthing room and it's as if the sun has suddenly come out. I'm holding both my darling babies close, one nestled in each arm. As I bend over to each side to kiss my sons, tears spill down my cheeks.

'I don't want them to be adopted, Sister Aileen!' I wail. 'I want to look after them … if I can.'

I hug them to me protectively.

'My wee children … you're beautiful, so beautiful … my beautiful boys. I don't want to give them up.'

Sister Aileen looks at me and shakes her head sympathetically. 'You're not much more than a child yourself, are you, Marie?'

'I'm nearly eighteen. I'm not a child.'

Sister Aileen sighs. She leans down and kisses my forehead. 'Will your family help you, dear?'

'Me ma, back in Ireland, knows. She was right mad when she found out I was expecting. Said she'd do what she could to help, but only if I gave it up. 'Course we didn't know there were two of them then. I can't ever go home though. Me da doesn't know. Ma said he'd kill us. She's the one gave me some money for to come here to London. Said there was plenty of people wanting a baby. But I can't! I can't give up my own child … my own *children*, Sister. That's why I'm come here to St Agatha's, when I heard there was this mother and baby home in London. What am I going to do, Sister Aileen? How am I to care for two babies?'

Chapter 2

1970
Marie

My feet ache something terrible from trudging the streets to Kentish Town Council Housing Office. It seems to be miles. My thin shoes are wet through. In the cold, the damp leather has chafed the bare skin of my feet, rubbing it raw in places. I've no socks or stockings. Rain dribbles from my hair, soaking through my collar, gathering in a freezing rivulet on my neck and back.

Never mind, I tell myself, trying to be brave, *the Housing Office will make sure we have a roof over our heads and a bed to sleep in tonight.* I pull the baby blanket closely around Barry, and tuck him further inside my gaberdine coat. He's wedged in on my right side. There's a sad space on the left. I'd shoved a jumper down to try to fill it. It's where Donal should be.

At last we get to the council offices. It's a dreary, forbidding scene. Barry's screaming by now, wailing at the top of his voice; he must be hungry, as well as cold. The official sits unsmiling behind his desk, while I stand, holding the baby. No chair for me.

The man raises his eyebrows at the sound of the baby crying, and sighs wearily. He looks at me like I'm dirt.

'The baby's hungry,' I explain. 'He's crying because he's hungry. Is there somewhere I could feed him?'

'This isn't a bleeding nursery, love,' he says. 'If you want somewhere to stay tonight, we've got to get on with filling in this form. You can go outside somewhere now and feed the baby if you want, but then you'll risk losing this bedsit and it's the last one I've got on my books. Your choice. There's plenty more folks needing accommodation; you're not the only girl looking for somewhere to stay in London, I can tell you.'

He glares at me.

'No, please, mister, I really need this room,' I say. 'Please, hurry up and finish the form.'

'Now you look here, missy, don't you take that tone with me! I'll finish the form when it's finished and not before. You girls don't know how lucky you are; having babies left, right and centre, and expecting the welfare state to support you. There's no gratitude in this country no more, no appreciation at all.'

'Oh no, I *am* grateful, mister, really I am. I'm just worried about the baby.'

'Yeah well, the sooner we get this done the sooner you can take the sprog away, and we might all have some peace.'

***

When the forms are finally complete, I thank him and leave. Barry is still howling. A few bedraggled people, mostly women, are sitting on a bench in the corridor, waiting to be seen, to be granted some sort of support from the council. Their eyes follow me enviously as I hurry for the door, clutching my precious piece of paper.

'It's all right for you,' their eyes seem to say. 'You've got through this nightmare; you've got *your* permit ...'

Outside, I struggle to arrange Barry inside my coat while holding the carrier bag containing our few possessions – I don't dare put it down. The main thing is I've now got the housing token and the address.

We aren't allowed to go to the house until six in the evening when the landlord will be there to let us in. That means another two hours of tramping about in the cold and wet. It's already starting to get dark. I'm exhausted, but never mind, it doesn't look too far to walk to the accommodation, thank God. The man from the council had shown me on a street map. Maybe under his rough exterior he did have some sympathy.

I'm feeling faint. I've had nothing to eat since breakfast, and that was just a crust of bread. I know I have to eat or my milk might dry up – and I can't risk fainting while carrying Barry. Maybe I can find somewhere to shelter and keep warm while we wait for six o'clock.

Kind Sister Aileen had given me five pounds *'just to tide you over, my dear girl'*, when I set off from St Agatha's, but now I've only a few coins left, after paying a week's rent at the hostel, and buying a bit of food. I don't know when – or how – I might be getting some more money. There's an 'emergency fund' but I'd have to go back to the council tomorrow and fill out another form to apply for that – there were too many other people waiting, and the office was due to close soon. The idea of standing in that queue of hungry-eyed people yet again, for a meagre hand-out, fills me with dread. I decide I'd better try to find something cheap to eat – if anywhere in London is cheap.

I set off in what I hope is the right direction for the accommodation. It's an area of small, closely built terraced houses. Some of them look quite old and shabby. After a while I notice the lights of a row of small shops. It looks – and smells! – welcoming. I can see a baker's shop that appears to be open. We head straight for it and as I step through the door a beautiful fragrance of fresh, hot bread wafts towards me, making my stomach growl with anticipation. The wonderful warmth envelops me and I hug Barry close. A plump, middle-aged woman with a kind face is standing behind the counter. She smiles at me.

'Hello, my love, nasty night, ain't it? What can I do for you?'

'May I just have a quick look at what you've got …?'

I hastily scan the price labels of the items in the glass counter in front of me, comparing them with the scant coins in my palm.

''Course you can, love. You just take your time – no rush.'

Barry is whimpering and snuffling now, too exhausted to scream. He squirms restlessly inside my coat.

'Oooh, is that a *baby* you've got in there? Ahh, bless him, let me see …'

At the sudden unexpectedly kind tone of the woman's words, I almost begin to cry. Sniffing, I open my coat and reveal the tiny, red, protesting face of my son. The woman hurries around to the front of the counter and takes him from my arms.

'Oh, he's *gorgeous!*' she croons. 'What's his name?'

I can't hold back my tears any longer. 'Barry.' I gulp. 'He's called Barry. Oh, I'm sorry, I'm sorry. You're being so kind. No one else has said nice things to me, not for days and days. It's just that he's hungry and I need to feed him, and they wouldn't let me at the council, and we're getting a room from the council, but we can't go there yet … so … so … could I please just have a bread roll? I think I've got enough for that.'

'Oh, you poor love. They're miserable bastards at that Housing Office, aren't they? Anyone'd think they was giving you their own house! 'Course you can have a bleedin' bread roll, love.' She stands rocking the baby and looking at me. I'm sobbing softly by now.

'Now, I was just about to close up, so you come through the back and get warmed up, darlin'. You're wet through, and you look frozen half to death. And this little fella's got a wet bum. I'm gonna make you a nice hot cup of tea and you can feed baby Barry, and put a clean nappy on him. I'm Sylvia by the way. What's your name, dear?'

8

'Ma-a-rie …' I sniff.

'Marie? That's a lovely name.'

Sylvia bustles me into the room behind the shop: a narrow kitchen with a plain wooden table and two chairs set against the wall.

'Sit down, Marie love. Have you got any dry nappies?'

I shake my head, tears running down my cheeks.'

'No,' I sob, 'I've only got four, and they're all wet. I've not had anywhere to wash or dry them.'

She shakes her head. 'Oh dearie me. Not to worry. You feed the baby. Then I'll change him for you. I know I've got some old towels out the back, what we can cut in half for a nappy. I know what it's like to care for a baby when you're on your own, with no money, believe me. No, it ain't easy when there's no man about to help you. Not that they're much bleedin' help, are they, love? Once they've done their bit, they're quite happy to bugger off and leave you to it.'

Sylvia bustles about in the cramped kitchen, while I feed Barry. He sucks rhythmically at my breast. What bliss to sit down. I feel the warmth of the room wrap itself gently around me and close my eyes.

***

The next thing I know, Sylvia has put a plate in front of me and is gently squeezing my shoulder. Barry, warm and fed, is fast asleep in my arms, his mouth slack.

'Here, give the baby to me, love, and get stuck into this – it's a steak pie and some mash an' gravy – nice and hot. Do you good, it will. A lot better than a miserable old bread roll, eh love? And there's some lovely hot tea for you as well. I've put two sugars in, for energy. You look like you need it. Now just get that lot down you.'

Sylvia takes Barry, washes and changes him, and then sits down

9

cuddling him on her lap, rocking him back and forth slowly. She watches me as I finish eating, shaking her head.

Relaxing now in the warmth, I remember the good friend I made at St Agatha's – Elsie – and her warning to me as we chatted in the cold yard of the home, our three babies bundled up in a blanket between us, like a row of sausage rolls.

I tell my new friend – Sylvia – what Elsie had said.

'*You do know they'll never let ya keep them, don'cha? Not when your mum and dad won't 'ave them in the 'ouse.*'

'*They're mine; they're my babies, Elsie. They can't take them off us. You're allowed to keep your Milly, aren't you?*'

'*Yeah, but that's just 'cos me mum said she'd support me and the baby. And 'cos me mum's just down the road in Shoreditch, not away off in Ireland like yours. They'll not let the likes of you keep them, Marie, not on your own. Anyway, they get a "donation" off the adopting parents, don't they? Sister Bernadette will make effin' sure she gets 'er money, I betcha.*'

We gazed at our babies in silence for a minute.

'*Mebbe they'll let you keep one of them,*' *mused Elsie.* '*You said you've got the milk to feed one at least.*'

'*They're twins, Elsie. They can't separate twins … can they?*'

'*They can do what they flippin' want. They're the ones in charge around 'ere. We've got no power, no power at all.*'

***

It's dark as I step out into the street again. I turn and give Sylvia a hug.

'Thanks for everything, Sylvia. You've been so generous and kind – how can I ever repay you?' Tears threaten to flood from my eyes again.

'Never mind all that, darling … it's nothing, really. Now, are you sure you know the way to Bailey Street? It's no more than ten minutes' walk. Just round that corner, turn left and then right by the post box. And don't forget where your old Auntie Sylvia is, will you, love? I expect to see you and this young man in the next day or two anyway, but you just come straight back now if there's anything you need – or if there's any problem, anything at all.'

I smile to myself as I walk along. Life isn't so bad after all. Barry and I have full stomachs, a place to stay for the next two weeks, and I've made a lovely new friend. If only ... *no*, I remember how Elsie had told me never to dwell on the 'if onlys'. She was right. I'd done the right thing, hadn't I? I'd made the right decision? Well, I didn't have a choice; it was the only decision I *could* make.

***

Thanks to Sylvia's instructions I soon find Bailey Street. It's a long, narrow row of small terraced houses, with another identical row opposite. Most of the houses look a bit shabby and neglected; paint peeling from the doors and window frames. I walk along the side with even numbers, looking for number 22. It doesn't take long. The front door on this house could certainly do with a fresh coat of paint. The windows could do with a wash too! There's no bell so I knock loudly on the door. It's opened by a thin, unshaven man in his forties. He frowns fiercely at me.

'Yes?'

'Er ... Mr Finch?' I say hesitantly. 'I was told you have a room. I've come from the Housing Office. Marie Tully's my name.'

I wave the housing token I'd been given by the Housing Office in front of the man's face.

'Oh yeah. Well, you're late,' he says, squinting at the token.

'Oh, I'm very sorry if I'm later than you expected, Mr Finch. They told me not to arrive before six o'clock.'

'Yeah? Don't know why they said that. Tell you anything they like, that lot. Anyway, it's OK – you better just come on in, love. Wipe yer feet. It's a devil keeping the floor clean; there's that much coming and going.'

The grey, threadbare carpet is indeed heavily stained. Narrow stairs rise steeply straight ahead of the front door, beside which an even narrower, gloomy passage leads to the back of the house. I notice what looks like a tiny kitchen at the far end.

The man steps aside to let me enter the house. I squeeze past him. He pulls a rope switch, and like a music hall performer, I am suddenly illuminated as I stand in a pool of light from a bare ceiling bulb above my head. Mr Finch looks closely at me.

'Blimey girl! They didn't tell me you was bringin' a *baby*. That's not really part of the contract. Oh well, now you're 'ere love … never mind. You'll 'ave to keep it well quiet, mind, or the other guests might complain.'

He exhales noisily. 'Right, now, the ground floor is where I live, so all these rooms are out of bounds – don't forget that, will you? OK, follow me, I'll show you to your room.'

He stomps noisily up the stairs and onto a small, gloomy landing, lit by another unshaded bulb. There are five doors that lead off the landing and Mr Finch opens the one at the very end on the right.

'Bathroom …' he informs me. 'It's every guest's responsibility to keep it clean. You share it with the other three residents.'

The bathroom is so tiny, Mr Finch has to step back into the gloom of the landing again, in order for me to enter. I wonder briefly whether anyone could actually sit on the toilet and still shut the door, without drawing their knees up to their chin. Next to the toilet is a tiny, stained washbasin, less than twelve inches across. I do a quick mental calculation of whether I could bath Barry in it. I decide we will manage. Opposite the basin is a shower scarcely big enough for a normal-sized human being to turn around in it! The shower is screened from the rest of the room by a plastic curtain, frayed and shredded at its lower edge, and made stiff by age. Patches of black mildew stain the walls and ceiling.

Mr Finch motions to me to come out. He leads me to the door

marked '4', furthest from the bathroom. He jangles a set of keys in his hand and produces a separate one for me.

'Right, come on then, girl. This 'ere is your room. This is your key. I don't ask for no deposit, 'cos I know me guests don't have no money. *But*, it's ten pounds to pay if you lose it.' He glares ferociously at me. 'Ten pounds! So make bloody sure you look after it. And keep your door locked at all times. Fred, over there in room one—' he lowers his voice and points to the door next to the bathroom '—can get a bit frisky when he's got a few pints inside him, know what I mean? He doesn't mean no harm, but some of the girls don't like it.'

He opens my door. The room, like the rest of the house, is tiny. There's a narrow single bed, a small table and stool, and a tiny chest of three drawers. It looks as if the room was intended for a child. There is just enough room to walk between the bed and other furniture to the window, provided the occupant shuffles sideways like a crab. In fact, the window is only half a window; the other half disappears into a partition wall. Clearly a larger room has been divided into two at some stage of the house's history, perhaps to squeeze extra guests in.

Oh well, I think, *just as well that we have so few possessions. There's nowhere to put anything.*

'There you are,' says my landlord cheerfully. 'Nice and cosy. The bed's got two sheets and two blankets, and a pillow, and that's your towel.'

He indicates a faded, greyish piece of material folded on the bed.

'I see … er … thank you, Mr Finch, but … er … do you have … *a cot*? For the baby?'

'No, I don't. It's not listed by the council as one of the requirements.'

'Oh …' I say, crestfallen.

Mr Finch looks at the baby thoughtfully. He's not an unkind man.

13

'Tell you what though, love. I've got a cardboard box down-stairs. Got it from the supermarket this morning. Should be about the right size – he's not very big, is he? You can have that. You might have to put the bedside table on top of the chest of drawers, like, if you want the baby on the floor next to the bed, that is. I'll bring you an extra blanket too.'

I hesitate for a moment, and then realise there's no alternative.

'Thank you, Mr Finch, that's very kind of you.'

***

Barry is quite snug in his cardboard box that night. I'm relieved to see that the blue blanket Mr Finch has brought is clean. It's thin and worn, but I fold it carefully, so that part of it forms a soft mattress over the base of the box, leaving a layer on top to serve as a cover. My own bed is hard and lumpy, but after feeding Barry, we both sink into a deep, exhausted sleep. I don't wake until the baby's hungry cries penetrate my consciousness a few hours later. It's still dark. At least it's easy enough to lean out of the bed to lift Barry from his little makeshift cot beside me and wrap the bedclothes around both of us while I feed him. Still plenty of milk, I note with satisfaction. I must have been given a boost by that wonderful steak pie Sylvia gave me, God bless her. I close my eyes and recall the delicious savoury smell of it, the succulent cubes of meat, the crisp pastry, the rich gravy soaking into the mashed potato. It was more than I'd eaten in all the frugal weeks of my stay at St Agatha's. Just thinking about it makes my mouth water.

Barry settles straight back to sleep after his feed, but I'm troubled by anxious thoughts of the future, and the past. Instead of relaxing into sleep, my mind keeps returning to the dreadful scene with Sister Bernadette – the confrontation that led to Donal being taken from me.

I stared at Sister Bernadette across the expansive, hostile plain of her desk. I could see her thin lips moving, but it was as though she was talking a foreign language, or perhaps as if she was underwater, the sounds making glugs, plops and bubbles ... not real words; there was no meaning to them – nothing I could comprehend.

'So you see, Marie,' she said 'you should be truly grateful that you'll be relieved of the care of one of your children. You are indeed fortunate that this very kind couple, with excellent background – well-to-do people from a fine, respectable ... Christian family, have chosen to adopt one of your sons. They have been shown photographs of both boys, and perhaps surprisingly, they have chosen the second-born child, who is of course the less robust of the two. No doubt their choice comes from a deeply charitable sense of sympathy, and a wish to help the most needy of the two. Very worthy, very admirable. Thank goodness there are such people are in the world, hmmm?'

She glared at me, as if waiting for some indication of gratitude, which was not forthcoming.

I glanced down at my babies, each sleeping peacefully in the crook of one of my arms.

'Of course, whether they will retain the Christian name you have given the boy,' Sister Bernadette continued, 'is entirely up to them. They may well decide to rename him, to make him theirs. That is their right, you see ...'

On and on she went, relentless, merciless. I tried to understand what she was saying, but I felt so faint, so nauseous, I couldn't take it in. Her words fell like raindrops on a puddle, creating momentary discernible rings and then disappearing, lost for ever – nothing my brain could hold on to.

'But ... but they're twins, Sister. They can't be separated, they're both my babies. I'm their mother. I can take care of them. I love them, both of them ...'

'Yes, well, of course that is the selfish view I might have expected from you, Marie Tully. If you truly love them as you say, you must consider what is best for them, not for yourself ... never mind what

15

you *want! These good people are wealthy, respectable, secure; they have a beautiful home. They long for a child to love. Your boy will want for nothing. He will have the best education, a fine future. What can you possibly give him? You haven't even enough milk for both infants!'*

Sister Bernadette snorted and glared at me. She shook her head in scorn and exasperation.

'A life of poverty and insecurity! A squalid flat somewhere, at best,' she continued. 'Just how do you expect to support one baby, let alone two?'

She turned and fixed me with a cold stare.

'Perhaps, just perhaps, you can manage to care for one child, taking in washing at home, or doing some other lowly work … cleaning floors maybe …'

I was silent for a moment, contemplating the bleak picture of life Sister Bernadette was painting for me.

'Yes, oh yes, now you can see it, Marie, can't you, hmmm? That's how life would be for you. Is that what you want for yourself, for your boys? No, I don't think so …'

She paused to allow these words to penetrate.

'I know you're not all bad, girl, but just think; think of the future. With only one child, and some help from the state, you may be able to manage – though don't for a minute think it will be easy!'

I looked down at the tops of my tiny sons' heads. I shook my own head slowly. My lips trembled. Tears cascaded down my cheeks. Sister Bernadette seemed to sense a weakening of my rebellion. Her tone changed.

'So, just think of this, Marie,' she crooned softly, soothingly. 'If, if, you agree to let the baby go – to go to this wonderful home that's being offered – not today, not tomorrow … but in about four weeks' time … if you agree to sign the adoption paper – just for the one child – well then, I think we can agree for you to keep the other one. All that would remain, is for the baby in question to have a thorough health and development check.

16

'What about that now – hmmm? In fact, we can even give you some help by way of finding somewhere to live, just to start with, of course, for you and the other baby – applying to the council you see, and maybe even getting some support for childcare to enable you to find a little job ... Now wouldn't that be a fine thing? What else can you possibly do, girl?'

So here I am now: living the life Sister Bernadette foresaw for me.

How am I ever going to earn enough money to support us? London is so expensive. Somehow, I'll have to pay rent somewhere, and buy food to keep us going.

I don't know a soul in London, apart from Elsie, who lives with her mum and dad in their small council house in Shoreditch, and my new friend Sylvia. I'll have to find my own place somehow. *How* is the critical question. I've neither qualifications nor experience to apply for jobs, and anyway what work could I possibly do, with the baby to care for?

I try to think positively; if I was an African woman in the bush, I'd simply tie the baby onto my back with a length of cloth, and get on with working in the fields, or cooking over a fire. I rather wish I *were* an African woman. At least it's probably *warm* in Africa.

But I don't think London has any fields to work in. I'll have to find something different to do. What am I good at? I have plenty of experience in cleaning, after all that skivvying at St Agatha's. I could scrub a floor for England and Ireland put together – that's for sure! I'm not a bad cook either; I helped me ma enough times at home. But the thing I'm best at is *sewing*. I had a real way with a needle, Ma always said. Maybe somehow I could use that skill ... but how?

Chapter 3

1972
Marie

If it hadn't been for Sylvia, I'd never have met Mrs Goldstein, never have considered the opportunity of working for her. How different my life would have been. We saw the advert for a housekeeper in the paper. It caught my eye, but without Sylvia, I would never have dared to contact Mrs Goldstein about the job. I thought there was no chance that she'd even consider me when she heard I had a baby, now a toddler – an illegitimate baby, who would have to come to live in her house too. It was Sylvia, always an optimist, who encouraged me to ring the number.

'Go on! You don't lose anything by giving it a go … Nothing ventured nothing gained!'

I was trembling when I told Mrs Goldstein about Barry. She paused in our conversation, as if she needed to absorb this information. I waited for her to say she couldn't have a mother with a baby for the position, but she didn't. After a minute she said, 'Well, how lovely that you have a little child, my dear! I am very fond of children. Please do come to see me, and we can talk together and decide whether we like each other. I'm quite sure that we will.'

She gave me directions for finding the house. I thought she sounded nice. She sounded gentle and kind. She sounded foreign too.

'Why don't you come here tomorrow morning at about eleven o'clock, Marie, and we can have some coffee together? Blackheath is the other side of London, south of the River Thames. You will need to take a bus to Charing Cross or the underground to Trafalgar Square, and then it's a short walk to Charing Cross. Then from Charing Cross station you take a train to Blackheath station. It's not very far – maybe twenty minutes on the train.'

Hearing this, I suddenly panicked and couldn't think of what to say. A soft 'ooh' of disappointment escaped my lips, though I hadn't meant it to.

'Marie? Are you still there, my dear?'

'Yes … sorry,' I said. 'I'm here. I … I was just thinking about the train … I was just wondering … er …'

'Ah … I think you are worried about buying a ticket. Am I right?'

'Yes. I'm sorry, Mrs Goldstein. I … I was just wondering how much it might cost …?'

'Marie, can you maybe borrow the money from someone you trust? I will pay you back the cost of the journey tomorrow – whether or not we decide that the job will suit you. Do you think you can do that? I really would like you to come. I think I will like you.'

I looked at Sylvia. She had helped me so much already. Was it fair to ask her for a loan on top of everything else? I absolutely had to try for this job. What other chance of work did I have? Meanwhile, Sylvia was nodding her head madly like a mechanical puppet. She must have understood what was going on.

'Thank you so much, Mrs Goldstein. I will ask my good friend

Sylvia to help me … and then I'll pay her back as soon as I can. If you're sure, I'll come to see you tomorrow at eleven.'

Sylvia started jumping up and down like a dervish, grinning and gesticulating 'thumbs-up' at me.

'That's good,' Mrs Goldstein said, 'and bring little Barry, won't you? I would have been so disappointed if you didn't come. You have a very kind friend in Sylvia, I think. Now listen carefully and I'll explain exactly how to get here. Have you got a pencil and paper?'

Sylvia leapt up and hugged me when I put the telephone down, pulling me into a crazy dance.

'It's a real chance for you, darlin', and they don't come often, do they?' she said. 'Somewhere to live, *and* a job into the bargain! She sounds such a nice lady. Don't you worry about the fare money – I'm not bothered about it. I want to see you and Barry settled.'

***

I step off the train and on to the platform at Blackheath station carrying Barry in my arms. We make our way out onto the hectic street, busy with shops and cars, and a crush of people scurrying about. My hand clutches the precious instructions, crumpling the paper into a damp ball, even though I know them off by heart. Barry is alert and curious, turning his head eagerly from side to side, trying to take everything in. He's starting to walk quite well, but it's too far to the house and I don't want to be late. So I have to carry him. He's getting very heavy now.

By the time we're out of the bustling centre of Blackheath, and into the quieter streets, twenty minutes have passed. I'm getting tired, but we're nearly there. We come to a leafy, spacious street. Linden Avenue, that's right, it's Mrs Goldstein's street. The houses are large and detached, quite varied in shape, but each one is set in a verdant garden, with bushes and trees. It's very different from the tightly built, older terraces I remember of Mr Finch's area, where most of the front doors opened straight onto the pavements – and even more different from the council houses round my block in Shoreditch.

I check the address on my scrap of paper. Number 19 Linden Avenue. This is the house, a fine, double-fronted brick building. The front garden looks lush and thick with large shrubs. Early spring flowers, like bright stars, dot the lawns. A curving path winds through this foliage towards an imposing front door. I gaze up at the wide windows on the upper floor. There are further smaller windows under the roof, set into the eaves. Barry wriggles, wanting to be put down. He toddles on up the path, stamping his feet.

The house looks quite old, maybe built in the last century, but it looks very well maintained. As we approach, I notice the window frames are all freshly painted white, as is the front door.

I hesitate nervously on the front step, trying to imagine us ever actually living in such a grand house. Before I've had time to ring the bell, the front door is flung open by a tall lady, quite old, maybe seventy or even more, with grey hair piled on top of her head. Mrs Goldstein. She's smiling broadly and reaches out both her arms to welcome us.

'You must be Marie – and Barry! I'm Erna Goldstein. I am so very pleased to meet you. What a darling little child! Hello, Barry; hello, my sweetheart. Welcome to my home. Come in, come in! Let us have some coffee together, and we will talk – and then I shall show you around.'

She leads us to a comfortable sitting room and tells me to take a seat, then sits herself down on the sofa opposite. There's a tray with coffee things: a white pot and two cups and saucers, with a plastic mug of juice that she gives to Barry. She points to some toys on the floor in the corner of the room.

'Those are for Barry to play with, if he would like. Now, tell me a little bit about yourself, Marie. Do you have experience as a cleaner?'

21

For a moment I had forgotten that this was supposed to be an interview.

'Yes, Mrs Goldstein, I have always helped my mother at home, being the eldest girl in the family.'

'Have you now? I'm sure she taught you lots of useful skills.'

'She did,' I reply eagerly. 'I can cook quite well … erm, but nothing too fancy. I can clean windows and hoover and … and scrub the house. I'm used to doing washing and making beds … and I'll do any other jobs that need doing. I'm good at sewing too …'

I explain I've been doing a part-time job as a domestic help and nursemaid for a lady with a small child of three, while she's at work. That enables me to pay the modest rent in a temporary, small bedsit the council has given us in a block in Shoreditch, near my friend Elsie, but now the council need it back, so Barry and I have to find somewhere else to live.

Mrs Goldstein just smiles and says, 'Well, I'm so glad you found me! How wonderful to have so *many* skills and such useful experience. Now when you've finished your coffee I'll show you all round the house. I hope you'll like the little flat you and Barry will be living in.'

So I guess that means I've passed the interview, that I've got the job! It seemed to happen without me noticing. Barry and I move into Mrs Goldstein's house two weeks later.

***

Many mornings, as I emerge from sleep, I wonder briefly if it's true, that it isn't a dream. We really do live in the beautiful house – warm, comfortable, and safe.

In the two weeks since we've been at Mrs Goldstein's we've already developed a routine. I begin each day by getting Barry up from his cot, and then washed, fed and dressed. Then while he sits strapped into his highchair or plays on the floor with his toys, I make Mrs Goldstein her usual light breakfast of coffee, a boiled egg and a slice of the dark brown rye bread she prefers, and which I have learned to buy at a small delicatessen in the village, run by a Polish couple.

Twice a week I hoover and dust the whole house, each time concentrating on a different room for a more thorough cleaning. Several of the rooms in the large house are unused, except very occasionally when a distant relative or old friend of Mrs Goldstein's comes to stay. She doesn't have a lot of washing, but I do it regularly, carefully making up her bed every week with fresh sheets and pillow cases.

She often asks me to join her while she has her mid-morning coffee, or to accompany her on a walk to the nearest shops, or occasionally to the park. I love these times. One of Mrs Goldstein's friends kindly gave me a pram, which her grand-child had outgrown. It converts into a pushchair, so I can take Barry wherever we go without the strain of carrying him. He's growing bigger and heavier by the day. No wonder, the amount of food he eats!

In the evening I cook us all a meal. Gradually, I've been expanding my repertoire, at first under instruction from Mrs Goldstein, and then by studying her numerous cookery books. She is used to different food from the plain fare I grew up eating and cooking, so I'm learning to make all sorts of unusual dishes – wiener schnitzel, Hungarian goulash, coq au vin, and other foreign-sounding – and *tasting* – dishes. I love their exotic names, and the ingredients: veal, red and green peppers, spices, garlic, and even *wine*! I've never tasted such things before. Generally, though, we both prefer to eat quite modestly and simply. Usually Mrs Goldstein eats her supper from a tray and listening to the classical music she loves, while I take my share, and Barry's, upstairs to our warm, cosy little 'flatlet' at the top of the house. Up there we have everything we could possibly need.

Mrs Goldstein even bought us a little colour television. It's a great wonder to me, bringing the world in all its reality into our home. I'd never seen such a thing before – the few televisions I'd seen in other people's houses back home had had dull black and white pictures, even though we all thought them a miracle at the time. Of course, Barry loves the cartoon shows like *New Zoo Revue* and the *Bugs Bunny Show*, but after he goes to bed I watch my favourite programme: *Bewitched*.

My housekeeping tasks only keep me busy for part of each day; for the rest of the time I'm free to play with Barry or take him out. I've also been developing my dressmaking skills, and have been using them to earn some extra money. Mrs Goldstein has recommended me to her friends. At first just repairs and alterations, and with the money I saved I managed to buy a second-hand electric sewing machine.

Now I've also been asked to make an outfit for one of Mrs Goldstein's friends, for her daughter's forthcoming wedding. She asked me to make up a pattern she'd bought, together with the material: a fine blue silk. I know how important the dress is for such a special occasion so I want it to be perfect.

Dear Erna Goldstein. How I bless the day I answered that advert for a housekeeper to care for an elderly lady. I learn she was a refugee from bad times in Europe. I know that she had escaped to England more than thirty years before, but I know little else of those times. Perhaps one day she'll tell me about just what happened to her all those years ago.

On more than one occasion Mrs Goldstein insists that this is 'my home'.

'You must do exactly as you want, Marie; you don't need to ask permission for anything you want to change in your flat. You should feel free to ask your family members round if you like. Or invite friends – perhaps for tea or coffee. In fact, you could ask them to visit, if you want. It's *your home* remember.'

'That's very kind of you, Mrs Goldstein, thank you. But all my family are still in Ireland, and I don't really have any friends here in London yet – apart from Sylvia, of course, and my friend Elsie who lives with her baby in her parents' house in Shoreditch.'

I tell her all about Sylvia, how kind she was, and still is, to me. How she helped me when I was all alone and that we have been friends ever since.

'Ah, *Sylvia*! She's the special friend you were with when you rang me, isn't she? She sounds so nice. Why don't you invite her round for lunch one of these days? Or even to stay for a night or two if you like?'

A few weeks later, on a Saturday, Sylvia comes for a day and we have a lovely time, walking around Blackheath, with Barry in his pushchair, exploring all there is of interest. We walk to Greenwich Park, so Barry can have a run about, chasing the birds and squirrels. While he's happy and absorbed, Sylvia and I have time to talk. She and Elsie are the only people in London, apart from at St Agatha's, who know about Donal, how his loss tortures me.

'You look well, Marie,' she says.

'I am well … and happier than I've been in a long time, thanks to you mostly, Sylvia. If it weren't for you I wouldn't be here. My life is transformed, because of you.'

Sylvia looks straight into my face. 'Oh really, don't be so silly. I'm just glad all's going well for you.'

'As well as it could possibly be without Donal.'

She nods her head and reaches out to hug me. 'I know, love, I know. Come on, Marie – let's have a go on that roundabout! Give me a spin!'

She picks Barry up and swings him in the air. We race to the little playground nearby. It's the happiest time Barry – or I – have had for a long time. We stay in the park all afternoon.

Then we head back to the house and all have tea together. I can tell Erna Goldstein enjoys Sylvia's company too. After that visit Sylvia comes to stay for a weekend every two or three months. Mrs Goldstein is always very welcoming.

Sylvia and I love to walk on the heath together. Barry loves it too. He seems mesmerised by the sky, leaning his head back and gazing upwards.

I understand why he is drawn to the sky. In the peace of Blackheath, in its open spaces and vast skies, my heart gradually settles. It has become my home, although I still miss my family back in Ireland.

'It's good to see you like this, Marie,' Sylvia says.

'I love to walk on the heath,' I tell her. 'That's what local people call it, anyway. It's not what I understand a heath to be, not at all like in my homeland. After all, there's no heather, no bracken, no shrubby golden gorse bushes. Just this great wide, manicured stretch of grass, an endless grassy meadow – with neither sheep nor cows to graze it!'

Sylvia laughs. 'Yes, and with roads and cars criss-crossing it.'

We stand and stare up at the sky, rising huge and dominant, sometimes steely grey and forbidding, but more often a great swathe of blue, and gentle. I get Sylvia to stand with me in the middle of the grass and we stretch our arms out to the sides and up to the heavens above. Then little Barry watches us with a cross face on him. He frowns at me, as if he thinks I'm a crazy woman – which perhaps I am!

'You know, Sylvia, sometimes I'm *almost* happy,' I tell her. 'There's just the one area of my life causing me pain and anxiety, and I can't stop it. That feeling of loss eats away at my soul every day and every night – and the sadness never seems to lessen. If anything, it consumes me *more* and more as our separation wears on. Sure, I chide myself for not being satisfied with my perfect, adorable Barry. Just look at him! Isn't it a disgrace – a sin even – not to be grateful for the life I now have, and especially with my fine, lovely little boy?'

'It's not a sin to mourn your missing child, Marie, your Donal. Your love for Barry can't wipe out your love and longing for Donal.'

She squeezes my arm.

'There's another shadow hanging over me …'

'What's that?'

'It's hard to put my finger on it, Sylvia, but I feel a concern about Barry. Oh, he's beautiful, healthy and thriving, yet, yet … I wonder if there isn't something not quite right with the child. As a baby, you know, he was forever looking around for no apparent reason, kind of looking over his shoulder, as if he expected to see someone there. Often his little face would suddenly crumple and he would cry inexplicably.'

Barry ran round us laughing and whooping.

'Well, he looks lively and happy enough just now,' Sylvia says with a smile.

'Yes, anyone who saw him now would say that. But, as he's grown into a toddler, he has a peculiar little game that he often plays by himself, holding out one of his toys, as if to some imaginary child, and then snatching it back, saying something like "*No not **you**!*" or "***You** not having it!*", with a glowering look of fury on his little face. It really worries me, Sylvia.'

'Mmm?'

'Well, at first I thought it amusing and quaint, but as time goes on he often repeats the game, and it just seems a bit odd. It's as if there's a terrible anger in the boy, which neither I, nor even Barry himself, can understand. Sometimes Barry's anger expresses itself against *me*, his own mother, Sylvia. It happens particularly when we have quiet times together, Barry and I. I suppose it's when thoughts of the dreadful empty gap in my life surface and preoccupy me. I really do try hard to control them, for fear of upsetting Barry, but I can't always hold those thoughts at bay.'

I can't stop the tears starting. When Sylvia hugs me, a deep sadness, a desperate longing, winds itself around my heart like a snake, squeezing it so painfully that my tears start to flow. Then Barry frowns and narrows his eyes and watches me closely. Of course, I reach for him and try to draw him into an embrace to reassure him, but his small body just stiffens and resists me with amazing strength.

'On two occasions,' I tell Sylvia, 'his hard little fists pummelled me and he shouted, "*No! Shadow boy there!*" Whatever could the child be thinking? Such an odd little boy.'

'He's a lovely boy, but he's very sensitive, Marie. Maybe you shouldn't make too much of these behaviours. He notices if you're upset or preoccupied.'

I know Sylvia is right. So I decide I'm right never to mention to Barry that he has a brother, a twin. It would only upset him further. He isn't ready for this information. He wouldn't understand the terrible choices I had to make, that in the end I made the only choice I could. Surely it was the right choice?

Maybe I'll never tell him. Or perhaps when he's older, much older ..., perhaps then I can explain.

Chapter 4

1972
Robert

'These things take time, Mrs Carlton,' the social worker assures Clarissa soothingly. 'You may need to be patient. None of us know just how traumatic early separation from the birth mother can be. And remember, your Robert had a *twin* brother. They had nine months in the womb together. Being parted from such a close sibling can affect a child in all sorts of ways, even one so young. Also, you have to understand that some children take a long time, perhaps even years, to settle, to feel fully secure, to attach themselves to a new parent.'

Clarissa glances at her husband, who sits at a slight distance, watching Robert in the play area. She is not prepared to be fobbed off by such platitudes, not this time. The child had been less than two months old when they'd adopted him, for heaven's sake! It's now two years later. She and Simon aren't 'new parents'. Surely Robert had barely had time to attach himself to his birth mother? He probably hadn't even noticed a change in mothers,

29

let alone been traumatised by it! Nor is she impressed with Miss Phillips' half-baked theories on the emotional effect of sharing a womb with his brother – such twaddle! Does she think they were happily playing 'uterus hide-and-seek' in there?!

It isn't as though she and Simon haven't tried – tried time and time again. Have they not committed themselves totally to the welfare of their adopted son? All right, maybe she isn't the most lovey-dovey sort of mother … a brief hug and kiss at bedtime, or a little cuddle when drying him after his bath; that's how Clarissa shows her affection, and that is surely enough. Have they not devoted over two years to the child's every need? She has no intention of allowing this young woman, a mere slip of a thing, with her fake smile and condescending expression, to patronise her. Absolutely not.

'Do you have children, Miss Phillips?' Clarissa asks through gritted teeth.

'Er … no. Not yet …' The young woman smiles a little nervously. 'But actually, I'm getting married in the new year, and we hope to start a family soon after that.'

'I'm sure you do … as we did ourselves. But in our case it wasn't to be. So we had no alternative but to choose adoption. We really did expect to love and care for a baby in need of just that – love and care. We had hoped to adopt another child too in time, perhaps a little girl. To make a real *family* one day.'

Miss Phillips nods her head vigorously, as if this is exactly what's to be expected, to be *encouraged*.

Clarissa regards her icily. Does this woman – this girl – think she needs her *approval*, that it means anything at all to her?

'However,' she continues, 'we haven't started a *family* with this child,' she says. 'It's almost as though we have started a *siege, a battle*! Every morning we pray that this day will be different, but it never is. In fact, it seems to get worse day by day. Sometimes it feels as if he's in *mourning*. Although of course that's ridiculous. Yet … I don't know … perhaps he is. Maybe unconsciously he

30

still misses his "birth mother", though I can't imagine why. What did she ever do for him?'

A muscle beside Clarissa's mouth begins to quiver. She struggles to control her voice. Simon is watching her steadily.

'Sometimes it's almost as if he *hates* us. Most days he cries and whimpers from morning 'til night. If I try to cuddle him, he arches his back, shrieks and struggles until I put him down. All he wants to do is play – not *with us*, you understand. No, on his own and in his own way – with toys, bricks or trains or some other objects on the floor. If Simon or I try to play *with* him, he turns his back or pushes us away. It's so very disheartening, so very dispiriting. Do you understand?' Her voice seems to break and fade away.

Miss Phillips nods.

'Yes, I do,' she whispers.

Clarissa appears not to notice. She carries on as if she has not heard.

'His play seems repetitive and without purpose; just making lines of toys, or sorting them into odd groups,' she continues. 'If I try to intervene, to actually *play* with him, he screams, or even pushes my hand away. If he doesn't get his own way he has the most almighty tantrums, which really frighten me. I don't know if he's unhappy, or if there's something wrong with him? Could he be … damaged, do you think? Or perhaps he's autistic?'

'Well, no. I don't think so. He was fully assessed just before you received him, and again six months after,' Miss Phillips replies, consulting her notes. 'His development was found to be normal, if not *advanced*,' she says with emphasis, gazing at the Carltons with wide blue eyes, as if they must surely see that advanced development in a child is something to be welcomed, something to be celebrated.

'Well, we've tried and tried for over two years now, but I'm sorry to say we both feel we've reached the end of the road as far

31

as this little boy is concerned.' Clarissa Carlton's voice is weary.

Miss Phillips looks aghast. 'You mean, you mean … you want us to *take him back*?'

Simon Carlton stands up abruptly and speaks for the first time. 'We do not want you to "take him back", as you put it, Miss Phillips. He is not an electric kettle to be returned to the manufacturer when found to be faulty! We wanted him to be our son. We gave him a new first name, Robert, and our family name because we believed he would be part of our family. We still want a child desperately – a baby to bring up in our home, as our own. We don't expect a perfect child – we know there's no such thing as a perfect child. However, there's nothing more we can do. We feel this child is not happy with us.'

He pauses, looking desperately sad. 'And I'm afraid we are certainly not happy with him.'

Mr Carlton draws in a deep breath and sighs it out again. For a moment he looks as though he might break down in tears, but he clasps his arms around his body and shakes himself slightly, as if to gather his emotions in deeper, to push them out of sight.

'A different home, different parents, may be much more successful than we have been. We really do hope so. He is clearly a needy child; needy in some way we appear unable to fulfil. Of course, we care about him. We wish him a happy life – but it seems it is not to be with us.'

Clarissa Carlton watches her husband with admiration.

Simon is now gazing at the little boy, who is absorbed in some activity arranging bricks on the floor in the 'play corner' of the room. He remembers how at first he had approved of the orderliness of the child. Hadn't he been a bit like that himself as a small boy? But no, *he'd* been deeply attached to his mama. He *loved* the few occasions his mama and papa chose to play with him.

He turns back to Miss Phillips. 'Please set in motion whatever procedures are necessary in this situation,' he says briskly, 'and let us know when to sign the paperwork.'

He strides towards his wife and helps her up from the sofa. She is sobbing quietly. Putting his arm around her, he leads her towards the door. He pauses briefly to pat Robert on the head. Clarissa looks down at the child. Without a further word they open the door and leave.

The small boy glances up momentarily from his game on the floor and then looks down again. The departure of his adoptive parents seems to have little effect on him. Miss Phillips gazes at him and shakes her head.

'Oh, you poor little beggar,' she says under her breath, 'what's going to happen to you now?'

***

That same evening, Miss Phillips drives Robert Carlton to an orphanage on the edge of the town. All he brings with him from his adoptive parents is a carrier bag of clothes and toys, and the name they had given him.

Robert is placed in a dormitory in the Pre-school Unit along with eight or so other 'difficult to place' infants. The programme is highly regimented, the theory being that young children respond to predictable punishment or reward – *training* in other words – rather like dogs. They need routine, firm handling, and to know exactly what is expected of them. The staff enforce the rules rigorously, and sometimes harshly, although not all are without care and kindness.

It is noticed that Robert is an attractive child, and carers in the orphanage feel he would be likely to be accepted by foster parents. Immediate efforts are made to identify a suitable foster family with whom Robert can be matched. It is felt that, ideally, Robert should be placed with a family where he is the only child, or the youngest child.

After a few weeks in the children's home, during which Robert does not really settle, a placement is arranged with the Collins family, consisting of mother Brenda, a part-time nurse, father George, a builder, and their daughter Lacie aged six. They had previously fostered two small sisters aged five and one. After a largely happy and settled year, the little girls moved on to a permanent home with adoptive parents. George and Brenda are confident that their new two-year-old foster child will be just as successfully integrated into their family.

For the first week of his stay with the Collins family, Robert screams almost continuously. He strains furiously at the harness of his highchair at mealtimes, shaking and rocking so violently his foster carers are afraid he will topple over. One of them has to hold firmly on to the chair at all times. When food is placed in front of him, Robert sniffs it and then flings the dish onto the floor.

'Poor little love,' says Brenda, 'he must have been that disturbed by being rejected by his adoptive mum and dad, no wonder he's upset.'

She tries to tempt him with a range of foods, and decides maybe he's missed out on some vital early baby experiences, and needs to revert for a while. She places him facing outwards on her lap, crooning softly to him, while George tries to insert a plastic spoon loaded with sweetened milky semolina into his mouth. Robert squirms violently, shrieking, arching his back and screwing up his face in fury, while George patiently pursues his open mouth, awaiting the chance to empty the spoon inside it. At last the spoon deposits its contents on Robert's tongue. His eyes open in surprise and rage. He takes a deep breath and blows the entire mouthful of semolina straight into George's face.

The semolina is abandoned and Brenda prepares a modest but varied feast of small pieces each of rusk, banana, cheese, apple, chocolate, and bread and butter. Her theory is that Robert needs to be reassured by giving him *choice*. She places a spread of these foods on the tray of the highchair.

'There you are, Bobby love, you just see what takes your fancy.'

34

Robert eyes the scattering with a suspicious frown. He fingers them and sniffs them. Brenda nods knowingly. '*Exploring,*' she mouths to George.

Robert pops the piece of chocolate into his mouth and sweeps the rest of the food onto the floor.

That evening, Robert allows George and Brenda to feed him the remainder of the bar of chocolate piece by piece, despite Lacie's outraged objections.

'You said too much chocolate's bad for *me*. I thought you said it would make me sick? You never let me have more than two little squares. How come he's allowed to eat a whole bar? *It's not fair!*'

'It's just to try and get him to settle, love. He's a sad little boy. He'll not always need chocolate, you wait and see.'

For the next few weeks, Robert survives on almost nothing but chocolate. The Collins family have to endure his frequent screaming and his hitting, biting or spitting at anyone within reach, his destruction of toys and tearing up of books. By the end of just over a month, they reluctantly admit defeat, and return him to the children's home. Brenda and George decide to have a break from fostering.

***

Throughout the coming years in the care of the local authority, several further attempts are made to place Robert with foster parents, but none of these placements last for long. Each time, the foster carers report a range of worrying behaviours: persistent bed-wetting, destructive behaviour, stealing, tearing clothes and books, flinging toys and other objects, aggression towards other children and adults, swearing, stealing, spitting, soiling, screaming … the list goes on and on.

In time, Robert progresses from the Pre-school Unit to the Primary Wing. The staff and other children in the home address him variously as Robert, Robbie, Bobby, Bob or Rob.

He comes to expect this variability of his name. It appears to him to reinforce an absence of clear identity, a failure – of himself and others – to know exactly who he is. He isn't sure whether it matters.

Chapter 5

1972
Marie

Local people refer to Blackheath as 'the village'. But it's hardly what I think of as a village. To me, a village is a little cluster of houses, with a church of course, and perhaps a small shop, and with luck, a pub – in the middle of the countryside – such as I remember from back home, and often think about and still miss terribly.

There's certainly no rural feel to this 'village', what with its cafés and shops of every description, most of them noisy, crowded and expensive. And always the restless press of traffic. There's any number of pubs and bars and restaurants in the village. In the evenings they heave with young people, who spill out onto the pavements, smoking, drinking, and talking with the loud, confident voices of the well-off.

Although I suppose I myself am also still young – considerably younger than many of these merrymakers no doubt – I feel no part of their groups. I feel no connection. It's my friends back home I miss the most – the girls with whom I chatted in the school playground at break times. We talked about periods, about which boys we fancied, about the records and clothes we loved but could never afford, and about sex, when we could finish a sentence without collapsing into nervous giggles. We discussed what life might be like for us when we left school. My special friends – Deidre and Gwen – and I would try to envisage life as adults, as *women*. No way did we want our mothers' lives – but then, what else was there for us? It was unimaginable. The thought that I might end up here, in London, in a grand house, with a little son … and without another … never occurred to me.

What with motherhood and responsibility, with the sadness of leaving my home and family – and the memory of the trauma that never leaves me – I think I have aged before my time. I'm barely in my twenties, yet I feel I've become a mature woman, almost middle-aged. Today we've been for a gentle walk, Erna and I, with Barry toddling or in his pushchair. It's too soon for lunch when we get back. Erna squeezes my arm as I shut the front door.

'Come and join me for a cup of coffee, Marie. I enjoy your company. Let's have a chat. I'd love to hear more about your life in Ireland.'

So I bring in the tray and we sit amicably together, while Barry plays with his little heap of toys in the corner of the sitting room, chattering to himself.

'So tell me, my dear … I'd love to hear more about your life in Ireland and your family.'

I begin with the easier part: my home and family. I close my eyes and think back to our little farmhouse – set in a small valley, with meadows and streams low down, and heather and bracken on the hills all around. It was a mile or so to the village, but with all my brothers and sisters, and Ma and Da of course, it never seemed remote to me, just homely.

'Well, I guess you might think our house was picturesque, um … Erna, for all we were poor and me da had to scratch a living from the earth. That was how he always put it – "scratch a living".'

Erna nods her head and smiles encouragingly.

'I was one of seven children in the family. I was a "middle child", and the oldest daughter, you see. There were two lads older than me, and four younger sisters.'

'Oh you were quite a tribe then,' she says.

'Yes, you could say that. Da always hoped for another son, but each time Ma gave birth it was another girl. He never reproached her, mind. We were a close family. Although he was a gruff man, not one for soft talk, he loved Ma. He loved all of us, even us girls. That is, until I disgraced myself, becoming pregnant – and me not married, nor even engaged.'

Erna tuts and shakes her head. 'No, no, Marie. You mustn't say that. You're judging yourself far too harshly.'

I decide to be quite open with Erna about what had happened. It's the first time I've told anyone the whole story. Well, apart from Sylvia, but this feels different, Erna Goldstein being my employer and all. Once I start I can't stop. I tell her everything; I don't hold anything back.

'Well you see, Erna … a travelling fair came to the village near my home – that was such a rare and exciting event in our little quiet backwater, you can't imagine. It filled all of us young people with huge excitement. I went with my friend Deidre. We were both just seventeen and innocent. The fair was such a great thrill.'

'Oh, I *can* imagine – it must have been!'

'Well, we couldn't afford more than a couple of rides. We just loved wandering arm in arm around all the stalls and rides. We were so excited by the atmosphere, the smell of the candy floss, so sweet and fragrant. We swayed and jigged to the blaring loud pop music; we heard it so rarely. The men working the rides give us winks and grins. We couldn't stop giggling at them!'

Erna smiles and nods.

'We got talking to a couple of the young fairground workers. I was completely bowled over when one of the men – he said his name was Billy – offered me a free ride on the waltzer. Billy was definitely the handsomer of the two. He came to whizz my car round lots of times, and he laughed when I screamed and said I'd be sick …'

I pause, uncertain whether to continue, whether she'd think me bad.

'Go on, Marie. It's all right.'

I take a deep breath. 'He asked me if I wanted to see his caravan. Of course I said yes I did, but that I hadn't the time just then – I had to get back home to help Ma with the tea. "OK, come back tomorrow then," he says, putting his arm around my waist. I was melting, Erna, honestly I was. I nearly fainted with the thrill of it.'

'Of course. You were so innocent, my dear.'

I nod. 'Deidre said she couldn't go back with me the next day; she had to go to the market with her ma. She said I should be careful, but I laughed at her, told her not to be such a fussy old biddy, and that she was just jealous. She didn't like that – not at all. It was a bit mean of me, wasn't it, but secretly I was pleased I was going back on my own.'

'So did you go back?'

'Yes. The following day I walked around the fair, terrified I might not see Billy, that he might have forgotten about me, or found another girl he liked better. But suddenly, there he was! He'd crept up behind me and kissed the back of my neck. I turned and he smiled and stroked the hair off my face. He had such a way with him. The sun made golden flecks in his dark eyes. I felt I was dissolving, Erna, I did really. Billy reminded me he'd promised to show me his caravan, if I wanted. I said yes, I did want. No hesitation. What a silly girl I was!

'The caravans all looked so quaint and exotic, with their colourful decorations. Billy was kind and funny, and charming. He told me I was beautiful. No one had ever said anything like that to me before, Erna, no one. It was "love at first sight" for me, that's what it was.'

40

She smiles and shakes her head gently. She reaches out and takes my hand. I'm starting to cry, but I carry on.

'Such an exciting life I imagined for myself: travelling around the country in the pretty caravan with this dark, handsome, young man who adored me. He'd said so, clear as anything. I believed him.

'That was where it happened, of course – in his gypsy caravan. For the rest of that week we met up every day after he'd finished his work on the rides. Then we'd creep back to the caravan. Billy bought me drinks I'd never tried before. They made me feel warm and dizzy and excited. Billy told me I was his special girl. I felt special.'

'Oh, you poor child,' Erna says.

I take some deep breaths and continue talking.

'After Mass on the Sunday, I walked from my home the mile to the village to see Billy. The plan was, I was to go away with him the following morning. That's what Billy had said.

'I knew I would have to tell me ma that night. I was a bit nervous about that. Sure, Ma might be upset, about me joining the travelling fair and all, but she'd understand once she saw that we were in love; she'd come around to the idea in the end. I was sure she would. Besides, Billy had said he'd take me back to visit the family regularly so I needn't worry. He'd explained everything.

'When I got to the village, the shock nearly killed me, sure it did. *There was nothing there, Erna.* The village green was there all right, but it was *empty*, completely empty. The roundabouts, the coconut shies, the helter-skelter, the bumper cars, the waltzer and the gypsy caravans – all gone. Just a few old cans lying about, and lots of rubbish blowing in the dust. The whole fair had disappeared, moved on, and Billy with it. It was as if it had never existed; as if it had been a dream, which perhaps it was. But I soon found that the dream was to become a nightmare.

'Oh dear, I can believe that,' says Erna.

'It was some weeks later I realised I hadn't had the "curse"

41

for the past two months. Sure, why do they call it the curse, do you think, when it's *not having it* is the true curse? I waited one more month to be absolutely certain. There was no doubt about it, I was pregnant. I told Ma. She'd suspected. She'd heard me being sick in the privy. She slapped my face straight off, when I told her, and called me a wicked girl. Then she cried and she hugged me, and called me a foolish, silly baggage, and she cried and cried, and so did I.'

'Oh dear, what a situation. Your poor mother was frightened for you, Marie. What happened next?'

'Ma and I concealed the pregnancy for as long as possible. Eventually, she gave me the money for the fare to England, "to sort myself out". She advised me to have an abortion – and *soon* – before me da noticed. My skirts were already getting tight. I couldn't fasten them. Ma gave me a couple of "safe" addresses in London to go to. Women knew about these things; sure, I wasn't the first in this predicament in our area, Ma said. No way was I to return home with the baby, she told me. It'd be different if there was a father for me to marry. As it was, Da would never have me back in the house – I had to get rid of it. But I couldn't bear the thought of killing an innocent child – my own child. Never.

'I made some enquiries of my own, and found out about a mother and baby home in London instead – St Agatha's. It was run by nuns – so surely they'd be sympathetic? They'd be bound to look after a good Catholic girl, despite my wickedness. That's what I thought. But it wasn't like that. Not at all. I had twins you see, Erna. Barry is a twin. The head nun forced me to give my other baby away, my darling Donal. I had to give him up to be adopted. I never wanted to. I miss my Donal so much.' I'm sobbing bitterly. I can't speak for several minutes.

I wipe my eyes and blow my nose.

'There,' I say. 'That's my whole story, Erna, my whole shameful story. God only knows what might have become of Barry and me if it hadn't been for Sylvia – and you.'

I wait for Erna's response. Yet she doesn't seem shocked, not at all. She never even mentions the word 'shameful'.

'Thank you, Marie, for telling me your story so honestly. I knew you must have had a very difficult time. You've been through a terrible experience, and at such a young age. But you did everything you could to keep your children safe and well cared for. You thought first of *them*, and not of yourself. You should feel proud of that, and not guilty.'

I can't speak. A lump rises in my throat and sticks there.

'We all make mistakes,' Erna continues. 'You were only seventeen, innocent as a child. You must not blame yourself. You knew little of the world, still less of men – and you were looking for love. We all seek love. It does not mean you are wicked. You are a good mother – always remember that.'

I think Mrs Goldstein is a wise woman, and a lovely, kind woman, but I don't think me da would agree with her.

Chapter 6

1976
Barry

I like going to school for lessons. I love my teacher. Her name is Miss Lamb. She understands about me. She knows how much I like to learn things like reading and writing, and number work. Reading is easy. I love books. The words make pictures and stories in my head. Lots of the other children struggle over the words, but it's so easy! You just have to look and the words jump out of the page.

It's the same with numbers. The other children are *so slow*. They must be really stupid. They take ages to count the apples and oranges in the pictures Miss Lamb holds up. Even then they can't just *see* that if you put three oranges and five apples in a basket, it makes eight fruits altogether! Sometimes it gets so boring waiting for other children to tell Miss Lamb what they can see, that I just have to shout out the answer. I know you aren't supposed to do that, but I can't help it.

Sometimes Miss Lamb says, 'Well done, Barry,' in her gentle voice. 'You're very good at the numbers, aren't you? But try not to shout out the answers. You have to give Milly a chance to answer, even if it takes her a bit longer.'

I know Mammy is pleased when Miss Lamb tells her how clever I am. She's proud of how quickly I learn new things.

Today, at the Mammy and Daddy time, when they come to talk to the teachers, I can hear what Miss Lamb says to Mammy. I don't have a daddy.

'He's the sort of child who soaks up new information like a sponge,' Miss Lamb tells Mammy. 'He's racing ahead with reading and number work. It's just taking him a bit longer than most children to make friends, but that will come in time with encouragement, I'm quite sure.'

Mammy looks very happy, so maybe she will stop telling me to *give other children a chance to answer* when she can tell I already know the answer? Grown-ups don't make much sense – and when I ask them what they mean they tell me to shush.

'What did you do at school today, Barry?'

Mammy always asks that question when she comes to fetch me.

'At playtime, I mostly walk or skip around the outside of the playground. I like walking on the blue line best,' I tell her, and she smiles at me.

I don't tell her about another good game I sometimes play. I don't think she would like it. It's where I stop to stare at one of the other children. They don't always like that, but I do. I like it when they look scared of me. I know Mammy would tell me I shouldn't play that game.

I don't like it if someone else is standing in my way on the blue line, when I run round my favourite route. So, then I bend my knees and lift up my arms to look like a monster. I put on a fierce monster face and roar at the person in my way. This makes them move out of my way, which is good – but sometimes the other child bursts out crying and runs to tell Miss Lamb or another teacher on duty in the playground. Then I get told off, when it isn't my fault.

Once, Miss Lamb asked Mammy to come into the classroom after school to talk to her about my game.

'Of course, he means no harm by it,' Miss Lamb told Mammy, 'but perhaps you could talk to him about good ways to approach other children and make friends? For example, with a "smiley face" rather than a monster face?'

Miss Lamb must have thought Mammy didn't know what a smiley face was because she was smiling a lot at Mammy, to show her. Mammy started doing her smiley face too and said, 'Yes, of course, I'll talk to Barry about it at home.'

I don't like it when Mammy or Miss Lamb tell me off about things that aren't my fault. It makes me cross. Sometimes I get in a rage. Mammy doesn't like me getting in a rage. She says, *'Calm down, Barry,'* but I can't calm down, because the angry feeling is there, inside me, bubbling away, like tomato soup boiling in a pan.

***

When we get home Auntie Erna gives me a hug and says, 'Hello, Barry my dear.' She's always kind. I really like Auntie Erna and she likes me. Mammy says that makes her happy because Auntie Erna is a bit like a granny to me, and Mammy is sad that I can't see my own Granny and Grandpa, because they live far away in a place called Ireland. I've never met them, so I don't really mind not seeing them. I like just having Auntie Erna.

I heard Mammy tell Miss Lamb about Auntie Erna, and that she thinks I get on so well with her because we're both 'intellectuals'. Mammy says she wonders if she isn't clever enough herself, or that maybe she didn't work hard enough herself at school to be clever like me? But Auntie Erna always tells her off when she says that – she says Mammy *is* clever.

After dinner – it was spinach and I don't like spinach – I go down to Auntie Erna's sitting room on my own. I love to do that. I walk up to her and stand in front of her 'til she notices me. When she looks up at me I say, 'I've come to see you, Auntie Erna.'

'So you have, Barry my dear. Come and sit down with me.'

She always says that.

Auntie Erna reads books to me that Mammy thinks I'm too young to understand. Long books like *Treasure Island*, *Moby Dick* and *Oliver Twist*. They do have some hard words in them, but Auntie Erna explains what they mean. I love listening to stories. Today we're reading *Oliver Twist*. I sit on the floor at Auntie Erna's feet and rest my head on her knee, looking up at her whenever she shows me a picture.

Stories are a bit like dreams. In my head, I can see the desert island, or the huge whale swimming in the waves, or the hungry little boy called Oliver, with his empty bowl, asking for more gruel. Gruel is like porridge. I can hardly wait for the next chapter.

I love Auntie Erna's sitting room. There's a big piano near the window. It's called a grand piano because it's so big. In one corner there's a chessboard on a shiny wooden table. I love looking at the figures. One of them is like a horse. There's a king and a queen too. Auntie Erna has been teaching me how to play chess. It's quite a hard game to learn, but Auntie Erna says I'm picking it up really well. She used to play chess with her poor dear boy, Aron, but he died long ago. I think Mammy said he's in heaven.

Auntie Erna is starting to show me how some of the music notes are written. I can find lots of those notes on the piano. The part of the piano with white and black notes that you press is called the keyboard. One day I might be able to play real music like Auntie Erna. She used to play concerts, but she can't do that so well now because her fingers got hurt. They're too crooked to play as fast as before.

When it starts to get dark, Mammy comes in to say it's time for my bath.

I shout 'No!' because I'm having a lovely time, and it's not fair.

'Be a good boy, Barry,' Mammy says. 'It's getting late. Auntie

Erna must be tired. We have to let her have some peace and quiet …'

Mammy tells Auntie Erna that she worries I might be disturbing her or being a nuisance. That makes me very cross because I know I'm *not* being a nuisance. I start to cry and shout. Auntie Erna speaks to me in her gentle voice.

'Now, Barry, Mammy knows what's best. You need to have a bath and a good sleep, so we can have more fun tomorrow. You know I always enjoy your company, but tomorrow is another day. We'll have more time for reading and chess, and the piano, tomorrow.

'But I'm not tired!'

'Good. That shows you can come back again tomorrow. Will you do that?'

'All right …' I say, but I still feel a bit cross with Mammy.

Chapter 7

1976-82
Robert

The regime at the children's home is rigid and stern. Robert is considered a deeply troubled and troublesome child. He is frequently punished, sometimes severely. It's noticed at the home that however severe his punishment, he never cries. It is also recorded that at times, when he thinks he is not being observed – for example when alone in bed at night – Robert cries bitterly to himself under the covers.

Robert is intelligent, but his severe emotional and behavioural problems manifest themselves in all environments – in the orphanage, at school and in foster homes. One after another, the foster placements break down due to Robert's challenging behaviour. Almost without exception, the foster parents reach a stage – usually quite soon after his arrival – when they announce they can no longer cope with the child.

In school, Robert is also often in trouble – for swearing or defiance towards his teachers, and for aggression towards other children of his own age or older. Yet he can show moments of kindness too; for example, comforting younger children who hurt themselves, rescuing and feeding abandoned young animals, or offering to help some of the older carers in the home with difficult or heavy tasks.

At times he demonstrates subtle humour and understanding; he can apply himself to subjects he enjoys at school with great concentration. Gradually, he succeeds in many areas of school-work, sometimes showing exceptional ability. Yet his behaviour continues to be highly unpredictable and fiery. There is concern about early signs of potentially criminal characteristics.

At eleven, Robert is moved – without notice or explanation – to a bleak children's home in rural Northumberland, in the far north of England. It is a home specialising in accommodating the most troubled and difficult of 'cared-for' children. He becomes increasingly withdrawn, rarely speaking to other children in the home or to the staff. He spends most of the time when not at school reading books, but his behaviour becomes increasingly unpredictable.

The following year, when Robert is just twelve years old and in his first year at a nearby secondary school, older and highly experienced foster parents are approached and asked to take him on. This is seen as a last-ditch attempt to save the boy from slipping into further delinquency and possibly a life of crime. He already has a record for occasional shoplifting and pickpocketing, as well as being regarded as aggressive.

Many of the other children in school are scared of Robert, though in fact his acts of aggression are only in retaliation to attacks on him, usually by older children, who often target him to see his response. He never hurts smaller children, and in fact, often protects them. Yet, from his first days at secondary school, he acquires a reputation for fighting

Chapter 8

1976
Marie

It's Saturday and Sylvia has come for the day. It's such a joy to have her company. She's so funny and warm, but also wise in her down-to-earth way. Barry loves her too; she's one of the first grown-ups he got to know, from when he was a baby in fact. She acts like a big kid with him; of course, he loves that.

It's a fine day, so we make a picnic lunch and head for the nearby play park. Sylvia reminds me to bring a bag with stale bread to feed the ducks on the pond. We let Barry have a good run about, let him climb on the climbing frame, push him on the swings and spin him round on the roundabout. The playground is busy with lots of other children. After a while Sylvia and I find a seat and sit drinking our tea from a thermos.

'He's a little watcher, isn't he?' she says. I follow her gaze to Barry. He's standing with his back to us, looking at two children hanging upside down from the climbing frame, singing at the tops of their voices.

'Mmm, I suppose he is. Takes him a while to join in. Actually, he sometimes acts like he doesn't really *like* other children.'

'Oh no, Marie. He's just a bit shy.'

Barry turns to look in our direction. Sylvia and I both give him a little wave. He smiles and heads for a small roundabout. A mother and her twin girls are playing nearby. They are barely more than toddlers, a couple of years younger than Barry, maybe three or four years old.

'Ah, look at them, Marie. Pretty little things. Look at that great fluff of fair hair!'

It gives me a start to realise they are identical twins. My heart starts to pound as I immediately think about *my* twins. They should be here together too. They should be playing together. Sylvia must know what I'm thinking. She squeezes my hand in hers.

The little girls are racing about, chasing each other, giggling and having a whale of a time. Barry is very interested. He watches them. I'm delighted to see him join in their chasey game, running around them in a circle. That really pleases me – I so like to see him playing sociably. He picks up a bit of speed and catches up with the wee girl nearest to him. Suddenly he seems to bump into her and give her a little push. She's sent flying down to the ground. She sits up slowly, looking shocked, her eyes searching for her mum. Then she starts wailing. Her mum and I both jump up and hurry towards the children. Barry is standing watching the little girl, his finger in his mouth.

'Oh, Barry,' I say, 'you have to be more careful. What do you say?'

'Sowwy …' he says in that kind of sing-song voice and looking at me, a little smile on his face. Maybe it's embarrassment. Then he says, 'Didn't mean to.'

I turn to the girls' mum. 'I'm so sorry. Is she all right?'

She's picked her up her little daughter and is cuddling her. 'Oh don't worry,' she says, 'she'll be fine.'

She gives Barry a kind smile. 'Accidents happen, don't they?'

'But, Barry, you're getting to be a big boy now. You should be more careful.'

He gives me another little knowing look.

***

Later, when Sylvia has gone home, I talk to Erna about it.

'It upset me, Erna. I know he's just a little boy, and the child's mother was very understanding ...'

Erna looks at me closely.

'So everything was all right then; just a little accident?'

'Well, I wasn't sure ... I just wondered ... whether it really was an accident. It seemed a bit ... mean.'

'Hmm? Children can appear to be unkind sometimes, when they are just trying out behaviours. It can be satisfying for them to see what reaction their behaviour causes. Maybe Barry was just experimenting? I'm sure he didn't intend to be mean.'

Chapter 9

1981
Barry

If only it would rain, then it would be indoor playtime and I could go inside, maybe stay in the library and read a book. No chance of that today. There's hardly a single cloud in the sky. The sun is making sharp dark shadows from the tall, red-brick school buildings across the playground. We'll have to go out. As usual a group of boys are playing football, thumping the ball into a goal area chalked on a tall wall at one end of the school building, yelling to each other to 'pass!', 'shoot!', 'kick!' at the tops of their voices.

I walk along the outside of the pitch, which is marked by white lines painted on the asphalt. A football rolls past just in front of me.

'Here! Barry, pass it over! Come on – kick it here!'

I take no notice. What a stupid activity, kicking a ball from one goal to another.

'Barry! Come on, you creep! Kick the fucking ball!' yells Guy

54

Robbins. Immediately a piercing whistle brings the footballers to a sudden standstill. Mr Lawless strides over towards Guy.

'We'll not have language like that in the yard, or anywhere else in school, Guy Robbins,' he says. 'Inside, *now*, and an hour's detention tonight.'

Guy groans and slouches towards the entrance, deliberately banging into me on his way and muttering, 'That was your fault, you moron. Just wait … I'll get you for this.'

'Make that a *two*-hour detention, Guy,' calls Mr Lawless.

All the boys who were playing football are looking at me with fierce, angry faces. They'll be after me on my way home. I'll have to leave sharpish after the bell, and run all the way. At least Guy will be out of the way.

It's double maths in the afternoon. The other kids always moan at that, but I love it. Maths is a language I understand. Most people seem to find it boring. I love the patterns, the logic and order of numbers. Mr James, my maths teacher, is the only one who understands.

We're doing algebra today. Mr James has written a long problem on the board. It's wonderful, like a mysterious puzzle to unravel. My heart starts beating with excitement. I get straight down to it. The rest of the class grumble and groan, but it doesn't take me long. I raise my hand.

'Well, surprise, surprise,' Mr James says with a smile. 'Have you worked it out already, Barry?'

'Yes, sir.'

'Well done, son. Come and write it up here on the board.'

I take the piece of chalk from Mr James, and write the algebraic problem out in numbers, explaining each bit as I go along, trying to help the others. Then I write the answer.

'Correct, as usual, Barry,' Mr James says. 'Good boy.'

He pats me on the back and gently nudges me back towards my desk at the back of the room. On the way I stumble twice over feet deliberately stuck out to trip me. As I pass through the rows of desks, I hear the muttering of 'swot', 'teacher's pet', 'Mummy's boy' and other insults hissed at me.

That afternoon, after the bell goes, it takes me a while to pack up my bag. I know I'll never be quick enough to beat the bullies, so I decide to borrow a couple of books from the library. Maybe by the time I leave, the others will have got fed up and gone home. But that plan doesn't work. A group of boys and girls are waiting at the school gate for me to emerge.

'Nancy boy!' one yells. 'Weirdo!' 'Cissy!'

'Youuu, got no dad no more – thaaat, means your mum's a whore!' someone sings.

Sean, a friend of Guy's, suddenly leaps out from behind the school gate. He sticks his foot out in front of me and I go flying. The metal bolt on the gate catches my forehead and my chin crashes to the asphalt. There's a moment when everyone is frozen in shock, including me. Then they start flinging mud from the flower bed at me. I get to my feet and run round the corner as fast as I can. I keep running.

When I get home I pull the front door open and slam it shut behind me, panting. Mum is just taking a cup of tea to Auntie Erna. They both look up in alarm as I fling myself on the sofa. I can't hold back the tears. My clothes are all muddy and my face must be mud-smeared too, and now the tears will make even more of a mess of it. I have a large bruise and graze on my chin, and a deep cut on my forehead.

'I hate it! I hate it!' I shout bitterly.

'Barry, sweetheart, whatever is the matter?' Mum asks. 'What's happened?' She gasps. 'Your face!'

'I never want to go back to that school.'

Mum rushes over to me, gently touching my face and peering at the torn knees of my trousers. 'Oh no! Oh, Barry! Oh, you poor love!'

Auntie Erna gets up and sits next to me on the sofa. She pats my leg. 'Has someone at school been unkind to you, my dear?

Children can be very cruel sometimes, can't they?' She speaks softly and calmly.

Auntie Erna always seems to know why things are difficult for me. She understands. That makes me feel better. Mum just seems to fuss.

'The others hate me because I'm cleverer than they are. They don't want to learn. They think I'm weird because I like learning. I wish I could go to a different school.' My chest is heaving and I'm trying to hold back tears.

'Oh, Barry love, you know that's not possible,' Mum says. 'It was the only local school that had a place. I know some of the children are a bit rough, but I'm sure they don't really hate you. Maybe I should go and talk to the head teacher,' she says, looking at Auntie Erna.

'No!' I shout. 'That would just make it worse – they'd hate me all the more for being a sneak!' Why couldn't Mum see that?

'Do you know,' says Auntie Erna, 'I have an idea.' She pauses. 'But first, let's think about this, Barry. I know that you are a clever boy and you are quick to learn your lessons at school, but you need to learn another lesson – and that is not to talk about being cleverer than the other children.'

'But it's true, Auntie Erna!'

'It may well be true, but other children won't like to hear you say it – it might upset and annoy them. They might think it's a little boastful, Barry.'

I look down at my feet. I think about this, and nod.

'But now listen, both of you. *This is my idea.*'

Chapter 10

1982
Robert

The social worker is called Mrs Wilson. She's quite nice – she actually talks to me.

'Now, Robert, I've known the people who have offered to foster you for many years. Mr and Mrs Carter, they're called, and they are truly lovely. They may let you call them Len and Betty,' Mrs Wilson says as we're driving along.

We seem to be travelling miles through the Northumberland countryside. The council must have decided to put me in the back of beyond, where I won't cause any trouble.

'Yes,' she continues, 'they're very experienced. They've fostered dozens of children over the last thirty years or more.'

Thirty years or more! I reckon that means they must be *very* old, probably over sixty. I'm not too keen on the idea of living with such old people … but it can't be worse than the children's home. I hated it there; it was like living with total strangers who didn't give a toss about me. So I decide it can't hurt to give it a try. Len and Betty Carter? Yep, definitely old fogey names. Oh well, let's see what they're like …

Mrs Wilson drives me for what feels like hours down narrow, twisty roads through countryside and one or two villages. Nothing except hills and woods, and fields with loads of sheep, and occasional villages. At long last we come to a row of small houses on the edge of a village.

'Used to be miners' cottages, these,' Mrs Wilson tells me, 'but now that nearly all the pits have closed, it's a mixture of people living in them. Pretty, aren't they, Robert?'

'Hmm … dunno.'

'Nearly there …'

We follow the road around a corner and up a small hill, with a row of about a dozen cottages at the top. Mrs Wilson stops the car in front of the end house.

'Here we are, Robert,' she says. 'This is going to be your new home.'

She turns round to look at me. 'Try and make the most of it, love, won't you? Len and Betty are really nice, and I know they'll like you.'

How on earth can you know that? I think. I've not met many people who like me. My heart is racing and butterflies are swirling in my stomach. I feel a bit sick. As we approach the front door, I can see a woman watching us through the front window. I'm scared, but don't want to show it, so I hunch my shoulders, look down at my feet, and slouch moodily behind the social worker. I glance up at the window again for a moment. The woman has disappeared.

Suddenly the front door is flung open and an oldish woman rushes out and steps onto the path towards me. She's short and has grey hair. A tall man who also has grey hair appears behind her.

The woman hurries straight towards me and before I have a chance to think of resisting, she presses me into her bosom and gives me a huge hug. I bet I've gone bright red. I push my hands deep into my pockets. I shuffle my feet and look at the ground. The man hovers behind her as if he's waiting for his turn. I push my hands further into my pockets and hunch my shoulders even further.

'Hello, Robbie, my darling!' the woman says. 'My name's Betty and this is Len. We're so glad you've come to live with us, pet. This is your home now.'

'Aye, laddie,' says Len, now joining in the hug. 'Welcome, welcome.'

'Now, my darling,' continues Betty, taking no notice of my reluctance to respond, 'if it's all right with you, we're going to call you *Robbie*, because it suits a young lad like you. Mebbes in the future you'll want to be Rob? That'll be for you to decide later, if you want to, pet. But for now, we'll just stick with Robbie, shall we?'

She doesn't pause for an answer.

'Eeee, Robbie, what a bonny lad you are! Isn't he bonny, Len? Clever too, I'll be bound. Well, the world's your oyster, Robbie, my darling. You could do anything you set your mind to, am I right?'

I'm so astonished at the warmth of this greeting, and that these friendly, elderly people seem to think they know immediately who I am, and might become, that I remain speechless, silent, looking from one to the other. I can feel an uncertain smile waxing and waning on my face, like the sun disappearing and then reappearing from behind a cloud. *Their* smiles are anything but uncertain. They positively *beam* at me, as if I'm the best thing that could have happened to them.

I feel suddenly as though I'm a real person for the first time in my life. It's the most extraordinary feeling I've ever experienced. It's as if they really *want* me. I feel I can tell they actually want me. I have a struggle to hold back tears, and they aren't tears of sadness.

'Come on, Robbie, pet. Let's not wear the doorstep down! Come on in and I'll show you your room.'

Len picks up my bag. 'Aye, up you go with Betty, lad. I'll bring your stuff.'

Betty leads the way up a narrow staircase. She points out the bathroom and toilet, and opens a door.

'In you go, pet.'

She stands to one side to let me past. The room isn't large, but it's flooded with golden light from the sun, just starting to go down in a clear sky. There's a double window looking out onto green fields and heather-covered hills beyond.

'Best view in the house, this room!' says Betty, squeezing my arm.

'It's a nice room, er … Betty.'

She beams at me. 'We want you to be really happy here, Robbie,' she says. 'What sort of thing do you like doing best, sweetheart? What did you like doing at the children's home?'

'I didn't like much. I liked reading, because then I could be by myself.'

'Oh, that's a bit sad. Sounds like you must have been lonely? Well, you can read as much as you like here, Robbie, but there's plenty else to do, and Len'll not let you get away with not seeing his allotment! It's his pride and joy!'

She gives me another squeeze. I don't pull away this time. I guess I'll have to get used to the hugs.

'Now you get settled in, pet, and then Len will take you for a wander about – and to see his allotment,' she says with a smile.

She turns to look behind us and then whispers confidentially in my ear. 'Just tell him how grand it is, Robbie, even if you don't give a toss. It'll make his day.' She giggles and gives me a wink.

***

That first evening is quite hard work for me. Len and Betty are lively, talkative people. I've never experienced being included in a conversation before. I like them all right. I like the house and

61

especially my room, I like Len's allotment, I like the 'toad in the hole' Betty makes for supper. But I sense that they want me to be happy with them and act like 'one of the family'. That feels quite a strain at first. I'm not used to it.

'So tell us something about the children's home, Robbie,' Betty says at teatime. 'Did you get on all right?'

'I … I hated it. We had to share a bedroom, four of us boys. The others were OK, but they weren't friends of mine. Some of the staff were all right, but they were like … strangers. That was how it felt. Living with strangers. They weren't cruel or anything, but they could be hard. There was no fun there.'

I was finding my thoughts difficult to put into words, yet I wanted to try; I wanted to tell them.

'There was no warmth, no understanding, no personal feeling, no …'

'Eee dear, Robbie. Sounds like they took basic care of the bairns, but mebbe didn't give them any *love*. Am I right?'

'I suppose so,' I muttered.

How could she know straightaway exactly what's on my mind, but I'm too embarrassed to say?

***

When I wake the following morning, I'm glad to remember where I am. The bedroom – my bedroom – looks sort of friendly. It needs something on the walls though. Some posters maybe. I don't think Len and Betty would mind if I put some up. I'm also pleased to remember it's Saturday, and that I won't have to face starting at the new school for another couple of days. I go downstairs. Len's sitting at the kitchen table, reading a newspaper.

'Morning, Robbie, did you sleep all right?'

'Yes thanks.'

'Well, there's no school today or tomorrow. What do you fancy

62

doing, lad? Will I take you for a tour of the village? Not that that'll take very long – there's not a lot to it!'

'Yes, OK, and then can we go back to the allotment?'

Len's face creases with pleasure.

'I liked it there …'

''Course we can, lad, 'course we can.'

Betty comes in from the garden, holding a large empty basket. I guess she's been hanging out some washing. She puts the basket down and puts her arms round my shoulders and gives me a hug, the first of the day.

'Here he is, the bonny lad!' she says, smiling broadly at me. 'Now, what'll you have for breakfast?'

Whatever Len and Betty might have been told about me, and even though they're quite old, from the very first day, they just seem to accept me for who I am. Most people are quite scared of teenage boys, I've discovered – and I'm nearly a teenager. Not Len and Betty. They treat me with affection and humour such as I've never experienced before.

***

I'm really nervous about my first day at the new school, but I try not to show it. In the end it's not too bad. Len walks to the bus stop with me. There are two other lads waiting, one about my age and one a bit older, and a girl also about my age. They all greet Len in a friendly way, looking at me with interest, but no hostility.

'This here's a new pal for youse kids,' Len tells them. 'Robbie's his name, and he's starting at your school today.'

I feel my cheeks start to burn, but the other kids just grin at me.

'Hiya, Robbie, welcome to Hartland High. I'm Danny by the way,' says the boy of my age.

'Yeah, Hi. I'm Buzz,' says the bigger lad.

'Hi, Robbie! My name's Paige,' says the girl.

I'm amazed at how friendly they are. Maybe the arrival of a new boy is a big event in this area.

It's the same in the school itself. Hartland High's not very big, being in a small country town. The teachers and the kids all seem keen to talk to me.

Over the coming weeks, I settle quite well and begin gradually to make some friendships, though it's still hard for me trust other kids enough to get really close. Len and Betty always encourage me to bring any friends home 'for tea', like we're all little kids! I don't mind, and the others seem to enjoy it too, especially Betty's baking!

Len and Betty ask me loads of questions about my time at school: what lessons I've had, who I sat next to, which ones do I like best, are the teachers nice … that sort of thing. They expect me to talk back to them as well. I can't get away with being moody and silent. Over the coming months, any grumpiness on my part is greeted with concern and understanding, and often with good humour, but they're never fazed. If I come home from school looking upset or angry, there's no question of stomping up to my room to spend time on my own, as I've often done in the past. No, they'll have none of that! They always insist that I sit down and talk to them, while they try to prise the reason for my unhappiness from me.

'Come on now, Robbie, my darling, out with it! You tell your auld Auntie Betty what the problem is … go on. Now, let's see … have any of those bad lads at school been nasty to you? No? Well then, have you fallen for one of the gorgeous girls? But mebbe she's not interested … Is that it? Doesn't fancy you like you fancy her, hmm? Though I can't think why she wouldn't, handsome lad like you – it's her loss, the daft lass!'

So gradually, the cause of my bad mood is coaxed from me, and they either comfort or reassure me, or we all end up laughing uncontrollably together.

***

For the first time in my life I feel a part of a family. Even Len and Betty's adult children greet me warmly when they visit.

'It's good for them to have a youngster to care for at their age,' their eldest son, Harry, tells me, patting my shoulder confidentially. 'It'll keep them young, like.'

'Aye,' adds their daughter Shirley. 'I'm right glad there's a sensible lad like you living with them; keeping an eye on them an' all, Robbie. Anything wrong, anything worrying you, just give us a ring. You've got me number.'

No one had ever considered me *good* for other people or anything else before, and least of all *sensible*! But I like their genuine faith in me. I like Len and Betty in a way I've never liked anyone before. I feel a closeness, which warms and softens my heart. I feel I have to live up to the family's positive opinion of me. I *want* to be liked by them. It's the first time I'm conscious of caring what anyone else thinks of me. It's the first time the concept of *love* has any real or special meaning for me.

***

In the second year, we have a new form teacher, Mr Lewis, who takes a special interest in me from the start. He also teaches English and drama, my favourite subjects. I really like Mr Lewis, perhaps because I can tell he likes me. Mr Lewis tells me I have 'great potential'. Nobody has ever said that to me before. Mr Lewis discovers how much I like reading books. I'd never told anyone about it – he must just have noticed I spend a lot of time with my nose in a book. He takes trouble to find out what sort of books I enjoy, and helps me to make selections from the school library. Mr Lewis encourages me to 'research' topics in my schoolwork, like in history or geography, by finding relevant books in the school or public library.

Mr Lewis meets with Len and Betty regularly on parents' evenings too – they never miss an opportunity to attend. I'm always included in the conversation, and I'm surprised to find that Mr Lewis has an amazing amount to say about me. I don't understand how Mr Lewis could know so much about me, when I don't even know it myself! I wonder if perhaps he just makes it up as he goes along.

'Robbie's an exceptionally bright lad,' he says, nodding at me, 'especially when you consider his past. He's really blossoming this year in all his work, but in particular, he's showing outstanding ability in English and drama. I'm sometimes astonished by how wide his vocabulary is for a lad his age. He reads widely, and has a real talent for writing, whether stories and imaginative accounts, or factual descriptions. He's got a truly vivid imagination. My one main concern is that his confidence is still so fragile.'

He looks at me sympathetically as he says this. He reaches out and clasps my shoulder. I probably turn beetroot-red. I can feel my cheeks burning.

'You've got to believe in yourself, Robbie. Try to think the best of yourself and what you can do. Be ambitious. Always *expect* the best, rather than expecting the worst.'

I shuffle uncomfortably on my chair. Mr Lewis nods and smiles at me, as if this is just what he would expect. Then he turns to Len and Betty.

'Robbie doesn't always realise just how good he is, how *able* – but he is. I've been amazed to see how he can hold an audience – in drama, for example. He's got a really special talent. He could be an actor; he's such a fantastic mimic. He can copy any accent, maybe because he's moved around a lot. He has the other children in stitches sometimes.'

'Eeee, Robbie! D'you hear that? Isn't that grand, son?' Betty squeezes my arm affectionately.

'Aye,' says Len, 'he's got a funny way about him all right – but you've got to apply yourself too, lad.'

'That's right,' says Mr Lewis, 'the fact is there's no limit to what Robbie is capable of, if he does apply himself. He can go on to

66

do his GCSEs, and then his A levels. In fact, there's no reason why he can't go to *university* one day.'

Len claps me on the back. 'Just listen to that, Robbie me lad. There's a great future for you. Never mind if the past has been tricky. The past is past and gone; it's *now and from now on* that matters. Work hard at all your schoolwork, even the bits that aren't your favourites – your greatest interests, like. Could be "Professor Robbie" one day if you put your mind to it!'

***

I soon get to know Len's two great interests in *his* life since retiring from the pit, one being fishing and the other being working on his allotment. Over time I learn to love sharing both these activities with him. Len teaches me how to set the bait on the rod, how to identify the best places along the river to catch different sorts of fish, how to hold on when the line jerks and pulls – and then how to draw it in carefully, smoothly, always steadily, though I'm wild with excitement. Actually catching fish for us all to fry with chips for tea is the ultimate joy for me, but most of all I love sitting quietly at the riverbank, listening to Len's stories of his life down the mine. It's like stories of another era to me. No other adult has ever talked to me of things that mattered. All around them, the mines have been closing down.

'They're tekkin' the heart out of the communities,' Len tells me, shaking his head sadly. 'Soon there'll be no work for lads round here, no jobs at all.'

Beyond the village, the beautiful Northumberland countryside stretches for miles. Despite living half his life underground, Len is a countryman at heart and he knows about every aspect of it. He teaches me to recognise birds by their plumage and their song, and to be *quiet* in the countryside; to listen to the sounds around me and distinguish one birdcall from another.

Betty's great love is flowers. At each time of year we bring her armfuls of whatever blooms are in season and I learn the names and characteristics of plants I'd never even heard of before. Len and Betty's fireplace or windowsill is never without a colourful vase of flowers to brighten it in the spring. As well as decorating the house, we gather plants for food, like young nettles or wild garlic to make soups or flavour stews.

As the year progresses into the later summer and autumn we bring wild blackberries, raspberries and damsons for jam, bottling and making tarts. Later in autumn we find edible mushrooms, which Len helps me to identify, using a much-fingered guide dating from the long-gone days of wartime rationing. At first, I'm scared to eat them, convinced we'll all drop dead from poisoning. But under Len's confident guidance, I soon learn to recognise the edible field mushrooms, big boletus, and the curly, yellow ones that they call 'scrambled egg'. More importantly, Len shows me how to recognise and keep away from the *poisonous* ones!

At home Betty and I wash the mushrooms carefully without bruising them. Then we pat them dry gently with a clean tea towel, and fry them for tea with onions, eggs, and a bit of rosemary from the bush next to the kitchen door. From that day to this, the smell of rosemary is always enough to set my mouth watering, like a Pavlovian dog.

Chapter 11

1982
Marie

After Barry telling us of his unhappy experiences at school, he and I both wait eagerly and nervously to hear what Erna Goldstein is going to suggest to help him.

'So this is my idea,' says Erna. 'Why don't we arrange for Barry to take the exam for Wentford Grammar School and see if they can offer him a place. I'm sure he'd do very well at the entrance examination. What do you think of that, Barry?'

Barry looks shocked. Then he beams at her like the sun is shining out of him. 'Oh yes!' he says. 'I'd *love* to go to Wentford Grammar School!'

'Now wait a minute, Barry,' I say. 'Erna, I'm sorry, it's a lovely idea, but it's just not possible for Barry to go to Wentford, much as I'd love him to.'

'Why not, Mum?' Barry wails, looking from Erna to me and back again.

'Because, darling, it's a private school and it costs a lot of money, and that's just the fees. There's the uniform and sports equipment, and other expenses no doubt as well. I just can't afford that sort of money. I haven't got it.'

'Of course not, Marie. You didn't let me finish. I am very fortunate that I have been left with more money than I need for myself. One day perhaps I'll explain how that came about. The important thing is that you, Marie, and Barry, have come to mean so much to me. I can't think of any better way of spending some of that money than by helping you both now. It would make me happier than I can say.'

Erna reaches to me and takes hold of my hand.

'So, Marie, I would love to help you and Barry in this way. I will pay for his fees and any other expenses related to his education. Please believe me, nothing would give me greater pleasure.'

***

Barry had been at Wentford School for nearly two terms, and was settling in so well. He'd studied hard for his entrance examination and had not only passed, but won a substantial scholarship. Erna paid for everything else. I could never fully repay her kindness, but I wanted to get something for her to show my gratitude.

One day, as I'm walking through Blackheath Village, looking in the shop windows. I stop at a flower shop and study the beautiful displays. A friend of Mrs Goldstein has just paid me fifty pounds for making her a two-piece suit. I know exactly what I want to do with the money. I choose a large bouquet made up of what I know are Mrs Goldstein's favourite colours – 'hot' colours to remind her of sunshine: red, yellow, orange and peach. I ask the lady to wrap them in fine paper, finished with a deep turquoise ribbon.

At home, I secrete the flowers into a vase filled with water to keep them fresh, and hide them in the cupboard under the stairs. I set about making a cake with freshly cooked plums and ground almonds, with a crumble topping. Then at teatime, while Barry is doing his homework upstairs, I bring in the cups and plates as usual, with the cake on the top of the trolley.

'Oh my goodness, Marie! You have been busy. You know how much I love plum cake.'

'I do, Mrs Goldstein.'

'*Erna!* Go on, Marie – must I keep reminding you to always call me Erna? Surely we are good enough friends for that?' She smiles.

'Of course we are ... *Erna.* It's just that as well as thinking of you as wonderful, generous friend, I sometimes think what a fine and grand lady you are, and how much I admire you. Anyway, I made the cake specially for you ... and I want to give you something too.'

I dash out of the room and fetch the bouquet of flowers from the cupboard. I place the bouquet on the low table to one side of Erna's chair.

'Oh! My goodness ... how beautiful! But it's not my birthday. What have I done to deserve such gifts?'

'It's just because you *are* such a good kind friend, and you have been so unbelievably generous to me and to Barry. Do you realise how much you have changed his life, Erna, and mine too? He was so miserable at his old school, so angry and isolated. Now he goes to school each morning with a skip in his step. He is soaring ahead with his lessons, and he's appreciated by the teachers and the other children. I'm hoping he might even bring a friend home soon – which has never happened before. I can never thank you enough for your generosity.'

'You have already thanked me quite enough, Marie, and you know that giving Barry the opportunity to attend Wentford School has been a huge joy for me. In any case, you know it was his own intelligence that helped him pass the entrance examination and even win a scholarship.

'So thank you for the beautiful flowers, and I can't wait to have a piece of that delicious-looking cake – but let's say no more about generosity and gratitude. Come, cut us each a piece of cake and let's have our coffee.'

I hand her a cup and a large slice of the cake.

'Thank you, Marie. You know, you and Barry are so special to me; in fact, you have become like my family. I don't have the company of my dear son Aron, but I am so happy to have your company. And, because you are so special to me, and have told me something of your own history, I would really like to tell you a bit more about myself. First I think I should explain to you, as my friend and companion, how I come to be living here in England in the first place … on my own, without my family.'

'Well, that seems very personal, Erna, very private, isn't it? I wouldn't want you to have to relive unhappy times or painful memories … You don't have to tell me anything about yourself you don't want to. I would never pry.'

'No, I know you wouldn't pry, Marie. It's because I like and trust you enough that I'd like to tell you about myself, as you have been open with me about your past.

'Did I ever tell you about my husband, Marie? His name was Andreas. We were very happy together, especially when our son Aron was born in 1927. I was a young woman of twenty-seven then. Andreas was a doctor and I was a pianist. We loved each other very much. We lived in Berlin during the 1930s. At first life was good; Andreas's parents lived nearby, we had good friends and we both enjoyed our work. One great sadness was that Aron showed signs of not developing normally physically. When he was two, he was diagnosed with a serious progressive wasting disease called muscular dystrophy. There was no cure. Things became even more difficult for us towards the later years of the 1930s. We were Jewish – do you know what that means, Marie?'

I feel a moment of acute embarrassment. I know the colour must be rising up my neck and suffusing my cheeks, as if I'm sitting with my face too close to a fire.

'Oh, you know, Erna, I'm sorry to say I'm not a very educated girl,' I say. 'Of course I've *heard* of Jews, and I know they suffered something dreadful in the war ... but I have only a vague notion of what it *means* to be Jewish and why you're not exactly like us Christian folk.'

Erna smiles. 'You are right, Marie, that we have some different beliefs to Christians, and some different ways of worshipping, as do people of other faiths. The problem is, many people distrust anyone who is different to themselves. So I'll tell you what happened.

'Hitler, the leader of the Nazi party in Germany in the 1930s and '40s, encouraged people to hate the Jews. He made out they were the cause of everything wrong in Germany. He made them into "scapegoats" for every problem. Do you know what that means, Marie? And many people liked having a group of people to blame for all that was wrong in their world.'

'Yes, I understand what you're saying, Erna. In Ireland people sometimes talked about the gypsies that way too. I always thought that was nasty. The gypsies are no different to the rest of us really.'

'That's true, I think you are quite right. Well, the situation for Jews became very difficult – very dangerous – in Germany. At first it was just calling them unpleasant names; you know, insulting them, goading them. Then gradually, many Jews were pushed out of their jobs, especially high-grade jobs like doctors, teachers, lawyers and so on. That meant many people lost their income – and then they could not support themselves or their family properly. Andreas was forced to leave his job in the hospital. He wasn't allowed to continue practising as a hospital doctor, even though most of his patients loved and trusted him.

'Luckily for us, he could earn a little money treating private patients in secret in our apartment. It was dangerous, and he only charged what he thought people could afford, but at least we could buy a little food. At this time too, many Jewish children and young people were being denied education. They were forced to leave their schools or universities. Things got worse and worse ...'

I shake my head and sigh.

'One night, a good friend of ours was viciously attacked in the street opposite. Many people saw it happen, but most were too frightened to do anything to protect or help him. Andreas and a former colleague crept out at night, carried the injured man home and treated his injuries.'

'That's wicked, that is, that's terrible. You must have been terrified.'

'It was wicked, and it was very frightening. Suddenly, we could no longer trust people we'd known for years; we couldn't even be sure of people who had once appeared friendly to us. We were especially concerned for Aron. He was particularly vulnerable because of his illness, which meant he was confined to a wheelchair from the age of about ten years old.'

'Oh, the poor wee boy ...'

'During the later years of the 1930s, life for us in Berlin was becoming more and more difficult and dangerous, as it was for all Jewish people. We hardly left the flat during daylight hours, even to buy food. Day by day, week by week, the Nazis gained more control over the population. These days, we might say they were being "brainwashed", especially the young people.

'The Nazis characterised the Jews as the cause of Germany's economic problems, and therefore the cause of poverty among ordinary people, deserving only disgust and hatred. Aggressive mobs of youths roamed the streets, looking for Jews to humiliate and victimise. Andreas's patients would creep into our apartment building late at night, and come up to our flat for him to treat their ailments, but it was very risky.

'Increasingly, we heard rumours of Jews being rounded up and sent to "camps" far away. We didn't know exactly where to – only that they did not return. Some people even referred to them as "death camps", but no one really knew what went on in them. Andreas's parents told us two couples, elderly like themselves, and living in their street, had been dragged away, crying and begging to be allowed to remain. Of course, that really terrified my in-laws.

'We were aware that the troubles and dangers would only escalate, so, even though we had little money, over the previous two or three years we had gradually, bit by bit, been transferring money to England via good friends we knew we could trust. Do you remember my friend Mrs Heller, Marie? For whom you made the lovely wedding outfit? She and her husband had already left Germany and were living in London. They were a great help to us. We were making a plan to leave Germany ourselves, for good. Although Berlin had always been our home, we felt there was no option but to emigrate and make new lives where it was safe, in England, and perhaps ultimately in Palestine.'

There are tears rolling down Erna's cheeks. I wrap my arms around her, hot tears of sympathy welling up in my own eyes.

'Oh, you're so brave to speak about it, dear Erna. Sure, it must be so distressing for you to remember those tragic times.'

'Yes, but I want you to understand, Marie. I must tell you how it was, even though it is upsetting.'

She takes some deep breaths and wipes her eyes.

'By that time, Aron was nearly thirteen. A week before our planned departure, the three of us were making our way back home after visiting Andreas's parents in their apartment nearby. It had been a dispiriting visit, one of many. The old couple would not hear of leaving Berlin, despite their fears. It had always been their home. They said they were too frail to make such a hazardous journey and they thought perhaps people were exaggerating the dangers. Surely things could never become so bad as Andreas and I seemed to imagine, they told us. Why, they had lived in Berlin all their lives. Of course, there had always been isolated incidents of anti-Semitism, they said, but things usually settled down in the end. There was no need to overstate the problems, to imagine the worst. They thought it was best just to keep their heads down and stay indoors out of sight as much as possible. Life was bound to improve again in time, they were sure. We should go to England, if we felt it was the best for us, but they believed we would soon return.

'Andreas was very worried about his parents' unrealistic assessment of the situation – and also worried about leaving them behind.

'On our way back that evening, we talked and talked as we walked. It was dark, and I was pushing Aron in his wheelchair. We were feeling frustrated by Andreas's parents' attitude – and by our impotence to change it. We were so preoccupied by our discussion, that I suppose we were less vigilant than usual.

'We had turned off from the wide, tree-lined Unter den Linden boulevard, into a maze of smaller, darker side streets, and we hadn't noticed a small group of Nazis following us.

'Suddenly this mob – made up of young men and teenagers, several in uniform and carrying weapons – ran towards us, shouting and jeering. They grabbed hold of Aron's wheelchair, rocking it violently from side to side. He was helpless. He could do nothing to defend himself as they taunted him mercilessly, mocking his disability. They just gave whoops of laughter, seeing his fear.'

'Oh no,' I gasp. 'That's so cruel. Your poor boy!'

'It was awful. Aron was absolutely terrified. Andreas was so brave – he placed himself directly between the Nazis and Aron, pushing them away as they came close, telling them to leave us alone, that we had done nothing to them.

'I had managed to grasp the handles of the wheelchair to try to hold it steady, but now they turned their attack onto Andreas, beating him over the head with rifle butts and metal batons. They were like savages, completely without mercy. Andreas fell to the ground; blood was pouring from his head.'

Erna paused and pressed her handkerchief to her face.

'I screamed at them to stop. That made them turn their attention to me for a moment. Several of the men began beating my hands with their weapons as I tried to cling to the wheelchair.

'Seeing Andreas so still and bleeding, I tried to approach him. I bent down to hold him in my arms. The attackers were suddenly shocked at the extremity of what they had done. It was clear to see that Andreas was dead, his skull broken. The attackers stood gaping at him for a moment, lying on the cold pavement, and then they ran away laughing.

'I was shaking, deep in shock. I knew Andreas was dead, and I hated having to leave him there, but there was nothing else I could do. My hands were irreparably injured, but I managed to limp home, pushing Aron's wheelchair with my elbows. Friends crept out later in the night to retrieve Andreas's body for burial. I was bereft at the loss of my beloved husband. I knew I would have to protect and care for Aron, and to try to arrange our escape and emigration, all alone. I could hardly think of my life without Andreas, but I was determined to take Aron to a place of safety.'

By now I'm trembling and trying to control the tears. Erna is so brave. I put my arms around her and we hold one another in a desperate embrace. I can't bear to think what she had gone through. After a while, Erna bravely gathers herself together and insists on finishing her story.

'With help from some gentile friends in Germany, and English friends who vouched for us, I managed to obtain the necessary documents for Aron and myself to emigrate to England. I cannot describe the pain of leaving Berlin without Andreas – and how much I missed him.

'Not long after we arrived in England in 1939, I heard that Andreas's parents had been forced to leave their home. They were taken, with others, to one of the camps. It was only much later that I found out they did not survive.

'My fingers had been broken in several places. A medical colleague of Andreas had bound them the day after the attack, using wooden spatulas as splints. My hands healed slowly, but they were very badly damaged; I would never be a concert pianist again. I was fortunate to be able to find regular work as a music teacher in England and earn enough to support myself and Aron. The Hellers helped me find a small flat to rent in Blackheath, close to where they lived. We had seven years together, Aron and I – precious years despite them being war years. Aron's muscle control, including his breathing, deteriorated relentlessly year after year. He died in 1946 at the age of nineteen. It broke my heart.'

'Oh Erna,' I say, embracing her, 'I'm so sorry for your losses. So many tragic losses.'

I feel such sorrow to know of the tragedies Erna – the kindest person I have ever known – has endured in her life. I think that perhaps we feel a special closeness because we are both mothers who have lost a precious son. Yet, I realise that when Erna lost her boy Aron, she lost him for ever, and had no other child to be the focus of her love, while I have Barry. I do regard myself as being lucky to have Barry, but of course, having one child cannot compensate for the loss of another. Even so, I tell myself, I must appreciate the gift that Barry is. I must always be thankful for him and treasure him.

I stand up and hug Erna.

'Dear Erna, thank you for telling me your story. I feel honoured that you trust me enough to share it with me. It can't have been easy to relive those sad and tragic times.'

Although my relationship with Erna had been – initially at least – one built on convenience, and although there's a difference of more than fifty years in our ages, over time we two women have become extremely fond of one another. In fact, as she said, we have become very close, if unusual, friends. Friends who trusted one another completely, even with uncomfortable truths.

***

After she told me the story of her life, Erna explained how she was able to buy such large house in Blackheath, and live in relative comfort. The money her husband Andreas's parents would have passed on to their son and his family, was made over to her after the war. The Goldsteins had been well-to-do businesspeople until their arrest and murder in the late 1930s.

Tragically, in 1943, Erna's own parents also died in the concentration camps, leaving their estate to Erna, their only daughter. In addition, during the years after the war, the German government paid considerable reparations to those who had suffered under the Nazi regime and had lost everything. The house in Berlin, where Erna and Andreas had lived after their marriage, was eventually sold, and the resulting money also came to her. So Erna became rich and comfortable in material terms, but her wealth was tinged with such extreme sorrow, such tragedy. Maybe being able to use it to support Barry's schooling has brought her some joy.

Chapter 12

1985
Robbie

Some days, Len takes a thermos of tea and a packet of sandwiches, which he calls his 'bait', to the allotment nearby. Len keeps his gardening tools in a small shed, in which are also two wooden folding chairs. During school holidays or at the weekends, I love going with him on these visits. Len marks off a patch of the allotment for me to cultivate myself. He shows me how to sow potatoes, carrots, leeks, spinach and lettuces; how to nurture them and watch them grow bigger. Soon the two of us are competing to see who can grow the biggest potatoes and leeks!

When my specimens win the size competition, Betty says, *'Eeee, our Robbie's got a real talent for growing, hasn't he?'* She's always on my side. When Len's vegetables win, Betty shakes her head and says, *'Oh well, the lad grows for flavour and quality, not just size!'* Len just gives me a wink.

A small Victoria plum tree stands in a sheltered corner near the shed. It provides some shade for the two of us as we sit quietly side by side eating our 'bait' on a hot summer's day. In the late summer its branches bend nearly to the ground with the weight of the ripening plums. At home, I help Betty wash and stone the plums and stew some of them for pies and crumbles, or to eat with rice pudding. But the bulk of the crop is used to bottle for the winter, and to make jam. That's a big job. I love the whole process of washing the jars and sterilising them in a warm oven, putting the fruit, water and sugar in a huge copper pan, and boiling the mixture until it miraculously sets on a cold saucer – and the little house is filled with the sweet, fruity fragrance.

One fine day during the holidays, while we're sitting under the plum tree, Len says, 'You know, Robbie, you've been working that hard at school lately, and doing so well, I think it's time for a treat, for doing something special. Why don't we all have a day out? I know our Betty would like that. How about we plan for an outing first warm day next week.'

'OK, that sounds great. Will we surprise Betty?'

'We will that. Good idea, lad. Where would you like to go? The hills, the country, or the sea?'

I'm bursting to go to the sea. I've never been before. 'Well … um, what do you think Betty would like best?' I ask him, praying for the answer I want.

Len screws up his eyes and looks at me thoughtfully. 'Hmmm, well now … let me see … I think she'd like the sea. Yes, definitely, she'd like a trip to the sea.'

'Yes, that's just what I thought,' I say.

***

The following day is hot and sunny.

'Phew!' says Betty. 'It's going to be a scorcher today. Not a cloud in the sky.'

'Just the day for a trip to the seaside then, I reckon,' says Len, winking at me. 'Best pack up your bikini, lass. Robbie and I will sort out the motor.'

Len drives his ancient Morris out of the front garden into the street. He checks the tyres, plugs and starter motor. Then he and I take the car to the nearby garage to top up the oil and put some petrol in.

'Time for an outing come round again, has it, Lenny, man?' the garage man says.

'Aye, Jimmy, that it is. Grand day for taking our Betty out for a spin.'

Then it's back home we go to give the car a final wash and polish.

'Time to get your swimming trunks and a towel, Robbie,' Len tells me.

'I'll put some lunch together then,' says Betty, making for the kitchen.

'Nah, don't do that, lass. It's your day out too. We'll have our lunch in a café or pub and save you the trouble of making it.'

'Ooh, but Len, the expense!'

'What did you marry a rich man for, if not to be spoiled once in a while, pet?'

Betty giggles at this and raises her eyebrows at me. 'Eeee, what's 'e like, eh Robbie darlin'?'

They act like teenagers sometimes – it always makes me laugh. We all have a lot of fun together, more than I've ever had in my whole life before.

But the thing is, Len and Betty *aren't* teenagers, even though they're interested in everything, and full of life and fun. I never really think of them as old, because most of the time they don't *seem* at all old. If I'd thought about it more carefully, more realistically, maybe it wouldn't have come as such a shock.

***

One day, when I'm fifteen, I get back from school to find there's no one at home. That's unusual – they're always there. Everything is quiet, ominously quiet. The back door is unlocked, as it always is, but why isn't Betty clattering about in the kitchen? I go in, feeling strangely uneasy. The silence gathers around me, sending prickles down my spine as I stand in the middle of the kitchen, wondering what to do. Perhaps I should look upstairs? Yet I dread what I might find.

I haven't even put my school rucksack down when Mrs Willis from next door comes knocking and calling, 'Cooo-eee!'

I hate her; she's a right busybody, and she always has a complaint to make about me, for any number of reasons: kicking my ball into her front garden, playing music too loud, or using my catapult to make stones 'ping' on the road sign at the crossroads nearby – any misdeed she can complain about, anything she can criticise. Betty never takes any notice.

Mrs Willis stops in the middle of the room and folds her arms on her chest. She leans her head back and looks down her nose at me.

'Len's had a stroke,' she tells me.

My legs go weak and wobbly, like they're going to give way. I can't breathe properly. I'm not sure exactly what a stroke is. It sounds quite nice, like a gentle caress – but I know that isn't what it means, I know it's bad.

My heart is thudding like a drum. The back of my neck feels hot and sticky, while the rest of me shakes uncontrollably, as if I'm freezing cold. It's a proper shock, but no way do I want to show Mrs Willis what I'm feeling. I can't bear for her to see how upset I am. She's enjoying herself, I can tell that – being 'the bringer of bad news', the mean old cow.

'An ambulance came – eeee, Robbie … top speed it was doing! Lights flashing – it were a proper emergency. Came to take Len to the hospital,' she says, her head on one side, that twisty little smile on her face, her eyes watching me. 'Betty must have dialled

'999,' she continues. 'Aye, she went with him, in the ambulance like, poor soul.'

I can hardly take in what she's saying. I have to concentrate on not swaying, not falling.

'Reckon it must be serious,' Mrs W goes on. 'You should have heard the siren!'

I want to punch her, right in her nasty smiling mouth.

She hands me a few coins Betty had left with her – for me to take the bus to the hospital. I run from the house and straight down the road to the bus stop, feeling sick with worry. Len *can't* be ill; he's strong, healthy; he's tough. There must be some mistake.

***

'No need to raise the roof!' the nurse says severely, as she opens the door onto the ward. 'I heard you ring the bell the first time! We're looking after sick patients here, you know.'

'I know … sorry … I-I just want to see Len,' I say, wiping my face with my sleeve.

'Five minutes, no more,' she says, looking at me a bit more kindly. 'He's not very well, sonny. Don't get him all excited, and don't tire him out, will you, there's a good lad. Is he your grandad?'

'No, he's my …' What was he? 'I'm … his foster son.'

The nurse puts her arm round my shoulder and leads me past a desk, where other nurses are talking and looking at someone's X-ray film on a screen. She pushes me gently into a ward with six beds in it, and points to the end bed on the right. Most of the men in that ward look half-dead – lying with their eyes shut and their mouths open, or staring vacantly at the ceiling.

I'm crying now; I can't stop myself, as soon as I spot Betty. She's sitting by the side of Len's bed, holding his hand. She gives me a sad little wave.

I hate seeing Len lying there in the hospital bed. I hate it. His arms are brown against the white sheet, from working outside on

84

his allotment. They look strong and muscular. He isn't a *feeble* old man. After all, he was a miner in his day, he's used to pushing heavy coal wagons about, and chipping away at the coalface. Len's arms are covered in tattoos from his time in the navy – one is a red heart with *'Beautiful Betty – my darling lass'* written inside. He's always been a tough man; he's had a tough life, but he's got a soft side too. He's shown it to me.

Len's face looks different now – he looks like an old man all of a sudden. His mouth is open and his cheeks look saggy. His face is nearly as white as the sheet.

'He doesn't look like Len,' I whisper, frowning hard to try to stop the tears coming. Betty stands up. She hugs me tight and sobs into my chest.

'Eeee, Robbie, Robbie. Our poor Len … what are we going to do, pet? What's going to happen?'

Well, what can I say to that? I don't know, do I? All I know is … I'm scared. I'm terrified.

***

Four weeks after Len's stroke they bring him home from the hospital in a special ambulance. I watch the driver push the wheelchair down the ramp. Len is slumped in it, his head flopping over to his right shoulder, all limp, like he's asleep, yet his eyes are open. Betty's standing at the front door, her hands pressed over her mouth, tears rolling down her cheeks. Len opens his mouth as if he wants to speak, but no sound comes out. All his features droop downwards over to the right, as if his face is too tired to stay straight. Only his eyes seem to have the energy to move. They dart about, as though they're frantically looking for the answer, but can't find it.

At that moment I know for certain Len and Betty's life is never going to be the same again – and neither is mine.

***

A few weeks after Len is brought home from hospital, I'm back in the children's home. It's Len and Betty's daughter Shirley who suggests it's *'for the best'*. Betty didn't want to let me go, she says. But she can't cope – she hopes I understand. I do and I don't. It's all Betty can do to look after Len, Shirley tells me. I tell her not to worry; I can look after myself, I'll be fine. There are tears running down Betty's cheeks when the car comes to pick me and my bag of stuff up.

'Don't you forget, Robbie my pet,' she sobs. 'You're a right good lad, right good. You make sure to stay that way. Keep working hard at school. You keep outa trouble, won't you? Promise me now, darlin'. Remember, you'll always be welcome here. You'll always be our canny lad. We love you, Robbie. Come and visit soon, won't you, son – there'll always be tea in the pot, and a piece of cake. That's if I can manage it ...'

Her voice trails away sadly. To tell the truth, I'm blubbing too. It feels like I've been crying for days. I walk over to see Len, lying on the sofa. He strokes my face with his good arm. He tries to say something, but it's just odd sounds that come out, like he's gargling. Len stares at me and a big tear squeezes out of his left eye and rolls slowly down. I hug him.

'I love you, Len,' I sob, and fly out of the room. Betty follows me. I give her a last hug. She hangs on to me for a long time, like her life depends on it. She's trembling. Her body feels small and frail now. I feel her bones moving about under my arms.

'I love you, Betty,' I say, my voice all jerky. I've never said those words to anyone before. I turn and run out to the car.

***

I visit them from time to time at first. Betty always makes a fuss of me, and Len smiles his sad, lopsided smile. They hug me and stroke my face, but things are never the same, of course. Two years later Len has another stroke. He's taken back to the hospital. They tell me he died peacefully in his sleep during the night.

Betty never really recovers from that. Never. She seems to get old overnight. She goes to live with Shirley and her family in the east end of Newcastle. Shirley rings now and then to tell me how Betty is, and to ask about me. I go to see them on the bus, but I can't bring myself to visit more than a handful of times after that.

Betty has always been a lively, funny, energetic woman. She's been full of the joy of living. Now she's just a shadow of herself: a frail, shrunken, white ghost. It's as if life has played a cruel trick on her, and she can't understand why, or what she's done to deserve it. From being cheerful and enjoying all the simple pleasures in life, she has become old, confused and withdrawn. It really breaks my heart.

Less than three years after Len's death, Betty passes away in the night, at Shirley's house. I go to the funeral and cry and cry. I lose contact with Shirley and the rest of the family in the end.

Chapter 13

1985
Barry

I remember the start of my first term at Wentford Grammar School, how I lined up with the other children in my new uniform with a tie and a blazer, with the school's special badge on the pocket, and suddenly felt at home. I loved my new leather satchel. It contained a whole bundle of exercise books, as well as some interesting school textbooks. My new form teacher introduced me to my classmates and asked them to be helpful and friendly to me, because 'it's hard to be a new boy in a new school'. I didn't expect them to do as he said. I was astonished that his request seemed to work. Several of the other children came to talk to me in a friendly way during break. No one called me names at Wentford.

Three years after that introduction, I'm still happy to be here. There's the usual group of boys who like to play football in the yard, and they even invite me to join them. The difference is they don't abuse me when I politely decline. There are plenty of boys too, who like me, have many interests *other* than football! I'm suddenly among other human beings with brains!

Due entirely to Auntie Erna, my life has been transformed. I have been spared the torture of life in my former school. To think that at first Mum didn't even want to accept her offer! She took some persuading to agree to Erna paying for me to move to the grammar school. Well, it wasn't her who had to suffer being the odd one out, the only boy with a brain and the desire to use it. In the midst of morons and savages.

Gradually I have found out who are the more serious boys in my year – those who are bright enough to be in the top set, as I am for every subject. Over time some of those boys have become friends and companions, although I'm very aware of the difference in our backgrounds. It can be quite embarrassing.

Some of my classmates invite me to their homes, and Mum is forever *tediously* trying to persuade me to ask them back to us for tea! She still keeps pressing me to invite them to our home, completely oblivious to how uncomfortable I might find it. Most of my friends come from well-to-do families, with highly educated, professional parents: lawyers, consultants, managing directors and suchlike. They live in homes that match their backgrounds, as you might expect. They talk about the kids from council estates as 'plebs'. I'm hardly going to reveal that my mother cooks and cleans for her employer.

Mum doesn't seem to appreciate that no way do I want to expose my friends to our poky little flat, to be entertained by stories of her peasant life back in Ireland, and fed beans on toast, or similarly unsophisticated fare. She's perfectly capable of cooking proper evening meals, but seems to feel anyone under about sixteen should be given 'simple tea', as she ate as a child. I'm certainly not going to reveal that I'm actually descended from Irish peasants.

I find the gap between my mother's experiences and my own grows wider day by day. Of course I'm fond of her, but I do resent the way she is constantly harping on about everyone having a 'sadness' in their life, which she says maybe she'll tell me more about 'when I'm older', but that now is not the right time.

I've always been aware of some vague feeling that I'm not enough for her, that somehow there's something *missing* – as if she wants my sympathy. But as she's not prepared to elaborate, what can I do about it?

I think perhaps I'm growing away from her and maybe that's natural at my age, but it's almost as though she *pushes* me away, so she can't be surprised if there's sometimes a distance between us. It's not my doing.

I do find her lack of ambition irritating and frustrating too. She tells me she did well at school and was considered bright, though it was probably basically a simple sort of hedge school and could hardly have had demanded high standards. Anyway, what has she done *since then* to improve herself and her qualifications? Absolutely nothing – except being pathetically proud of her sewing abilities. It appears that she does have a bit of a gift for designing clothes, so why not develop that side of things further? No, not even that. I don't think I inherited my intellectual leanings from her … so from whom I wonder?

Luckily, Auntie Erna has always been a kind of parent-cum-grandparent to me, and one who fulfils the more intellectual side of my life. From early on she recognised my ability, and the need to stimulate me with demanding cerebral activities. I've always enjoyed her company, although I suppose her own intellect may start to deteriorate now that she's getting so old.

Chapter 14

1989
Barry

My Dear Barry,

I'm so glad you've settled well at university and are finding your studies interesting. You were so ready to be stretched intellectually, and to make your way independently in life. I can just imagine how satisfying it is. I'm sure you have some interesting discussions with your fellows!

Of course your mother loves and misses you dreadfully – as do I – but she is so proud of all you have achieved, and does not resent you having to be in London to fulfil your ambitions. It is inevitable that parents and children have some differences as young people spread their wings and get ready to 'leave the nest'. I hope you appreciate that Marie wants nothing but that you follow your dreams. She had so few opportunities to pursue study or a career herself, but don't forget too, that you have been fortunate in inheriting her genes. She is extremely able and I am sure you will come to see that more clearly in time.

I don't want to lecture you, Barry – you will have many at university who are much more able than I to take on that role! So study hard and enjoy all the opportunities your new environment offers you. I hope you will have a wonderful time. Enjoy yourself.

With fond love,
Your Auntie Erna

PS: I hope you received the cheque I sent you at the beginning of November? You maybe forgot to mention it in your last letter.

What a relief it's been living away from home this last year, though sometimes I do miss my conversations with Auntie Erna. There were some painful, overemotional goodbyes of course, especially with Mum.

Erna is right that I was so ready for living independently. Sharing my life with two women, each clingy in their own way, for the first nearly twenty years of my life has felt pretty stifling at times. Just leaving the house with my suitcase and stepping on the train at Blackheath station felt like an extraordinary liberation. I'm sometimes impelled to take deep breaths to clear my lungs, my heart and my head of the cloying atmosphere.

It's just fantastic being in an environment so totally focused on cerebral pursuits. None of this could have happened without Erna, and I am eternally in her debt, as Mum never fails to remind me. I'm sure Erna has no intention of actually asking me to pay back what she's spent on me. I certainly hope not! Maybe one day, when I'm earning pots of money, I'll offer to pay her back … but I don't suppose she'd accept it.

Erna loves receiving letters from me, telling her all about the current focus of my studies, and about university life in general. I do actually enjoy sharing details of my courses and experiences with her. She always responds with great thought and intelligence to my comments about the lectures I've just attended, and about my latest research.

What would I have done, growing up, without Erna? Of course it's not just about the money, though that's been a crucial enabling factor – but it's been about the nature of my relationship with her. I think this last year, despite being apart for most of the time, we've actually grown closer, if that were possible.

Of course I do miss and love Mum too, in a way. Somehow, she always seems to be withholding some part of her heart. It's not an easy relationship. Well, perhaps it's not surprising, her own experience having been so far removed from mine. It's as if she can't always connect with me … or maybe it's the other way round.

Erna has paid for whatever part of my course is not covered by my grant. She sends me regular generous contributions for my living expenses. Stupidly, I must have forgotten to mention her last cheque. They make quite a difference, so, luckily, I can manage financially without too much difficulty. I certainly wouldn't have survived if I'd had to depend on Mum's support alone. She has no idea of the cost of living independently in London as a student, although she should have some understanding, having been nearly destitute when I was a baby. Apparently we were practically sleeping on the streets.

When I left the house to start at university, Mum and Erna each handed me an envelope to open on the train, or when I reached my accommodation, to give my finances 'a bit of a boost' at the start of my course. Erna's envelope contained £200; Mum's contained £50. That says it all.

***

Most of the others on my course are men, but there is a small group of girls too. I get to know one of them quite well during freshers' week. She's called Helena, and both her parents are clearly high-earning professionals, so she's had a lot of financial support throughout her childhood, and at university.

We start going out together during the first term. She's very good-looking in a conventional sort of way: long blonde hair and a good figure. I really fancy Helena. Although she isn't the brightest star in the sky, at first, we get on well, and the regular sex is great.

She went to a posh girls' public school in Surrey. On our first date Helena revealed that it was one of the most expensive girls' schools in Britain. Her parents must be loaded.

'It was such fun!' she told me, sipping her glass of top-quality white wine. I watched anxiously as the wine rapidly disappeared. It had cost me more than I'd ever spent on a whole bottle previously!

'I was quite sporty,' Helena said, her cheeks growing pink. 'I was in the school lacrosse team. We had such a fabulous time!'

I sense we don't have a lot in common and it soon becomes clear that she's quite 'high-maintenance'. All that money behind her from Mummy and Daddy, but she still clearly expects me to pay her share most of the time, whatever we're doing, and 'economy' is not a word in her vocabulary.

'It's just what a gentleman should do,' she would say coyly.

'Maybe I'm no gentleman. Maybe I'm just your bit of rough.'

She likes that – at first. Then she starts complaining I'm 'too rough'.

It's quite a turn-on seeing how far I can go playing the rugged 'hard man' role. I get bored with Helena after a while though, and decide I'm not prepared to waste any more time, or money on her. I start looking around for someone more exciting, and less costly. There are plenty more fish in the sea.

***

I wouldn't say I make particularly close friendships at university, but I meet people whose company I enjoy from time to time, and with whom there are no trying emotional entanglements – just interesting discussion, light-hearted banter, plenty of alcohol and an introduction to a range of increasingly strong substances. I'd started on occasional joints in sixth form, but it's at uni that I start exploring some of the harder stuff.

Mum – and Erna – would be horrified, no doubt.

Chapter 15

1992
Marie

I run to Erna's sitting room, the letter clutched in my hand.

'Erna! Erna!' I shout.

She looks up from her newspaper in alarm. 'What is it, my dear? What's the matter?'

'No, nothing's the matter. Nothing at all. Barry's been awarded a First Class Honours degree at university! Just think – our Barry! What an achievement, and he says he's been offered a top job at an international bank!'

'Oh, that's wonderful. Where will he be working? Is he coming home soon?'

'He says it's in the City! He says he's going to find a flat to rent, somewhere to share with a friend, I think. Oh, Erna, I'm so proud of him. I just don't know where he gets his brains from!'

'I do! Barry gets his brains from you, my dear. In any case, Marie, you have brought up your clever son, and encouraged him in all he does, and that's *your* wonderful achievement.'

'Mmm.' I smile thoughtfully.

'Oh, Marie, you never seem to realise how clever you are. You may not have had the chance to finish your education, but just look at what you have achieved yourself. Your dress designs are in demand all over south London! I always felt you could have become anything: a teacher, a nurse, a lawyer … anything. Maybe now that Barry is through university and progressing professionally, you could think of opening a little boutique, or at least selling some of your designs in an existing boutique.

'Or, if you wanted, what's to stop you retraining for a different line of work? You could do anything you wanted. I would gladly support you.'

On these occasions I feel a great knot of anxiety build in my stomach. I sit there, a weight like a stone inside, heavy, dragging me down. I suppose I take on a doubtful expression, because Erna studies my face intently. She looks as if she clearly recognises that expression – she knows me so well – and realises that now is not the time to push her arguments further. She puts it aside for the time being, but I know she'll return to it again another day.

My self-confidence has always been fragile, and still is to this day. I feel so uneducated. The only thing I've ever been really good at is sewing and dressmaking, even years back as a young girl at school in Ireland.

It had felt good to excel in something. I was a hard-working and careful pupil, always in the top few of the class in other subjects. I loved to read, and the teacher praised my writing and number work too so I wasn't stupid, whatever Barry thinks!

I suppose I might have been even cleverer if I'd attended school every day, but what with my four little sisters – Bridie, Ava, Nuala and Grace – Ma often kept me home to help her.

The domestic studies teacher praised my sewing all the time. She let me use the new electric machine – there was only one for the whole school. I knew my skill in dressmaking was something exceptional, and that gave me a special feeling.

97

Sure, hadn't I made little frocks and nighties for my younger sisters by cutting up old sheets and curtains that neighbours had discarded, or Ma's old clothes? After a while I even made my own patterns, drawing them carefully on sheets of old newspapers. Ma said the clothes I made were better than shop-bought and anyway there was no money for buying new clothes in the shops. She said I had a real way with a needle. Coming from her, that meant something; she was sparing with her praise was Ma.

Those first months in Blackheath with Erna, when Barry was a toddler, I realised I could make something of that skill. Sure enough my work is valued by the fine ladies who are Erna's friends, and visit the house. It feels so special to know I can do something and do it well, when they can't, however clever and educated they are!

Barry has certainly made the most of the opportunity Erna gave him. He always worked hard at school: completing his homework assignments on time and getting good marks in all his subjects. I was, and am, truly bursting with pride in my clever son, but I'm always careful not to show off to others.

I always loved Barry to show me his schoolwork, though he was often reluctant to do so. I have to admit that when he *did* show me his exercise books, often I could hardly make head nor tail of what he'd written, especially some of the science and mathematics! It could have been Egyptian hieroglyphics for all I understood of it, and Barry would often raise his eyebrows at my ignorance. I tried to ask intelligent questions but they must have seemed foolish to him.

Of course I always praised him and admired his work. Yet, especially now that Barry is making his way in the world, I can't help thinking of poor Donal, and how he might be faring with his education, and work perhaps? He'll be twenty-two, just like Barry, now! Was he clever as a boy like his brother? Surely he must be intelligent too; they're identical twins after all. Did he attend a good school like Barry? Did his adoptive parents help him to achieve all he was capable of? They're so well off, surely they could afford the best for him. I wonder if he's been going to university too, like his brother? My heart aches to know more of him and his life. Is he happy? Does he look exactly like Barry? What sort of a young man is he?

***

It's a fine warm day, so Erna and I decide to have our morning coffee in the garden. There's a secluded corner sheltered from any wind, where the heat of the sun is softened, being filtered through the leaves of two beautiful silver birch trees. I put cushions on the seats and accompany Erna out, holding her arm to make sure she doesn't trip. She is a little less steady these days – she's over ninety, although you wouldn't guess it.

I settle her in her favourite seat and show her Barry's letter. She reads it with a great smile on her face.

'My goodness, Marie, what a smart son you have. He's such a credit to you, and the way you've brought him up.'

I leave her to read the letter again, and bring out the tray, a woollen shawl over my arm, which I wrap around her shoulders. She's so thin and feels the chill, even on a summery day like today.

'Thank you, Marie. You're always so thoughtful.' She watches me with her keen eyes. 'Is everything all right, dear? You seem a little preoccupied lately.'

'Oh, I'm all right, Erna …' I begin.

She narrows her eyes and puts her head on one side. She peers at me as if to say 'Really …?'

'Well, all right … I have been worrying about Barry a bit.'

'Hmmm. Not for the first time, I think. But why just now, when he's doing so very well? His degree, his job. He's making a success of his life, isn't he?'

'Well … yes. But, as you know, Erna, there's a side to Barry that worries me sometimes. He can be hard; he can be … well, I don't want to exaggerate, Erna, but almost cruel sometimes.'

'Certainly I know he doesn't suffer fools gladly! He can judge other people harshly at times. Maybe that's a part of being as very able as he is. But *cruel*, Marie?'

'Well, not all the time of course, but there's a tendency to hardness that I've noticed in him; now, as an adult sometimes, but even years ago as a young child …'

'Mmm?'

'Well, for instance, you might remember I've mentioned how once, when he was just a little boy, and Sylvia and I took him to the playground, there was another mum and her twin girls playing nearby? They were barely more than toddlers and Barry a year or two older. He started playing "chasey" with them, but then he seemed to push one girl over …'

'Yes, I do remember you telling me about it, Marie. I thought you were maybe reading too much into an accidental childish incident. I mean children often try out behaviours, even naughty ones, to see what happens.'

'Perhaps that's so, but there's been a bit of a pattern to these incidents of unkind behaviour … Remember that time when Barry was about seven, and Mrs Holt from next door brought that little new puppy to show him?'

'Oh yes, I do – it was so tiny. Such a sweet little thing! Barry was delighted with it, wasn't he? He said he'd love a puppy himself.'

'Yes, that's right, and at first he played nicely with it. Do you remember, he rolled a ball for the puppy to chase? Then the puppy got tired, so Barry sat on the sofa with it on his lap, and the puppy went to sleep. Barry cuddled it gently at first.'

'Oh yes! And then it suddenly gave a loud squeal, and it wriggled out of his lap still crying.' Erna is looking thoughtful now.

'It did, and it moved to the other end of the sofa, away from him, and licked its paw. It watched Barry. It was scared of him, Erna.'

'Mmm, yes, I do remember – Barry said maybe the puppy had had a bad dream … I thought that was quite funny.'

'Well … he could always think up a clever idea. You know what I worry about most, Erna, is that Barry might have been affected by me having to give up his brother for adoption, and by my constant longing for Donal ever since.'

'But haven't you told me that you didn't feel Barry was ready to hear about that? You've never actually told him about his twin brother, have you, Marie?'

'No. At first I believed he was too young to understand, and then later I wondered if it might make him more insecure and troubled. Perhaps I was wrong not to talk to him about it. I think I was afraid of upsetting him.'

'Well, it's not really my business, but I do think you should be open with him about now he's an adult. Maybe it would help him to settle some of the confusion he may have experienced as a child. And you know something else, Marie? While you have spoken to me about how you came to be pregnant with the twins, you've never told me in detail about how you were compelled to give one of them up – what effect it had on you.

'If you feel able and willing, why don't you practise telling the story by first describing to me what happened?'

I take a deep breath.

'All right,' I say hesitantly.

I close my eyes and think. I picture the forbidding mother and baby home … Immediately, I am transported back to Sister Bernadette's office all those years ago, a trembling, frightened young girl, a young mother, not yet eighteen. I can picture Sister Bernadette's hard, scornful face. I tell Erna exactly what happened on that terrifying day. She listens to every word, barely taking her eyes off me, occasionally shaking her head.

At last the story is finished.

'She was right in what she said, Erna, cruel though it was. In the end, what choice did I have? I couldn't have cared for Donal as well as Barry. But that decision nearly killed me.'

Erna struggles up from her chair and hobbles towards me. She bends over and hugs me. Our tears mingle on our cheeks.

'Oh my poor darling,' she says. 'You poor girl. You must tell Barry this story. He will understand that all you have done is for love – love for him and love for his brother.'

'I do want to tell Barry, but I just wish I could find Donal first. I was never allowed any information about the adoption – what his new name is, where he lives, that sort of thing. If only I could send him a little note to say how much I've always loved him. Maybe he'd like a photograph of me, and Barry? I wondered if I should try to ask a private detective to look for him. I've some money saved from my dressmaking.'

'Perhaps I can help you there. I would gladly pay for someone to search for your Donal. I believe there are special people who may be able to help trace missing relatives. What with computers these days, it may be possible.'

'Thank you, Erna, but you've already been very generous and paid so much to help me and Barry. I feel this is something I should maybe pay for myself.'

Chapter 16

1996
Robert

The woman from the council housing department tells me her name is Julie. Julie is emphasising the flat's good points, of course. She refers to it as 'an apartment'.

'So this here is the kitchen …'

Like I hadn't noticed. Or maybe she thinks someone who's been sleeping on the streets might have forgotten what a kitchen is. But she means well, and I'm not going to give her a hard time.

'I know it's quite … compact, but it's not badly designed and fitted out, is it? Look, here there's the fridge …' She opens the door. The fridge could do with a good clean.

'Oh, with quite a roomy freezer section. That'll be handy, won't it?'

She's really trying, poor lass. She starts demonstrating the gas cooker next, and then we continue to the 'sitting room', but there's nothing to sit on apart from the wooden floor. The floorboards look a bit rough and ready – you could end up with a nasty splinter in your bum sitting on that floor.

Julie is enthusing over the view from the window. I humour her by looking out. There's a tiny, rusting play area and a small, neglected 'garden area' as she describes it. It's more of a yard with some scrubby grass, trampled earth and a sad-looking tree in one corner, its trunk bending almost to the ground, as if carrying the weight of all life's problems. *I know just how you feel, man,* I think.

'It's communal,' Julie tells me brightly. 'So on a fine day you could take a chair out. You might meet some of your neighbours down there for a chat and some company.'

I hope not, but I say nothing. Nor do I mention that I don't even own a chair. I'm waiting for her to go, so I can settle in and unpack the black plastic sack containing my few pathetic possessions, but she walks through to the bedroom. A lumpy-looking single bed is pushed against the wall. There's no bedding. Next we inspect a small bathroom. The bath looks like a chimney sweep has been having a good soak in it.

'Oh dear. Someone hasn't left it very clean …' she comments.

'It'll be fine, I'll give it a scrub. Thanks for showing me round the flat, Julie. It'll be a whole lot better than the underpass. 'Specially when it's fucking raining.'

She looks shocked for a moment, then pulls her face together and retrieves her smile when she realises I'm making a joke.

'Yes, at least you'll be warm and dry in here. Well, I'd better leave you to settle in, Robert. Here's the key for your front door, and this one's for the downstairs door to the block. Don't forget the guys from the "Home In" charity will be coming over tomorrow morning with a few bits of furniture and stuff to help you. If there's one spare, they might even bring you a telly. Fingers crossed.'

To my relief, she leaves. I stand still, close my eyes, and listen to the silence in my new home.

There's a kettle at least, and some Nescafé, but no milk, so I make myself a mug of black coffee and start to consider what

I'm going to do with the next twenty-six years of my life, or even the next six! I haven't exactly made a brilliant success of the first twenty-six That's got to change.

At least I'm off the streets. That's got to be a positive start, and applying for – and eventually *getting* – council accommodation was another step up the ladder.

I don't want to end up like some of those sad geezers I met on the streets. 'Specially the old guys: sick, freezing, stinking, starving, half-crazy most of them, living from one hit of booze or drugs – or both – to the next. Like old Harry, with his mangey dog Skip – his only friend in the world. There's supposed to be emergency accommodation – night shelters – to crash in overnight, but most of us were too scared to go to those, except as a total last resort. Too many hard men happy to slice you up if you don't give them some cash, or some drugs.

Nobody *needs* to sleep rough, is what the council says. I'd like to see *them* bed down in one of those places.

Slowly, painfully, I clawed my way out of the bottom of the sewer. It was a slow process. I accepted some temporary accommodation, got myself cleaned up a bit. My life became a series of short-term, low-paid jobs plus some voluntary work in a nearby homeless shelter, supplemented by some meagre benefits. Finally I was offered this small, basic flat by the council. It's not much, but it's a whole lot better than a pavement or underpass – and it's going to be my home for a while, so I'd better make the most of it.

I open the bag with my few possessions in it and start to unpack. The first thing I take out is a photograph of Len and Betty, which accompanies me everywhere. I'd put it in a frame years ago. They're standing at his allotment with their arms around each other, smiling broadly. It brings a lump to my throat. I kiss the photo and put it on the mantelpiece. How soft is that?

The sound of children's voices outside drifts upwards. I go to look out of the front window. There are three little kids down in the so-called 'play area' down below. Basically just two lopsided swings and a rusty climbing frame. A woman who I assume is the kids' mum is watching them, but then she says something in a foreign language, maybe Arabic, and disappears into the flats. The youngest kid is about three or four. He starts climbing up the fence separating the play area from the road. The older boy and girl are trying to stop him, but quick as a flash he's hoisted his leg over the top and is down the other side. His brother is calling him to come back, but the little fella's enjoying himself picking up stones and chucking them into the road. Cars are speeding about an arm's length from the kid.

I grab my keys, run out of my flat and down the stairs as fast as I can. When I get to him, thankfully the kid hasn't walked into the road. I pick him up and lift him back over the fence. By now his mother must have heard the older kids shouting as she's come out and is watching with her hands over her mouth. I think she might be annoyed with me for touching her child, so I start to explain but she grabs my hand and shakes it.

'Oh thank you, thank you,' she says, hugging the little boy. 'You very good man, very good man.'

'It's OK,' I say, 'no problem. He's a little adventurer, isn't he?'

Her husband emerges from inside and sees what's going on.

'Thank you very much, sir,' he says. 'Jabril is naughty boy – always escaping. The road is dangerous. Thank you.'

He says something in Arabic to his wife and then turns back to me. They want me to have a meal with them that evening. I tell him it's OK, there's no need, anyone would have done it, but they insist, so I go. Their names are Hakim and Faiza.

The family is from Iraq. They haven't long been in England, so they know how it feels to be outsiders. They're very hospitable and welcoming. That evening, we have a delicious spicy vegetable stew with rice, sitting in a circle on the floor. Little Jabril insists on sitting in my lap. It feels good to have made some friends.

***

The next day, with my precious benefit money in my pocket, I head to the corner shop for some supplies – bread and a carton of milk. On my way back to the flat, I see an old woman struggling with two lumpy shopping bags. I know she lives in my block – I've noticed her before.

'Hello,' I say. 'Can I help you with those? They look heavy.'

'Aye,' she says, 'they're heavy, all right.'

She eyes me up and down suspiciously, looking torn between wanting my help and wondering whether I might run off with her shopping, I bet.

'My name's Robbie,' I say. 'I've not long moved in. I think you live in the flat below mine.'

'Oh aye, now you come to mention it, I think I've seen you.'

'Here, let me take those in for you.' I reach for the bags. She looks at me and then releases her grip on them.

'That's right kind of you, lad,' she says with a smile. 'I'm Nora by the way.' She flexes her shoulders and hobbles along beside me.

'Well, it's really nice to get to know the neighbours, Nora, being the new boy on the block.'

'You'll find most folk are quite friendly, Robbie.'

Nora rummages in her handbag for the key and opens the front door.

'Thanks, pet, I think I can manage them from here.'

'You open the door to your flat, and I'll just put the bags straight on the kitchen table for you.'

'You're a good lad and no mistake. You'll have to come in for a cup of tea in a day or two.'

'I'd like that, Nora.'

***

My flat is in a pretty rubbish part of the city: generally run-down, poor housing, cheapo shops, the odd pub, and hardly a blade of grass to be seen, so I even appreciate the 'garden area'.

107

Still, people around here are OK. Friendly if they get to know you long enough to trust you.

People from all over the world.

Lots of refugees. Colourful fruit and vegetable shops. I like that. I feel like a permanent refugee myself. What I could really do with is a job. I don't expect to make a lot of money, with me not having any qualifications, but any money would be a help, and maybe a job would make me feel more settled.

It felt good to help Nora earlier. I quite like older people, and they seem to like me. I wonder if maybe I could find a job helping to look after them somewhere?

That afternoon, I go for a walk hoping to see some job vacancy signs in shop windows, and get some ideas about what might be available. Not a lot, seems to be the answer, but at least I'm getting to know the area.

There's a library just around the corner, a short way along the high street. Even though I love reading, I can't remember the last time I read a book. Mr Lewis would be disappointed in me. He was always so encouraging.

Inside the library I stop and look round at all the shelves stuffed with books.

'Hello. Can I help you?' A woman behind the counter smiles at me. I get the impression I'm a special event.

'Yes, erm … I've just moved in nearby. I love reading books and wonder if I could borrow one or two?'

'Certainly you can, that's what we're here for. We're always pleased to have a new borrower. Just tell me your address. Once you've got your own library card, you can borrow books straightaway.'

That's what having a proper address can do for you! The woman says she's the chief librarian. She produces a printed map of the area for me, and points out various places of interest: a community centre, a swimming pool, a historic church, a walk to the riverside, and the high street from where buses go to the city centre.

'Thanks a lot. It's really useful to know a bit more about what this area has to offer. Oh, do you know if there are any care homes for the elderly nearby, where I might get a job?'

The librarian indicates several on the map and circles them with a red biro. 'Do you have experience working in that area?'

'Well no, not exactly … but I get on well with older people.'

I expect her to say I don't stand a chance of a job without experience, but she doesn't. In fact she gives me some very good advice.

'I've had quite a bit to do with the Job Centre,' she explains, 'and if you don't mind me saying this, I suggest that first you ask what type of work might be available in the home, and whether they have any vacancies. Explain any relevant experience you might have, even if it's not actual working experience. Then, crucially, offer to work on a voluntary basis for a month or two, so that they can see how you interact with the residents, and if necessary, they can train you in any aspects of the work in which they feel you might need more knowledge or experience.'

'That seems a very wise strategy,' I say. 'Thanks for the advice. Do you think any of the homes are better than others?'

'Hmm. They're all pretty good, but this one here—' she points at the map '—this is called Golden Days – terrible name!' she says with a laugh. 'But it has a very good manager, and a lovely, happy atmosphere. We have a volunteer delivering library books to some of the residents. That's something else you could consider doing in time. Also, if you need any help putting a CV together, just come back in and ask. I or one of my colleagues would be happy to give you a hand.'

I thank her profusely for all the advice and information. I go home with an armful of books to read, and a feeling of hope in my heart. It's been a long time since I felt so positive.

***

Three weeks later and I've managed to get a trial week working for Golden Days Care Home. The manager, Lorna Fuller is really welcoming.

'The key is getting to know each resident personally, Robbie – understanding their background, personalities and interests. That's what I tried to do when I first came here.'

After she's shown me the ropes, I'm paired with Belle, an experienced carer, who I'll be shadowing for the rest of the week.

'What Belle doesn't know about working with elderly people isn't worth knowing,' Lorna tells me.

***

I love the job at Golden Days. Lorna is a bright, caring woman. Not only does she make a point of getting to know the residents well, she also insists on having regular contact with family members, ideally in person, or on the phone if they live too far away.

Belle is generous in every sense of the word. Big in build, big in heart, and big in personality; she seems to genuinely love the old people she supports. She's a very physical person too, always stroking and hugging the residents.

'One of the things elderly people miss,' Belle tells me, 'is *touch*. It's so important. Imagine having lived with a partner and family, and then losing them; coming all alone to a place like this – or even living alone at home – feeling that nobody loves you, nobody really cares for you, nobody holds your hand or touches you in any way.'

'I can relate to that.' I say it in a jokey way, but of course it's true.

'Oh, Robbie, you poor darling, you've always got *me* to love you,' she says with a grin.

'Thank you, Belle. Very nice for a poor boy with no one in the world wanting to touch him.'

''Course, Robbie, it's got to be absolutely non-sexual touch, you understand. Just warm, affectionate, accepting touch. The sort of hugs your mam would give you.'

'Oh, and I thought you fancied me, Belle.'

'Cheeky! I'm serious. In a sense, even though they're older than us – *much* older than *you* – we've got to be almost like a mother to them, a gentle, loving mother. That's what they really need.'

'I'll do my best at being a mother, Belle. But never having known my mother, I'm short on experience.'

'Oh, Robbie, I'm sorry. Didn't you even have nice foster parents?'

'Mostly no, but I did have just one set of lovely foster parents, Betty and Len. They were ace. They did love me and I loved them. The nearest thing I had to parents or grandparents. But I didn't have them for long.'

Belle put her arm round my shoulders.

'Well, thank heaven for Betty and Len, Robbie. You just think of what their love meant to you when you deal with our old folk. I know you're going to be a great carer. You've got a good heart, believe me; old Belle can tell.'

Chapter 17

1996
Marie

We haven't seen that much of Barry recently. I know he's busy with his job, and it's right that he wants his independent life. What young man of twenty-six wouldn't? But I do miss the regular contact with him, and I know Erna does too. Just now he's having his flat redecorated so I offered for him to come and stay at Erna's for a few nights. To my delight he's accepted.

There's been a particular tension, a distance between us lately. It's very painful to me. His moods seem very up and down. Some of the times we have met up, he doesn't seem quite with it. I've even wondered if he's been drinking. Those pressured City jobs can be so stressful.

I'm hoping these few days together will be a chance to straighten out some of the problems and renew our closeness. I know I've got to talk to him about his brother, and I want to, but I'm anxious about how he'll react; he can be so unpredictable. Maybe I should have told him long ago, but I suppose I was afraid he might be very critical of my decision. He might hate me for it. So I delayed and delayed; it never seemed to be the right time. I endlessly question the rights and wrongs of that decision.

***

Barry appears to be in a good mood when he arrives, which delights me – in fact, he gives me a big hug that lifts me right off the ground!

'My goodness, Barry, what a strong man you've become!'

'Didn't you notice? I've been quite grown up for a few years now.'

'Yes I had noticed, of course I had. Listen, Barry, why don't you go down and see Erna first? She's dying to talk to you, and she tires easily these days, you know. She goes to bed early. I just have to finish making supper; it'll only take ten minutes. It's a vegetable lasagne. I got a pile of beautiful vegetables at that market just round the corner from your flat. Have you been there? It's lovely fresh stuff. You and Keith should eat more fruit and vegetables. They're good for you.

'Yes, *Mummy*!' he answers in a little boy's voice, and goes stomping down the stairs noisily.

Hopefully, when he gets back from seeing Erna, we'll have a relaxed meal and time for a proper conversation. I hope he'll tell me more about his work. I know he thinks I don't understand any of it, but I wish he'd try to explain it to me.

***

I put some music on in the background, and light candles on the table to try to make the atmosphere peaceful when Barry comes back.

'Auntie Erna seems much older these days, Mum. She's getting really frail now, isn't she?'

'Yes, she's very frail, in her body at least. But, maybe that's not surprising at ninety-six. Her brain and her spirit are as robust as ever, though.'

'Mmm. Part of me expects her to go on for ever. She's an amazing woman.'

'She really is. I'd love to hear more about your life, Barry. How is the job going?'

'Oh it's OK. It's hard work, making money for the clients and the bank. I don't have a lot of spare time.'

'So what do you actually do?'

'Oh, let's not talk about it, Mum. It's basically shifting money from one fund to another. Assessing clients for investments, that sort of thing. You wouldn't really understand.'

'Well, I might, if you explained it, Barry.'

'Maybe another time. I'm quite tired.'

'I expect they work you too hard?'

'It's a culture of long hours for everyone. There's not much time for leisure activities … Mmm, this lasagne is really good, Mum.'

'I'm glad you like it, son, but you haven't eaten very much. You're nearly as thin as Erna. Have another helping.'

'I've had plenty thanks. A coffee would be nice though.'

We move from the supper table to the comfortable armchairs. Barry carries in the tray with coffee for him, and green tea for me. I've started drinking it lately. People say it's good for your health. I don't like it much, but at least it's hot.

I pass Barry a cup of the strong coffee he likes.

'Doesn't it stop you sleeping?' I ask him.

He smiles. 'Not really, I guess I depend on my regular fix of caffeine.'

'As long as it's nothing stronger,' I say.

He turns his head to look at me, as if shocked by my comment.

'A joke, darling.'

'Oh right, yeah …'

His long body relaxes into the armchair. What a handsome

young man he is. There are times it quite takes my breath away. Suddenly the image of another handsome, dark-haired young man flashes through my mind … a young man with those same brown eyes flecked with gold. I shake my head to push it away. Not now … keep a clear head.

'Barry, love, I want to talk to you …'

'I'm glad to hear it, Mum. I didn't think we were going to sit in silence all evening.'

'No …' I take a deep breath. 'Barry, there are things I maybe should have told you about long ago. I didn't keep them from you to be secretive or to hide the truth from you, but just to wait for what seemed the right time, a time when you were old enough to understand … understand properly. I suppose I wanted to protect you. Maybe I was wrong …'

'Mum, what on earth are you talking about? Whatever it is you want to tell me, just say it. You're starting to scare me.'

'Well, there's nothing to be scared of, but I do want to tell you about what happened when you were born. I've never told you the whole story.'

'What do you mean?'

'Yes … well, the time when I became pregnant, as a young girl of only seventeen. I've told you a bit about it, but now that you're a grown man, I need to – I *want* to – tell you the full truth about how it happened … and who your father was … and what happened after you were born.'

'OK …' he says slowly.

'You know about my ma and da and all the rest of the family back in Ireland. You know about what simple folk we all were, deeply religious and old-fashioned. I've told you how your dad charmed me and swept me off my feet. Perhaps he took advantage of my innocence, but I can't put the blame on him alone; I *wanted* him, Barry, I can't pretend I didn't.'

I hold nothing back. Barry sits motionless in his chair, his face grim and inscrutable.

'I was so frightened when I realised I was pregnant, and even more so when Ma told me to go to England, to London, to have an abortion, or my da would never have had me back.'

Barry nods a little wearily, like he's saying, *I've heard this bit.*

'So I went to London all right, but I'd already decided that no way would I "get rid of" my child. Instead, I found out about a mother and baby home run by nuns. I was convinced they would be kind, that they'd support me.'

Barry listens in silence. His face is unreadable. He stares straight ahead.

Trembling, I continue with my story. I tell him about Sister Bernadette, who was strict and unsympathetic, and about Sister Aileen, who was so kind and protective towards me.

'It was a great struggle,' I tell him, 'but, oh, what a joy it was when you were born, Barry, when I held you in my arms – a perfect, darling baby. I loved you the moment I set eyes on you.'

'Well, I'm glad it ended positively anyway,' he says with a small smile. He looks ready to stand up.

'But, Barry, that's not how it ended … There's something else.'

His face changes. He looks uneasy. 'What now?'

'After a few minutes, the labour pains started up again, and a second baby was born.'

Barry frowns at me, his eyes narrowed. 'You mean … I had a twin?'

'Yes, Barry, I had twin boys; identical twins.'

'So … he died?'

'No, oh no, he didn't die. You were both small, but healthy. I tried my best to feed and care for you, my two darling little sons, but Sister Bernadette was very mean. She told me there was no way I could keep and sustain *two* babies. She insisted I would have to give one of you up for adoption.'

Barry was watching me carefully, barely blinking. He'd gone white as a ghost.

'I had no money, just one friend, Elsie – you remember Elsie,

Barry? She'd had her little girl there, in the mother and baby home, just before you were born. She was kind to me, a good friend, and we've stayed in touch from time to time. Sister Aileen was kind too, but Sister Bernadette insisted that I had to give one child up. She said there was a couple waiting to adopt a baby, rich people who desperately wanted a child. I had no choice in the matter. I had to agree, or I'd have lost both of you.'

'How did you choose? How did you choose which of us to keep and which one to give up?' His voice is hard and grating.

'I didn't. The couple who adopted Donal – that was your brother's name, Donal – it was their choice ... I don't know why they chose him. Sister Bernadette said it was because he was smaller and more needy, so they felt they could help him more. I only know I had no say in the matter.'

I take a few moments to wipe my eyes and collect my thoughts.

'I was told the couple would change his name, and I could never know what that new Christian name was, nor his surname. Sister Bernadette said I'd never be allowed to trace him, never. She said I wasn't to even *try* to trace him.'

'But did you ever try?'

'I did ... and Erna tried to help me. We hired a researcher to try to trace him, but it seems all Donal's birth and adoption records were destroyed, most likely by Sister Bernadette. She was onto a good thing. Finding rich people who were desperate for a child, who'd make a big donation to the mother and baby home. She wouldn't have wanted anyone looking into the finances. The researcher was clever in uncovering some dates in a ledger at St Agatha's though. Every little step took a long time to achieve. I decided not to tell you about Donal until we found him. Maybe that was a wrong decision ...'

Barry looks darkly at me but doesn't comment.

'Anyway, by checking the dates the researcher found it was clear when Donal was adopted, and then we discovered that the adoptive parents decided not to keep him.'

'So, if those rich people had chosen to adopt *me*, and not … Donal? You would have let them?'

'Darling, I had no choice, no power in the situation. That's how it was. Things were different then.'

Barry makes a face. 'What did you actually do to stop them?'

'What could I do? I was seventeen, I was all alone, far from home, and I had no money.'

'Maybe you could have tried to get some help.'

His expression seems to say *you didn't really try*, or maybe it was just my own feeling of guilt interpreting it that way.

'Barry, you must believe how totally heartbroken I was to have to give up your brother. I nearly died of grief when they took him. It was the worst day of my life. My only comfort was the thought that Donal would be with people who really wanted him, who would dearly love and care for him. I felt sure, that as wealthy people, they would cherish him and give him a good and full life; better than I – a penniless young girl – could possibly give him.'

Barry stares at me in silence for a moment after listening to this account.

'But you felt that that life was good enough for me, did you?'

'No, Barry, that's not fair. I loved you then and I love you now. I would much rather have kept you *both* with me, whatever my limitations. I would have done my best to look after you both – as I have tried to do for you …'

He stares down at his knees.

'In any case,' I say, 'the *worst* thing the researcher managed to discover was that Donal did not have the happy, full and good life I imagined for him. Those people gave him up when he was just two years old, and returned him to the local authority. I wasn't allowed to know his name, or where he'd been moved to. I only know he was in the care of the local authority, which means in children's homes, and perhaps with foster parents.'

Barry stands up abruptly.

'I know it must be a shock for you, Barry ... but I hope you understand ...'

'Well, thank you for telling me. Better late than never, I suppose. That explains a lot. I'm tired. I think I'll go to bed now. Goodnight.'

'But wait a minute, Barry, I did do something – I wrote a letter to each of you, to try to explain, and to tell you how much I loved both of you, and would always love you. I wrote it while you were still a baby. It was for you and Donal to read when you grew up, or if anything happened to me ... Of course I never had the chance to give Donal his letter, but this is yours ... if you want to read it?'

I take an envelope out of my bag.

He stares at the envelope. Then he shrugs and takes it. 'OK ... I'll look at it in my room.'

Chapter 18

1996
Barry

My hand trembles when I slide the letter out of the envelope and gaze at the page of Mum's childish handwriting.

London, June 1972

My darling Barry,

If you are reading this, you will already know that you are one of twins, and that your twin brother is called Donal. Whether you have known this for some time, or have just learned it, I want to tell you a bit about your birth and Donal's and the weeks that followed it.

The days immediately after your birth were happy, joyful days. You were such adorable, beautiful babies, both of you, and I loved you so very much. St Agatha's – the mother and baby home – was a dismal place, but I thought nothing of that. Although I was only a young girl, and without the support of my own mother, I wanted to be the best mother in the world. I spent every minute of each day with you – cuddling you, feeding you, singing to you and playing with you. I can't tell you how much I loved you; I adored you both.

But the happy time soon came to an end when Sister Bernadette, the head nun – a hard, unsympathetic woman – told me I would have to give one of you up. She said a rich couple had applied to adopt Donal. Sister Bernadette allowed me no choice in the matter. She insisted I wasn't capable of caring for both of you boys. They would take Donal away in four weeks' time, she said. I was desperate.

The time came nearer, day by day, as I knew it had to. I was full of dread. It felt almost like waiting for my execution.

I'd named both of you boys: Barry and Donal. The adoptive parents chose to adopt Donal because they felt sympathetic as he was weaker. Sister Bernadette warned me that they had decided to rename their adopted child, as was their right. It broke my heart that nothing would be left of me for Donal, of his rightful mother, not even his name. I was afraid he would grow up thinking his mother had abandoned him, didn't want him, and didn't love him – that I had rejected him. That idea was unbearable, Barry.

For four precious weeks I spent every possible minute with you boys. Whenever I lifted little Donal and held him close, I tried to breathe him in, to hold his scent inside me. I studied every bit of his face and body; I tried to commit every detail to memory, to keep Donal in my heart for ever. I can still see him, as if it were yesterday.

Of course I loved and cherished you, Barry, just the same. I was comforted by knowing that you, at least, would be with me as you grew, thank the Lord. It pleased me that you would always know how much I loved you, but it saddened me that Donal, your brother, would not.

Sister Bernadette complained that I spent too much time

and attention on Donal. She said it would make the separation all the more difficult for both of us, as if there was any way to make taking him from me easy. Sister Aileen was so much more kind and understanding. She often came and sat with us, taking you on her lap, Barry, to leave me free to hold Donal for a few minutes, to cuddle and kiss him those last precious days.

I wanted to meet the adoptive parents – I did so want to know who was going to keep my Donal, and to be sure that they were kind, loving people – but it wasn't allowed.

When at last the dreaded time came, I stood on a chair watching at the high dormitory window, holding you, Barry – my darling, precious remaining child – hugging you to me. By stretching up on my toes, as far as possible, I could just see the ground far below, the tarmac drive curving round the front of the tall, grim faade of the building.

All the girls in the dormitory were gathered around my chair, like an army of support. I could feel their sympathy, their pity. I knew they were on my side, but there was nothing they could do to help.

Outside, I heard the sounds of the front door opening and muffled voices drifted upwards. My heart began thundering like a drum in my chest. A tall man in a dark overcoat emerged, followed by a woman in a camel coat and brown knee-high boots. She was carrying a white bundle. A black car was parked near the entrance. I knew nothing of cars, but it looked large, shiny and expensive to me.

I opened my mouth and a terrible howl came out – out of me: a chilling sound, inhuman, like the cry of a desperate, wounded animal. I stood up higher on my toes and leaned the top half of my body further out of the window, while the other girls clung to my legs. The woman outside holding the baby – holding my Donal – stopped walking and glanced upwards for a moment. Then she walked quickly to the car.

The man helped her into the back seat. Then he went around to the front and got in. Sister Bernadette gave them a wave and they drove off. They were gone, with my Donal.

That's how we lost him, Barry. All these years you should have had the companionship of your dear brother Donal. All these years the three of us should have been together, together as a family. I pray we will be reunited one day.

Thank goodness I still had you with me, darling Barry. I don't know what I would have done if they had taken you too. I think it would have been the death of me. I love you so much.

Your mother, Marie

I stare at the letter for a long time. Why now? Why hadn't she told me before? It would have explained such a lot – that feeling of a gap, a vacancy, someone absorbing her thoughts and affection. Donal. He was like a shadow, haunting my life all the years gone by. Someone lurking in the background, hidden, unreachable, yet ever present.

No way can I sleep after taking these revelations on board. So much for cutting down on the drugs. Now's not the time for that. I rummage in my case and slide open the zipped pocket at the bottom. My heart's pounding. Better lock my door. I don't want Mum walking in. Just the sort of thing she might do.

Shall I go for my usual line? No, not tonight. I need something stronger. There's a syringe, ready prepared. That's good. My hands are shaking. I roll up my sleeve. The needle slides in. I lean back into the pillows and sink into blissful oblivion.

Chapter 19

1996
Marie

Sometimes it feels as though my life is spiralling out of control. Barry is so angry and resentful, and that causes me terrible pain. I've stopped trying to explain any more to him about the choices I had to make. It just seems to provoke him further. I'm trying to ignore his anger and bad mood, and just continue to show him the love I feel for him. Despite all the worrying things I have discovered recently.

There's no doubt I've had concerns about Barry over the years, but it is this year that the worries have really come to a head. It's not as though he's a teenager any more; he's a young man of twenty-six, settled into his job and his flat, doing so well in many ways.

But now I've found evidence of something that perhaps I'd always dreaded most. It must have been a subconscious dread, because I have no memory of actually formulating the thought. Yet, when it happened, it's as though everything fell into place. Not that that's any kind of comfort. When I discover the secret, it's the most terrible shock imaginable. At the same time, perhaps I had sensed something of the sort for some months, maybe even years. It seems to explain some puzzling things about Barry's behaviour.

He has given me a key to his flat, in case I'm passing and need to call in, although he's given me instructions never to drop by unannounced unless absolutely necessary, some sort of emergency for example. He could be out, or engrossed in some essential work project, he says, and wouldn't want to disappoint me.

So until today, I've never actually been to his flat since the day he moved in and showed me and Erna Goldstein around it. Not that there's any sort of emergency or great urgency today. It's just that I've been to a market not far away and decided to take some nice fresh fruit and vegetables to Barry and his flatmate, Keith. It's a weekday, so I don't really expect them to be home.

I'm sure they won't mind. It'll be a nice surprise for them. I'm convinced neither of them is very bothered about a healthy diet, and that worries me. Eating better would do them both some good. Barry's very thin and pallid – and Keith's not much better. How I'd love to feed them both up a bit on some good home cooking. In the meantime, some wholesome, natural foods are the best I can offer.

One thing that has occasionally crossed my mind is whether perhaps Barry is gay. I don't know what went on at university, but certainly I know he's never brought a girl home. Is Keith maybe not just a flatmate, but a *lover* too? Not that I'm prejudiced against gay people; I wouldn't love Barry any less. My main anxiety is just whether Barry might have contracted AIDS. Could that be why he looks so thin and unwell? That idea terrifies me.

Also, it worries me that while *I* might accept Barry being homosexual, not everyone else is so broad-minded. I feel being gay would just make his life so much more complicated and difficult.

Also, I have to admit that I ache and yearn for Barry to produce a grandchild for me – I can't help it – and as I've never seen hide nor hair of a girl in his life, that's starting to seem more and more unlikely.

I open the door to their flat and call out 'Yoohoo!' but there's no reply. All is quiet. I walk all around the flat, feeling a bit like an intruder.

Now I don't like to criticise, and perhaps young people these days have different standards, different values, but there's no doubt about it: the place is a right *pigsty*! Those boys are supposed to be professionals. It's basically a decent apartment, quite posh in fact, and heaven knows what rent they pay for it! It's not just some grotty student dive. They really should respect it. They could even pay someone to do a bit of cleaning for them if they aren't prepared to do it themselves, maybe even some cooking occasionally – they could certainly afford it.

The first thing I notice is that Barry and Keith have separate bedrooms. While it doesn't exactly prove anything, I'm pleased to see that, and feel a bit reassured. Maybe I was getting myself anxious and upset over nothing.

I roll up my sleeves and decide to give the place a good clean and tidy-up as a nice surprise for the two young men. Would it be a pleasant surprise though? Surely they won't feel offended, or that I'm poking my nose where it doesn't belong? Lots of lads of their age don't seem to think much about tidiness or keeping their environment spick and span, it just isn't a priority for them. True enough, they both work hard at their jobs, put in long hours, and probably don't have much time for housework. A bit of help surely can't hurt, just this once.

Well, I scoot through the kitchen as fast as I can. In fact, I'm enjoying myself, washing the dirty dishes, putting crockery neatly away in the cupboards, cleaning the cooker, the surfaces and scrubbing the floor. Then on to Barry's bedroom. Well, there's stuff all over the place: clothes, books, papers, dirty coffee cups and plates, scattered on the floor, and every other surface. Hadn't I taught him to put his things in their rightful place? I soon realise

I can't make much cleaning progress, without first clearing some of the mess away. So naturally, the first job is to find places to put all his bits and pieces neatly away.

I open one of the drawers in the chest ... and my heart nearly stops. It's a complete shock. I feel physically sick at what's inside. Little plastic bags of white powders; some marked with an 'H', others with a 'C'. At first I tell myself it must be some sort of medicine. Then – horror of horrors – right at the back of the drawer, there are three hypodermic needles, together with packets of tobacco and cigarette papers, some sort of burner, and a bundle of stained metal spoons, done up with a rubber band. I stare at each item in turn, trying to think of a logical explanation for them, my stomach convulsing. I'm afraid I might be sick. My hands are trembling. It's hard to breathe.

I've led a pretty sheltered life in some ways, it's true, but I'm not totally *daft*, nor totally innocent. It doesn't take much to realise this is a stash of drugs: *Barry's stash of drugs.* Exactly what they are, I'm not sure. I guess it must be hard drugs of some sort. Could the 'H' stand for heroin? What else would it be? What would 'C' stand for, if not cocaine? An icy chill crawls down my spine. My legs feel like blancmange. I slam the drawer shut; I've seen enough. I sit on the bed for a moment, trying to stop trembling, to steady my breathing, to calm myself down.

All of a sudden, a little flutter of hope flits through my throbbing brain; fragile, like a delicate butterfly. *Maybe the stuff is Keith's!* That's it. Of course! Why didn't I think of that? It doesn't even belong to Barry! Thank heavens for that thought ...

Yet ... yet ... this isn't Keith's room, I know that; it's Barry's room. It's Barry's drawer. These are all Barry's belongings. I recognise them. I'm deceiving myself. The lovely, fragile butterfly crumbles and falls to the ground like dust. Of course everything in the drawer is Barry's. The drugs are Barry's. There's no doubt about it. My son is a drug addict.

Well, that explains a lot. No wonder Barry needs so much

money, no wonder he's so withdrawn and his moods are so unpredictable. No wonder he sometimes looks frail and ill …

I try to replace all Barry's things exactly where I found them, and shut all the drawers and cupboards. Like a thief, I retrace my steps and make sure his bedroom is exactly as it was before. Of course I can't unwash the crockery, or dirty the floors I'd cleaned. I'll have to admit to spending some time in the flat. I leave the fruit and vegetables as planned. Feeling nauseous and dizzy, I leave the apartment and hurry home.

***

After my discovery, I have terrible difficulty getting off to sleep at night. Chilling fears for Barry's future preoccupy me constantly. What kind of a world might he be involved in? A world of sickness and addiction, dealers, drugs gangs and violence? Oh my God, isn't losing Donal bad enough? Please don't let me lose both my boys …

Even when I manage to sleep, frightening words like 'overdose' and 'junkie' and 'AIDS' infect my dreams, and linger in my mind when I wake, allowing me no peace or rest, night or day.

Yet, in some ways, Barry seemed unchanged. He behaves just as he always does. He rang me to thank me for the bag of market foods, and for doing the washing up. He didn't seem to notice anything else.

He appears to be coping with work and with his life in general, just as usual. Perhaps I've made a huge mistake; maybe the little packets are something quite harmless. Some sort of powder to relieve flu symptoms or an upset stomach. Perhaps, after all it *is* Keith who is taking them, and maybe Barry is keeping them in his room to stop his friend from taking too much. That must be it – there's bound to be a logical explanation. I've been torturing myself unnecessarily.

But as time goes on, I worry more and more about Barry.

Sometimes he looks so gaunt. There are shadows under his eyes. He doesn't always look well. There's a tremor about him. He becomes impatient when I suggest he should see a doctor for a check-up. He tells me there's nothing wrong with him and I should stop fussing. I try my best not to get agitated about him, but I sense something is definitely not right.

Barry rarely speaks of girls. His world at work seems to be mostly a man's world. Of course he's young yet, but I would so love him to have a special young woman in his life, but where on earth would he meet her? He hardly ever goes out or social-ises. *How lovely it would be if he were to meet a nice girl and they married and had children. Then I would be a grandmother,* I think, even though I'm only forty-three! Yet, what a joy that would be for all of us.

I decide not to bother Erna with my concerns. Her health hasn't been so good lately. Despite that, she's been eager to offer help to Barry with putting down a deposit on a flat of his own.

'Why spend money on rent month after month, my dear?' she says to Barry. 'It's just money down the drain. Whereas if you have a mortgage, it goes towards a home you will own yourself in time.'

Bless Erna, she's always so wise, and always so *generous*.

London prices are achingly expensive and rising rapidly all the time. Barry finds a small but charming flat in Putney, in a pleasant leafy area near the river. He couldn't have managed it without Erna's help.

Chapter 20

1999
Robbie

Life hasn't been great lately. There have been some significant changes at the Golden Days Care Home, and definitely none for the better. The home has been absorbed into a big trust incorporating six care homes, all of them are run by a new manager, Cameron Black. He's been appointed to replace Lorna, for whom I had so much respect, and great liking. Cameron is a totally different type from Lorna. He's not hands-on at all. In fact he'd never dream of getting his hands dirty.

He dresses in a sharp, expensive-looking suit, and sits in his office most of the day. He has nothing to do with the residents; he wouldn't know any of them by name, or their families. He doesn't have much direct contact with the staff either. He prefers to communicate via emails or staff meetings. He calls one this morning, insisting on full attendance.

'Over the last twenty years or so of Lorna's management, a great many activities and outings have been developed and funded.

While well meant, I do not regard most of these activities as part of the core responsibilities of this institution. I believe we need to get back to our core functions.'

Cameron looks round the room with a severe expression.

'I'm not saying all the money spent on activities like the drama club has been wasted. Just that when funding is limited, there are far more important areas in which we could invest ...'

I'm horrified; I'd set up the drama club with Lorna's blessing. The residents love it – it gets some of those old people talking, people who've been silent for as long as anyone could remember. Also, the music sessions, the art groups, the trips to the sea or the park, and the regular family get-togethers, all of which are so valued by the residents and their relatives – it seems all these are too wasteful, and have now disappeared from the new care home brochure.

'From now on, the emphasis has to be on economy,' Cameron announces. 'The Trust doesn't believe in wasting investors' money. Without this unnecessary and staff-intensive expenditure, we can manage with five fewer members of the team.'

Cameron looks round at all of us for approval. Most people, in deep shock, and wondering if they may be one of the five, stare silently at their feet.

'Additionally,' he continues, 'in future our meals contract will be with a centralised catering firm, who will deliver ready to heat and eat meals for all residents. This is a much more efficient way of providing nutrition and will replace the current extravagant use of on-site chefs, who have clearly been pandering unnecessarily to the whims and preferences of individual residents. Imagine the savings resulting from this change!'

'Er, excuse me, Mr Black, but some of the residents have particular dietary needs ...' begins Amina, one of the long-standing carers.'

'Yes, yes,' Cameron says impatiently. 'We'll check which are genuine dietary needs. Probably most are just plain fussiness, which costs us a lot of money. So normalising the menus will result in major savings.' He looks round the room as if expecting applause.

'We can then afford to give the entire care home a complete makeover: redecorate, smarten it up. Think how that will boost our residents' morale! Quite clearly a more efficient use of limited resources.'

***

Many staff are let go, including me. Belle resigns.

'I can't work this way, Robbie,' she tells me sadly. 'All they're interested in is outward appearances to impress shareholders. No thought for the lives of the poor old residents.'

And so I find myself jobless again, with no money coming in. Luckily, over the three years I've been working at Golden Days I managed to save a bit of my wages each week, never having been a big spender. I count it regularly, and amazingly, it's now nearly three thousand pounds! I've put the cash in a large brown envelope and stashed it under one of the floorboards in my sitting room. It's a bit of security for me while no money's coming in; it enables me to pay the rent for a while – but it's certainly not going to last for ever.

I go regularly to the job centre, but there's not much on offer at the moment. I register with a home care agency, helping elderly or disabled people in their own homes, four days a week. Not having a car, I can only take on people who live fairly near to me, and not too far from one another. Between visits, I travel as rapidly as possible on foot, or occasionally a short bus journey. Most visits are strictly fifteen minutes; a few are twenty or thirty minutes. I rush about toileting and washing the client, preparing a quick meal, or putting them to bed.

In between tasks, I try to talk to them, provide a little window of company. Most live alone and are deeply lonely. I can give so little, yet the clients are pathetically grateful. I get paid only for the time actually spent with the client, not for travel between visits. It's disheartening work, but I do my best.

One day a week I go back to visit some of the residents at Golden Days. I organise a little show for them to sing and act in, on a voluntary basis of course – that bastard Cameron wouldn't dream of paying me for it. Anyway, the residents love it, and so do I, so I'm happy enough to carry on. At least it makes me feel that I'm making some small positive contribution to the world.

I met a young woman during my time at the care home. She's called Tracy and works part-time as a cleaner at Golden Days. Tracy's had some difficult times herself; she's got a little girl of about three, who's looked after by Tracy's mam. I feel a bit sorry for the child; Tracy's not exactly the maternal type. She seems happy to leave the little girl with her grandmother most of the time. Sometimes Tracy stays overnight at my place. Other nights I don't know where she goes. I reckon she'd be keener on me if I spent more money on her – she's often asking me to take her clubbing or out for a meal. Sometimes she's asked for a loan to buy herself a dress or trousers. Well, I know I'd never see any of that so-called loan again. I feel a bit mean always refusing, but clubbing's not my scene at all, and I never buy myself new clothes. If I really need something, which is rare, I head for the charity shop. Anyway I need to keep my float for the rent. Memories of sleeping rough haunt me constantly.

I wouldn't be surprised if Tracy chucked me any time soon. It doesn't really bother me; there's no commitment on either side. Having said that, I do enjoy a bit of female company – I've had little enough of it over the years. Although I can't pretend Tracy and I have anything much in common. She's not interested in books, films, history or discussions – or any of the things I like, in fact. She enjoys going out for a drink (or five!), going clubbing if she gets the chance, watching stuff on television, and sex. The latter suits me fine, but I'm not in love with Tracy, nor, I have to admit, do I find her very interesting company. But she's cheerful on the whole and seems good-hearted. At least, I thought she was.

Hoping to warm her heart, I take Tracy out to a film, despite her reluctance. It's a well-reviewed film with good actors, and I hope she might be won over if she enjoys it. She doesn't enjoy it.

'It was dead boring,' she complains. 'Nothing fucking happened. It didn't make sense. Why did she stay with him if she didn't even like him? Seemed pointless to me. There might at least have been a murder or summat. I'd'a murdered him, no problem!'

Tracy's in a bad mood for the entire walk back to the flat. She cheers up a bit when I offer her some vodka. She finishes the bottle and comes to bed in a much better mood. We make love and she goes straight to sleep. It takes me a bit longer to settle, but I'm tired from my work, and soon sink into a deep sleep too. At some point of the night I'm aware of her getting up.

She kisses me gently and whispers, 'Toilet ...' I sink back to sleep.

A reluctant dawn is creeping through the gap in the curtains when I start to wake. I have a bad feeling, a sick feeling, deep in the pit of my stomach. I stretch my hand out towards Tracy, but she's not there.

'Trace?'

There's no reply.

'Tracy!?' I call, much louder this time. Still there's no reply.

I jump out of bed and run to try the bathroom door. It's open and the bathroom is empty.

'Tracy?' I shout, my heart pounding.

I run to the sitting room and yank the curtains open. There's no sign of her. I hardly dare look ... But I have to. I see the floor-board is sticking up on one side. I know what to expect, but can't believe it's really happening. I don't want to look. I kneel down and remove the floorboard. I screw my eyes tight shut and slowly push my hand into the hole, feeling all around. The envelope holding my three thousand pounds has gone, and Tracy with it.

Chapter 21

1999
Barry

Looking back on my life so far, I admit there are some points at which I may have made bad decisions. Of course Mother would say it all went downhill after I became so dependent on drugs, and to some extent perhaps she's right. It's true I've been using cocaine heavily recently. It eases some of the anxieties and depression, and still seems to allow me to concentrate on my work. At least none of the senior managers have noticed – they certainly don't complain about the money I'm still making for the company.

What my mother has never appreciated though, is the extent to which *she herself* is to blame for all that went wrong in my life. Of course her strict Catholic upbringing created a potentially bottomless pit of guilt, but on the other hand, she has rightly had plenty to feel guilty about.

Instead of presenting herself as an innocent victim of our wicked father – a blameless child – perhaps she should have accepted that she alone was responsible for the decisions she made.

Yes, she was ignorant and limited in many ways, but it's not as if she was totally ignorant of the 'facts of life', for heaven's sake. She grew up on a smallholding with sheep and cows. Reproduction was going on all around her. All right, she was young, but she wasn't a child. She was a young woman capable of making a decision – capable of resisting his advances. But she didn't resist, and the consequences were obvious and could have been foreseen.

In due course, my twin brother and I were the innocent and unfortunate results of her actions. Quite understandably, the staff at the mother and baby home where my brother and I were born advised Mother to put at least one of us up for adoption. She regarded that as a tragic choice she had to make, yet there was every reason to expect that Donal, as she had called him, would be well loved, nurtured and devotedly raised by his adoptive parents.

As it happened, the placement was not successful. We don't know exactly what went wrong, but it must have been bad for the foster parents to give him up. Perhaps Donal was a disturbed and difficult infant, perhaps he was resistant to the affection his adoptive parents tried to show him. Of course we knew nothing of this until many years later. Rather than feeling glad for him and the opportunities adoption might have offered him, and rejoicing that she still had *one* child, Mother spent years mourning the child she had given away, rather than focusing on and celebrating the one she still had.

In her circumstances, Mother is incredibly lucky to have found Auntie Erna by chance, and to have been, in effect, adopted by her. Without Erna's help and support … well it hardly bears thinking about. Mother accepts Erna Goldstein's support and generosity without question. Yes, she's kind to Erna and is clearly fond of her. She is grateful for her generosity, always was, and tries to repay it by doing some work around the house, fashioning herself as a kind of housekeeper. But where is her personal ambition?

She claims to love children, so why didn't she at least train to become a nursery nurse or teacher and gain some independence?

If she loves me, as she constantly told me, why did she endlessly mope after Donal? Not that I'm jealous of Donal. How can I envy a faceless name, a shadow, a ghost?

Certainly my mother's constant preoccupation with the absent brother (I almost wonder sometimes – did he ever even exist?) was an ongoing irritation to me growing up, even though I didn't know at the time that I had a twin! It was Auntie Erna who really appreciated me, who tried to know and understand me as an individual, who took a genuine interest in me and truly valued me as a person. It was Auntie Erna too, who recognised the potential in me, despite having emerged from a gene pool of somewhat limited intelligence and ambition. It was Erna too, who determined that my brain should be encouraged to develop to its true capacity by arranging for me to attend a good school, a private school.

Though this generosity was well meant, it created another problem for me, one that Auntie Erna could not have been expected to foresee, but perhaps Mother at least should have – not only foreseen, but understood. Going to an expensive and prestigious school meant mixing with boys of very different backgrounds to my own: boys from high-achieving professional families, and those with a family history of moderate wealth.

Mother could never understand my reluctance to invite these boys back home. Well, was I to show them to our poky little flat ('cosy' she called it) at the top of the house, for my mother to appear in her 'pinny', and serve them with bread and butter or beans on toast? She never had the faintest idea how embarrassing – how humiliating – that would be. Of necessity I became a bit of a loner. At least it gave me plenty of time to concentrate on my schoolwork. I always did exceptionally well academically. Mother is pathetically proud of my achievements.

Back to the unfortunate choices … Almost everyone experiments with interesting substances in their youth; it's part of natural exploration, part of growing up. Neither Mother nor

137

Auntie Erna would have approved of that, let alone the harder stuff that rapidly followed, but it wasn't until I was working in the City and had money to spare, that I moved on to cocaine and occasionally heroin.

It's all perfectly civilised. None of that lurking in filthy back alleys to score, worrying if being knifed and robbed was part of the deal – I'm sure that's what Mother imagines! No, my dealer wears a suit and tie – he looks more like a suburban bank manager than a dastardly crook.

I suppose like everyone else, at first I convinced myself that I was in control of my habit … I could stop any time if I chose to. It was just an enjoyable recreation like any other. Mother fussed tediously that I was looking frail and poorly. She offered to pay for me to go on holiday somewhere bracing and healthy. Not that I needed her money. But I did agree that a break might do me good. I arranged a week's walking in the Cheviot hills in Northumberland. The first time was back in the early Nineties.

It was one of the best decisions I ever made. The peace in that rugged, unspoiled landscape restores my soul, while the wholesome food and vigorous exercise re-energise my body. That visit was the first of several expeditions I've made to that northern extremity of our country. Generally I even abstain totally for the duration of my trip, but my abstinence doesn't last long once I'm back in the hectic, stress-inducing capital.

After Mother challenged me, having found my stash while secretly snooping around my flat, I did cut back for a while. She made such an almighty, ridiculous fuss about it all – calling me a junkie and all that overdramatic rubbish. Once an Irish peasant, never a sophisticate, I suppose. I think I've convinced her that my drug-taking is all in the past.

***

It was meeting Anaïs that really made me try to change my ways, take a more determined approach. In those first, early days of our relationship she was such a delight. Beautiful, charming, funny – I was crazy about her. So bright and lively, so warm and loving. I adored her.

She's come to be a kind of drug to me herself, one I can't get enough of. Maybe I have an obsessive personality, but Anaïs really gets under my skin. I think of her constantly, have done from the moment we were together. I admit I may be overly jealous, misguided at times. I'm constantly terrified she might leave me, go after another man. Well, she's so attractive, so gorgeous, any man would want her.

Anyway, I've left poor old Keith to rent our shared flat on his own. He can afford it. Meanwhile, thanks to Auntie Erna, as usual, I found a much better apartment in the posher part of Putney. It wasn't long before Anaïs moved in with me. It means that earning more money is absolutely essential. I work long hours, but she earns much less, teaching French part-time in a school, and giving some private individual coaching lessons. It's the only drawback to our relationship. I can't see any likelihood of her bringing significantly more money into our household any time soon. Anyway, despite being financially stretched, it's worth it. I'm so in love with Anaïs, and besides I have hopes of more money coming my way from Auntie Erna in time, maybe quite soon. She's seriously getting on – not very far off a hundred after all!

Unfortunately, what with working such testing hours, anxieties over money, and fear that I might risk losing Anaïs – the stress started to oppress me. Inevitably, the drugs have gradually taken over again, as they always do eventually, I suppose. I've been kidding myself that I could control them, just take them occasionally. What a fool. It appears that my drug habit has had some effect on my health. My GP has referred me to a kidney specialist, as he suspects there are some problems. I'm waiting for an initial appointment.

Chapter 22

1999
Marie

In recent months – all through this difficult time in fact – Erna Goldstein is getting older day by day. I'm starting to wonder if she'll even make it to her hundredth birthday. She's such a positive person. She talks of having a *family* (in which she sweetly includes me and Barry) *celebration party*. Yet I can't help noticing the signs of ageing, despite my preoccupation with Barry. There's no denying it any longer. For some time, Erna has found walking more difficult, especially the stairs.

Luckily, there's scope for alterations in the large house to make life easier for her. We've had the smaller downstairs sitting room converted into her bedroom. I sewed her some fresh bright curtains in her favourite deep apricot colour, and made a matching duvet cover for the bed, although she always tells me not to go to so much trouble. Of course I always reply – truthfully – that it's a pleasure to do anything to help, and no bother at all.

It pains me to see my dear friend grow thinner and more

bent. I make her all her favourite foods to try to tempt her to eat more, but increasingly, her appetite grows smaller. A few of her very elderly friends still come to visit. They sit in a huddle with Radio Three playing in the background as they chat. I bring them little china cups of coffee or tea, and sometimes small pieces of the lemon or marzipan cakes Erna loves, or some light vanilla biscuits I've made, making sure they're crisp and light, but not too hard for their old teeth.

These last months too, Barry has largely cut himself off from me. It causes me terrible pain. I know the revelation about his twin brother has been a huge shock for Barry, one he hasn't been able to deal with. I know too, that he's depressed and that always leads to him taking more drugs than ever. I can see it in the shadows under his eyes and the hollows of his cheeks. I see the tremor of his hands and hear it in his voice. Perhaps he believes it's the only way he can cope with his confusion and resentment, but I'm so afraid for his health.

Barry is still fond of Erna. He comes by regularly, and generally, after greeting me briefly, he hurries to her sitting room. They sit together for an hour or two talking, listening to a piece of music and discussing it afterwards, or occasionally playing a game of chess. I don't begrudge these visits – they are one of Erna's greatest pleasures – but I am so sad to feel the gulf between Barry and myself. He's hardly spoken to me since I told him about Donal. Whatever Erna's increasing physical frailty, her brain is as alert as ever. Her sharp mind is not oblivious to the changes in Barry either.

'Is he quite well, my dear? He looks so gaunt and haunted at times. I wonder if they are working him too hard at that job of his? Perhaps he could do with a holiday?'

I try to reassure her. 'You're right, Erna … you're right he's not been quite himself lately. Too many late nights perhaps. But don't you fret yourself; he's on the mend. I've made him promise to eat better and to get himself out of doors regularly for some fresh air and exercise. He's going on one of his visits to Northumberland shortly, and he's promised to take himself in hand ...'

'Hmm ...' She looks at me doubtfully.

***

In her declining years, Erna has depended more and more heavily on my support, and I'm so glad I have been there to give it to her. As she grows more frail and infirm, I care for her needs as best I can. I feel it is a privilege, and never a chore to help her. Erna is always appreciative.

'Thank you, Marie. You are so good to me. So full of love and kindness. Nothing is ever too much trouble for you, my dear. You know I have always said you would have made an excellent nurse.'

Most of all I *hate* to hear Erna speak of her own death, which she does ever more frequently as the years pass by. She is forever assuring me that I will never need to worry about my own well-being in the future; that I will be 'well taken care of' when she is gone.

'Sure, don't speak to me of you not being here, Erna. I can't bear to think about it. No, I refuse to give it a single thought just now, for the idea fills me with sadness and emptiness. You were ever so generous to me and Barry all those years ago – and so you have been ever since. I couldn't have done without you then, no I absolutely couldn't. But I can't do without you now either, believe me. It's not the money that I want, dear Erna, it's you! You and your friendship.'

'Bless you, Marie, I don't want to make you sad, but we must be realistic and practical. I am a very old woman. None of us lives for ever – you know that. You are very precious to me, and I simply want you to know that you will never be left without means to support yourself in comfort when I am no longer here.'

Erna Goldstein is indeed very old. The year itself is a constant reminder. As she's always telling me, she is as old as the century.

Having been born in the year 1900, each of her birthdays corresponds to the year! She takes a delight in this idea, whereas I feel terrified; I feel there is no escaping a growing, frightening awareness of just how old she is getting, and of a future without her, which I can't bear to contemplate.

What with my anxieties about Barry, and my increasing worries about Erna, it is a great joy when a much happier event brings warmth and excitement to our lives, brings us all together in fact, and allows me to file the 'drug problem' away somewhere in the recesses of my brain, for a while at least.

Unexpectedly, Barry suddenly introduces a beautiful, charming, lovely young French woman – Anaïs – into our lives. I can see she is very special to him as soon as I see them together, more than special in fact. That brings such great pleasure and hope to me. I love the girl from the moment I set eyes on her.

Anaïs tells me she had come to England to be an au pair a few years previously. She'd liked England so much she had stayed and eventually trained as a teacher. She taught French, which she greatly enjoyed, though she says English children are very naughty! Parents and teachers are much stricter in France, she tells me, but she smiles when she says it; she's clearly fond of children, even naughty ones. My heart soars with hope at that thought.

For a while our lives become calmer and closer. Anaïs likes me, I can tell. She likes coming to see me – and Erna – at home. Barry has always been polite and warm with Erna of course. He respected her as well as being very fond of her – but the new relationship with Anaïs seems to make him easier *with me* too. The change in Barry is as clear as day. He no longer maintains a cold distance from me. He's back to calling me Mum and talking to me. He tells me Anaïs had fiercely reproached him for the way he was treating me. He should mend the relationship, she told him, build bridges. It was clear to her that I love my son; he must surely see that too. What joy to have Barry restored to me.

He adores Anaïs. It's obvious by the way he looks at her. He's started to look better in himself too – he's put on a bit of weight and got some colour in his cheeks at last. It's such a pleasure for me to see. She softens him.

One evening, the young couple come for supper at Erna's instigation. I leave Erna, Barry and Anaïs talking, while I go to prepare the main course in the kitchen. A few minutes later Barry comes out to see me.

'D'you need any help, Mum?'

'Well thank you, son. You could just chop some of that lettuce and add it to the salad bowl over there, please.'

As he gets busy with the salad, I stop what I'm doing and study his face for a moment. The strained look I have grown so used to seems to have evaporated.

'What?' he asks, with a careful, sidelong smile at me.

'Nothing, my darling, nothing at all. I'm just happy to see you looking so much better. That's all. It's amazing what a good woman can do for a man, don't you think?'

'Now who could you possibly be thinking of?'

'I think we both know that, don't we?' I say. I give him a hug. For once, he doesn't stiffen or resist. He kisses the top of my head.

We carry on with our preparations in silence for a few minutes. Then he draws a deep breath, straightens up and looks at me. 'She's the light of my life, Mum. I feel very lucky to have found her.'

'You *are* lucky, son …' I say carefully, watching him, judging the situation. It's now or never. I *have to* confront him, get it out in the open.

'So … so maybe now you can finally deal with the drug problem, can you? Go on one of these "rehab" courses? Before they do some real lasting damage …'

I hear Barry's sudden intake of breath. The knife he's been holding clatters onto the table. Colour drains from his face. He stares at me. In that moment I realise he has no idea that I'm aware of his drug use.

'What do you … I mean …? When …?'

144

'I'm not completely stupid, Barry, though you might think it, nor am I blind. I'm your *mother*. I've known for some time. I'm worried about you, and if Anaïs knew, she would be worried too – that's if she's prepared to take the risk of staying with you at all.'

He picks up the salad knife and looks down, the knife slack in his hand. He appears deep in thought.

'I'm really hoping you and Anaïs might stay together,' I continue, 'get married perhaps ... maybe even have children in time. I can tell how much she means to you. But ... but Barry, would she want a ... *junkie* as a husband, as the father of her children?'

His expression changes instantly and he glares at me through screwed-up eyes.

'For Christ's sake, Mum, shhhh!' he hisses, looking round at the door. 'I'm not a fucking junkie ... I just ... you know ... use a few *recreational* drugs, just to relax me. You know nothing about it ... I mean ... everyone takes them sometimes these days. It's just London life.'

'You watch your mouth! And don't talk to me like I'm an imbecile. I know the difference between an occasional ... *joint* ... and taking *hard* drugs regularly ... *injecting* them even, Barry.'

He stares at me in surprise, maybe even with a new respect. There's a pause, each of us with our thoughts. After a minute or two, he begins more quietly, 'Well, I'm definitely going to cut down on them. *I am, Mum.* I was planning to already. Anaïs really matters to me; she matters such a lot. I'm not going to do anything that risks our relationship.'

'I'm glad to hear it. But never mind *cutting down*, son, *cut them out*! If you need help doing that, then make sure you get it. I understand there are experts and clinics who could support you. But whatever you do – *cut – them – out*!'

Barry glances furtively at the kitchen door again. 'OK, OK ... you're right. Of course I will. I'll look into rehab. Don't say any more about it ... but you don't need to worry ... I promise.

Don't say a word to Anaïs about this, Mum, *please. And,* don't mention it to Auntie Erna, will you?'

***

I know Barry tried. Perhaps he succeeded, for a time. He and Anaïs marry at Lewisham registry office just a few months after our discussion. It's a very quiet ceremony, as they wanted, only Erna Goldstein and me to witness it. Erna, bless her, has given them a wedding present of another generous contribution to his flat in Putney, although with Barry's large salary, I'm not sure he really needs help. Erna also insists on them having a further money gift, for them to use for a holiday or honeymoon.

After the very simple marriage celebration, they decide to go on honeymoon to France. Sadly, Anaïs's mother died of cancer when Anaïs was still at school, but this visit is her chance to introduce Barry to her father, and other family members, as well as having a few days to themselves in the warmth of the Mediterranean.

The new apartment is now their shared home – Barry left Keith behind in the rented flat. I don't know how he disposed of the drugs and equipment. Maybe Keith took them over. I don't want to know anything more about it.

***

Things go very well during those early days. Anaïs brings us all such joy. She delights me and Erna, with her warm smile and the way she tosses her lovely dark auburn mane when she laughs – which she does a lot! Barry seems a changed man. It's such a relief to me. He can hardly take his eyes – or his hands – off Anaïs. He's more relaxed than I ever remember him being before, and there's a softer, kinder side to him that he's never shown before, except perhaps to his Auntie Erna.

I thought I couldn't have been happier, when, about a year after

146

they married, Barry and Anaïs come to tell us they're expecting a child! I'd noticed Anaïs's stomach had become a tiny bit more rounded recently, but hadn't dared to hope. The two of them hold hands and giggle like excited teenagers when they tell us the news. I'm in tears of joy – I'm going to be a grandmother! Erna hugs me, and them. She insists we open a bottle of the expensive sparkling wine she keeps for really special occasions.

'Well, if this isn't the most special of occasions, I don't know what is!' she says, full of smiles and delight.

I notice Anaïs only drinks about a thimbleful for a toast, the good girl, already thinking of the welfare of the baby she's carrying. She has a sweet way of stroking her growing belly, as if caressing the child itself, calming it and sending it off to sleep. I know she's going to make a wonderful mother. I can tell.

What a happy, thrilling evening for us all. I think my heart will burst with pleasure.

The only shadow clouding my happiness is thoughts of my missing boy, my dearest Donal. Somehow our family joy over the forthcoming child only emphasises the empty chair at the table. That's how I think of Donal; an ever-present part of our family, yet absent, missing.

Where is Donal? If only I could hold him, hug him, and tell him how much I love him too. If only we could make our family truly complete.

***

Just as my head is full of thoughts of my missing son, there's a new excitement, a new revelation. *A letter from my sister Bridie arrives!* I've thought so often of Ma and Da and all the family back in Ireland. I knew Da was unlikely to soften his attitude to his 'shameful daughter', but I'd hoped the rest of the family would have been more tolerant, more understanding. Yet, though I've written regularly to Ma and my sister Bridie over the years, I've never heard a word back. I think they must have all forgotten about me, erased me from their lives. It pained me greatly. Wouldn't Ma be missing me, and the grandsons she's never seen? If it hadn't been for Erna Goldstein, I think I'd have died from missing my ma. Yes, even with all the support and kindness – and love – Erna has given me, I *long* to see Ma – and my little sisters.

Bridie's letter is a huge shock. Da has just died, she writes. After I left Ireland, and he learned the reason why, he wouldn't have my name mentioned in the house. He told Ma and my sisters he'd found out that I'd emigrated and had left no address. Wasn't that just wicked of him? There was no way to contact me, he told them.

Long after, when Da died and the family went through his papers, they were shocked to find every single letter I'd written over the years, dozens of them, hidden away in his desk drawer. It broke their hearts.

They all loved me, and longed to see me. When would I come to see them all in Ireland? Bridie wrote. I certainly hope to. Maybe after the new baby arrives, that visit is something to consider.

What with Bridie's letter, and the arrival of Anaïs in our lives, and the imminent birth of a grandchild, the next few months are such an exciting time. Much as I adore my boys, there's a part of me that remembers the pleasure of having *sisters*, and how I enjoyed looking after them, playing with them, and making pretty clothes for them. Never having had a daughter – I've sometimes missed having another girl or woman who could share some of the more 'feminine' interests with me. Anaïs now fills that 'daughter-shaped' space in my life perfectly, although I don't know that I've even been aware of it *being* an empty space before.

She works part-time at a nearby school and tells me amusing stories about what the children get up to, and what she's been doing with them. Soon, I know most of their names and person-alities. Sometimes we go out for a cup of tea or coffee together, or shopping – especially with the baby on the way. Both of us enjoy looking at all the maternity and baby things: clothes, toys and equipment. It thrills me that she asks my opinion about what are the best and most necessary things to buy, as if I'm the expert! I had *nothing* for my own babies when they were tiny, not even proper nappies.

Anaïs is delighted when I show her two pretty cot duvet covers and pillow cases I've sewn for the coming baby, one for summer in a fine, flimsy material and one for winter in a warmer, brushed fabric.

'Oh, Marie!' She hugs me. 'They are so beautiful! And all those tiny clothes you have sewn and knitted already! What a lucky baby to have such a clever *grand-mère*! What a lucky girl I am to have such a kind, thoughtful mother-in-law. Oh, I hate these words, don't you, Marie, *"mother-in-law"*? It sounds so formal and cold, when you are a lovely *mother* to me, a *real* mother!'

My heart is fit to burst with joy at hearing these words. They bring tears to my eyes. Anaïs is such a warm and affectionate girl, and I have come to love her dearly.

***

Three months later, we three are all in the delivery room at the local hospital: Anaïs on the bed, Barry one side of her, holding her hand and encouraging her with every contraction, every push, me on the other side offering what words of wisdom I can as I bathe her brow with a cool sponge. I push away all thoughts of my own confinement all those years ago.

After eight hours of struggle, to all our joy, a perfect baby girl is born. I don't know who shed more tears, Barry or me – but of course they are tears of happiness. They call their little daughter *Nina*. A beautiful name for a beautiful child.

Chapter 23

2000
Marie

'I'm so sorry,' the doctor tells me in a hushed tone, 'but she may not live more than a few hours. I'm afraid she won't last the night.'

I myself won't speak those words aloud at all, as if saying them is confirmation of the reality; that my employer and dear friend Erna Goldstein is dying. The district nurse is very caring. He offers to remain with me during the night.

'Thank you,' I say, 'but I can manage. I will look after her. I always have.'

I show the doctor and the nurse out. They write down a number and tell me to telephone at any time if I need them.

I'm terrified. How can I possibly manage without Erna? How can I *live* without her? I cannot imagine life without Erna. Although I am now a mature woman of forty-six, it feels as if I am losing an adored grandmother and much-loved close friend all at the same time – yes, and even a *mother*, having missed my own mother for so many years.

I won't leave Erna's side. Sylvia has been staying for the last few days. She offers to help, to relieve me, to allow me to rest. I'm glad of her company in the house, but I let no one else care for Erna, not even Sylvia. I want to be alone with her.

Most of that night she sleeps, her breathing an irregular groaning sound. I sit on a chair resting my head beside her on the bed. Every now and then her eyelids flutter open for a moment, and very weakly, she mutters something like, 'Oh … hello, my dearest, I'll be with you in a minute …'

Could she mean me, or is she thinking of her beloved husband and her boy, Aron? Is she anticipating that she will be joining them shortly? If joining them means leaving me, I don't want it. I want her to love me enough to stay with me.

There is little I can do for her, but I make sure she knows I am with her all the time, that she is never alone. Every now and then I moisten her lips with a small sponge soaked in cool, fresh water. Then I stroke her hair and her face gently. I hold her hand and kiss it.

In the bleak, early hours of the morning, her breathing slows further and becomes even more laboured. Very carefully, I lie down next to her and gently put my arm around her. I whisper softly in her ear, '*I love you, I love you, dearest Erna, I'll always love you*,' over and over again. Perhaps these little attentions bring greater comfort for me than for her, but she gives a peaceful little smile, which I know is for me, even though her eyes remain closed.

In the end, the pauses between each of her breaths become agonisingly long, until at last, terrifyingly, silence fills the room. I press her arm and even shake her a little.

'No! Don't stop! Don't stop … Erna … Erna … please breathe again, please, *oh please*,' I urge her.

But no more breaths come. Silence surrounds me. I know she is gone.

I sit for some time, a terrible emptiness enveloping me – I don't know how long. Gradually the empty nothingness inside me fills up with an awful, unbearable sadness. It pours into me like a stream filling a pond and I begin to cry, the sobs coming from deep within me, shaking me, racking my whole torso, until I feel my ribs will break. I rock backwards and forwards like a madwoman, moving in time to my own hoarse moaning and sobbing. I *am* mad – mad with grief. All of a sudden I hear my voice, as if it comes from another body, crying out in great anguish.

'Donal! Donal! Oh my boy, my beloved son, please, please come back to me … I need you. I need you so much.'

The funeral takes place almost immediately. It's the Jewish way as I know, and Erna left strict instructions. The rituals mattered to her as she got older, although she had not been a frequent attender at the synagogue. The burial is a sad affair; cold, dull, drizzly weather matching the mood of the occasion. At the grave-side Barry stands on my right side, Anaïs on my left, with tiny baby Nina – who has brought me infinite joy at this time of sadness – strapped firmly to her chest, warm inside her coat – just as Barry had once been clasped to my chest all those years ago, on the verge of destitution until I found Sylvia, after which Erna finally became our saviour, our rescuer.

Barry supports me as I weep, holding me upright, his own face set rigid and grim, his hand gripping my elbow like a vice. Anaïs cries softly too. Her hand is a more gentle caress, stroking my arm, reminding me of her love. I worry that I am embarrassing them, especially Barry – making an exhibition of myself in public – but I can't help myself.

After such a long life, only a handful of Erna's very elderly friends are still living, and remain fit enough to be able to stand with us at her graveside. Sylvia is with us, of course, dabbing her eyes with her handkerchief. I tremble uncontrollably, in part with the cold, in part for my overwhelming sorrow and distress. I can hardly believe I'll never see her again, my beloved friend, never talk to her, laugh with her. It's unreal; it cannot be.

As the coffin is lowered, I picture Erna's kind, expressive face inside it, now motionless and cold, and I feel suddenly that I can't bear to be parted from her. I reach my hand shakily towards the coffin, trying somehow to connect with her. Barry pulls my arm back and gives a sigh of irritation. Anaïs's arm encircles my waist gently. Dear girl, thank goodness for her support and understanding.

***

For the next two weeks I scarcely leave the house. I wander without purpose from one room to another, like a ghost, unable to settle. Some nights, I lie on Erna's bed, hugging her pillows to me, as if cuddling a baby; wrapping myself in her duvet, and breathing in the delicate, woody, sandalwood scent of the cologne that she favoured, and which lingers there still.

I am quite bereft, and find it hard to carry out the simplest, normal day-to-day activities like washing or eating, which makes me deeply ashamed. Sure, hadn't Erna herself suffered a much, much more profound loss all those years ago, I chastise myself. And yet hadn't she carried on bravely? She had never given in to her grief, never.

I dread having to turn my mind to moving from this house in which I have lived so happily for the last quarter of a century. I don't even think about money; what does it matter? In any case, I suppose I'm confident that Erna will have arranged to leave me a small bequest. She'd always assured me I'd be well looked after, that I shouldn't worry, and so I don't. Whatever that bequest might be, however small, together with my now regular earnings from dressmaking – most of which I have saved – it will surely be enough to put down a deposit on a modest house or flat, or to pay a reasonable rent for somewhere small but decent? I won't think about all of that until I have to.

***

Six weeks after Erna's funeral, Erna's solicitor, Mr Adams, calls me and Barry into his office to read the will.

'First of all, Mr Tully, Ms Tully,' he says, 'may I extend my most sincere condolences to you both for your sad loss. I know you and Mrs Goldstein have been very close friends and companions for many years. She was a most admirable person.'

'Thank you, Mr Adams, it's kind of you to say that.'

It is only then, as Mr Adams begins to clarify the will, that I discover what the future holds for me. I learn that there is not to be the expected 'small bequest'.

Far from it. It takes me a while to absorb this news. I can scarcely make sense of what Mr Adams is saying, so unexpected is it, so totally unreal.

What emerges is, that apart from a number of generous charitable donations, and a bequest of £10,000 for Barry and his family, *I am the only beneficiary* of Erna's will. Apparently, the large, valuable house in Blackheath, and a considerable amount of capital, are now entirely *mine*. It hardly seems possible to me. Overnight, I've become a rich woman.

Chapter 24

2002
Marie

One thing that's caused difficulty over all these years, is that Barry has seemed somehow to *sense* my love, my longing, for Donal. It's not as though the strength of my feelings for Donal ever diminished my love for *him* – for Barry – in the slightest. Yet even as a tiny child, somehow he seemed to know when I was distracted or distressed by my thoughts of his brother. I always had to try to conceal my feelings from him, for fear of throwing him into a violent rage. Now that he's a grown man, now more than ever, he seems to hate me talking about his brother, or even thinking about him.

Barry has had so much that's good and positive in his life, yet he can't seem to appreciate it. His needs are like a bottomless pit, like a deep, deep well. No matter how much good, clear water is poured in at the top, the well never remains full; it seems to leak away, to need more, always more.

One of Barry's over-riding needs – and one that really bothers me – is *money*. He's obsessed with the stuff; always wanting more, never satisfied with what he's got – and he's got *plenty*! He's ridiculously jealous of those who have even more than him (like *me*, since Erna died), and mean with what he himself has. It isn't as if he even enjoys spending it. He isn't a man for fancy meals out, the theatre, expensive holidays, or extravagantly posh clothes. Mind you, he does believe in 'quality' for himself, like his top-quality suits, and his car is his pride and joy. I suppose he reckons it sends a message to the world – *'Look at me; I'm successful'* – and he likes that.

I wouldn't mind that so much if money gave him any real pleasure, but it doesn't appear to. What saddens me most is that he never buys Anaïs or Nina nice things. No beautiful jewellery or pretty dresses, no lovely weekends away in the country, or holidays in the sun. Not even special flowers or chocolates once in a while. I only wish that he would; small gestures make such a difference, send a positive message, show affection and caring. I feel they deserve to be treated sometimes, and heaven knows, he can afford it.

Barry certainly did exceptionally well in his studies, I know that, and he must be doing well in his job too; he's been promoted several times. He's now in a senior position at a top City bank. God knows exactly what he does; he never talks about his work, and I've stopped asking. Barry and Anaïs have bought a lovely house about ten minutes from me, where they and Nina live. He earns an absolute bomb – no exaggeration. Yet money was the start of many a row between him and his wife. Not that she's a spendthrift – far from it – but he criticises almost anything she buys for herself, or Nina, or for the house.

I couldn't ask for a better daughter-in-law. I'm very fond of her. She's a lovely girl: gentle, kind, affectionate, funny – and a good mother to Nina. Barry can be so hard on her – and the child – always nagging them about something or other. Anaïs has lost that sparkle she once had. She looks so sad much of the time. I hate to see it.

Over time, I start to notice how wary Anaïs, and even little Nina, have become of Barry. That's been the start of serious worries about their relationship. They look downright scared of him at times. On a couple of occasions recently, I see Anaïs has bruises on her face or arms.

One time when they come to visit me, I notice she has the remains of a black eye. It's starting to turn that yellowy colour. She's rubbed foundation on it to try to disguise it, but I can see.

While Barry is sorting drinks in the kitchen, I ask Anaïs about it. She gets that look of a frightened rabbit on her face, glancing round quickly to see if Barry is in the room. Then she says she walked into a doorframe, that she wasn't looking where she was going. But that doesn't fool me, not for a minute. Nina has developed a permanent guarded look too. She's watchful, especially if Barry approaches her mother, as if she's expecting an attack at any moment, poor mite. Something is going on, something bad, and I don't like it. I can't bear it.

While Barry's out of the room, I go and sit next to Anaïs on the sofa. I hug her and speak softly to her. Tears well up in her eyes. She stares at her feet. She shakes her head ... she won't tell me. A fierce rage grips my heart. I leave her and Nina in the sitting room, walk into the kitchen and shut the door. Barry is opening a bottle on the table. I storm up to him, grab his arm with all my strength and pull him round to face me. He looks surprised, really shocked – and a bit scared himself!

'Barry Tully! Don't you *dare* ever, ever, *ever* raise your hand to your lovely wife – or your child – ever again!' I spit the words straight into his face like bullets. I'm right ferocious, even though he towers over me.

'If you do, you can be sure you'll get nothing from me, *nothing*. I'll write you straight out of my will for ever. They'll get the lot! Do you hear me? Do you understand?!'

Well, he doesn't like that. He's furious. His face goes white and he stands over me like he's going to hit *me*, and all. He's *shaking* with rage, using all his self-control not to punch me – I can see.

***

I know Barry was already very angry with me before this. Not long ago, I'd asked him round to show him my will, which the solicitor had updated for me recently, according to my instructions. The main change in it is that I'd decided to put one or two conditions in there. I'd also added in a couple of special bequests. The first is for £10,000 to go to Sylvia, as my special friend, if she's still alive at my death. I don't suppose Barry is too worried about that one; after all, Sylvia's more than eighteen years older than me.

I told Barry I'd made a substantial sum of money – £20,000 – available to go direct to Anaïs *immediately*. It's to give her some freedom, some security, and, I'm sorry to have to say it, some independence from Barry, for all he's my son. Without making some legal arrangements, I can't trust him to do right by his wife or his young daughter, and that's a great sadness for me.

My darling little Nina will get a similar lump sum when she's eighteen, to help her with whatever she wants to do – whether to further her education or training at university or college, to develop her career, to set up a business, to buy her own flat, or *whatever else she wants it for*. I know she'll use it well, she's such a sensible girl already. Maybe it doesn't sound that much in the circumstances, what with today's prices, but I'm sure Anaïs will always help her out if need be – and besides, this will be *an advance*; she'll be getting more from my will in the long run.

I've already helped my dear, loyal friend Elsie and her family whenever I could over the years, and she'll get another £10,000 now, for a special holiday, home improvements, or a few little luxuries – whatever they want in fact. A further £20,000 in my will is for Elsie to set up and run a small charitable trust to help impoverished unmarried mothers – in a desperate situation like we two girls had been – so they can *keep* their babies, and have somewhere safe to live. Of course, Barry doesn't approve of that idea, not at all, but it means a huge lot to me, and Elsie's always wanted to do it if only she had the money. If there'd been help like that for us and some of the other girls all those years ago, maybe I'd never have had to give up my precious Donal.

Apart from the special bequests, at my death this figure will be divided equally between Barry, Anaïs, and of course, Donal too, if he is ever found. The one condition I imposed on Barry for him to receive his own share, is that he should search for and *find* his brother. If – God forbid – through his search Barry finds that Donal has passed away, that share will be re-divided equally between himself and Anaïs.

Barry is furious that Anaïs is given equal financial status to his own in my will. Yet, to give him his due, although he hates the conditions I placed on him, he has devoted a lot of time and effort into trying to track his brother down. I suppose the thought of the extra money is a major motivation for him – which is exactly what I hoped it would be – but I admit I'm impressed by the determination he's shown. In the process of searching for his brother, Barry frequently comes up against frustrating dead ends, but he's never given up.

***

Maybe all the stress is partly to blame, or maybe it's just an unfortunate coincidence, but back in spring, a routine breast screening examination reveals abnormal tissue at the back of my left breast, requiring further investigation.

Sylvia accompanies me to my hospital appointments. A scan shows a significant lump, and a subsequent biopsy confirms that it's cancerous. The oncologist, Mr Bassington, is an amiable, fatherly man in his late fifties.

'This is a sizeable growth, Ms Tully,' he tells me, as Sylvia, sitting beside me, squeezes my hand. 'Had it been in a more prominent position, you might have noticed it much sooner. As it is, I'm afraid it may have been there some time, and therefore there is a chance that it will have spread.'

I hear Sylvia's sharp intake of breath. She's crushing my hand in hers.

Mr Bassington pauses to allow me to absorb this information.

'I think the best thing is for you to have an MRI scan to ascertain the exact extent of the tumour, and then for us to operate as soon as possible. I'm afraid you will almost certainly need a mastectomy, so that we can remove as much as possible of any cancerous tissue. That will be followed by a period of chemotherapy, which will aim to target any rogue cells that may have spread. In time, you may want to consider an implant. They're very successful these days.'

I find it difficult to take in all he is saying. I try to picture the 'rogue' cells: wicked little creatures with cruel, snarling faces, attacking my vulnerable, helpless flesh. *Implant,* he says. There's something else to picture.

'Sure, and why would I want such a thing, Doctor? Here I am nearly fifty and never married. I don't think I'll be wanting a perfect bosom to attract a husband after all these years without one – and never missing one, if the truth be known.'

Mr Bassington smiles. 'Perhaps not, Ms Tully, but it's something to think about in due course. Many women simply want to be restored to their former … er … *symmetry*. Not necessarily for a husband or partner, but perhaps for themselves …'

'Oh, I'm quite symmetrical enough, I think, what with having an arm and a leg each side. That'll do me. But, will I live, do you think, Doctor? *That's* what I need to know. Or should I be after saying "*Mister*" to you, being a consultant and all?'

'"Doctor" will do just fine. I think we have a good chance of treating you successfully, but I'm afraid nothing is absolutely certain. Cancer is a serious disease.'

Sylvia gasps and blows her nose noisily.

'Yes, yes, I know,' I say. 'And I know you doctors don't like to be pinned down to exact figures, but tell me now, at a guess, what would you say are my chances?'

'You're right, Ms Tully, we don't find it very helpful to put an exact figure on these things, but I'd say a fit lady like you has a very good chance of surviving, for many years yet.'

'Fifty-fifty would you say?'

Mr Bassington smiles again. 'Yes, perhaps … even better odds than that I'd say. Maybe sixty-forty, at least – in your favour.'

'Oh well, sure, that would be worth putting a bet on! That'll have to do for now. Come on, Sylvia, stop *snivelling*, for God's sake – let's go home.'

***

How could I possibly have got through the last years without Sylvia? No way at all. She's been everything a good, loyal and kind friend can be, and I'll never stop loving her for it. I often think about how I could demonstrate to her just how important she is to me.

When Erna was alive she always welcomed Sylvia into her home. She often said how much she liked Sylvia, what a good and 'special' person she was, but I think Sylvia felt a bit self-conscious in her presence.

'She's so refined,' Sylvia would say, 'and so intellectual. I mean, it's not that she's *snobbish* in the least, I'm not saying that, but I sometimes feel like a proper Cockney with her, rough and common!'

'Erna would never judge you in that way,' I often assure her. 'She likes people for who they are, not for how they speak or what kind of a family they come from. She always says she suffered enough because of people's prejudices in the past, to ever hold such views herself. She likes you very much. She admires you for being such a good friend to me, as I do too.'

When Sylvia and I first met and I was only eighteen, she'd seemed much, much older; she'd seemed grown-up to me. I thought of her as a mature woman, although in fact she'd only been thirty-six. Thirty-six seems unbelievably young to me now that I'm so much older than that myself! Sylvia had spontaneously befriended me in such a warm and motherly way, that I'd thought of her as middle-aged, even elderly, at the time. How our perception of age changes as we move through life, and the so-called milestone birthdays go by!

***

I always loved Erna Goldstein's big, old house, and I'd been very happy there. Yet, since she died, I find I don't want to stay there on my own – but neither do I want to move to a completely different area. I'm so used to Blackheath after all these years. It's all I know of London, and I feel at home here. So, in time, the fine old house is sold – for what I regard as an *enormous* amount of money. I find a smaller, more modern one not too far away. It's in a quiet street and has a pretty, sunny garden at the back, just the right size for me. I make an offer and move in within three months.

By this time, Sylvia is sixty-eight – but just as she'd seemed older than her years when I first met her – now she actually seems *younger*, or perhaps ageless. She's just Sylvia. Even though we're both getting older, it's as if I'm catching her up in age! Since I moved to the new house, my friendship with Sylvia has really taken off again, but in a different sort of way. We're both on our own and know how lonely that can be.

The baker's shop has been taken over by a chain, and they want a younger person to serve in it. Sylvia is asked – well, *told* – to retire. She has a modest pension, and the bakery, having valued her long service, give her a small lump sum by way of compensation for being required to stop working before she had wanted, and also to make up for her having to leave the little flat above the bakery, where she's lived for so many years.

Sylvia starts renting a council flat in a high-rise block. She's on the ninth floor and has a good view, but she struggles with the stairs when the lift is out of order, which is frequently. I know too, that she's finding it hard surviving on her pension.

So I decide to invite Sylvia to live with me. It isn't just that I want to help her, I'm genuinely fond of her and we enjoy one another's company. What could be a better arrangement?

'You'll have your own room and bathroom. We can be as independent as we want, but we're here for each other if we want support, or just company,' I tell her.

'I wouldn't want to take advantage of you, Marie. Anyway you've got your granddaughter and daughter-in-law nearby. And Barry of course. You don't really need me.'

'Yes, well, some of them are more help than others, as you know. It's not just about *needing* you; it's that I'd *love* you to be here, as my good friend. Sometimes I might need your help and support, yes. Sometimes you might need mine. Heaven knows, you've given me enough over the years.'

***

Sylvia knows all about the worries I've had with Barry – from when he was a baby and a tiny wee boy, then through his adolescence, and even now, as a mature man. She understands too, that the deep well of sadness in me about losing Donal has never left me. How could it? He's my child, my own son, just as Barry is, and I can't help but love him too, even though I haven't seen him for over thirty years.

I had always known that Donal's name was changed by his adoptive parents, and at first the authorities are not prepared to divulge what his new name might be. That makes it very hard for Barry to trace him. We also knew that the initial adoption had broken down after just two years, and that Donal was returned to the care of the local authority. It appears he spent years in some dreary children's home, the poor, poor child.

This information breaks my heart. I remember that terrible day at the mother and baby home as if it were yesterday, when the wealthy-looking couple came to fetch him. It felt as though they not only took my child from me, they tore a part of my soul out and took that away too. Yet, over all the years, I had comforted myself with the belief that although *I* couldn't be a loving mother to Donal, at least he was being loved and cared for by people who desperately wanted a child; people who could afford to give him everything he might want and need in life.

However, that was not the case, not at all. Poor Donal's childhood has been spent in dismal institutions with the exception of some brief, apparently unsuccessful, attempts at fostering. Why, oh why did I ever agree to give him up? All this time, my precious boy could at least have had a loving mother, even if a poor one. How many nights had I cried myself to sleep thinking of him, and wondering if he believes his mother never wanted him? That thought is unbearable.

Chapter 25

2004
Robert

Dear Robert,

You may be surprised to hear from me. I know we have never met – perhaps you don't even know of my existence – yet we are not strangers. I imagine this letter may come as a complete shock to you. My name is Barry Tully and I am your brother – your twin brother! We were separated soon after our birth. I have also only learned of your existence recently.

You may wonder why I have contacted you now. Well, sadly, Mum died of breast cancer two years ago. She was only fifty-one. I found myself thinking about you more and more. I wanted to get in touch with you, my only known surviving relative, (apart from my four-year-old daughter, Nina) as soon as possible, especially as I'm not in very good health myself – and none of us knows what the future holds. I think about you often, and hope you are fit and well yourself.

Let me tell you a bit about myself. I live in London. Like you, of course, I am nearly thirty-four. I married in my twenties, but sadly the marriage has run into difficulties. At the moment, my wife and I live apart. My wife, Anaïs, is French, but she lives in Blackheath, in South East London, together with little Nina, while I now live north of the Thames, near Swiss Cottage. I've been lucky with my educational and career opportunities, and currently work for a large international bank in the City. I earn well, but I can't say that's brought me a lot of happiness.

I don't know what you have been told about your/our background. Our mother, Marie Tully, was unmarried and only seventeen when she met our father. He was a 'rolling stone', working with a travelling fair that visited Mum's village in Ireland. He charmed her, an innocent and uneducated girl at that time. Predictably of course, after a brief affair, he 'hit the road' and disappeared. Mum never saw him again.

She soon found out she was pregnant. Her parents, especially her dad, were very strict. Mum had to travel to London on her own, where she gave birth in a dismal home for single mothers – St Agatha's – run by nuns. The senior nun was very harsh. She insisted Mum give up at least one of us babies for adoption. There was no choice.

By pure chance, I was the child she kept, and you were the one given to adoptive parents. The nuns told Mum it was 'for the best' and convinced her that you would have a better life with people who could afford to care for you properly. Her father wouldn't have her – or us – back in the house. She could never return to Ireland. To her lifelong, desperate regret and sorrow, she was unable to support and bring up both of us. It broke Mum's heart to give you up.

You may have judged her harshly over the years, Robert, but I promise you that all through her life, Mum never stopped loving you, thinking about you and longing for you. Just having me was never enough for her. I know that.

She was desperate to find you. Years later she hired a researcher. He found out that your adoption had broken down, and you had been returned to the care of the local authority at about two years old. Mum was devastated. She had always comforted herself with the belief that at least you would be wanted, loved, and well cared for.

Please believe me, Robert, Mum tried very hard to trace you and reclaim you, but rules were stricter in those days. She'd given you the name Donal, but she was told that the adoptive parents would have changed it, so there was no point in searching for 'Donal Tully'. She was told no one would allow her to know your new name, that you were being fostered, and it would disturb and disrupt your life if she were allowed to have contact with you. So she had to give up, though it was a continuing sadness throughout her life.

Times are different now, and the internet makes all sorts of things possible. After a long search, I was able to trace you through a specialist social worker, who told me your name is now Robert Carlton. Mum always only thought of you as Donal. If only Mum were still here, she would be so happy to find you. But though that's never to be, you and I are brothers, Robert, twin brothers – so you do have a family and someone who cares about you.

Robert, the main reason for this letter is that I would really like us to meet and have the chance to talk. I know you live in Newcastle, and by coincidence, Northumberland, the hinterland to your great city, is a county that I have walked in and much loved in recent years, never realising that my own brother was a mere thirty or forty miles away! I would love us to meet in Northumberland, Robert, and perhaps to walk together on another occasion. However, not knowing anything about you, it seems best to meet somewhere less remote and more accessible in the first instance.

I thought Durham would be a good place for us to meet,

being on the direct train line from London, and only fifteen minutes from you in Newcastle. I have enclosed a copy of a street map of Durham, and marked, a café about ten minutes' walk from the station, called Wearview Café. I suggest, on this occasion, we meet there for a light lunch at about 1 p.m. on Wednesday 7th February – it would be a chance to talk and begin to get to know one another. Please give me a quick call on my mobile (number below) just to confirm you will come, Robert.

I very much hope that you will come – meeting you would mean so much to me. However, at no time are you obliged to continue our contact, should you prefer not to.

Robert, I can't tell you how excited and thrilled I am at the prospect of meeting you after all these years. Please, please come.

Your brother,
Barry Tully

The letter arrives completely out of the blue. It's totally swept the feet from under me. Why now, after all these years? I stare at the letter. I *frown* at it, as if I might make it disappear. I feel deeply unsettled. In fact, the letter really provokes me. No one has shown much interest in me before. I know nothing about any relatives. It's never occurred to me that I might have a *brother* – or any family at all for that matter. In all the years of my growing up, I've never been told about a brother, let alone a *twin brother*. My first instinct is to tear the letter up and put it in the bin or burn it – just forget the whole thing. I glare at the letter, trembling accusingly in my hand.

Why should this man, this Barry, this *stranger*, imagine I'd be interested in him; now, at this stage of our lives, as each of us are into our *thirties*, for fuck's sake?! Surely he can't really be my brother? Probably some sort of scam. I hold the letter over the fire once more; a miserable smouldering affair, as usual, giving out bugger all heat. My fingers are itching to let go of it, to be done with it and forget all about it. But, at the last minute, I have second thoughts, tighten my grip and pull my hand back – just as the flame is about to devour the letter for ever. I blow on it, scattering a small cloud of ash and singed paper fragments into the air. They drift slowly to the floor, like dirty snowflakes. I give a deep sigh and read the letter one more time.

I'm not sure exactly what I feel. Shock, anger, disbelief, total confusion, it's almost as though it has personally offended me. It's a long letter. I read it countless times. Each time, it leaves me feeling more agitated. Oh yes, he certainly has a way with words, this brother of mine. No doubt about that.

He's right that I know little about my history, about my 'birth family'. All I've been told is that my mother had been young and unmarried, and that she'd been abandoned by my feckless father before I was born. That was it.

So, he was a 'rolling stone' was he? Sounds a bit like me. Maybe I take after my dad ...?

Yes, OK, no doubt our mum was young, and maybe she'd had a rough time, *but she didn't want me*, did she? She can't have done, or she'd never have agreed to my adoption. Didn't she realise how much I *needed* her when I was growing up, how much I wanted her? Even if she'd been forced to give me up, surely she'd have tried – *really tried* – to find me? Well, my brother says she did try. Maybe she did, how do I know?

I'd never made any attempt to trace her myself. What was the point? I wouldn't know where to start. So that was that. I don't feel much for her ... well, not usually. Just occasionally I did wonder about her ... sometimes in bed, I'd long for her, for a mother. But why should I have feelings for her? Fancy giving away your own child. What mother would do that?

No one had ever mentioned a twin brother before, not in all those years. Is it true – do I really have a brother? I notice Barry hasn't added any address or details to his letter, apart from the mobile phone number. Maybe he's just some crank, a weirdo, an attention seeker. Maybe the whole thing is a hoax. Bound to be, in fact, with my luck.

Yet ... I hold the little map of Durham in my hand. That's real enough. Shall I go? Shall I meet my brother? *The 7th of February is just two weeks away.*

I can't get the letter out of my mind. Whatever I do, bits of what he wrote creep back into my consciousness. One thing strikes me is that without *me* even knowing of this Barry's existence, *he* has been thinking about *me* for some time – years perhaps – and I'm not sure I like that idea. No, not at all. It feels a bit like an intrusion. Almost as if Barry has been secretly watching me, observing me without me knowing – like a *voyeur*, like a *stalker*. That thought sends shivers down my spine.

But ... on the other hand ... Barry does really seem interested in me, really keen to meet me, to *know* me. Not many people have ever expressed interest in knowing me before. In fact, it's as if Barry thinks he *does* know me, as though he feels *connected* to me somehow. I don't think *I've* ever felt connected to anyone in my life, not really ... except to Len and Betty. I wish I was still connected to them.

Is it possible that I might *like* Barry? That he might feel like ... not a friend exactly, but ... well ... like a *brother*? What harm could there be in meeting him? If he really *is* my twin brother – my *identical* twin brother – well, that means the two of us must have started life as exact equals – in other words, with *nothing*! Then, at some point early on, everything changed.

Donal Tully. Is that really my name? I can't get my head around it. He sounds like a stranger ... Who is he? Who am I really? No harm in finding out a bit more about myself, I suppose. Suddenly I feel excited, *eager* even.

***

The following morning I wake early. I haven't slept well and can't sleep any longer, my head's that full of questions. There are no *answers* coming, none at all, just tension. I get up – I need to do something active, stop the nerves jangling.

Money's one thing that has been on my mind. I go into the kitchen, pull out the cooker and gently ease the loose skirting board out with a screwdriver. My hand gropes around in the dust and rubble. Eventually, there it is, I find what I'm looking for. My fingers close around a crumpled A5 envelope. I haven't counted what's in it since Tracy made off with my previous stash. I know it won't contain much. My very minimal wages caring for needy and elderly people in their homes, plus even more minimal allowances from the state don't allow me much in the way of *savings*. I open the envelope and carefully count the contents. *Ninety-seven pounds*. That's my entire worldly wealth – apart from day-to-day cash. Barry wouldn't think much of it, I bet! Just small change to him. Still, it's more than enough for a ticket to Durham, and lunch in a café.

I can't get the thought of my possible meeting with Barry out of my head. There's a permanent tight feeling in my belly. My heart's beating overtime. What will my brother be like? I try to picture someone who looks exactly like me. It isn't easy. It's strange how you can look at yourself in the mirror nearly every day, yet would you recognise yourself walking down the street? I'm not sure I would. Besides, even if he looks more or less the same in terms of features, likely there'd be all sorts of differences too. Barry's bound to dress differently for a start. He might wear glasses. His hair is probably cut at some fancy, expensive barber. I wonder if his voice will be exactly the same as mine? That would be weird. He probably won't have a local accent, unless maybe a London accent.

He's obviously intelligent. Well, I'm not thick myself. He must have been good with money – so that's a difference; I've never had any money to be good with.

How different Barry's life must have been to mine – what with his high-flying job in the City. What could we possibly have in common?

Yet perhaps I *should* meet him? Perhaps I should see it as an opportunity not to be missed. Imagine standing face to face with him. What would we say? Would we shake hands? Hug? Who could tell what might come out of that meeting, that relationship. Anything might be possible, I suppose.

As I think about the reality of meeting him, the prospect of experiencing the actual *presence* of my brother, I feel the tightness in my belly rising to my chest, followed by a racing of my heart as excitement takes hold. The truth is, I'm not just excited, I'm scared – *scared sodding stiff*.

Chapter 26

2004
Barry

I hesitate briefly outside Wearview Café, hoping he won't be there yet. I made sure to arrive early; I need some time to gather my thoughts. It's exactly as I remember from a previous visit: a small, stone-built cottage on a steep, quiet back street. True enough, a tiny stretch of the River Wear, sparkling in the winter sunshine, is just visible in the distance from outside the café, allowing the name a small degree of accuracy.

I adjust my sunglasses and push the door open. The owner, a friendly woman in her sixties, with grey hair clamped loosely into a bun, is behind a counter stacked with cakes and biscuits, and other snacks. I remember her from my last visit to Durham. It was a long time ago. I'm slightly anxious that she might recognise me, but she doesn't. I adjust my hat to a jaunty angle.

'Oh hello there! Lovely day, isn't it?' she says with a friendly smile. 'What can I do for you today?'

'I'm … er … meeting someone here for a bite of lunch.

I'd rather wait 'til he comes before ordering. He may be a few minutes late. Have you got a quiet table for two? I'm afraid I forgot to book.'

'No problem, pet. We're quiet today. There's a little room at the back with a secluded table. Nice and peaceful,' she says, pointing down the corridor leading to the rear of the building. 'You go and get settled down. Just order whenever you're ready. All right?'

I thank her and make my way down the passage. I pass one small room on the left, with three tables, two of them occupied by women deep in conversation, and a further room on the right of the passage with a large family group sitting at two tables pushed together. I continue to a small, dark room at the end, lit only by a narrow window and the flames of a coal fire. There's just one table, and it's unoccupied at present. I sit down, put my hat on the seat next to me, and study the menu. My newly grown beard is itching. I give it a rub and remind myself to try not to scratch it or fiddle with it.

A few minutes later Robert still hasn't appeared and I start to wonder if he's decided not to come. I open my case and take out the letter that arrived from my hospital consultant this morning, and start to read. The words seem to swim in front of my eyes. My hands are trembling slightly. I've barely read a paragraph when approaching footsteps sound in the corridor. I hastily fold the letter and stuff it into my trouser pocket. A man of my age and height, a man who clearly looks like me, hesitates in the doorway. He looks at me and takes a few steps into the room.

'B-Barry?' he asks nervously.

'Robert!' I say. 'Robert … this is wonderful! I'm so happy to see you.' I stand up and move round the table towards him.

We're standing face to face, staring at each other in silence. I'm not sure whether to extend my hand for a handshake, or to launch straight into a hug. I feel myself swaying, my legs suddenly weak and shaky. Sweat rolls down my spine.

'Barry … are you OK?' He looks at me anxiously.

I gather myself and try to smile reassuringly. 'Yes … yes … Robert, I'm fine. This is all quite a shock, isn't it? I feel quite overcome and shaky, but I'm absolutely fine. All the better for seeing you!'

I step forward and put my arms around him. He hesitates and then hugs me back, his embrace more uncertain than mine. He snuffles into my shoulder. For a moment I have no words for this situation. Those I had carefully prepared have deserted me. My brain has turned to mush. I can think of nothing to say to my brother.

'Robert …' I take a deep breath and start again. 'Robert … Robert … thank you for coming. This is wonderful, isn't it?'

'Yes … yes … I … I don't know …' He gulps, rendered even more inarticulate than me. He wipes his eyes with the back of his hand.

I lean back a little, placing my hands on his shoulders. In the face of his reticence, his nervousness, I take charge. I notice the violent trembling of my brother's body, tears now rolling down his cheeks.

'Come, sit,' I say gently, releasing him and returning to my seat. It's a double wooden bench seat. I pat the cushion beside mine. 'Come. Come and sit down.'

He takes a seat, turning his head to look expectantly at me. We are now side by side.

The fire is blazing like a furnace, making the small room uncomfortably hot. I rummage in my pocket and bring out a handkerchief. There's something ridiculous about its red spotted design. I mop my face just before the café owner steps through the doorway.

'Now then, gents, what can I get you? Eeee, but you're nice and cosy in here with the fire, aren't you? Open the window if you get too hot.'

'I'd like two poached eggs on toast please,' I say decisively,

175

consulting the menu, 'followed by a piece of that delicious-looking coffee walnut cake … and a pot of tea for us both …?' I look at Robert for confirmation, holding up the menu for him to see.

'What about you …?'

'Yes. Same,' he blurts, without looking, 'please.'

'Oh well, that's straightforward then, isn't it?' says the woman with a cheery smile, and bustles out of the room.

Although the gloom blurs some of the details of each of our faces, I can tell he looks very like me. I wonder if he's surprised by my beard, hurriedly grown in preparation for our meeting. It must obliterate half my face. I remember I'm still wearing the large sunglasses. They might strike Robert as odd, if not ridiculous, in such darkness. I take them off and slip them into my breast pocket.

'I didn't expect you to have a beard,' he says. 'Have you always had it?'

'Well, not when I was a kid,' I say with a smile, 'but for a while.'

I peer at him and then put my sunglasses on again.

'Sorry about these,' I say. 'Looks stupid in these conditions I know, but … erm … I've recently been diagnosed as having … er … *glaucoma* and they're supposed to help.'

I wonder briefly if actually having glaucoma would mean Robert, as a twin, would also have it. Do identical twins always have the same ailments? As far as I know, my eyesight had always been good, with no need for glasses of any sort. The 'glaucoma' is a pretence to explain the sunglasses.

Robert is staring intently at me. 'Barry, did our … er … mother … have cancer for long? Did she suffer?'

'For a few months. She had some treatment … It helped, but you know, not in the end. She was brave though.' I pause, looking at him. He looks so sad. 'Robert,' I continue, 'I'm sorry it wasn't possible to make contact with you until after our mother had died. It's very sad that you couldn't have met her.'

176

He nods and looks thoughtful. 'What was she like?'

'Marie? That was her name, Marie Tully. She was a very emotional person. Very loving and sweet-natured, although I didn't always find her easy. We had a bit of an up and down relationship.'

He nods.

'She only told me about you recently, but I know she never got over having to give you up to be adopted, Robert, never. Of course, she'd be out of her mind with joy to think of us sitting together like this. It's so good I was able to trace you, so good – just a shame it couldn't have happened a bit sooner … a lot sooner.'

'I never knew … anything about her. Nor about you, Barry.'

'Yeah. I know. It's strange to think of us each growing up, exactly the same age, yet knowing nothing about one another, isn't it?'

'Why didn't our mam, I mean Marie, tell you about me until recently?'

'Well, yes, good question … I think … perhaps misguidedly, she thought it would upset me when I was a kid. Then, I suppose even when I was a young adult, she wasn't sure how I'd react. I've been through some difficult times, so probably she thought such momentous news was more than I could cope with, that it would further disturb me. It was meant well, I suppose, but … misjudged.'

'Mmm.' Robert looks thoughtful. He fiddles with the cutlery. 'And did it?' He looks straight at me.

'Did it what?'

'Did it upset you, disturb you?'

'It was quite a shock, if I'm honest, finding out about you. But it certainly didn't upset me, Robert. It took me a while to process the idea of having a twin brother – as I'm sure it has you too? But far from being upset, I'm delighted, really I am. It's almost as though there was a gap, a vacuum, in my life as I was growing up – and that you've filled that now.'

He smiles and presses his hand on my arm for a moment.

'So, let's not regret the time gone by, eh? Let's just make up for lost time. Now that we've found each other, we must never lose contact, must we? Now, I really want to hear something about you, Robert. Tell me about your life. What about your adoptive parents? Why didn't that work out?'

'I honestly can't remember a thing about that time, Barry. I was only two when they returned me to the local authority. I suppose I was a difficult and disturbed child. I wasn't happy in the children's homes. They were very ... impersonal, not like being part of a family.'

So we talk, and talk. I make sure to demonstrate great interest as Robert tells me of his life up to now. It sounds depressingly bleak, and I can't help feeling sorry for him – that great series of dreary orphanages, the mostly unsuccessful foster homes, the lack of affection, of stability, or of real opportunities, despite him clearly being intelligent.

It was all so cold, so limited and pathetic compared to the warmth and almost cloying devotion I've been shown by Mother and Auntie Erna. I tell him about my education and how fortunate I've been to be supported by Erna Goldstein. Robert tells me he did have one or two positive experiences with good and caring teachers who showed a special interest in him and encouraged him. Thank God for them.

'The only really happy time I remember was with a couple of lovely foster parents, Len and Betty, when I was much older, twelve or thirteen,' Robert says, 'They were like a mam and dad and grandparents all rolled into one. I loved them to bits, but they died too soon.'

He looks so sad as he talks about them, yet he appears completely without bitterness, which amazes me. I reach out and squeeze his arm.

'I'm really glad you had that experience, Robert, even though it was too short.'

'Aye,' he says thoughtfully.

I laugh. 'You know, Robert, that's the first "Geordie-ism" you've come out with! I was worried I might not understand you – I expected you to talk with a strong Geordie accent when I heard you live in Newcastle! But it's hardly noticeable at all.'

We both laugh at that.

'The thing is,' Robert says, 'I moved that many times as a kid, all over the country, so many different orphanages and foster homes and schools, that I had to get used to a new local accent each time! I got pretty good at imitating them. You had to, or you were marked out as an outsider, and that made you a target – fair bait for the bullies. I found I could switch from one way of talking to another at the drop of a hat. Some of the kids could be pretty rough. I think I ended up with almost no accent at all.'

'Must have been really tough. Mum would have been so upset to know what you had to go through.'

He nods.

I tell Robert a bit about my own life.

'You've been very successful compared to me,' Robert says.

'If making money counts as success, I suppose I have …'

'But …?'

'But my relationship with my mother … *our* mother … was tricky at times, and my marriage to my wife, Anaïs, is not going too well just now … on the rocks, in fact, some might say. Mostly my fault, I guess. I've never admitted that openly to anyone that before,' I say, swallowing hard. 'Are you married, Robert?'

'No, I'm not, no children either. I've had some girlfriends, of course, but no real long-term relationship.'

We look at one another sympathetically. I feel a need to try to deflect the emotional turn our conversation has started to take.

'At least we share a lovely little daughter, Anaïs and I – Nina. She's four years old. She's adorable.'

'Well, you're a lucky man then,' he says, smiling at me.

***

After we finish our meal, I suggest we walk together along the river and past the imposing cathedral. Robert agrees, and we stand up and gather up our things. He spots something on the floor under the table and bends down to pick it up. He squints at a folded piece of paper.

'Some sort of letter,' he says turning it round in his hand. 'I think you must have dropped it, Barry.'

'Oh, yes … I think I did. Thanks.' I hastily stuff it into my bag. 'Now, I'll just go and pay. No, I *insist*, Robert! I'm a rich man, remember?'

***

Outside, the sun is lower in the sky but still shining brightly. I've put on my sunglasses, hat and coat again. I'm aware I must look a bit odd and formal compared to Robert. Perhaps the smart, expensive outfit was a mistake for a casual meeting up of twin brothers, especially the Homburg-style hat? Altogether somewhat old-fashioned and strange, what with the straggly beard and sunglasses too. I must have made a mysterious and unconventional impression.

'Do you want me to take your arm, Barry? I mean, the path's a bit rough and steep. I just wondered … what with your eyes and that?'

I'm taken by surprise for a moment, but I thank Robert and assure him I can manage.

We walk all around the riverside, circling the cathedral towering over us. I do most of the talking. Robert's not a garrulous type. Yet there's a warmth, there's an honesty about him.

We find a bench overlooking the river.

'Let's sit here for a few minutes, shall we? I'm going to have to get my train back to London shortly – and I'm just remembering that steep hill up to the station!'

'Aye, it's quite a pull all right,' he says with a smile. 'Thanks for coming all this way north to see me, Barry. I really appreciate that. It's been really … special.'

'Robert, what's a three-hour train ride between brothers? It's been fantastic to meet you, very special, as you say. It's really great that we're making a start at getting to know one another. I'm so happy about that. But there are years and years to catch up on, aren't there? Far too many for just one meeting. I suggest we meet again soon – *very soon* … say in about two months' time? What do you think about that?'

'Yes, I'd like that very much.' He gives me a sidelong look, half-pleased, half-embarrassed.

'Please don't be offended by me saying this, Robert,' I say carefully, 'but it seems to me that you've been pretty unlucky in your life, whereas I've had things fairly easy. From what you've told me today, I can tell that life hasn't always been easy for you over the years. I realise that I've been fortunate in having many opportunities, which you haven't …'

Robert glances briefly down at his cheap-looking, ill-fitting clothes. Probably from a charity shop, I realise. Then he raises his head and looks at my obviously expensive outfit, my leather case, my smart shoes, and he nods.

'Look, Robert, I don't want to embarrass you, but I really want to give you a little contribution *now*, to help make things a bit easier and … more comfortable for you …'

'Thanks, Barry … but there's no need. I'm OK, you know …'

'You're more than OK – I really admire how you've coped with such difficult times and stayed positive. Anyway, next time we meet,' I continue, 'I'd like us to discuss how I can help you get your life … erm … to turn in a much more positive direction.'

I hold a fat envelope and reach it towards him.

'Barry,' he says, his voice a bit shaky, 'I'm really happy to get to know you, happier than I can say. I'm really pleased you want to see me again … but there's no need … you don't have to … I don't expect …'

I put my hand up to stop him. 'Please, Robert, please take it. It's a pleasure to help you – *my brother* – in whatever way I can, I mean it. Now, I must just head to the gents' in that pub we passed, and then we better make our way to the station to get our trains home.'

Robert is still hesitating, so I gently press the envelope into his hand.

'Thank you, Barry, that's very kind, but all I really want is to stay in touch, to see you again and get to know you better.'

As we walk up the steep hill towards the station, I try not to show what an effort it is for me. I really must make an effort to improve my fitness. I notice Robert looking furtively at me every now and then.

***

At the station, my southward train is the first due to arrive. Robert waits on the platform with me. I hand him an ordnance survey map of Northumberland.

'Present for you, Robert. Maybe we can meet in Northumberland for one of our future get-togethers? I'd really like to share some of my favourite places with you, and this is one of them. But let's plan for a rendezvous, convenient for both of us next time – like Durham has been. Do you think early April would be good for our next meeting?'

'Hmm, I'll have to consult my social diary,' he says with a grin, 'but it sounds like a pretty good time to me.'

'Fine. Let's talk about the details of meeting up when we're next in touch.'

I'm pleased he feels relaxed enough with me to make a joke.

The train rumbles slowly into the station. We embrace warmly, without reserve this time.

'It's been so good to see you, Robert. I'll give you a ring in a day or two.'

I step up into the nearest carriage and turn to give Robert a wave.

Chapter 27

2004
Robbie

I think a lot about my meeting with my brother, with Barry. I
find myself thinking particularly about my – about *our* – mother.
I'm aware the relationship between Barry and Marie has been
complicated and not too easy. *My* predominant feeling about
her is sadness. Why couldn't Barry have found me before she
died? That really hurts. I would so like to have met her, to have
known her. Now that can never be. There's a great hollowness,
a deep sorrow inside me to think I'll never know my mother.
Marie. Knowing her name makes her real somehow for the first
time. A real mother I can never know.

What do I think of Barry? What do I *feel* about him? Certainly
I'm flattered and delighted that he likes me enough to want to
meet again, and so soon. Yet, there's something mysterious about
my brother – the oddness of his clothes, and something a bit stiff
and formal about his manner. Maybe it's to do with him being
a southerner – I haven't met many of them before – or maybe

it's because he's so much richer and more sophisticated than me. He's generous with his money though. That envelope he stuffed into my hand contained a thousand pounds!

In a way, he felt more like an *older* brother than a twin, but I put that down to the way he took charge, took control of the conversation a lot of the time we were together. Probably because he's more confident, and I was so nervous.

I wonder fleetingly whether maybe he doesn't want us to be seen together – not recognised as *twins* anyway? Why would that be? Perhaps he's a bit ashamed to have a twin brother who's so obviously less affluent, doesn't want it known that I'm his twin? It almost feels that way. Was that why he took trouble to look slightly odd and unconventional? Was it to make him look different from me? Doesn't really make much sense though, after going to so much trouble to arrange for us to meet up. None of it makes much sense. Maybe it's just too much to process suddenly, out of the blue. I suppose I may need much longer.

***

Just a week later, another letter from Barry arrives. My brother certainly seems keen on his letters. It arrives only two weeks after our initial meeting. Reading it, I realise Barry might have been too embarrassed to communicate the information verbally over the phone, even though he knows I've bought a mobile with some of the money he gave me.

I'm quite pleased to see that this letter is much shorter than the last one! But its contents really shake me to the core.

Dear Robert (or should I start calling you Donal?!),
    I can't tell you how much our meeting delighted me. I feel we really made a connection, don't you? It's very, very early days in our relationship, I know, but I do believe we'll go from strength to strength, getting ever closer over time.

It's because I really liked you, Robert, and admired you as a person, that I have some confessions to make. One or two important areas of my life (and yours) that I was not entirely honest about. I'm very ashamed of that now, and very sorry. I hope you will understand and forgive me. It was wrong of me, and I want to change all that, and be completely open and honest with you from now on. My only excuse is that perhaps I needed to see whether I fully trusted you first – and please believe me, I do.

I noticed that you never once made any demands on me; there was no sense of you being 'out for what you might get', no jealousy or resentment – despite the fact that, in material terms, you have hugely missed out in comparison to me. That really impressed me.

It may seem strange to you, Robert, but there are things I'm desperate to tell you, in person and as soon as possible. Would you be able to meet again, before the 7th April? (And keep that date to meet in the Cheviots, as we discussed.)

How about another meeting, in York this time, on Wednesday 3rd March? I know it's very soon, but as I say, I really want to put one or two things straight. This time, I've enclosed a return train ticket for you, just so you don't have the bother of having to go to the station and buy one. Oh, and I'm glad you've got yourself a mobile phone – I think you'll find it a convenience – and we can more easily be in touch any time.

York is about an hour's journey for you, more like two hours plus for me. I suggest we meet at Bettys Tea Room at twelve noon and have a bite to eat and a cup of tea or coffee (full address on attached paper). Due to work commitments, I'll have to leave by about 3 p.m. this time, so it's a bit brief. Please say you can come. Leave a message on my phone. Hope to see you very soon,

Your brother Barry

What's this all about? What *confessions* does Barry need to make? What has he not been *entirely honest* about? I'm intrigued, but also anxious. I try to think whether *I've* been open and honest with *him*. I can't think that I've tried to deceive him in any way. Why would I? But then, why would he? What has he told me that may not be true, or not 'entirely'? I'm intrigued by my brother Barry. What an enigma he is.

There are the train tickets, bought and paid for by him. Perhaps he thinks I've already spent the thousand pounds he's given me, and can't afford the train to York?! Or maybe it's just another way of putting pressure on me to meet him again, where and when he wants? He certainly knows how to get his own way. Anyway, I won't argue; I want to see him again. I'll go to York to see him. Those *confessions* are mysterious, and a bit worrying. Oh well, I'll soon find out about them. Curiosity may have killed the cat, but it won't kill me! At least, I hope not.

***

The date of our second meeting is rapidly approaching. I decide to buy a few decent items of clothing for our next get-together. The contrast between Barry's and my getup at our last meeting was a bit too blatant. I enjoy my trip into the town centre on the bus, and have a leisurely look round some of the shops. I even stop in a café for a cup of coffee. Barry's money gives me choices I've never had before.

Despite that, it really *hurts* me to see the price of a pair of men's trousers and a shirt or sweater! I almost turn around and head straight back to my favourite charity shop ... but I decide I should show Barry how his gift of money has already started to help me present a smarter, more positive image. I'm also on the lookout for a warm fleece to wear in the Cheviots. I see one or two, but even with the big gift of money Barry has given me, I just can't bring myself to spend so much, when I

187

already have an old one. Surely it will do? It's only *slightly* worn.

In the end I decide on a simple pair of dark brown trousers and a maroon crew-neck sweater. My shirts are all pretty old and shabby, but I've had enough of spending money. Who'd imagine it would be so exhausting! Anyway what a waste it would be – my shirt will be hidden under the jumper. I might just as well wear an old one.

Back home, I walk to the library, where Julia, my friendly head librarian, shows me how to look up Bettys Tea Room in York on the computer. From the map on the screen, I jot down a few instructions to find the way, on foot, from the railway station and into the narrow pedestrian lanes, where Betty's is situated. Julia photocopies the map so there's no excuse for getting lost.

***

In York, the lanes are crawling with people, ambling along slowly, pausing to look in shop windows, chatting, pointing things out. Lots of tourists talking excitedly in a range of languages I can't understand. I imagine this is what it feels like being abroad. Not that I've ever been.

I head straight for Bettys Tea Room. It's not far. This time I'm the first to arrive. The old house is on three floors; I head straight upstairs. It's early for lunch, so there are plenty of unoccupied tables to choose from, some fairly secluded. I find one in an alcove behind a pillar. That should be private enough. I've barely sat down when an eager young waitress comes and asks what she can get me.

'I'm waiting for my … brother. He … er … looks a bit like me, but he's got a beard,' I tell her. 'I'll just wait 'til he comes to order, if that's OK?'

'Yes, 'course it is,' she says with a smile. 'I'll come back in a little while.'

After a few minutes I hear footsteps on the stairs and then see

Barry standing and looking around the room. I lean forward and wave at him. He spots me and raises his hand in greeting as he approaches. The first thing I notice about him, is that *he's shaved off his beard!* What's that all about?

I stand up. We embrace firmly this time. A lump gathers in my throat. My heart is racing. It's almost as though I'm in love! I realise I'm very, very happy to see him.

'Barry, good to see you, man, really good.'

He smiles and looks at me as if he's checking whether my pleasure is genuine, as if he's wondering exactly what I'm thinking.

'I'm not sure if it was the "real you" in Durham last time, or whether it's the "real you" today?' I say with a sly grin.

'Oh …? Oh, what … oh right … *the beard*. Yeah, I'd just tried it out for a few weeks … you know, to do without shaving, and to see what I thought of it. But it started to drive me mad, itching, and getting food in it, and that …'

'I think it suits you better … without, I mean.'

'Yeah? Well, I guess we look more alike now …' He examines my face closely.

'It's like looking in a mirror, isn't it? Have you ordered anything yet?'

'No, I was waiting for you.'

I pass him a menu. There's a bit of a hiatus, while we both study the menus. Barry decides on soup and a salad. I go for soup and a sandwich. We indicate to the waitress that we're ready to order, requesting our meals along with two coffees. Barry's looking a bit uneasy. He fiddles with the cutlery. He looks down at the table.

'Robert, I've got to tell you. There's no way to justify this …' He takes a deep breath. What the hell's coming now? He raises his head and looks straight at me.

'I lied to you … I'm sorry. I lied to you about something very important.'

My heart's beating so loudly, I'm sure the other diners must hear it. Barry gives me one of his intense stares.

189

'I lied to you,' he repeats, 'because I wasn't sure I could trust you ... and I wanted to protect her. I wanted to protect our mother, and myself perhaps ...'

'I don't understand.'

'Our mother, Marie. She isn't dead, Robert. She's alive. Our mother is alive.'

'She's alive ...?' I whisper.

'I'm so sorry I ... er ... pretended she had died. I wondered if you might be ... well, I'm sorry Robert ... but, "out for what you could get", once you realised there was money in the family.'

'You thought I was some sort of *gold-digger*?'

'Well, yes, I suppose I was afraid you might be. I know it was me who contacted you in the first place, but I knew your life was bound to have been difficult, deprived perhaps. And then once I heard from you about your life, there was every reason for you to feel that you'd had a really "bad deal" in life, especially compared to me.'

'I'd never thought about it that way, Barry. It just never occurred to me,' I say quietly.

'That's exactly what I realised when we talked last time. You're a much nicer person than I am – you definitely are. I felt ashamed of my suspicions, Robert. I really want to make it up to you.'

'So was the cancer a lie?'

'What? Mum? Well, no, not exactly. It's actually true that she's not been all that well recently – I promise you, this is all true, Robert. I'm going to be totally honest with you from now on. Always. Mum *has* been treated for breast cancer. Her oncologist is confident that they've caught it early enough, and that all the cancer was removed during her mastectomy. She's having some chemotherapy to "mop up any rogue cells" as they put it. Apparently, she'll be closely monitored for a year or two, and then if she progresses well, perhaps less frequently, but still checked regularly.'

'So ... she's alive? Our mother is alive?'

'She is. Marie is alive.'

I nod. I'm feeling dizzy. I'm afraid I may pass out.

Chapter 28

2004
Barry

Robert has gone very pale. He looks as though he may faint.

'My mother is alive,' he whispers.

Tears start to roll slowly down his cheeks. I stand up and move to behind his chair. I put my arms around him and hold him firmly. I can feel him trembling. It's a terrible thing I've done to him.

'What happens now?' he says. 'What do we do next?'

'I think that's partly up to you, Robert. Maybe we both need to think carefully how we want to go forward. Primarily, I guess there are Marie's feelings to consider, and yours, of course. That's why I wanted to meet with you today, so we can discuss the way ahead – openly and honestly. Marie doesn't know we've been seeing each other yet. I felt I had to make sure *you* want to see *her* before telling her that you've been found.'

'She doesn't know? Of course I want to see her, but I don't want her to be upset,' he says, his chest convulses with a small sob. His whole body is shaking.

'*Upset?* To hear that you've been found? Robert, she's yearned and longed for you for her entire adult life. She'll certainly be shocked, but she'll get over that. She'll be thrilled, joyful, ecstatic, speechless with happiness. But definitely not upset.'

The young waitress comes over to us hesitantly. 'Is everything all right …? Can I get either of you anything …?'

'You could get us a bottle of champagne!' Robert says, near hysterical.

'Oh … I'm sorry, sir … I don't think we have champagne.'

'Don't worry, love, only joking. Maybe bring us some more coffee?'

She gives a sigh of relief and smiles. 'I'll bring some straight back.'

We both watch her scurrying back towards the stairs.

'So, Barry. What do you think is the next step? Where the hell do we start?'

'Well, as I said, in a way, I think it's your call, Robert, but I'm happy to make a suggestion.'

'What are you thinking?'

'Well, what I'm thinking is I know this is probably the most momentous piece of news in your entire life, and I'm sure you need some time to think it over, to process what it means *now*, and what it might mean for you in the future. This mess is my fault, entirely my fault for being so cowardly, and for misjudging you. So, it's right that whatever we do now should be up to you.

'Having said that, while I had to tell you the most important thing – that Mum is alive, and not dead as I pretended – I now *suggest*, we don't rush headfirst into emotional reunions *immediately*. Let's give ourselves – and I do mean *both of us* – some more time to get to know one another, to think about all the implications of this new grouping of relationships.'

He's looking at me intently, an agonised expression on his face.

'All these years, you've been on your own, Robert. Now

192

suddenly, you're part of a family: a family of strangers. That's quite something to take in.'

'Mmm, yeah … you're right. I suppose there's a lot of new relationships to negotiate.'

'Yes … and as I said in my letter – I hate to admit this Robert – there are some other things I wasn't totally honest about.'

Robert puts his hands over his face.

'Jesus! What else?'

'Well, for one thing, I'm not too well myself …'

'What d'you mean? What's wrong with you?'

'I won't beat about the bush, Robert. I've had a bit of a drugs problem … no, not a bit, *a lot* – I've had a serious drugs problem … an *addiction* for some years.'

'You? What … what kind of addiction?'

'Cocaine … heroin too. I am trying to get a hold on it, but it's hard. Hard drugs, hard problem.'

'I've known quite a few druggies, you know, when I was living rough. You don't seem the sort of person on hard drugs, Barry. I'd never have guessed it.'

'There is no "sort of drugs person", Robert, and I've learned to be quite good at controlling outward appearances.'

'Does our mam know?'

'Yes. She let herself into my flat some years ago, while I was at work. She was bringing some fresh fruit and vegetables that she'd bought at the market nearby. She decided to give the place a clean-up – typical mum you know …'

I pause in horror at what I'd said.

'No, I don't know.'

'I'm so sorry, Robert, 'course you don't. It was just a stupid figure of speech.'

'It's OK. I know it wasn't deliberate,' he says. 'Does your wife know?'

'Anaïs? Yes, she's come to know – because it's made me even more of a bastard than usual. That's why she doesn't want to put

193

up with me any longer. I'm not proud of the way I've treated her.'

'Phew. What a situation.'

'The thing is … there's something else to tell you.'

'Bloody hell, Barry. What else?'

'It's not really something new – it's something connected with the drug-taking.'

'What?'

'Well, all these years on heroin and cocaine has really fucked up my health. My kidneys have pretty much packed in.'

'Jesus! How serious? Can they treat you? You had a letter from the hospital, didn't you? I remember seeing it now – at that café in Durham. What did it say?'

Robert looks at me, frowning. His mouth is quivering. I can tell what he's thinking. *I've only just found my twin brother – am I about to lose him?*

'It is serious, Robert, very serious. My specialist has made it clear that a kidney transplant is the only hope.'

'Well, that's not so bad then, is it? They can do kidney transplants, can't they? They do them all the time. When are you having the operation?'

'They *can* do it … but the thing is, there's a great shortage of kidneys, especially for people with my unusual blood group. In fact, it's a rare blood group, so highly unlikely that a suitable donor, someone who's a blood match, will be found in time.'

'But … that's impossible. There must be people who could be donors! People with the same blood group … there must be!' He looks like he's about to burst into tears.

I'm scratching at the wood grain on the table, looking at my brother. He's staring at me. His hands are shaking. His mouth is twitching.

'It's me, isn't it? I'm the one who's a match. Identical twin brothers have the same blood group.'

'Yes.'

'So … so that's why you need me! That's why you sought me

out, right? You need my fucking kidney! You never cared about meeting your long-lost brother; you just needed a part of my body! That's all you wanted me for, right?'

'Robert, you remember I said there would be no more lies? I said I promised to tell you the absolute truth from now on? So I'm going to do that.

'Yes, your kidney could save my life. But when I first found you I didn't know just how bad my kidneys were. Then, on the morning of our first meeting, I got the letter from the hospital – the one you found on the floor. It didn't pull any punches. Without a transplant I haven't got long.

'At first, I thought I would see what you were like as a person. I wanted to persuade you to give me one of your kidneys, but I didn't know what it would take. Knowing you were bound to have been hard up for most of your life, I thought maybe all it would take would be to offer you enough money. I'm sorry, Robert, to admit this – it's horrible I know – but I really thought that, having led such a miserable, poor, deprived life, you'd be bound to agree. But then we met, and by the end of that meeting, I realised I was starting to really like you. To be honest, I was drawn to you as to very few people before. I could tell you weren't hooked on money the way I've been. You weren't motivated by material gain in the same way as me. I admired how you didn't seem resentful about me having had everything, and you so little in life.'

I was running out of breath. I had to stop and breathe deeply for a while. Robert watched me, frowning.

'I found I really *wanted* you to have some of the advantages I've been given, Robert. I *wanted* you to meet our mother, while at first I'd thought to keep you apart from her in case she persuaded you against giving up a kidney. I thought that after all those years of missing you, maybe she wouldn't want to risk losing you by having a major operation. That's why I told you she was dead. Why would she? *I* don't want to risk losing you either. It's a terrible thing to have done, Robert – to you, and to her. I know that now.'

I couldn't go on. My voice cracked, and I could hardly breathe. I put my hands over my face and sobbed like a baby.

Robert put his arms around me. 'It's OK, man, it's OK. I understand. I'd probably have done the same.'

'No, you wouldn't. I know you wouldn't. We may be twins, but we're different.'

Robert gives me a little shake to make me look at him. 'Well I tell you what, brother Barry, you're not going to pay the bill today. I'm going to – from that ridiculous amount of money you gave me. Let's get out of here and have a walk by the river before you have to get your train back. That'll give me a chance to think about your proposal.'

'No! No way. Don't think about it now. I'm not going to let you make any decisions about that today, Robert, unless it's definitely no, which I'd absolutely understand. In fact, not before our next meet-up in the Cheviots. You have to promise *not* to make a decision, nor to tell me about it, until after that walk in the hills in April.

'And if you still want more time after that, it's fine. I want you to know I'd completely accept a negative answer, with no hard feelings. There's still a faint chance of finding a donor from the data bank, so there's no pressure on you.'

Chapter 29

2004
Robert

As we walk, Barry tells me a few other untruths on his conscience. For example, the beard at our first meeting had been hastily grown to make us look less alike, less obviously twins. At the time, he seemed to think that if anyone saw us and later remembered us as twins, it could be assumed he'd somehow tricked me into giving up a kidney. Totally irrational perhaps ... but part of his guilty conscience. Well, I'd already sensed part of it. Also, he doesn't really have glaucoma, he tells me, that was just a pretence to explain why he was hiding behind sunglasses on a cloudy winter's day – another part of his disguise.

I could start to wonder if Barry is a pathological liar, but I prefer to put the 'pretences' down to his initial distrust of my motives – even though he was the one who had contacted me in the first place! I'm trying hard to believe he really is determined to be truthful from now on. If my life were on the line that way, how far might I go, might any of us go, to save ourselves?

197

As to the issue of whether to agree to part with one of my kidneys, I need to think hard about it, and maybe do some research into the effects of living with only one kidney – as well as the implications for Barry of *not* having a well-matched transplant. I decide to talk to Belle, one of my few loyal and totally trustworthy friends, who also has some medical knowledge. I know she'll give me some straight opinions.

***

After Barry's revelations in York, I spoke to Belle to ask for her advice. She's always calm and wise, and straight to the point.

'It seems to me you've got strong feelings for this newfound brother of yours, Robert, am I right?' she said.

'Yes, I guess I have. He's the only family I've got; at least, he's the only one I've *met* so far. I have a *mother*, Belle, but I've not met her yet. That's the next big thing to happen.'

Belle gives me one of her huge smiles, and then changes to a serious face. 'Yes, that's wonderful news, Robbie – a mother *Barry told you was dead*, right? That was a terrible, terrible thing to pretend to you.'

'He knows it was a bad thing to do. It's all sorted out now, Belle. He's explained why he told me that. He's a bit of an enigma, is Barry. I think he's been used to having his own way. I'm making sure I stay in control, but I have been giving the question of the possible kidney donation a lot of thought.'

'Sounds to me like you're leaning towards agreeing to it. You know I trained as a nurse, Robbie, don't you? I worked with the transplant team for a while. It's true people can certainly live fine with only one kidney, but that's not to say it's a minor thing. It's a major operation for you as well as for him, remember. Also, you've got to be well sure your one remaining kidney is in good shape, and will see you through the rest of your life.' She pauses and looks at me.

'But without a doubt, assuming it's a match, it would give your brother the best chance of life.'

That's enough for me. I've made a decision.

Chapter 30

2004
Marie

I can't remember the last time Barry came round to my house. So today feels like a treat – a special occasion. He rang to say he had something to tell me. Something important, he said. I'm delighted, if a little apprehensive. Is it good news or bad? You never know with Barry. Either way it feels like a special occasion, and special occasions in Erna's house always meant cake. As Easter isn't too far away, I decide to make a Simnel cake. Like Erna always was, Barry is fond of almonds and marzipan, has been ever since he was a little boy. He used to love rolling the little marzipan balls for the top of the cake in his hands.

'The little balls represent Jesus's disciples. We need to make eleven.' I tell him.

'Why not twelve balls, Mammy?' Barry asks, even though he knows full well. 'There were twelve disciples.'

'Yes, but we don't want Judas, do we, Barry?'

'Why not, Mammy?'

'Because he was bad, son, that's why. He betrayed Jesus, didn't he?'

'Yes, that was mean, so we won't put him on our cake, will we?' he says with satisfaction, popping Judas into his mouth.

***

I cut Barry a piece of the cake and pour coffee for us both. It's a mild day for early spring, so we sit with the doors to the garden open, letting the sunshine flood in.

'Mmm, Simnel cake. That's a treat, Mum.'

'Here you are, Barry love, and there's plenty for seconds. You look like you need feeding up.'

He looks dreadful. Worse than usual; frail and ill. I've not seen him quite so pale before. I sit next to him on the sofa.

'Pity you didn't bring Anaïs and Nina too, Barry. It's a while since I've seen them.'

'Probably not as long as since *I've* seen them, Mum. You know we're not seeing each other just now.'

How I hate the bitter tone he uses when he speaks about Anaïs these days.

'Well, more fool you. It's a crying shame.'

'Look, Mum, let's not talk about that today. I haven't come to talk about me and Anaïs. I've something very important to tell you.'

'Not more bad news, I hope, son.'

'I think you'll agree it's not bad news at all. In fact, it may be the best news I could bring you.'

'Oh, I could just do with some good news. Come on then, spit it out.'

'I've found him.'

At first I don't understand. I look blankly at Barry for several seconds. Then I feel nausea washing through me. Is it …? Can it be …? I can't get enough oxygen. My lungs aren't working properly. I pant and gasp frantically, trying to suck more air into my lungs. I think I'm about to collapse, or maybe have a stroke. I stare at Barry, and open my mouth, trying to speak, but no sound comes out.

'Mum, I've *found* him,' Barry repeats. '*I've found Donal.*'

'Donal!!' I hear the word come out of me, an unearthly howl. I clasp my face in both hands, trying to keep it upright, but some force throws my head back. I gasp for air. I can't think of any words. Is it possible? I'm afraid I may be losing my mind.

'Oh God! Oh God! Oh dear God! Are you telling me the truth, Barry? Is it true? You've found my Donal! My boy! My baby!' I hear myself scream.

Barry's looking at me anxiously, like *he's* wondering if I'm losing my mind too, wondering if maybe he shouldn't have told me. Yet how else could he have shared his news?

Barry gets up and kneels on the floor in front of me. He puts his arms around my waist and holds me firmly against his chest. He strokes my hair. I'm trembling and moaning, swaying backwards and forwards despite his grip on me; I can't control it. He squeezes me tightly.

'Ssshhh,' he croons. 'Ssshhh, Mum. It's all right. Yes, I've found Donal, I really have, and I've *met* him! He's doing really well.'

I sit bolt upright, and try to focus my mind on what he's told me. I look him straight in the face.

'He's *well*? He's all right? What does he look like, Barry? Is he just like you? Where is he? Is he here, in London? Does he want to see me? He doesn't hate me, does he? Please tell me he doesn't hate me.'

'Whoa! One thing at a time … I'm going to answer all your questions, Mum,' Barry says quietly, 'I promise. I'm going to tell you all about Donal. Everything I know. But I need you to calm down a bit. I'm going to get you a drink, some brandy. It'll make you feel calmer. We'll each have some, OK?'

Very slowly, as if he's afraid I may return to the madness of before, Barry releases his grip on me. He stands up, watching as I continue to rock backwards and forwards on the sofa. He disappears into the kitchen and returns a few moments later with two small glasses.

He sits on the chair directly opposite me.

'Here,' he says, handing me a glass. 'Drink this, Mum. It'll make you feel better.'

The smell of it nearly makes me gag, but he's right. I swallow some and it courses down my throat in a red-hot stream. I cough and choke, and then sip some more. Its heat is a comfort, reaching every extremity of my body.

'Thank you, darling. That's better. I'm all right. Please tell me about Donal now.'

***

I'm going to see my son, my Donal, very soon. First, Barry is going to meet him in the wilds of Northumberland in four days' time. It's been arranged for a while. Donal lives in Newcastle. Barry's already spent some time with him. He wanted to meet Donal before telling me, to make sure he was all right, not resentful, not revengeful about being 'given away'.

'I was really impressed by Donal, Mum,' Barry tells me, 'for all he's had a difficult life, he's got a lovely, kind, thoughtful personality.'

'Has he ...?' I whisper shakily. 'Yes, of course he has. I knew he would have.'

I picture him. I hear his voice. Every thought of him, my Donal, brings fresh tears of joy.

'So far we've met twice in all, Mum. The first time in Durham and then after that, in York. I've spoken to him on the phone several times too.'

I nod, soaking up every word Barry says.

'Meeting up the first time was very strange, almost unreal – a strange experience for both of us, very emotional. But we got on well, straightaway. We're growing closer all the time. He's dying to meet you, but he's also very nervous. He's never been to London. He wants me to take him down, as he feels a bit at ease with me now. I know you can hardly wait to see him, but do you think you can bear to wait just another couple of weeks?'

'I've waited over thirty-five years now, so I have, and had no choice in the matter. I guess I can wait another two weeks. But it will be hard, Barry. I *ache* to see him – now, right here in front of me. Until then I can't quite believe it's true. But I know it is. Thank you, dearest Barry, for making my dreams come true, for making it possible.'

For once *he* takes the initiative; he stands up, walks over to me, and gives me a huge hug.

Donal's adoptive parents named him Robert, but he'll always be Donal to me. Why, oh why couldn't they have told me that his adoptive parents gave him back to social services when he was only tiny? Why didn't they tell me years ago? Why couldn't they return him to me then? All those years we could have been together – *wasted*.

Still, I'm not going to focus on those lost years, not now. I just can't wait to see my boy, to hold him, to love him. I'm really proud of Barry too, for the sensitive way he's handled getting to know his brother. I'm touched that he's been so thoughtful and protective of me. For all Barry's faults he's got a good heart. He can be difficult, but there's good in him too. I just wish he were stronger, fitter. At least a day or two of fresh air and walks in Northumberland should do him good.

After their short break up there, Barry is going to bring Donal to London to stay in his flat with him. Time for Donal to get to know all his family, but gradually. Starting with me of course. I don't know how I'll contain all my feelings for Donal for the next two or three weeks! If only Erna was here to meet him. How thrilled she'd have been.

I'm bursting to tell Sylvia about him, and Anaïs, and Elsie. But I'll not tell anyone, not yet, not 'til he and I have met. One step at a time. Oh, what joy! If only Erna were still with us – how she would have loved to know Donal.

Chapter 31

2004
Robert

Just four days before we're due to meet up in the hills, Barry rings my new mobile to check I'm still coming. He sounds tired.

'Don't forget I gave you a detailed map of Northumberland, Robert,' he tells me. 'There's a map reference for the exact spot in the Cheviots for us to meet in April. You'll see it's marked on the map with a red circle. You have kept the map, haven't you?'

'Yes, I've got it. That's fine, thanks.'

'I've written the date and time for us to meet and some clear directions to get there. You *can* drive, Robert, can you?'

'I *can* drive … I mean, I've passed the test. But I don't have a car of my own. I'll need to hire a car to get there. Unless we meet in Newcastle instead, Barry, and you can take me up to that place in the hills in *your* hire car?'

He pauses before replying, as if he's seriously *considering* my suggestion, but I sense he doesn't like it. I've noticed Barry always likes to have his own ideas about arrangements, and doesn't appreciate deviating away from his set plan.

'I really think it's best if we travel independently, Robert. You know … my train from London might be delayed and I wouldn't want to keep you waiting.'

'Hmmm, well … either one of us could be delayed on the way to the Cheviot meeting place. But anyway, it's OK, whatever's easier for you, Barry. You're the one who's got further to come.'

'That's right. Well now … er … as you've got to hire a car … I'll send you …' he starts to say.

'No, no, Barry. It's fine, absolutely fine. No problem. You've given me more than enough already, man,' I interrupt, anticipating his offer of further funds.

'Hmm … all right then, if you're sure.' He sounds mildly put out. 'So, you're all set for our get-together are you, Robert?'

'Yes, I've got the car hire planned booked. I found a different outfit to yours in the end.'

'Oh? Not the one I suggested near the Central Station? It seemed so convenient.'

I smile at this anticipated response. 'Well, it is convenient for your return journey, Barry. But you know me – I'm always after a bargain. I found a hire company that was cheaper, further along the river. Anyway, it's no problem; I've got an OK car in mind.'

I want to resist his tendency to control me, and he doesn't like that. He doesn't like me asserting my own arrangements.

'You know, Robert, you've got to get out of that "find the cheapest" mindset. Money's not going to be a problem for you from now on. Start thinking about what's most convenient – and best quality – first.'

He sounds slightly fussed and flustered. I try teasing him out of it.

'Are you sure you're OK to *drive*, Barry? What with the glaucoma?' I ask him.

'The what …? Oh yeah, ha ha, very funny … *the glaucoma*.

I'm absolutely fine driving. Anyway Robert, it'll be great to see you again. Drive very carefully, won't you.'

'Yeah, you too. See you April 7th.'

It's all very well for Barry to tell me to reform my cheapskate 'mindset', but habits of a lifetime take more than just a few weeks to change! I'm used to making my own decisions, and not sure I want to trust Barry's view of the world all the time. When I check, the Quayside car hire looks very expensive to me. All right, I've enough money now, thanks to Barry. He's made it possible for me to have choices, which I enjoy, but I've no intention of asking him for *more* money. Why waste it if I can find a cheaper firm?

There's another issue too. I don't have a valid driving licence, even though I did pass my driving test. The ramshackle outfit I've found probably won't give a toss about details like that.

So I decide to go down to the riverside and look for myself. Not the smart dolled-up area of the Quayside, with the huge glass, slug-shaped concert hall, expensive restaurants, and the Millennium Bridge, changing colour as you watch it. That's what tourists and visitors see as their train rolls over the rail bridge into Newcastle station. Probably think it's a right posh city. Probably have no idea what lies beyond – but I do.

Where *I* go is the messy, upstream part of the Tyne; where down-and-outs doss down behind piles of old bricks or rubbish bins; where hopeful old guys swing fishing rods out over the black water; where scruffy kids bunk off school to kick a deflated ball around and chuck stones into the water's edge – laughing and running away if they splash passers-by with mud.

I noticed it a while back: a rough, tumble-down garage with a notice claiming they did car rentals. At least it looks *cheap* – or so I think. That's what drew me to the place in the first instance, but it soon becomes clear that renting any car at all is going to cost an arm and a leg! The car rental guys turn out to be right sharks – they tell me they usually demand a credit card, which I don't have, *of course.* They'd have known that just by looking at me.

So I have to leave the rotten car rental outfit a large deposit just to book it for April 7th. They act like they're doing me a favour! Truth is, they've got me over a barrel; they tell me I'm lucky to find any company willing to trust me without a credit card. I know that's true. Of course it's daylight robbery. Just as well Barry has given me all that money. Money might not mean much to him, but I haven't spent so much in one go for years – and that's without any petrol!

Just as I thought, the car rental boys don't even ask to see my driving licence, or else I'd have had to show them the one I'd found on the ground in a Sainsbury's car park a while back. If they'd known about that, *and* that I'd hardly ever driven a car in recent years, they might not have been so happy to let me drive off in their miserable old Skoda! Bunch of cowboys.

***

The night before Barry and I are due to meet, I lie awake half the night, worrying about the drive, only finally nodding off at about four in the morning. Then I sleep on until the alarm wakes me at half past eight. I sit up with a terrible start, my heart thumping.

Calm down, Robbie, man … relax … relax … I keep telling myself. *Plenty of time to get there.*

I don't put on my best new trousers and jumper – no point, it could get muddy in the Cheviots. I'd found a good pair of trainers at the Oxfam shop that fitted. The woman in there knows me well; she let me have them reduced to two quid. They don't look too tatty; in fact, they look nearly new – quite a smart grey with a black flash – but they'll be no good at all if it's wet and boggy up in those hills.

Just as well I've no eggs or bacon left – I've no appetite, I'm that excited. I force a quick piece of toast and jam and a mug of tea down me, and I'm done. Luckily I'd written out the route in detail the night before – when I needed to turn, all the road numbers and villages I have to pass through – it took me hours. The librarian had shown me how to do it, following the map, and I soon caught on. I feel well proud of myself. I haven't done stuff like that since I was at school.

I do a quick check around the cramped, fusty little flat, and make sure I've got everything I need.

The hire car is still where I'd left it, thank God. In this area, there's always a chance someone might have slashed the tyres – or even nicked the car.

I sit quietly in the driver's seat for a few minutes, gripping the steering wheel, until my heart slows down, and my hands stop shaking. It may be five years since I last drove, but surely, I tell myself, you never forget – it's just like riding a bike … only faster.

'Get a grip,' I mutter. 'Deep breaths; in – out, in – out.'

I put the key in the ignition and turn it on.

'Slow and steady, Robbie man, slow and steady,' I say aloud as the car edges forwards. 'You don't want them boys in blue after you.'

***

It doesn't take long to leave the city behind – urban congestion replaced by woods, fields, and rolling open spaces. A feeling of freedom and excitement sweeps over me.

The reception on the car radio starts to fade out the further north I drive. Never mind, I'm not much bothered about that. No need for music or chatter; there's so much else to experience and I'm enjoying myself. There isn't too much traffic on the roads, especially after I turn off the main A1 onto the narrower country roads. Only about half an hour outside the city and the whole world has changed. It's mid-spring; a few fields are still brown earth, with neat plough lines and channels, as if a giant in a tractor has run an enormous fork carefully up and down, up and down. But most of the fields are showing a green tinge, where some crop is starting to grow, even though I'm too far away to tell what it is.

The sun is shining in a pale blue sky. Puffy white clouds drift across the sky, like in a kid's picture book. There are sheep everywhere – and tiny lambs following their mums about in the lowland grass fields close to the farms. I pull into a lay-by for a while to watch them. I notice how the ewes keep a careful watch on their lambs if they stray. Must be a natural maternal instinct, I think, to watch over your babies. Even animals are seriously distressed to be separated from their offspring. How did my mum cope, I wonder?

There are cows and horses too in some of the fields, standing motionless as toy animals. They look so calm and peaceful, as if contemplating the purpose of life. 'Take you a long time to solve that mystery, guys,' I mutter.

High above the road, some sort of hawk is circling slowly, looking for prey. I love the country, yet I've not been out of the city for ages. When was I last away from the built-up area? Must have been years and years ago, probably when I was living with Len and Betty.

Thoughts of the countryside set my mind drifting to my time with Len and Betty. I can still picture their faces like they're right in front of me. They were so nice; they were the best. It brings a lump to my throat to think of them. I remember how they used to take me out to run about in woods or have picnics on the beach. Sometimes they even took me to visit friends or relatives of theirs for tea. The special thing about Len and Betty is they gave me *choices*. First time in my life I'd ever had choices. All right, they weren't *huge* choices, but they mattered so much to me.

'*What do you want to do today, Robbie? Want to come down the allotment, help me dig some taties?*'

'*What kind of cake d'you fancy, pet – chocolate or jam?*

'*Want to give this mix a stir?*'

'*Shall we cycle down the coast today, or the river?*'

211

Gently asking my opinions, never just barking orders at me like I'd been used to. It was the first time I experienced being regarded as a member of a proper family. Of course, Len and Betty had their own family: two middle-aged sons, Harry and Bob, and a daughter, Shirley. There was a tribe of grandchildren too – younger than me, many of them. At first I was wary of them, and a bit jealous too, truth be told. I wanted to be their only kid, and special, but they all included me in family discussions and get-togethers. They made me one of them.

They weren't scared of teenagers like most of the foster carers; they really *liked* me. I could tell. They actually liked talking to me, and – something that I thought was amazing – they *listened* to me. They were so affectionate, I couldn't help but respond. Len would call me 'Laddie-me-Lad' and Betty called me 'Pet' or 'Robbie-Pet', or sometimes 'Darlin''. Len would give my shoulder a squeeze or ruffle my hair, and Betty was forever giving me hugs. Of course, I'd sometimes pull away and say, 'Give over'… or 'geroff' in a gruff voice. Well, you had to act tough, didn't you …?

But really I loved their affection. It was like how I imagined grandparents might be. *Should* be. I would have happily stayed with Len and Betty for ever. Maybe I wouldn't openly admit it, not even to them, but I really hoped they might adopt me – be my mum and dad for real, even though I knew they were too old. But it just wasn't to be. It was better not to think too much; so often I just ended up in a sad place. Maybe, just maybe, at last I'm going to be part of a real family soon.

I force my thoughts away from the sadness, and back to my journey. I check my directions. Still heading the right way. The little car struggles up and up for some time, climbing a tiny narrow road up into the Cheviot hills. The narrow road morphs into an even narrower stony track, making the wheels grind and crackle. Surely it can't be much further? We seem to be climbing for ever, not getting anywhere – except higher.

Suddenly, there it is – the small car park, all on its own, miles from anywhere – just as Barry described. From here, I know I'll have to walk about three miles even higher up into the hills. Phew, hope I'm up to it.

I stop the car and look around. A cluster of ash trees mark one edge of the car park. They lean eastwards in unison, like a row of dancers momentarily striking a pose. Three other cars huddle under the shelter of the trees. Opposite, the hill falls away steeply towards the expanse of the valley below.

With the engine switched off, the only sound is the shrieking of the wind. As soon as I try opening the car door, a fierce, bitingly cold blast nearly knocks me over. Dark clouds scud rapidly across the sky, briefly shutting out the sun. I quickly slam the door shut. In the relative warmth inside, I struggle to put on my jumper and then my fleece. Old and slightly moth-eaten though it is, it will offer some slight protection from the cold.

I sit back and start the engine again, steering the Skoda in an arc to nestle beside a blue Peugeot. Next to that is a slightly battered Fiesta, and beyond it, a shining black Golf. *That's got to be Barry's hire-car,* I think, *typical of him.*

I've packed a couple of sandwiches, two cans of beer and a bottle of water in a carrier bag, along with a thin nylon anorak in case of rain, the map Barry had given me, and all the money I have left. It's nearly midday according to the clock in the car. I decide to have one of the sandwiches and a can of beer before setting off, just to give me enough energy for the long steep walk ahead. I'll share the other can with Barry when I reach him. I try Barry's mobile number to let him know I'm on the last stretch, but predictably, there's no signal up there.

Remembering Barry's instructions, I lock the car and make for the footpath marked with a blue arrow. It doesn't look inviting; the land is covered in scrubby grass and patches of heather, some thorny broom bushes – and ahead, the steep, rocky pathway.

***

After two hours of walking, I wonder whether Barry would struggle with the climb too. Especially as he's clearly in poor health. Is he really up to such a rigorous walk?

My feet throb from the constant impact of the stones on the flimsy soles of my trainers and my thighs and ankles are aching with the unfamiliar effort of clambering up rocks and the steep, uneven inclines.

Serves you right for not keeping yourself properly fit, Robbie, I think grimly. The bitterly cold wind cuts through my fleece, instantly freezing the sweat gathering on my back. I'm worrying more about Barry, so I try the mobile again, but there's still no signal.

I don't encounter any other walkers – nor any other living creatures for that matter – except the occasional small cluster of sheep, who bleat in surprise at seeing a human being, and the odd rabbit scampering away in panic.

By two o'clock – Barry's planned rendezvous time – I'm exhausted. It's only knowing that the meeting place must be nearby that keeps me going for the last fifteen minutes or so.

At last, the hill levels out into a domed, grassy area. So even and symmetrical is the circular curve of this summit that it appears almost carved by human hands, although I know it must have been created by thousands of years of constant, harsh weathering. I also sense immediately that this is the right place. It's clearly the end of the path.

I stand for a few minutes in the centre of the hump, my legs trembling, my heart thudding in my chest – partly from the effort, partly from some anxiety about seeing my brother again. I turn my body slowly around on the spot, examining every view of the 360-degree circle. Where is he? Surely he wouldn't have given up and gone, just because I'm a few minutes late? Anyway, he would have passed me on the path if he had decided to go back to his car – there was no other path.

I walk in a circle through shrubby undergrowth: heather, ferns, and gorse. A pair of grouse rise out of the heather in alarm, giving me a right fright, calling their strange cry, just as I remember Len describing to me years ago: *'Go-back, go-back, go-back …'*

'Well, I'm not going back', I tell them crossly. 'Not after all the bloody effort of getting here!' I sit on a rocky outcrop to rest for a minute.

Still no sign of Barry. Surely he should be here by now. Irritation starts to gnaw at my insides. Is this Barry's idea of a joke? I grit my teeth and shake my head, trying to expel the thoughts. We were getting on so well. I sit on a slab of rock.

It's only now that I begin to realise just how important this brother of mine has become to me, how much I want to see him again, and above all, how much I want to get to know my mother. A sudden longing for her, for my family, tears painfully at my heart.

The feeling is almost unbearable. Barry has clearly decided not to pursue our relationship any further. He obviously doesn't like me as much as he made out. Why would he? I feel like weeping. But I stand up and shake myself.

'Pull yourself together, Robbie, man', I say out loud. After all, what does it really matter? I hadn't even known about my brother's existence for all those years before our meeting in Durham only about two months ago, and it hadn't bothered me then. Never gave it a thought. Why should it matter now? Yet … it does matter. It matters a lot.

I do one more circuit, my steps growing heavy and weary. Just as I approach the point where the footpath reaches the grassy summit, something catches my eye. Further down, almost hidden in the heather, I see a dark, bluish colour. Is it a carrier bag, or perhaps a rucksack?

I walk towards it, stepping carefully over the heather bushes, which threaten to trip me with their hard, twisty stems. The dark blue object grows larger as I approach. It begins to take shape … the shape of a jacket: a navy blue jacket. I creep cautiously

215

towards it, my eyes struggling to take in the reality of what they are seeing. Not just a jacket, but a man – a man wearing a jacket. It's definitely a man.

Lying sprawled on his back on the ground, gazing heavenwards with open, sightless eyes, is my brother, Barry.

Chapter 32

2004
Robert

I stare at the lifeless body of my brother.

Barry is lying on his back, one arm bent, his fingers clutching the strap of an expensive-looking rucksack, the other arm thrust up behind his head. The navy blue jacket – the Barbour he'd worn at our previous meeting – is open, revealing what looks like a grey Shetland wool jumper, with the collar of a checked shirt just showing at the neck. Instinctively, my hand moves up to my own neck, as if in an involuntary gesture of empathy, or perhaps just horror at what I'm observing. My breath comes in rapid pants, as if not enough oxygen is reaching my lungs. My whole body is trembling. Sweat trickles down my spine. All strength leaves my legs; they give way beneath me and I sink to my knees on the damp ground. Such great sorrow compresses my whole body that I am overcome with shaking.

'Barry …?' I whisper. 'Barry? Barry, *please* …'

There is no reply. Of course there is no reply. I've never seen a dead body before, but anyone could tell he's no longer alive. I creep a few inches nearer and crouch by his side. I look into my brother's face. It bears no sign of pain or struggle, which is a relief to me. Barry looks calm and peaceful. His face is smooth, free of lines. His mouth even seems to turn upwards faintly, as if smiling just faintly.

Despite being drawn and haggard, perhaps from the drugs, Barry's face is slightly smoother, less rugged than mine, I notice, at these close quarters. Perhaps it's just the effect of a comfortable life? All traces of the beard removed, I admire my brother's close, clean shave, that sleekness again; it's a perfect finish – unlike my own uneven stubble, the result no doubt of always having to use cheap razors.

His hands are clean and well-manicured: perfectly trimmed nails, neat, even cuticles.

I reach out and hesitantly touch Barry's hair. Just like mine, it's chestnut-brown, with the first streaks of grey at the temples. But unlike my straggly, greasy hair, Barry's is silky smooth, conditioned, cut to perfection – a soft wave above the ears and over the forehead. It is clearly an expensive cut, but a traditional style, which is somehow both gentle, yet masculine. It strikes me that Barry is a very handsome man. But, despite looking exactly like him, it has never crossed my mind to consider myself good-looking or handsome, nor do I believe anyone else has ever thought so either.

I kneel there, next to my twin brother, and sigh. A deep sadness settles heavily over me like a dark raincloud.

What am I to do now? *What the hell am I going to do??!* Just when I was looking forward to having a brother in my life, for all the years to come, Barry has been snatched away from me. And what about my mum? What about Marie? How can I meet her if Barry's dead? It seems desperately unfair.

It's not fair! I feel like wailing, like a disgruntled child promised a treat, only to have it whipped away. It is as though a dark, damp blanket has wrapped itself around me, a blanket not of comfort but of loneliness. A heaviness, a tightness, rises in my throat, and my eyes well up with tears.

'*What the hell am I to do?*' I repeat. I try my mobile phone again, but as before, there is no signal this high up and remote. Also the charge seems to have run down by now.

Perhaps I should make my way back to the car park and down the hill to call the authorities from the nearest village. But who would I ring? I wonder if anyone would even believe my story? That I just found him here. Me with my dubious background, and an envelope full of money in my pocket. The skin on my back crawls at the thought of leaving him here all alone. But if I talk to the police, who knows what could happen to me. What assumptions might they make? What can I do?

I feel utterly alone and desperate. I can't think straight.

Then an answer comes to me. There is something else I could do, something makes some sense out of this situation. Perhaps it's even what Barry meant me to do in such circumstances. Is this perhaps why he asked to meet in such a remote and lonely place? I stand up and listen, then walk back up to the mound and look around. There's no doubt about it; we are completely alone. I return to his body.

I hesitate for a few moments, wondering if I can really do this. Then slowly, gently, respectfully, I begin to undress Barry, careful not to twist or distort his limbs. First, the navy blue jacket. I slide Barry's arms out of the sleeves, and ease the back from under his body a little bit at a time.

'Lucky we're both thin, Barry,' I whisper to him. 'You're not too heavy, are you, mate?'

I place the jacket to one side on the heather, folding it carefully to keep any damp off the inside. Next, the grey Shetland sweater. That's a bit more of a struggle. It fits his body closely, but at least the wool is soft and pliable, allowing me to pull the sleeves off without too much difficulty. Then I have to work Barry's head out of the neck opening, pulling it over his chin first, and then lifting his head while easing that too out of the opening. I hold my brother's head on the palm of one hand – I'm astonished at the weight of it – but I manage to extricate it in the end. The checked shirt is easy enough; it has buttons from the collar to the hem. It's made of some sort of brushed cotton material. I stroke its softness against my cheek, feeling it catch slightly on my stubble. Beneath the shirt, Barry is wearing a white T-shirt vest of the finest, silkiest material I have ever felt. I bend down until my mouth is closer to Barry's ear.

'That must have kept you warm as toast, lad, eh?' I say to him quietly, stroking his arm.

I fold the vest and lay it on top of the shirt.

I stand up and take a step back. I feel unsure about removing the clothes from the lower half of Barry's body. There's something slightly indecent, embarrassing even, about anticipating his nakedness. Yet, we're brothers after all, perhaps it doesn't matter. So I begin to untie his laces and slip off his sturdy walking shoes, breathing in the rich smell of top-quality leather before setting them to one side. Next, I pull off Barry's socks and put one inside each shoe to keep them dry. His feet are white and narrow, just like my own, the toes straight. Size ten, I notice, exactly the same as my size. I loosen the brown leather belt and unzip the warm moleskin trousers. They slip easily down over Barry's narrow hips, then over his knees and feet. I feel in the pockets; they're empty. I give the trousers a shake and fold them carefully. Then I hesitate momentarily before removing his underpants, noticing they're made of the same silky cotton as the vest.

My brother now lies totally naked on the ground. How slender and vulnerable he looks. Can a dead man be vulnerable? What more, what worse can happen to him than death? I'm overcome by a sudden impulse to hug him, aware that, other than brief hugs when we were together, this is my only chance to truly, physically connect with my brother. I kneel down next to Barry and clasp him in my arms, trying to ignore the beginnings of rigor stiffening his limbs.

'I'm so sorry, Barry,' I say, my voice sounding gruff, the emotion catching in my throat. Tears are spilling down my cheeks. 'I'm sorry we'll never get to know one another better.' I pause. 'Not ever now. I guess it just wasn't to be.'

I sob quietly for a minute. Then I undress myself quickly, and dress Barry in my own shabby clothes. I worry briefly that Barry will become cold and wet with only my threadbare sweater, lightweight fleece, and thin nylon anorak to protect him from the harsh weather, while I will luxuriate in the protection of my brother's fine navy jacket. It seems so unfair. If only, I think, I'd been able to apologise to Barry for the poor quality of the clothes in which I had to dress him. He certainly wouldn't think much of them. But no, there's no way to do that.

I check the Skoda car keys are still in the pocket of the fleece, and leave them there. Then I run my fingers through Barry's hair, ruffling it so the style is closer to my own, my fingers registering the silky, clean feel of his hair. I move my hands vigorously throughout Barry's hair in a circular motion, until it stands up in untidy clumps. From my own trainers, now on Barry's feet, I scrape some mud, and push it into my brother's pristine fingernails, rubbing more dirt onto the palms of his hands, and some onto the bottoms of the trouser legs. I step back to study my handiwork.

I'm shocked at how scruffy, how rough, how *inadequate*, this reflection of me looks. Not much better than a tramp. That must have been what other people thought when they looked at me.

Quickly looking down at myself now, I realise that I'm still naked. I'm freezing cold too! I hastily dress completely in Barry's clothes, starting with his soft white underclothes and working outwards. It's as if everything has been made for me, *made to measure*. Each item of clothing fits perfectly, the belt even fastening on exactly the same hole as fitted Barry's waist. The shoes, Cinderella-like, hold my feet in a precise, gentle embrace, such as I've never experienced before – the softness of the leather an exquisite caress.

Finally, I slip my arms into the warmth of the navy jacket. Inside one of its pockets I find car keys with a VW Golf key fob, just as I guessed. Barry's hire car.

I open the rucksack and briefly examine its contents: a bottle of water, the remains of a packed lunch, a small silver flask containing what smells like brandy, and a wallet containing nearly two thousand pounds in cash! I've never seen so much money, or such denominations. Until I met Barry, a twenty-pound note was a rare enough presence in *my* pocket. It would certainly look suspicious for me to be found in possession of such riches. The very sight of it scares me rigid.

In the wallet too, there are several bank cards, Barry's driving licence, an open, first-class train ticket from Newcastle to London – presumably for his return journey. Also in the rucksack are some sealed envelopes on which are written 'for Robert' in handwriting spookily resembling my own, but considerably neater. I decide to open them later. I take a couple of swigs from the flask and feel its warmth cascade down my throat, the heat spreading throughout my body. Although I've had little to eat all day, I have no appetite for the food. Never mind, the brandy provides some fuel for my flagging body. I take a few more swigs. Then I pack everything back in the rucksack and sling it over my shoulder.

Just in time, I remember to extract Barry's letter to me from the inside pocket of the fleece. I check once more that the key to the Skoda is still there and that all the other pockets are empty. I take one last, long look at my brother, and give a deep, deep sigh, which seems to end in a sob. It's as if I'm looking at my own corpse. Then, at last, I start to make my way down the path. It feels like a lifetime since I'd last walked it.

By the time I get back to the car park I'm exhausted and it's getting dark. The Peugeot and the Fiesta have disappeared, only my Skoda and Barry's Golf remain. My hand trembling, I aim the key at the Golf, and press the button. The car chirps and the lights flash in response. I get into the driver's seat and switch on the interior light. In the glove compartment are all the documents from the car hire company. I quickly check through them. The car is due back by six o'clock tomorrow afternoon and Barry has already paid in full – that's a relief.

A sudden thought strikes me. I step out of the car and open the boot. Inside, is a smallish, soft leather holdall, which contains a change of clothes, some pyjamas and a washbag – clearly an overnight bag. That will come in handy.

'Right, Robbie man,' I mutter under my breath. 'This is final decision time. Once you turn the key in the ignition, there's no going back. You're committed.'

I take some more gulps of the cold air to steady my nerves, then get back in the car and turn the key. The Golf purrs into action. Suddenly terrified, I turn it off again. I haven't worked this out. What am I going to do? Not just now but tomorrow, the next day and the day after that? Most importantly, where do I go right now?

There's no way I can return to the flat, never again. That feels strange, but there isn't much I'd regret leaving behind, so perhaps it doesn't matter. Wait a minute! What about that photograph of Len and Betty? It's the only thing that really matters to me. I feel a sudden panic. It hadn't occurred to me that I might never go back. For a moment I consider whether I could drive back there and sneak inside in the dark, to pick up the precious picture. No, of course not. That wouldn't make any sense at all. Far too risky. I feel like crying. *Get a grip, Robbie,* I tell myself. *It's only a photo. Close your eyes and you can picture them; they'll always be in your heart.*

Next dilemma … where to go now?

Well, Barry must have lived somewhere; I've seen his address on the various documents. I'll just have to check. What about my other choices? I suppose money won't be a problem. There's two thousand pounds just in cash. How scary is that? Maybe I can get one or two of those bank cards to work for me too. I'm going to have to learn about spending money; learn how to be Barry. The prospect fills me with more terror than pleasure. First things first though – there's *tonight* to organise. Concentrate on that.

After spending a few minutes familiarising myself with the car controls, I put the key in the ignition again, turn it, and the engine softly growls into life, almost inaudibly. I press the clutch and ease the gearstick into first, second, third, fourth and fifth. Then I find reverse. Phew, hurdle number one overcome.

Next, I move forwards slowly, wind my way down the rough track carefully, and begin the descent from the Cheviots onto roads of ever-increasing size, past isolated farms, through tiny hamlets, then villages.

In the first village of any size, I notice a phone box. Please God let it be working … There's no directory of course. Only one thing to do. I dial 999. I'm shaking from head to foot. After a minute a woman's voice answers: 'Emergency. Which service do you require?'

'Police,' I reply. 'Urgent …'

There are some clicks, and a minute later another woman's voice answers: 'Northumberland Police services. How can we help?'

'I … I've … erm … just been walking in the hills, the Cheviot hills, and … I discovered a man's dead body, just lying in the heather.'

'Is the man definitely dead, sir?'

'Yes, definitely. He's … he's cold. Um … and he's getting stiff. His eyes are open.'

I start to sob. It takes a moment before I can continue speaking.

'I … I can give you the map reference for the spot he's lying …'

'What is your name, sir?'

'It … it … look, it doesn't matter. I'm just a walker …'

224

'I need your name, sir.'

'Look, it doesn't matter. I don't know the man. I don't want to get involved. I came upon him by chance. I … I need to get to … erm … *Berwick* urgently. I'm expected there … and I'm late. This is the map reference. Write it down. You'll find him there …' I read out the map reference.

'Just a moment, sir. We need to know …'

I read the reference out one more time and ring off. My hands are trembling violently. I'm afraid I'm going to be sick.

There's nobody about, thank goodness, and it's now dark. If the police want to identify the caller, they'll probably search the route northwards to Berwick. That was my intention, anyway. *I'm* heading south to Newcastle.

It's all I can do to turn the ignition key and grip the steering wheel. I take some deep breaths and slowly steady my nerves. I drive, not taking in anything during the first part of the journey. Eventually I come to the junction with the A1 heading southwards towards Newcastle. How different this journey feels from the previous drive. Was it really only this morning?

Exactly what to do, where to go, *tonight*? That's the next thing to consider. I'm effectively homeless again, but surely no need to sleep in the streets tonight. I could afford a night in a comfortable hotel – that would help set me up … a warm bath, a good sleep, time to calm down and think about my possible options, make a plan, think about the short-term future. After that, there's the longer-term plan to decide too … but maybe that can wait for now. That's it, one step at a time …

Approaching the outskirts of Newcastle, I turn off the dual carriageway onto the first urban slip road, leading to a leafy, well-to-do suburb of the city. I know there's a Country Park Hotel there; I've seen it on a number of occasions. Never had I thought of staying there myself of course, but tonight, I decide, it would be just right.

I turn into the hotel car park and pull up alongside a bevy

225

of other expensive-looking cars. Well, at least both the car and I look the part now, in Barry's clothes – I'm quite the country gent. Apart from my hair, that is. I look all around; there's nobody about. Quickly, I douse some water from Barry's water bottle over my head, making sure it's well damp but not dripping. Then I use Barry's comb to smooth it back neatly. Job done. I pick up the holdall and the rucksack, lock the car and try to walk confidently into the expansive lobby, my heart thumping.

I'm Barry, I'm Barry, I repeat in my mind.

Back at school, I'd always done well in drama. When I was with Len and Betty, my favourite teacher, Mr Lewis, told me I had a real talent for acting. I never managed to carry on with it after I left school. Now's my chance to put that early promise into practice.

First off, you need to lose any remnants of that Geordie accent. Put on a posher southern voice; a London voice, I tell myself.

A slender young woman in an immaculate black suit stands alert behind the polished wood of the reception desk.

'Good evening, sir,' she says. 'How can I help you?'

My mind suddenly goes completely blank. I can't think of what to say.

The girl's pale blue eyes widen for a moment, her mouth briefly a round 'oh' of surprise, before resuming her bland, detached expression. She regards me with a puzzled expression.

'How may I help you, sir?' she repeats.

'Sorry … er … miles away … I'd like a room. For the night.' I stutter. Then quickly add 'please.'

'Do you have a reservation, sir?'

'Er … no … I don't … I've been out all day. Haven't had time to book a room. Haven't had time to shave either, I'm afraid,' I say, rubbing my chin.

'Oh I see,' she says indifferently. 'Well now, just let me have a look …'

She consults a computer on the counter, her long red nails clacking on the keys.

'Was it a double or a single, sir?'

'Single, double, makes no great difference for tonight. Just as long as it's got a nice comfy bed and an en suite, it'll suit me.'

She raises her eyebrows and purses her lips. 'Hmmm. Let me see,' she repeats, frowning, looking at her screen. 'Ah. Yes, we do have a double room on the second floor. It has a view over the gardens. That's available.'

'Well, that sounds fine, love.'

'Room 211,' she says, 'if you could just let me have your credit card for a moment, sir.'

I reach into the rucksack and extract Barry's wallet.

'No problem.' I smile, scanning the cards nestling in each neat division with terror. Oh God, which to use? I pick one at random and hand it to the receptionist, suddenly overcome with apprehension.

Oh no … what about the PIN? I think, panic rising. Maybe Barry's included the PIN on one of his sheets of information in the overnight bag. If not, there's just the cash.'

'Of course, no money will be debited until you check out in the morning, sir,' the girl says.

She places the card briefly in the card machine, and hands it straight back with a cool smile. Relief floods through me. I'd half expected the machine to shriek *'Thief! Thief! It's not his card!'* for all to hear.

'Thank you, sir. A buffet breakfast is included in your booking and is served until ten in the morning, and this is your room key.'

She hands me a plastic card and points out the way to the lift and stairs. I raise a finger in acknowledgement and head for the lift. What a relief to get through that horrible ordeal. Still, I'd managed to maintain the southern accent pretty well.

After struggling for a few minutes with the key card, I finally enter my room. It's nearly as big as my entire flat! I shut the door and gaze around in wonder. A vast bed with an inviting snow-white, soft feather duvet awaits me. I can't resist flinging myself on the bed and bouncing up and down.

The small bar and fridge contain an array of alcoholic and non-alcoholic drinks. There's a coffee machine on top too. Also in the fridge are a range of snacks, including a ready-made salad with a tiny tub of balsamic dressing, and a superior-looking French cheese and aubergine 'toastie', with instructions for heating it in the microwave. Suddenly I realise how hungry I am – I've eaten nothing but a small sandwich and a few scraps of Barry's picnic since early morning. I prepare myself a supper of the toastie and the mixed salad, with a bowl of ready-prepared fresh fruit to follow. I even open a tiny bottle of red wine.

Once I've finished eating, I have a long hot shower in the luxurious bathroom, making use of all the small containers of soaps and shampoos. Feeling fragrant, fresh and more relaxed in the fluffy white towelling robe provided, I recline on the bed to study the contents of Barry's bags in more detail.

The first thing I open is the envelope in Barry's writing, addressed to me as follows:

For Robert – to be opened only in the event of my death.

That's really chilling – he'd actually *planned* for the possibility of his death! Inside was a letter. Barry was a right one for letters, and no mistake. I grit my teeth and start to read.

Dear Robert,

I never expected you to have to read this letter, and had sincerely hoped you wouldn't need to. However, if you are reading this letter, my plans haven't quite worked out and I assume I have not survived our rendezvous. As you know I have been treated for severe kidney disease, so I felt I had to make some sort of provision in case the worst happened.

Although I knew there was a possibility that I might die

sooner than planned, I very much hoped that I would live long enough for us to get to know one another better. Sadly, that is not to be.

Among the documents attached to this letter, you will find:

- *Full details of my home address – feel free to live in my apartment for as long as you need or want.*
- *Information about my work and work address.*
- *Any other information that I thought might be useful to you, such as financial and legal documents, passwords, pin numbers etc., to make your future years more agreeable.*
- *If I am no longer alive, I want you to feel free to help yourself to anything of mine, including money. (Anaïs and Nina are well taken care of by our mother's will.)*

Robert, my young daughter, Nina, is the main beneficiary of my will. I separated from Nina's mother Anaïs a year ago. I hope you may be able to make contact with her and Nina in time. Their address and contact details are attached.

Enjoy the rest of your life, Robert – I did really want us to get to know one another and develop a truly close brotherly relationship. I'm sorry that was not to be.

Your brother,
Barry

Reading his letter brought home to me the reality of Barry's death. I was overcome with the sadness of losing him just a few months after finding him. How was it possible? I broke down and wept for the first time since finding Barry's body.

Investigating the large envelope further, I found it contained a variety of detailed and complicated notes and information. Importantly, on top was the address of his flat, and instructions on how to get there.

There was also a further sealed envelope addressed to me. Inside that, I was relieved to see that Barry had left the password to access his computer, a ticket for a left luggage locker at Kings

Cross station, keys to his flat, as well as the combination for a safe in his apartment, and the PINs for his credit cards.

Barry seemed to have thought of everything. Why, oh why didn't he make the exact danger to his health clear to me before? Why didn't he give me the information contained in this envelope? If he had, maybe I could have honestly explained the situation to the police immediately after finding his body.

What have I done?

Chapter 33

2004
Robert

Despite everything, I fall asleep almost as soon as my head hits the pillow, not waking until after seven the following morning. I hadn't realised just how exhausted – mentally, emotionally and physically – I'd been from the terrible, nightmarish, life-changing events of the previous day. I wake feeling awful: depressed, panicky, and most of all, deeply saddened by the loss of my brother.

I glance round at Barry's clothes and luggage, just to assure myself it hasn't all been a dream, a nightmare, that it has really happened; Barry really is dead, and for better or worse, I have swapped identities with my brother. This realisation fills me with sorrow and dread all over again. I feel my future of pretence and anxiety is now unavoidable. There's no escape.

I feel overwhelmed by sadness for Marie, my mother. All these years, it appears she has longed for me, her missing son, and now, just as Barry and I were preparing for me to meet her soon, it is Barry who is lost to her for ever. How cruel is fate? Will she blame me somehow for causing his death? I still ache to see my mother, but will the joy of that event be tarnished for ever?

I need to make a list of everything to do before leaving Newcastle – perhaps for ever. To start with, I must make myself look more presentable, more like Barry. So I decide to get myself a good, professional haircut, somewhere nearby after breakfast. I dress in a set of clean clothes from Barry's overnight case. Then I smooth the duvet and lay the entire contents of Barry's luggage out on the bed. I help myself to a sheet of hotel writing paper and a pen. I have to resist the impulse to help myself to all the top-quality – and free – paper and pens. Old habits die hard.

I write a to-do list: pay hotel bill, get hair cut and shave, take hire car back. Once my list is complete, I pack my bags, slipping all the essential information for the day ahead into an envelope and securing it in the inside pocket of the casual jacket I've found in Barry's bag. If I lose any of those vital numbers and details I'll be well up the creek, I think.

I stand in front of the mirror to check my reflection – I hardly recognise myself. The jacket fits me perfectly, hanging crisp and smooth, at once smart yet casual. He certainly had good taste, did my brother Barry.

I leave the rest of the luggage in the room and hang the 'do not disturb' notice on the outside door handle.

Downstairs, a young man in a dark suit hovers in the lobby and greets me with a respectful 'Good morning, sir.'

I respond with a friendly casual wave and continue into the bright, spacious breakfast room.

Around half of the tables are occupied. It's mainly elderly couples, and a few younger, single people, who might be on business trips, but what do I know? A friendly middle-aged woman in hotel uniform greets me and asks my room number. She offers me a choice of tables, asks whether I would like tea or coffee, and explains that I am to help myself to the vast array of foods on offer at the buffet.

My usual breakfast is no more than a slice of toast and a mug of tea. I stare at the long tables groaning under numerous different breads and pastries, cereals, fruits and yoghurts, cold meats and cheeses, as well as hotplates offering a range of cooked food. The choice and volume almost sickens me.

Once again, I have to resist my initial pauper's urge to take advantage and pile as much as possible on my plate and while I'm at it, to slip some pieces of fruit into my pocket, and perhaps to wrap some slices of the delicious-looking cheeses in a paper napkin … But then I remember. I have to train myself to think like Barry. What would he do? Would he snaffle whatever he could, because after all, he had paid for it? No, of course not. He didn't need to. If he was hungry later he'd just buy himself some lunch.

So now, consciously and determinedly in my Barry persona, I help myself to a modest portion of smoked salmon (which I'd never tried before), scrambled egg, a slice of a dark rye bread – new to me – and some fresh fruit salad. All of it tastes wonderful, along with two cups of the excellent fresh coffee. So this is what it is to be rich, to have *enough* of everything. Yes, I suppose I could get used to this.

I take out my to-do list and look at the first item: pay hotel bill. Now I'm anxious that I've written down and rehearsed the correct PIN for Barry's bank card. I remind myself that if any problem with the PIN arises, I have more than enough cash to cover the hotel bill. Despite that, failing to provide the correct PIN seems so revealing, so suspicious.

At the reception, the young man turns the card machine towards me.

'You're looking a bit anxious, sir. Not a guilty conscience, I hope!' he says. He smiles at me.

Oh God, he's guessed, he's realised! I think, my heart thumping.

233

'What? What do you mean?' I say.

The young man immediately loses his smile and looks remorseful. 'Sorry, sir, just my little joke. Not a very good one, I'm afraid. No offence intended.'

'Oh, OK, none taken.'

Now what the hell was the number again? Breathe, breathe, and think …

'Actually I hope I do get it right. I'm forever muddling up my PINs! There's that many of these blooming cards to remember, aren't there?'

He smiles, unperturbed – politely tolerating a rich man's joke.

Then I take a deep breath, key in the memorised figures and wait. I nearly pass out from lack of oxygen, I've been holding my breath for so long.

The card machine gives a little click, and then whirrs into action. The whole transaction goes through without a hitch. I gulp for air, afraid I'll faint with pure relief.

The young man hands me a receipt with a smile, wishes me a good day and urges me to return soon to the hotel.

Phew, not too effing soon I hope, bonny lad, I think to myself. *I just couldn't stand the strain!*

Just as I turn to leave, I remember item two on my to-do list: 'get hair cut'. I turn back to the young man and ask if he knows of a good barber's in the area.

'Oh yes, sir,' the lad says eagerly. 'There's a very good Italian barber in the high street. Casa something or other. Turn left immediately as you exit from the hotel's drive. It's just about half a mile down, on the left-hand side. You can't miss it.'

I thank him, press a tip into his hand and leave the hotel with some relief. It's definitely not an environment I'm familiar or comfortable with.

***

234

An hour later I'm reclining, my body rigid with tension, in a barber's chair in Casa Degli Uomini, while Saïd, a swarthy Syrian – not an Italian at all – massages organic oils into my scalp with gentle but muscular fingers.

'Relax sir, try to relax …' Saïd implores me.

I decide to indulge in a professional shave as well. Having noted how I'd hacked at my face with the hotel equipment, Saïd tuts disapprovingly. He shaves me enthusiastically with a ferocious-looking cut-throat razor. Then he wraps hot towels around my face, followed by cold towels to 'close ze pores'.

My hair is then snipped, washed, and dried. Saïd pauses and steps back to assess his handiwork for a moment. 'Is good, is very good.'

It is good too. I've never seen my hair – nor my face – look like this. Every hair is perfectly in place; gentle waves undulate backwards above my ears. The lines that had appeared on my face in the last few years seem to have retreated. My forehead is smooth, my jawline firm and masculine. I look ten years younger. I look handsome. I look like Barry. It's money well spent. I shake Saïd's hand and give him a large tip.

As I walk back to my car, a sense of possession, of entitlement, creeps into my thoughts. I try to resist it, but a feeling of calm and well-being settles over me, like a soft, comforting blanket. I expected to feel – perhaps I *should* feel – tense and anxious, perhaps even *guilty*. Yet I do not, or at least, not as much as I expected. Who is this Robert inhabiting my skin? Who thinks he is claiming – or perhaps *re-claiming* – what is his due, what has been his due for half a lifetime? I'm not sure I like him very much, but I'm committed to being him.

Next stop is Barry's car hire shop behind the station. It's a totally different outfit from the providers of my Skoda. I feel a twinge of sympathy for the guys at that car hire place. I wonder if they'll ever get their car back.

The lenders of Barry's Golf communicate a different ambience.

Impressive cars wait in the parking area. The Golf now seems a modest choice. Inside, soft, calming music plays. A young man behind the curve of the polished wooden reception desk looks up and smiles as I enter the office.

'Good morning, Mr Tully, how did you get on?'

Momentarily thrown by the question, I wonder what Barry might have told people about the purpose of his visit to Northumberland. Has he left a trail of evidence? I decide the safest option is to keep to non-committal responses. I remind myself mentally to keep to my London accent.

'Fine, thank you. I've enjoyed the driving up here – the roads are so quiet compared to London.'

'Oh, aye. We haven't got the jams of the South East up here – not yet anyways. A lot busier than it used to be, mind. So you found your brother all right up there?'

What to say to this? I'm seized by panic that renders me dumb. I gaze down at the written car hire contract, as if absorbed in its details, buying myself time to think of a suitable response.

'Mmm? Oh, no … er … no, unfortunately. Turned out he wasn't very well. Not well at all.' I feel a lump rising in my throat. 'He couldn't manage the long walk in the end.'

'Oh, that's a pity. Still, now you've explored the North East a bit, I hope you'll make another visit before too long.'

'Who knows, who knows?' I look up with a smile. 'Now then, full tank, right?'

'Yes, that's good, thanks, Mr Tully. I'll just give her a quick check-over and we're all straight. You got long before catching your train back south?'

'Just long enough for a bite to eat and a pint.'

'Good timing. Sounds like you planned that well.'

I'm grateful the height of the desk disguises any trembling of my knees.

The young man checks the car and I hand over the keys and a tip. I'm discovering the power of money to make friends.

'Thanks very much, Mr Tully. Enjoy the rest of your day. Hope to see you again up in these parts before too long. Have a safe journey home.'

***

The train journey to London is uneventful, but I'm filled with apprehension. My life has taken on a momentum of its own. I feel out of control.

I've rarely travelled by train before, and *never* first class in my entire life. I've never been to London, yet I now face living there, possibly for the rest of my life. Is it a life I want? Certainly I want to meet Marie, my mother. I want to get to know her and I want her to know me. I want to be loved by her, as I've never been loved before. But … what if she blames me for losing Barry? What if she thinks I've caused his death? *Oh Barry, why did you have to go and die, just when I was so happy to have you for a brother?*

I'm suddenly jolted back into the present by a uniformed woman leaning over me with a smile.

'Excuse me, sir, I said, "Would you like some coffee?" So sorry if I disturbed you. You were miles away!'

I stretch my legs out and sip the coffee (in a *china* cup, not plastic!) and have one of the biscuits brought by the attendant.

I use some of the remaining journey time to revise the information left for me by my brother. I need to become completely fluent in all the details of my new life. How different this life is going to be? How have I got myself into this situation? I'm so scared, launching myself into an unknown, unfamiliar vacuum, perhaps for ever?

***

At Kings Cross station I present the ticket at the left luggage office, and am handed a small suitcase in return. I call into Smiths for an *A-Z*. London might just as well be a foreign country for all I know about it. I'll need all the help I can get to familiarise myself with my new surroundings. Then I head for the short taxi queue, the address of Barry's flat written on a small piece of paper clutched in my hand.

Chapter 34

2004
Marie

'When did you last see him, Anaïs?'

'Well, ages ago, Marie. You know we're not really seeing each other at the moment.'

'I'm so worried about him. He's been behaving so strangely lately. He's not been himself at all. He hasn't been for some time, but recently he looks so ill. I'd really hoped that going on the rehab course would be the end of his difficulties. In one way it did help. At least, I believe he finally got the drugs problem under some control. I'm not sure if he totally cut them out. I begged him to so many times, Anaïs. Begged him …'

'I know you tried, Marie; no one could have tried harder. But he didn't really listen to anyone else, did he?'

'No, but now I'm thinking … even if he did seriously cut down … maybe it was too late … for his health I mean. He looks just awful and he's got no energy. He told me he'd been diagnosed as having some problems with his kidneys, but he didn't really

239

explain what that meant. He's always been a bit secretive, hasn't he?'

'I know he's seen a consultant, Marie, but he hasn't told me much about it.'

'Yes, he said that to me too. You'd expect the consultant to have discussed what *treatment* might be available, but Barry's said nothing about that to me.'

'Mmm. Me neither. I'm so sorry, Marie, I can see you're really worried.'

'You know he found his brother Donal at last, and that they've met up together, don't you, Anaïs? I'd rather expected Barry would have brought Donal to see me by now, but there's been no word from him for a week or more. I thought maybe Donal would at least ring me too. I do hope nothing's gone wrong with the arrangements. The plan was for them to meet up in the hills in Northumberland and spend some "quality time" – as he put it – walking together, and birdwatching and so on. Barry loved that part of the country, but I worry whether he could possibly manage a trip like that in his state of health?'

'Did Barry and Donal get on well when they met?'

'They seemed to, according to Barry. Poor Donal hasn't had a very easy or happy life, by all accounts, not happy at all, but Barry said he's not resentful or angry. He's not bitter at all. Apparently he's just thrilled that his family has been found, and that he'll be able to meet us all.'

'It's just amazing, Marie. All these years you have longed for him and thought about him, and soon you will hold him in your arms! You must be so excited.'

'Excited definitely. I can hardly believe it's real. I've been trying to imagine what he'll look like, what he'll sound like, what kind of person he'll be – and all I come up with is someone exactly like *Barry*! But of course, although they're identical twins, there's no reason for them to be exactly the same in every way. Donal will have had such a different life, such different experiences and

240

that's bound to have affected him. To be honest, Anaïs, although I can scarcely wait to see him, I'm a bit scared of meeting him for the first time. Does that sound idiotic?'

'Not at all. I can understand you being nervous. But I'm sure you'll forget your fears the minute you set eyes on him.'

Chapter 35

2004
Robert

My first ride ever in a black London cab, and my exhaustion soon catches up with me. I close my eyes and let the drone of the driver's cheerful commentary wash over me, spurred on with only the occasional response from me.

At last the taxi slows and stops in a leafy street. The taxi driver parks outside a large four-storey house. Is it Victorian, or perhaps Edwardian? I'm totally unfamiliar with London's house styles.

''Ere we are – Swiss Cottage, right? Nice 'ouse, mate, *very nice*! Be worth a bob or two, eh? Mostly Russians and Ay-rabs around 'ere I reckon. Filthy rich some of them lot are and no mistake!'

I murmur my agreement and hastily assure the driver that the entire house does not belong to me – I occupy only one of several flats in the building. I'm not sure why it's so important to me that this man – a total stranger – should know that, but somehow it is. Perhaps I haven't yet fully settled into my new persona – certainly I don't want to be thought of as 'filthy rich' as a Russian oligarch or Arab sheikh! I pay the driver and add another substantial (but not too ostentatious) tip. The man thanks me cheerily and drives off.

I stand on the pavement, my luggage around me, staring up at the building that is to be my home for the next few days. I look all around. Barry's neighbourhood couldn't be more different from the one I left behind in Newcastle. Plane trees cast mottled shadows in the evening sunshine. The street ends in a cul-de-sac two houses along from Barry's. From there, a footpath enters an expansive park beyond, a grassy hill creating a pleasant, open view. Large houses, each individual in design, with well-maintained front gardens, stretch to the right and left. There's no litter, I immediately notice. It's clearly an affluent area.

I gaze up at the house. Barry lived here, I remind myself; he actually lived here. If only he still did, and I was just paying him a visit. Sadness, never far away, washes over me in a tidal wave of mixed feelings. What am I doing here without Barry? Should I just turn around and go back to Newcastle? But no, my mother, Marie, lives in this city. I can't leave without seeing her. *Get a grip, Robbie.* I feel lost, helpless and frightened. I'm desperate to get to the safety of Barry's flat … but will it be safe?

I hold the keys at the ready, so tightly they dig painfully into my hand. I stare at them. One for the main front door and another two – a Yale and a mortice key – presumably for the door to the actual apartment. There's also another small key. What could that be for?

The heavy wooden front door has a metal letter box. Next to the door is a set of twelve bells, each with the number of the apartment and the name of the occupant beside it. Next to number 12 is the name 'Mr B. Tully'.

The front door open, I step into the downstairs hallway and

look around: a fine cream and black tiled floor, looked after. Clean too. Against the wall immediately to the right of the entrance, is a set of dark, wooden post boxes, arranged in three rows of four, each one marked with a metal label bearing the owner's name and flat number. This is important information, I tell myself.

I'm still holding the bunch of keys, my fingers pressing the large Yale key, which had let me in. It looks as though the very small key is for the post box. I try the key on the box marked with Barry's name and number. It opens immediately. Inside are six or eight envelopes. I tuck them under my arm and relock the box. So far so good.

In the centre of the hall is an old-fashioned cage lift, around which curves an impressive marble staircase, with a highly polished dark wood banister. Three doors lead off the ground-floor hallway. I guess apartment twelve will be on the top floor. I'm not a great believer in lifts – always feel a bit claustrophobic in them. I prefer to use the stairs, no matter how long the climb. Three floors is nothing. I pick up my bags and begin walking up.

Suddenly, from above me, I hear the sound of a door being opened and then closed loudly, followed by a brief jangle of keys. Rapid, thumping footsteps are heading down towards me. My heart gives a lurch, but before there's time for panic to set in, a well-built man of about my age appears, leaping energetically downwards. He's dressed in shorts, a vest and running shoes. He grins, jogging on the spot, and raises his hand in greeting.

'Evening, Barry, good trip?'

My heart thuds frantically in my chest. *Oh God, he actually thinks I'm Barry … Think fast, man, and don't forget the accent. Who is he? What's his name? What does he know about Barry, about me? Play for time …*

'Not bad, thanks,' I say with a smile. 'Glad to be back though … Still pounding those pavements are you?'

'Yeah, you know me, glutton for punishment. Well, *glutton* at any rate! Guess that's why I have to keep all this up. I see the beard's gone, Barry. Must be a woman exerting influence, am I right, eh?'

He doesn't wait for an answer. We grin at one another and he's gone. I stand limply, waiting for the trembling to recede. Is it possible? This total stranger thought I was Barry? He's never met me in his life, but he thinks I'm my brother. Judging from the sound his descending footsteps made, I guess he lives on the second floor. I make a mental note to look at the names on the post boxes again tomorrow, memorise them. I'll have to check what the jogger's name might be.

I continue up the stairs. Four doors on the first floor, and another four doors on the second, which is also where the lift has halted. That means only one flat remains at the top – trust Barry to have the penthouse! Sure enough, at the top of the stairs, the landing has only one door to a flat – number twelve. I like the idea of being the only resident on that floor; it's a relief, it feels safer. Opposite my door is what looks like a cupboard, bolted shut, perhaps containing cleaning equipment. The door to the flat has two locks: a Yale, and below it, a mortice. I take a deep breath and open the door to my temporary home. Thank God, I think, thank God, I've made it. At least I won't have to sleep on the streets tonight. That's something. I can relax – up to a point – for tonight anyway.

I walk in and look around. So this is where Barry lived. This is the place he called home. The apartment turns out to be spacious but less huge than I'd imagined, and simpler in style, which pleases me. Not exactly my idea of a penthouse, despite being at the top of the building. Stylish and tasteful, but fairly modest – I like that. More of an attic flat, fitted neatly into the roof space, the sloping ceilings making for interestingly shaped rooms. It feels a relief. I'd expected possible flamboyant, showy extravagance – this feels much closer to my own taste. So me and Barry are alike in more ways than one. I explore thoroughly, searching for any clues that may tell me more about my brother.

It's been a long day. It's late when I lock the door of the flat, and I'm very tired, but my mind is too agitated to think of sleep just yet. I'm getting to know my brother's home, but what do I really know of *him*?

I pull out the letters and other paperwork I'd found on Barry's body, in his luggage, and now in the apartment. I know there are still some brown envelopes I haven't opened, whose contents I have not yet examined. Maybe they'll contain some clues as to Barry's true motive in wanting to meet up with me – and particularly in initially pretending to me that our mother was *dead*.

I begin by looking through all the letters and documents I've already seen, just in case I missed some vital piece of information. It's well after two in the morning by the time I've pored over nearly all of them – so far, there's nothing particularly significant or helpful in any – but I'm not about to give up just yet. I turn my attention to the brown envelopes.

The largest has a file inside labelled 'Medical'. This time its contents really are interesting, and provide some new clues, or confirmation at least. There are copies of several detailed medical reports indicating that Barry has serious kidney disease, apparently most likely to have resulted from his addiction to heroin and cocaine over many years. I'm learning more about a sinister, frightening side to my brother's life.

Also in the medical file I find a glossy brochure advertising the facilities at a luxurious private hospital and clinic – in the country *just outside Newcastle*. Barry was clearly planning to have some treatment there. Why near Newcastle, rather than in London, where he lived? The only logical reason is to make it near *my* home, and deliberately remote from his. There is also a series of letters between Barry and a renal consultant. The final letter from this consultant, a Mr Harrington, is chilling in its pronouncement:

Dear Mr Tully,

Further to your appointment on 09/12/2003, I am sorry to have to confirm that your full assessment shows significant late-stage kidney failure. This is a serious and now irreversible condition, which unfortunately is often seen in long-term users of drugs such as heroin, as we have discussed on previous occasions.

Your kidneys are now functioning at only a fraction of normal capacity, and this is likely to deteriorate further. Your body is unlikely to be able to sustain this situation for long. Regular dialysis is not a long-term solution, and the only real option at this stage is a kidney transplant.

I must emphasise that while the seriousness of your condition means we will make you a priority for an available donated kidney, finding an acceptable match is likely to take some time, particularly due to your unusual blood type. The best hope, therefore, is a living donation from a family member. It is much more likely that a compatible kidney will be found within your close family than the general public. Ideally, the donation could come from a sibling, whose DNA and blood group may not only match your own closely, but who is also of your own generation. Of course this may not be possible, so we shall continue the search for a donated kidney representing a close match, whatever the family circumstances.

I will arrange for our specialist transplant nurse to make a home visit to discuss these issues further with you.

In the meantime, I must emphasise again how important it is that you refrain completely and absolutely from further

use of heroin, cocaine or any other drug not prescribed by a
medical practitioner, to prevent further damage.

Yours sincerely,
Tristram Harrington
Renal Consultant

I stare at this letter. I haven't seen many letters from medical consultants, but feel sure that such a direct and forceful message from a doctor is unusual. He certainly isn't beating about the bush. I reread it. It appears Mr Harrington feels he has to lay the facts on the line pretty harshly for Barry to take notice – and act on them.

So now it appears I have a clear confirmation for why Barry had decided to contact me after so many years had passed; why he wanted to meet me so urgently. He'd definitely received Mr Harrington's letter before we met for the first time and I saw it in Durham. So, Barry had been, in effect, terminally ill with kidney failure. He'd told me already that his only real hope of survival had been a kidney transplant, but that his rare blood group meant finding a compatible kidney was unlikely. Mr Harrington explained this clearly in his letter.

The only real chance was using a transplanted kidney from a *close family member*, he wrote. By some extraordinarily lucky chance, it happened that Barry had an identical twin brother waiting in the wings, and unknown to most people. *That was why he needed me.* Did Barry have any other interest in me? Probably not. Transplanting one of my kidneys into him would greatly improve his chances of normal life. He needed *my kidneys* – or one of them at least. That was probably *all* he wanted from me, I realise, at least initially. I now believe it may have been his sole reason for contacting me. For all he said he'd changed when he found he liked me so much. Yet now I have a strong sense that he must have hoped to 'befriend' me, perhaps 'butter me up' as a loving brother (or even *bribe* me if he'd found me highly motivated by monetary gain, which he didn't), and persuade me to help him live, by giving him one of my kidneys.

It's all starting to make more sense now. I wonder if the plan was to have my kidney secretly removed in the private Newcastle clinic, and immediately transferred to Barry's body. No chance of our mother dissuading me to go ahead with it – she wouldn't even know. He was basically planning to use my healthy, living body as a means of harvesting 'spare parts' for his own failing one – and if everything went to plan no one else need know about it. Medical staff would probably be told it was all to be kept confidential to protect the identity of the rest of the family, and maybe to protect our mother from anxiety.

I sit in a daze, deep in shock. Would I have done it? Would I have given my kidney to this man who was my brother, but whom I barely knew? I'm not sure. Talking to Belle, I think I'd decided I would. How could I *not* save my brother's life? The more I learned of my brother, the more he puzzled me. In the event, I was never given the chance to fully consider such a self-less, charitable act through to its conclusion – Barry had died after we had met only twice, and were about to meet again. He may have died on that hillside only minutes before we were due to meet for the third time, only minutes before I found him.

Despite the fact that Barry explained the situation to me, I have a sinister feeling that he'd had his plan all worked out long before he revealed it to me; long before he even tried to meet me. It's certainly not a comforting conclusion. Now I can think of little else. Yet, even though I've found a clear explanation for why Barry had wanted to meet me in the first place, telling me that Marie was *dead* seems unnecessarily extreme. Perhaps I'm starting to get paranoid. Yes, he admitted it was to prevent a meeting between Marie and myself, but knowing how manipulative he could be, I wonder if he was going to maintain that stance until well after the operation had been carried out. He'd admitted he thought that once she met me, she would try to stop me from donating a kidney to him; that she would dissuade me. After all these years of our mum longing to see me, might she have been reluctant to think of my life being put at risk – even to benefit her other son?

Whatever Barry's initial motivation in telling me our mother was dead, he had clearly changed his mind, and I wanted to believe that he had come to like me too much to deceive me. In the end, Barry never got the chance to carry out any part of his plan. He'd died before a transplant was possible – and here I was, in his home, trying to sort out the mess he'd left behind.

Chapter 36

2004
Robert

Gradually, the flat becomes a familiar, reassuring haven; I feel safe, and increasingly at ease there. The first thing I notice is how light it is. The apartment is bright and airy. It has views and aspects in every direction, allowing light and, sunshine to surge in at every time of day. I love the compact kitchen overlooking the garden, far below. It's equipped with everything I could imagine, and probably much I would never even have thought of. A glass door leads from the kitchen to an outside space cut into the slope of the roof – a cross between a large balcony and a small roof garden.

This immediately becomes my favourite part of the apartment. It faces south and west, the best directions for sunshine, and below is the long, narrow garden that goes with this house. Beyond, stretches a patchwork vista of gardens varying in size, belonging to neighbouring houses and those opposite – creating an extensive, park-like green space full of mature trees and shrubs. I'm astonished and delighted. I've never imagined London like

251

this, knowing the city only from clichéd photographs of landmarks and familiar scenes: busy streets with red buses, Big Ben, the Houses of Parliament, Piccadilly Circus and so on.

From this roof garden, London presents a much greener and more homely, domestic side to its character. I fall instantly in love with it, as Barry must have done.

The flat has two large bedrooms – I choose the back one for myself, while Barry had clearly slept in the front bedroom; the wardrobes and drawers are full of his clothes. The bathroom is modern and stylish, fully tiled, with a toilet, bath and separate shower. There's a spacious, comfortable lounge, with two large sofas, and a dining area adjoining the kitchen. A huge, flat-screen television and some complicated-looking sound equipment occupies a shelving unit in one corner.

So, here I am. I'm desperate to contact Marie and find my family, but where do I start? I can't just phone her out of the blue and tell her Barry is dead. I don't want to convince her I'm Barry, even if it were possible. I want her to know *me*, Donal. I'm too scared to go out. What if someone who knows Barry is suspicious, realises I'm not Barry? OK, the runner was fooled, but he was in a hurry, and it was quite dark on the stairs. I decide to give myself a few days to work out a plan.

I'm terrified of being discovered as a fraud, an interloper. The day following my arrival I don't leave the flat at all. I tell myself I need to spend time familiarising myself with its contents, like the electrical equipment, but actually it's because I'm so afraid of being found out. I've lost any confidence I may have had, and feel desperately nervous of the foreign environment.

***

After one more day, I risk putting a tentative foot outside the front door. I have to; I'm running out of food. I focus on gradually getting to know the immediate surroundings. Every expedition presents unimaginable, unpredictable hazards; every encounter is a new and often terrifying challenge. I never know who Barry was acquainted with or was close friends with, so I have to proceed extremely cautiously in every situation.

Greeting people – or responding to greetings – is a social minefield.

There are a few local – and expensive – shops nearby. A bakery, a café with tables on the pavement, a newsagent, and a greengrocer with an amazing, colourful array of fruit and vegetables, some of which I don't even recognise, wouldn't be able to name, and have certainly never eaten. I fill a carrier bag with a variety of fresh food and pick up a couple of takeaway meals to reheat.

Further afield is the large, busy shopping centre of Finchley Road, not yet explores – maybe one day. Once I've risked stepping out into the unfamiliar and intimidating further streets, I might begin going for some longer walks too, but not yet. There's plenty of green space and parks nearby.

On my way back to the apartment from shopping, I stop at the newsagent for a paper, and sit down at an outside table of the local café to read it. Even in early spring, it appears that people sit outside at pavement cafés. The harsh wind of the North East doesn't penetrate these London streets. As I sit, I take note of the large sign over the door: 'Oliver's Place'.

The proprietor, a cheerful and effusive man, greets me in a friendly and familiar way. Clearly Barry frequented this café.

'Hello there, Barry! Long time no see! I nearly didn't recognise you without the beard! Suits you better though, I think. It made you look older.'

It's clearly Barry's 'local', but I only dare take a chance on whether the man really is the proprietor after I hear another customer calling him by his name.

'Hello, Oliver. Yes, I decided the beard wasn't really *me*. Been pretty busy lately too. Had a brief trip away, but it's always good to be back. How are things with *you*, Oliver?'

There, I'd risked the name, twice, and wasn't met with the response I'd dreaded, a look of puzzlement or confusion – phew! Clearly he *is* Oliver.

I'm becoming expert at unspecific, bland conversations, which are basically 'fishing trips', aimed at getting necessary information for future reference. Back at home, I make detailed notes in a large notebook, commit the details to memory, practise verbal responses, like an actor preparing for a part – which is exactly what I feel like much of the time.

'Not bad, not bad,' Oliver replies. 'Sally's so much better now she's finished the chemo …'

So, his wife or partner is called Sally and had apparently been treated for cancer. Something to log in the notebook, and remember for possible further conversations. I don't know how long I'll be living in Barry's apartment, and may need such information.

'Oh that's good news, really good news – give her my best, won't you?'

'Will do, thanks, Barry. Now, what'll it be today?'

'A flat white and a plain croissant please.'

'Oh OK, branching out now, are we …?'

So what the hell would Barry have ordered? I wonder.

'Well, you know, Oliver, a change is as good as a rest …'

He raises his hand and nods, then disappears inside. I settle down to wait for my coffee and look at the newspaper. Despite the early season, the sun feels warm and gentle as I flick the pages. Definitely a different, softer, southern feel to the air than I'm used to. I begin to feel more relaxed than I've yet felt in London. The pleasant feeling doesn't last long.

Suddenly, my heart gives an almighty jolt. The feeling of calm evaporates instantly. A short piece on page four has caught my eye:

Northumbria Police believe they have identified the man whose body was found by hikers in a remote part of the Cheviot hills in Northumberland on Friday. He is thought to have been Robert

Carlton, aged 34 years, of Scotswood, Newcastle upon Tyne. Carlton, unemployed, lived alone. Neighbours said Carlton was a kind man who generally 'kept himself to himself'. One neighbour thought he may have had mental health issues and possibly problems with drug and alcohol abuse. The police have established that Carlton was brought up in care, but so far, they have been unable to trace any relatives. At this stage, it is believed that Carlton died of natural causes, but a post-mortem is due to be carried out. A car hired by Carlton in Newcastle was found in a car park at some distance from his body. Police are still trying to trace a walker who rang Emergency Services after finding Carlton's body, but rang off without leaving a name. It is believed he may have connections with Berwick upon Tweed.

'Problems with mental health issues and possible drug and alcohol abuse …' I read, frowning. *What sodding cheek!* Who said that, I wonder? Where did they get that idea?

It's like staring at a notice of my own death. It's disconcerting to see it in black and white – chilling, in fact. So that's how the outside world sees me, is it? Nausea washes over me. My hands, holding the paper, begin to shake. Oliver reappears and puts a tray on the table.

'Here we are, old son … I say, Barry, are you all right? You're looking very pale. You look as if you've seen a ghost!'

'I think maybe I have …' I fold the paper over hastily.

'Well, you just sit quietly a while. Have your coffee; you'll feel better. Unless you'd like me to bring you a drop of something a bit stronger?'

'No, no, your good coffee will be just right. I'll be fine in a minute, thanks, Oliver.'

He pats me on the shoulder affectionately and goes inside. I open the paper again and sit for a long time reading and rereading the short article. Then I fold the paper several times, as if any onlooker glimpsing what I've been reading, would be sure to identify me as the fraud and doppelgänger I really am. So I've fooled Oliver too. I suppose that's a good thing. It's what I have to do. Yet it leaves me feeling desperately sad. *Who am I really now?*

I drink my coffee and put the croissant in the carrier bag for later; another example of frugal old habits I find hard to throw off. In any case, my appetite has vanished.

A smartly dressed old lady at a nearby table makes eye contact and cocks her head towards a small Jack Russell dog sitting at her feet. The little dog is staring intently at me.

'I'm afraid Jacky's noticed you didn't eat your croissant,' she says with a smile. 'I think he's hoping you might have asked him for some assistance!'

'Oh I see, would he like some?' I rummage in my bag for the croissant. 'He's welcome to have a piece.'

'Oh no, no, absolutely not,' she says. 'It's very kind of you, but he's just *greedy*. The vet wouldn't approve at all. Jacky's supposed to be watching his weight, you know, but of course I have to do that for him. He's much more interested in watching *food* I'm afraid!'

'He's lucky to have someone taking such good care of his figure,' I say with a chuckle.

I finish my coffee and stand up. The old lady looks disappointed that I'm not going to prolong our conversation. I realise she must be lonely and probably enjoys engaging strangers – but seeing the newspaper article has really spooked me. It's left me feeling tense and drained. I need to get away. I need the safety of the flat. I need to be alone.

I wish her goodbye, pat the ever-hopeful Jacky, and leave a tip and payment for my coffee for Oliver on the table. Perhaps the brisk walk home via the steepness of Primrose Hill will help release the tension.

Chapter 37

2004
Robert

After the shock of seeing the article, I remain sealed in the apartment, afraid of being seen outside. I know it doesn't make much sense – who would associate me with the newspaper article – yet it's made me very uneasy. Right now, after seeing the name of 'Robert Carlton', seeing the reference of his dead body being found up in the high Cheviots in Northumberland in the paper, all I want to do is retreat to the safety of the apartment, put a pillow over my head and hide away.

Once I feel brave enough to risk going out again, I decide it should be safe enough to head along the nearby canal towards the zoo. It's surely unlikely that I'd encounter people who knew Barry wandering about there. There are several routes to choose from. Sometimes I veer off into Regent's Park around the edge of the zoo. The highlight for me is hearing all the growls and grunts, the squeals and screeches, the whoops and calls of the inhabitants – and trying to imagine which animals might be making each noise. Apart from those born here, London must be a foreign environment for them too, just as it is for me. Would they recall their tropical jungle homes, the humid swamps, towering trees, rushing rivers or vast savannahs from which they have come? Do they long to return or have they adapted, regarding this vast city as their home, as perhaps in time I might too?

On my homeward walk, I turn left up onto Primrose Hill. Near the bottom of the hill, clusters of parents chat together, while their young children play in a large sandpit. It's a happy, homely scene. I watch them for a short while – but what I really need is to expend some vigorous energy, to disperse the feelings of shock and unease at seeing the newspaper report of 'Robert Carlton's' death.

It's true that was what I'd *wanted* them to conclude when I exchanged Barry's clothes with mine, but seeing Barry's (*my?*) death reported in black and white that way, naming *me* as the corpse, is sinister and very unsettling. More than strange. Really creepy in fact.

That decision I made high in the Cheviot hills is irreversible. It's set me on a path of deception I can't be free of, unless I reveal what I have done. Will that ever be possible, or will I have to maintain a lie for ever more?

I head up one of the steep paths that lead to the top of the hill, pushing my legs hard to walk as fast as possible. Soon my lungs are expanding and my chest tightening with the effort. My breathing becomes laboured, making clouds of condensation in the cool evening air. It's a steep incline, but a short distance. Nothing like the two-hour-long climb uphill to meet my brother that day. *That day* … it feels like a lifetime ago, yet I realise that less than a week has passed.

One or two Lycra-clad fitness freaks pass me, running up the hill as fast as they can, glancing around for admiration, then jogging down again and repeating the challenge.

'Go on then you show-offs – you try running up the Cheviots

if you think you're so effing fit,' I mutter grimly.

At the rounded summit of the hill, people cluster to look at the view: London stretched out below – a vast cityscape as far as the horizon. Actually, there isn't a proper horizon – just a jagged skyline of towering structures piercing the sky; there's the Post Office Tower – once, years ago, that was thought to be unimaginably high yet now it looks almost *tiny* – dwarfed by newer giants like One Canada Square and the Cheesegrater, and many more under construction. I'm starting to learn their names and recognise them. London scares me, but it also fascinates me. It's so huge, so exciting, so different from anywhere I've ever experienced; it could be another planet.

I feel like a prehistoric caveman, or some isolated tribal jungle dweller who's somehow collided with modernity, confused, over-awed, and often terrified … Much of the time I feel minute and insignificant – like a tiny ant, paralysed by fear, unable to move, alone, yet surrounded by millions of others who all seem to know their way around, know one another – but know nothing of me, and care even less. Could this vast, anonymous city really become my home for the rest of my life? Do I want it to, or am I *trapped* here for ever more?

***

By the time I get back to my street it's starting to get dark. Outside our building, a small, elderly woman is trying to open the front door. With a large bag over one arm, she's having some difficulty coordinating the turning of the key with pushing the heavy door. I consciously remind myself to maintain my southern accent.

'Here, let me give you a hand,' I say, leaning forward to push the door. She gives a start and turns to see who I am. She peers at me with a look of some confusion.

'Oh, good evening, Mr Tully!' she says with an uncertain smile as I hold the door for her. I almost look round to see if she's addressing someone else; I haven't got used to my new surname yet. It doesn't quite feel like me.

'Yes, I had to check it was you! I see you've decided against keeping your beard – I'm so glad! I'm pleased to see you – it's very kind of you to help me. That door is so heavy. At least there are still *some* gentlemen left in the world!'

I let her go into the hallway ahead of me and watch carefully as she approaches the letter boxes. She begins to open the box for flat 2 and extracts a couple of letters. I notice the name printed on her box – 'Mrs E. Winkelman' – and immediately commit it to memory.

'Are you keeping well, Mrs Winkelman?'

She turns with a look of mild puzzlement on her face. 'Oh, er … yes, thank you, very well …' She pauses and looks at me quizzically.

'You seem in a very good mood, Mr Tully.' *Mr Tully* again!

'I've just had a lovely walk, so I am in a good mood, Mrs Winkelman. And please do call me … Barry.'

This time she looks at me with some astonishment. I'm getting more and more nervous. What's the problem?

'Oh! Well, er … yes, all right. Er … then you must call me Esther, Mr … I mean, *Barry*.'

She smiles at me and heads for the door of her apartment. As I start up the stairs, she turns and says hesitantly, 'Perhaps you would care to call in for a cup of tea or coffee some time … er … Barry?'

'I should like that very much, thank you, Esther,' I reply.

She gazes at me and shakes her head slightly. She gives me another shy little smile, looking distinctly bemused.

I continue up the stairs, my heart beating frantically with nerves following the encounter, but also smiling to myself. Clearly Barry had not made a habit of pleasant socialising with most of the neighbours. Never mind, Mrs Winkelman wasn't complaining; she appeared to like the new, friendlier version of Barry.

***

I realise I'm going to have to make some decisions about what to do next, and *soon*. I can't go on living as Barry much longer. I'm going to have to make contact with my family. I *want* to make contact with them; with my mother, with Anaïs and her child. I'm going to have to reveal who I really am.

My contact with the outside world and its inhabitants often feels stressful and even hazardous, full of uncertainties and risks. But despite this, I'm beginning to almost enjoy myself – the peace and solitude of 'my' apartment in particular, and the feeling of safety and security it gives me. It's my refuge. It's almost starting to feel like my *home*. I'm becoming accustomed to the various complicated and sophisticated appliances in the kitchen – and spending more time cooking for myself than I ever had before. Barry had clearly enjoyed cooking; as shown by the array of cookery books on the shelf in the kitchen. Now, for the first time in my life I can afford to buy freely from the huge range of interesting and wholesome foods available in the shops and markets nearby.

In my previous life, my occasional treat had been fish and chips wrapped in newspaper; cheap and cheerful perhaps, and not exactly health food – but I loved it. Now I'm starting to take pleasure in choosing vegetables, fruits and salad items, many of which I've rarely, if ever, tried before. Stir-fries are regular features of my evening meal. Quick and easy to make, and better for me … though I still get takeaways sometimes.

This evening I'm really going for quality; I select a piece of fresh salmon from the fridge, baste it with olive oil and rub it with salt, crushed garlic and a squeeze of lemon juice. Then I wrap it in foil and put it in the oven to roast while I prepare the stir-fry. I find the preparations calming. I choose onion, aubergine, squash, fennel and tomatoes, and begin to chop them. This will do me for two meals at least, I reckon. I put the radio on and hum along peacefully to the music. I've decided Radio Three is more in keeping with my new persona than the Radio One and Two programmes I previously listened to, mainly because they were the only reliable frequencies my cheap transistor radio could reach. Now I find myself recognising and enjoying the classical music much more than I'd expected.

Suddenly the doorbell rings loudly, causing me to jump with the shock. I almost drop the wok I'm holding and shaking like a seasoned chef. To my alarm, from the tone of the bell I realise the unknown visitor is not just downstairs at street level, but up on my floor – and at the door of my apartment! That means it's either another resident of the house, or someone who has already gained entry from outside. It also means I can't pretend not to be in – they're bound to have heard the radio.

Who can it be? Perhaps Mrs Winkelman come to invite me for that cup of tea? Surely she wouldn't be back quite so soon. It could be anyone, and I dread having to bluff my way through another stressful encounter. I struggle to control my beating heart and hectic breathing. I switch off the radio and the gas, take some deep breaths and head for the door. Should I call out to my visitor, I wonder, to find out who it is? No, just open it, I decide.

My hands are shaking as I unlock the door. Light from the landing engulfs me as soon as I open the door, and draws a bright halo around an attractive young woman with dark auburn hair standing at the threshold. I've definitely never seen her before, yet oddly, I sense there's something vaguely familiar about her. She regards me steadily. Her look is careful, enquiring, almost hostile; it is certainly unnerving. We stare at one another in silence for a few moments.

'Hello, Barry,' she says, with a distinct French accent.

Chapter 38

2004
Robert

My frozen brain slowly churns into action. That French accent … Of course, Barry's wife! *Oh God – think, think, man … you've seen it several times in all the information Barry left you …* My brain's frozen with panic. What was she called? What was her name? *Hang on a minute … yes … yes, of course … it was …*

'*Anaïs!* Hello! It's good to see you … erm, how are you? Have you come far?'

She looks a little surprised. 'I have come from home, Barry.'

Oh God, what a stupid bloody question! Of course she's come from home. Where else would she have come from? Home … where the hell was that again? Oh yes, *Blackheath*, wherever that is.

'Barry?'

'Yes …?'

'Can I come in, please?'

'Yes, sorry, yes of course you can, Anaïs. Please come on in!' Idiot! Leaving her standing on the threshold!

Trying desperately to control my frantic breathing, I press my back against the wall to let her past. She looks curiously at my face as she squeezes by. Is my greeting overenthusiastic? I search my memory for more information about 'my wife' Anaïs, and her relationship with Barry. If only I'd brushed up properly on the information Barry had left. Oh my God, can I really do this? Shall I just explain to her, tell her everything, tell her the truth …? No, not yet. Now's not the time. Play for time … *Think, think.*

I stagger after her as she makes for the sitting room. My legs feel like giving way. Were they estranged, separated, divorced? Wasn't there something Barry had said about disagreements? What was it? I can't quite recall what that was all about. Was it money? Was it to do with his mother, *our* mother? I'm sure he mentioned divorce. Maybe they just didn't get along? There was so much new information to take in. Suddenly my mind's a blank. I'm going to have to tread very, very carefully. Or … perhaps … could this be a first opportunity to explain the truth? It would be such a relief.

I glance at Anaïs's retreating back as she walks ahead of me. She looks to be in her mid to late twenties. Young, but definitely an adult – a young assured woman. *You have to treat her appropriately,* I tell myself. This could be very tricky. I sense complications. What dangers lie ahead?

Anaïs sits gracefully on one of the two sofas, yet her posture is defensive. Long legs crossed and facing away from me, arms hugging her waist. Her expression communicates a mixture of emotions: anxiety, confusion, apprehension. She looks at me, clearly waiting for me to initiate the conversation, but I'm at a loss. A drink seems a safe place to start.

'Would you like a glass of wine, Anaïs?'

She shoots me a look of surprise, puzzlement. This conversation is a total minefield. Panicky thoughts follow one after the other. I feel sweat prickling on the back of my neck, trickling an oleaginous stream down my spine. What had I said that was wrong? Possibilities rampage through my brain. Does she not drink? Maybe she's a reformed alcoholic, or teetotal, or doesn't approve of alcohol?

Was it the use of her name? Maybe Barry never called her by her name; maybe he always shortened it or used a nickname. The endless possibilities hit me, one after another in rapid succession, like fire from a machine gun. I'm hyperventilating again, feeling like I might pass out. Then suddenly her lovely face relaxes.

'Yes, OK, Barry, thank you. Wine would be nice.'

With dizzying relief, I head for the kitchen. What might she like? I have no idea.

'There's a chilled Sauvignon, or a Bordeaux red!' I call.

'You know I don't like Sauvignon, Barry,' she says, standing in the doorway watching me.

'Er … yes, of course, only joking. Bordeaux all right for you?' I ask apprehensively.

'Perfect,' she says, with a hint of a smile.

I fuss about in the kitchen, putting two glasses of Bordeaux on a tray. I open a packet savoury snacks and one of roast cashew nuts, and pour the contents into two small pottery bowls. I hope she doesn't notice my hands shaking. She watches as I carry in the tray and place it on the coffee table in front of her.

'It looks like you're getting very domesticated, Barry.' She smiles uncertainly.

'I can just about manage to pour some wine and put out a few nuts.'

I hand her a glass. She takes a sip of her drink and puts it down on the table. I push both the bowls of snacks towards her but she shakes her head.

There's another awkward silence. I'm nervous about initiating anything with her.

'Well?' she says after a minute, her eyes on me. There it is: the enquiry I'd sensed was coming. Her eyes bore into me.

'Well what?'

She gives a little frown of irritation. 'Well, how did it go with your brother, Donal? When is he coming to London? Marie is desperate to see him, you know that.'

Oh Jesus … I'm heading towards deep, deep water here. I can't delay responding indefinitely – there's nothing for it but plunge straight in. I stand up in front of her. 'Anaïs …'

She looks up anxiously. She fixes me with an intense stare.

I pace back and forth uneasily.

She stands up and blocks my path. 'Barry? Barry? What is wrong?'

We gaze at one another. I feel tears welling up in my eyes. I can hardly breathe. She frowns. She reaches out and touches my arm, her face a question.

'Anaïs … I'm so very sorry …'

'What? What is the matter?'

'I'm not … I'm not …'

The tears threaten to cascade down my face. I can't stop them. She grips both my arms with her hands, her eyes searching my face.

'Barry …? You are not *what*?'

'No … I'm not … I'm not *Barry*, Anaïs.'

'What are you talking about? Are you crazy? How not Barry? How can it not be you?'

'I'm Robert … Robert. I'm sorry.'

'Robert …? You are Robert? So where is Barry? What are you doing here?'

She starts to look around the room, a panicky expression on her face, as if she expects to see him hiding somewhere, and this is all a joke, a bad joke.

'Anaïs, I'm so, so sorry,' I repeat. 'I have to tell you … Barry … Barry is dead.'

Her eyes widen in horror. 'Dead? What do you mean?'

'I found him up in the hills, where we were supposed to meet. He must have collapsed. He was just lying there on the ground, on the heather – in the open. He'd told me he was ill, but I had no idea how bad he was.'

I break down in tears.

Slowly, cautiously, she sinks down onto the floor too, shaking her head from side to side in disbelief.

I hesitate to touch her; it doesn't seem my role. But I am drawn to comfort her somehow. I bend over and take her hands in mine. Very gently I help her stand back up. She puts her arms around my waist. She's trembling. We, strangers until this moment, remain in a sorrowful, tearful embrace for some minutes. Then I guide her backwards to sit on the sofa. I sit next to her, my body angled towards hers, facing her.

Clearly she knew about me, but I tell her the whole story of our fragile new relationship, Barry's and mine. It comes pouring out of me. How he wrote to me and asked that we meet for the first time in Durham. How he lied to me, telling me Marie was dead.

But then he must have had second thoughts and told me the truth. I explain to Anaïs what Barry told me about his drug addiction and his serious illness, and how he hoped I might agree to donate one of my kidneys to him, to save his life. He was afraid Marie wouldn't let me do that – risk my life by giving up my kidney, I tell her.

'I could have saved him, Anaïs. I had decided. I was going to let him have my kidney, because I came to love him. We only met twice, but he was my brother. And even though he lied to me at first, I think he loved me too, And now it's too late.'

I take some deep gulps of air.

'When I found him, just lying there, it was so terrible. I didn't know what to do. My brain was in shock I guess, frozen. I hugged him. I wanted to be close to him. I was so afraid I might be blamed for his death somehow. I couldn't just leave him lying there with no one finding him, maybe for weeks, could I? I wasn't really thinking straight. I decided to change places with him, change identity. So people would think it was me, Robert, who had died and was lying there, not Barry, just at first, until I worked out what I was going to do. That's why I dressed him in my clothes and dressed myself in his clothes.

'I took his car, leaving mine in the car park. I found a phone box in a village and rang the police. I told them I was out walking and had found a body. Gave them the map reference and then hung up. I was too scared to say who I was, nor did I give them his name.

'I stayed in Newcastle that night in a hotel, then I took Barry's car back to the hire company, and got the train to London. Barry had left me details of his address, and almost every aspect of his life: keys to his flat, instructions, everything … so that's why I'm here. I wasn't trying to impersonate Barry. It just seemed the only thing I could do at the time, until I could find the best way of explaining everything to Marie. Anaïs, I so want to see my mother. I don't want her to hate me.'

Anaïs listens silently to this account, her eyes wide, scarcely blinking.

'*Mon pauvre, mon pauvre …*' she says, big tears welling and then slowly spilling down her cheeks. I'm not sure if she means Barry or me.

'I knew Barry had met you in Durham, was it?' She pronounces it Durr-ham.

I nod.

'And also in York, yes? Marie knew too. He told her about meeting you. She knew he was going to Northumberland to meet you in the hills, Robert. In fact, it was she who told me that – Barry and I were hardly speaking.'

Anaïs shakes her head from side to side, looking thoughtful.

'Marie was very worried about Barry,' she continues. 'We both knew he was ill, but he hadn't explained *how* ill, or exactly what was wrong with him. He and I didn't get on well any more. I only saw him when he came to see Nina, our little girl.'

'He told me a bit about that,' I tell her. 'Anaïs, do you think it's all right, me staying here in Barry's apartment for the moment? It seemed to be what he wanted. He wrote me a letter and gave me lots of information to be read if he had … died. He must have known it was a possibility. You don't think it's wrong?'

'I think it's all right, Donal, for the next day or two. But we must arrange for you to visit Marie as soon as possible. She needs to be told about Barry. That really can't wait.'

I notice she slips into calling me Donal more and more. I like that.

'I agree. I can't wait to see her either. Will you talk to her about it?'

Before she leaves to go home, Anaïs and I agree she will have a think about the best way forward, and will ring me at Barry's apartment so we can make the arrangements. We must talk to Marie very soon. She can't be left believing that Barry is still alive, and busy occupying himself with arranging a happy family reunion with her long-lost missing son, when all the time, he is dead. I must meet my mother as soon as possible, and she has to be told of Barry's death. I long to meet her, I long for her to know me as her son, her Donal, but will that be possible? Will she think I have brought about Barry's death?

269

Chapter 39

2004
Marie

There's a strong sense of something strange going on. I'm not sure exactly what it's about. I've noticed there seems to have been an 'atmosphere' lately, but I can't say just what it means.

Barry, for one thing. What's going on with him? He's always been a bit secretive, especially with me, but even so, he doesn't usually let more than a fortnight or so go by without visiting me – or telephoning at the very least.

And now, having told me he'd found Donal, Barry must surely realise how desperately impatient I am to see my son, missing all these long years. Why doesn't he bring him? Surely he wasn't lying when he said he'd found Donal? That would be too cruel. Yet, as the days go by, I'm almost starting to wonder. I couldn't bear it if he's raised my hopes only to dash them by telling me he hasn't really found Donal after all.

I know Barry had planned one of his walking trips up in Northumberland, but he rarely allows himself more than a week's holiday – ten days at the most. He must have been back for a fortnight or even longer, surely, but I've still had no word from him. I do hope he's all right; he looked so unwell the last time I saw him. I pray he's not back on the drugs. He promised me he'd stay clear of them, but I know I can't really trust him in that regard – those drugs have such a hold on him, he can't resist them. Once an addict, always an addict, I suppose.

I'm thankful I've had Sylvia for company; she's always such a loyal friend. Sometimes it's hard to remember she's almost seventy; she's that lively and fit as a flea for her age. Just a bit slower on her feet these days perhaps. Friends are so important. I feel blessed in Sylvia and Elsie.

The three of us had a lovely day out together last week. It was a fine day – sunny and not too cold, for all it was still only April. We got the coach at Lewisham station, and an hour later landed in Tunbridge Wells, very fast and comfortable – and all for nothing with our bus passes! Such a good scheme. At least there are *some* advantages to getting older!

The journey's always a treat in itself. You see a different part of London, and then out into the countryside, which looks so beautiful at any time of the year, but especially in the spring. Everything starting to burst into life and colour. I love it.

So there we were in Tunbridge Wells. I like the quaint country feel of the town. It's not too big for walking around, and there are some lovely shops to explore – though *'a bit on the posh and pricey side'* according to Elsie. Anyway, we were mostly just window-shopping – only buying a few knickknacks, some little presents for the family. It's not as though any of us is hard up nowadays, but I suppose we've all spent so many years being careful, looking after the pennies, it's hard to break the habit.

After the shops, it was off to our favourite pub for a good lunch of fish and chips. Eddie, the landlord, is a cheery soul. He always remembers us and gives us a warm welcome – literally! – a special table by the fire. We were practically melting!

So many new and interesting dishes on offer these days (Eddie says he's had to employ a Latvian chef!), but in the end we tend to prefer the traditional old favourites. The others noticed I didn't have my usual appetite that day, what with expecting to see Donal in a few days. Anyway, we worked off the meal in the afternoon, with a gentle walkabout and then sit on a sunny seat in the park, enjoying watching the children playing. It reminded Elsie and me of when our own children were small, and all the little tricks they got up to.

A dark cloud of sadness threatened to overtake me then, as I think of Donal and all the lost years. The longing for my precious boy has never ceased – never – and since Barry said he's been found, that longing is stronger than ever. Surely Barry is telling me the truth? Surely I will see my Donal soon. Sylvia and Elsie understood why I was so distracted by my thoughts on our day out. They're such good friends.

After a while, when the sun had gone and the afternoon started to grow cool, we found a cosy café and treated ourselves to a pot of tea and a piece of cake before the journey home. We all agreed how important it is to get away from time to time. Sylvia's been on her own for most of her life, and Erna's passing has left a huge vacuum in mine. Elsie's lovely husband, Greg, died of a heart attack two years back. He was only fifty-seven, poor love, and of course the children have all flown the nest now, so *she's* on her own at home as well. It does her good to get out. It does us all good.

***

Anaïs rang me this morning to ask if she can come to see me tomorrow, in the afternoon at two o'clock. I'm glad to hear her voice again – what a lovely girl she is – but oddly, she sounded a little different, a little strange this time. She paused before each sentence, like she had to think carefully about every word she spoke. Very unusual – she's usually so spontaneous. Also, it's unlike her to make such a formal 'appointment' to visit me. She knows she's welcome any time. I told her so.

'Any time will suit me fine. I'm always happy to see you – you know that. Are you coming on your own, lovey?' I ask her, hoping she'll bring Nina with her – she's so precious to me. Anyway, Anaïs pauses for quite a while as if she really has to think about it.

'No, I won't be coming on my *own* … erm … your … son's coming too' she says carefully at last. Well, that's an odd way of putting it – *your son* – isn't it? They must have had another argument. It's so sad.

'Shall I ask Sylvia to join us then?' I ask her. This time she answers straightaway.

'No, Marie, not today, if you don't mind. We just want to speak to you on your own this time, just the two of us.'

How mysterious she's being today!

'All right then, my darling, see you at two o'clock.'

It's unusual for her and Barry to visit me together these days. In fact, I can't remember them ever doing so since they split up. Maybe it's good news? I can only hope it is, but something in Anaïs's tone suggested it wasn't. Could it be something to do with Donal … some problem? I do hope not.

Well, at least I'll be able to ask Barry all about Donal. Maybe that will put my mind at rest at last.

***

I lay a tray with tea and a lemon cake I'd made a couple of days before. Lucky it's still fresh. I like to have something baked in case of visitors – and if no one comes, Sylvia and I always manage to finish it off between us! We're neither of us bother about dieting or silly ideas like that. Anyway, I've always been thin myself. Even in my older age I never seem to put on any weight. Sylvia isn't as slim as she used to be, but just 'comfortably rounded' is how she puts it.

The sound of the bell comes as such a shock that my hands are trembling when I fumble with the key to open the front door. I must have got more worked up than I realised after speaking to Anaïs in the morning.

Chapter 40

2004
Robert

I've seen no further reports about 'Robert Carlton's' death in the newspaper, so that aspect of the story has gone quiet. Probably a good thing. Allows me to feel more calm and ready – ready for the next steps in my return to the family fold.

After breakfast, just as I'm starting to think about the best way of making further contact with Anaïs, the phone rings.

'Donal, it's Anaïs. I've been thinking. We can't leave it any longer. We absolutely must arrange to see Marie and tell her about Barry, as soon as possible.'

'I agree ... I'd just been thinking that too. We really can't delay any longer.'

'No, but it's bound to be a huge shock. We must be careful how we do it,' she says.

'So ... how shall we start? What do you think we should we do first?'

'I think I will phone her today, and suggest we come to see her tomorrow, maybe in the afternoon.'

'Yes. That sounds good,' I say, absolutely terrified at the prospect.

'So we'll go to see her together, unless you'd rather talk to her on your own, Donal?'

'No, together is better this first time, I think, Anaïs. I may be her son, but I'm a stranger to her. It may be very stressful – for both of us.'

'However we do it, Barry's death is going to be a terrible blow for Marie. At least she will be so happy to have found *you*. Can you even imagine how she has longed for you?'

'I hope she'll be happy about being reunited with me. But in the circumstances, she may regard me as something like an evil omen, returning to her after all these years of longing, but in doing so, bringing about the death of her other son.'

'No! Don't say that, Donal. You did not cause his death in any way. You can't take the blame for that – and Marie will not blame you either; never, never, never – I'm quite sure of that. I know her very well – we are very close. It's very, very tragic about Barry, but he brought it completely on himself. It is not your fault. Anyway, maybe we need to talk a bit more together about how exactly how we tell Marie, do you think?'

'Yes that would be helpful, but is there time if we're going to speak to her so soon?'

'If you come here for a simple supper tonight. Can you do that? Nina will be here, but she goes to bed about half past six or seven o'clock, so we could talk then for a while. Would that be all right for you? I'll tell you how to get here.'

I love hearing Anaïs's voice. Her French accent charms me. I know so little about her, but it's as though through hearing her voice I can picture her face.

Anaïs tells me her address in south London and gives me instructions how to get there. For me, the prospect of a visit to her home is exciting and frightening in equal measure.

I feel a need to prepare myself. Somehow, I want to try to familiarise myself with this intriguing sister-in-law I've met so briefly. I search everywhere in the flat for photographs of Anaïs – in drawers, among papers, in the safe – but I find not a single one, not even any of Nina, nor Marie. Barry appears to have erased mementos of her – and all of his family – from his life. What a strange enigma my brother was.

I search for something suitable to wear for the visit, aware that I'll be wearing clothes that belonged to Barry – Anaïs's ex-husband – and that feels strange. Is it inappropriate? Perhaps I should go out and buy a new outfit? But how ridiculous, when there are stacks of clothes in Barry's wardrobe – more than I've owned in my entire life. In any case, there's no time to go clothes shopping, not if I'm to get to Anaïs's house in time for an early supper. I'm going to have to wear something of my brother's for the evening. I just hope I don't choose something that looks wrong, or causes offence in any way.

After trying on several outfits and studying myself in the full-length mirror, I settle on a pair of light brown casual trousers that look quite good on me. Then I come across a maroon brushed cotton shirt folded on a shelf in the wardrobe. It looks brand new. In fact, it *is* brand new! When I unfold it, I notice the shop's label is still attached. I try it on and it looks fine with the trousers. I know it's a twenty-minute walk from Blackheath station, and I'll be returning in the late evening, so I take a grey woollen sweater in a bag and put on a lightweight linen jacket.

***

If I wasn't so nervous, the walk from Blackheath station to Anaïs's house would have been enjoyable. They live in a leafy street of pretty, but modest, semi-detached houses, about a mile from the station. It's a quiet residential street – a cul-de-sac, so no through traffic. Children are out playing on their bikes and in the gardens.

Anaïs's front garden is colourful with a mass of bright flowers.

I stand on the step, my heart jittery as I wait for them to respond to the bell. After a minute, there's a lengthy jangling of keys as someone unlocks the door, followed by the thud of a bolt being pulled back at the top, and then the bottom of the door. Is everyone in London so security conscious?

Anaïs opens the front door, carrying a little girl of four or five tucked into her hip. She smiles and leans forward to kiss me, the formal French way of greeting: one cheek and then the other. Can she hear the hectic thumping of my heart? Nina watches me with big eyes, her finger stuck in her mouth.

'Nina, this is Papa's brother, Donal,' Anaïs tells her, as I follow them inside.

'It's Papa.'

'Not Papa, sweetie, it's Uncle Donal.'

Nina regards me cautiously, suspiciously.

'It's good to see you again, Anaïs,' I stammer, handing her a bunch of flowers I bought at the station. She looks surprised.

'Oh, Donal, they are very beautiful, thank you. Look, Nina – aren't they lovely? I'll put them in water.'

'Pretty,' she says.

I take off my jacket and Anaïs puts it over the banisters. She turns and suddenly stops mid-step, her eyes wide, one hand holding my arm gently.

'Oh …!'

I look around to see what has caught her attention, and then realise it's *me* she's looking at so intently. I immediately fear I've made some terrible error of dress code.

'You are wearing it.' She places her hand on my chest. Her touch sends shock waves through my body. I gulp and hold my breath.

She must have noticed my look of confusion.

'That shirt. I gave it to Barry. It's so long ago and he never wore it. I thought he'd thrown it away. Perhaps because I gave it to him.'

She looks at me, a sad smile on her face.

'I'm so sorry, I didn't know. I shouldn't have worn it … I just didn't have anything else to wear.'

'No, Donal, how you could know? I'm pleased you did wear it. It suits you.'

'Well, thank you. It's a lovely shirt.'

Nina is standing at a slight distance, closely watching us together, looking a little puzzled.

We continue into the sitting room. Anaïs does an expansive sweep of the room with her right arm, as if to indicate 'sit where you like'.

I sit on the floor, and hand Nina a box of little figures and animals I bought for her at Charing Cross station. She tips them out on the rug and smiles up at me for the first time.

Anaïs kicks off her shoes and sits opposite me on a low velvet sofa, her legs curled underneath her. Nina heads off into another room.

Alone with Anaïs for a few moments, I'm able to look at her properly for the first time. She's slender in close-fitting jeans. A casual top of vibrant colours in abstract patterns give her an exotic look. Her hair is dark, but glinting with a subtle auburn tinge from the light behind her. Her face is delicate, with a smooth forehead, high cheekbones and large, dark eyes.

Nina brings in three little toy figures. She puts two down on the low table and hands me the third. She laughs when I make the toys 'talk' to one another.

'*She likes you,*' Anaïs mouths at me.

Conversation between us is a bit self-conscious and stilted at first, but after a while, the atmosphere softens; we relax together. Nina trots in and out of the room, bringing things to show me. Anaïs watches me pensively.

'Have you seen any more articles in the newspapers, Donal? Do you think there has been an inquest yet? Are they going to investigate his death further? You know, look into exactly how and why he might have died?'

279

'Not that I know of, not yet. I'm buying a newspaper every day and making sure to look carefully to check for any more reports.'

'We must think carefully how we tell Marie, don't you agree? It will be such a shock for her, so terrible. Oh la-la – *la pauvre!*' She shakes her head and dabs at her beautiful eyes with a tissue. 'Well, let us not talk about it more just now,' she says, indicating Nina with her eyes. 'Now, it is time for supper – no, Nina? Come, Donal, you sit down here at the table. I must just finish the main dish – one or two minutes. Nina – please come to help me.'

I sit, as Anaïs indicated, to the right of what appears to be her place, and opposite Nina's chair, which has a cushion on it to boost her height.

After a minute Nina appears, carefully carrying a wooden bowl with a green salad. Her face is a picture of deep concentration as she climbs on her chair to place the bowl in the centre of the table. I wink at her and she smiles shyly, before dashing back to the kitchen.

The clatter of dishes and pans, mingling with the soft murmur of Nina and Anaïs's voices, drifts through to me. A homely, domestic sound. After a few minutes, Anaïs reappears, carrying a large earthenware dish, from which emanates a mouth-watering aroma. She sits down and smiles at me. Nina follows.

'*Piperade!*' Anaïs announces with a little smile. 'A traditional Provencal dish. Onion, garlic, peppers, mushrooms, tomatoes and beaten eggs. Very simple, but very tasty. Nina, please pass the bread to your uncle.'

'Wonderful. It smells delicious.'

Anaïs glances up at me, as if checking my comment was genuine. She gives me a small smile.

The fragrant, savoury mix is truly delicious, and instantly becomes one of my favourite meals. Served with a green salad and crusty French bread, it is perfect.

To finish, Anaïs has made a crème brûlée, crisped under the grill. I thank her for going to so much trouble.

After coffee, I read a book of Nina's choice – about a family of elephants living in the jungle. I love the feel of her warm little body on my lap, her head resting trustingly against my chest. Then Anaïs takes her up to bed. She seems to settle to sleep quickly. I'm conscious of not wanting to overstay my welcome.

In the sitting room, Anaïs and I get straight down to discussing how to talk to Marie. We ponder at length together how Marie might react – on the one hand, to news of the death of her one son, Barry, and on the other, to the sudden reunion with her other, long-lost son, Donal. How cruel is fate to give my mother the gift of one child, apparently so desperately longed for over thirty-four years, while at the same time snatching away her other child – flawed, problematic and difficult, but still deeply loved by Marie nonetheless.

I have to keep reminding myself that this is Barry's ex-wife, that there has once been a romantic relationship between them, one that subsequently became deeply troubled. The possibility of domestic abuse at Barry's hands has been alluded to, even by Barry himself.

As the evening wears on, we become more relaxed with one another. Conversation flows more easily, despite the fact that I'm careful, and nervous of saying the wrong thing somehow. Still, we begin to talk as friends, ranging many topics. She's much more travelled than I am – I've barely left the North East! I'm happy to listen to her anecdotes of adventures she's experienced when younger.

We both share a love of books, the countryside, and we each discuss some of our favourite films. She even laughs at some of my jokes.

When it's time to go, we embrace with genuine warmth rather than French formality – on my side at least.

'Goodbye, Donal,' Anaïs says, looking directly into my face. I hesitate by the door.

'Thank you very much, Anaïs, it's been a really … special

'evening,' I say sincerely, feeling the inadequacy of words, the potential for misunderstanding.

'Yes, it's been good to spend time with you, Donal. I have enjoyed our evening together.'

I edge on to the outer doorstep. Anaïs stands by the front door, smiling, yet gazing at me with a slight frown, as if trying to puzzle me out.

'So, Donal ... at least now, we have a plan,' she says, following me outside. We stand facing each other, compressed by the limited space. 'I will come to the flat tomorrow and we can go together to speak to Marie.'

I have a sudden thought.

'What about *Nina*, Anaïs? Will you have to bring her too?'

'Oh no. It's good that you think of her, though. Nina has school. That's why I arranged to meet at two. We can concentrate completely on talking with Marie. Also the school is not far from her house.'

'That's good – well done. You're very organised.'

'It won't be an easy meeting. We will have to tell Marie about Barry first. That will be the hardest part. Of course, she will be so, so happy ... about *you*, I mean, but also so very, very sad, about Barry.'

'I know, thank you for making the arrangements, Anaïs, but I dread having to cause her such distress.'

'Yes, it is horrible. But she is very strong, I think. You will see.'

I raise my hand in a final greeting and begin to walk away. As I turn briefly by the garden gate, she lifts her hand suddenly towards her face, as if considering whether to blow me a kiss, then pausing uncertainly. The raised hand gives me a last wave and Anaïs gently closes the front door.

Chapter 41

2004
Marie

The doorbell rings and gives me a start. I should have left the front door open for them, but Barry's always urging me to keep it locked for security and it's become a habit. I hurry to open it, feeling so excited to see them both. Especially Barry today – he's going to tell me all about Donal, and when he's going to bring him here. I can't wait!

The two of them are standing on the doorstep. It's so good to see them together – happens so rarely these days, sadly. I open the door wider. Anaïs is in front, and Barry hanging back a bit. He's looking down, as if he's anxious about something. That's not like Barry; it seems a bad sign, I think. Immediately I start to wonder if something's not right. I'm wondering if he's done something he doesn't want me to know about.

Anaïs hugs and kisses me warmly, as usual, and then steps around me into the hall. Barry follows, still looking down – but as he reaches me, he suddenly throws his arms around me and draws me into a huge embrace. He nearly lifts me off my feet. He clings to me tightly, as if his life depends on it. I can feel his chest kind of convulsing, almost as though he's holding back tears.

'Hello, son … hello, my dear darling,' I say, though the words are muffled because my face is buried in his chest. I can hear his heart beating. How affectionate Barry's being today, how emotional. It gives me joy; he's not often so demonstrative.

'Mum, Mum …' he says, stroking my head close to him – and then I realise he's *crying*.

'Barry …?' I manage to get out, starting to feel increasingly worried now. What's happened? What's wrong?

'Mum, Marie, Mother …' He gulps through his sobs. Now there's an uneasy squirming feeling in my stomach.

'I'm sorry … I'm so sorry …' Barry repeats.

I prise his arms from me and push him back and upright. It's hard, him being so much taller than me. It takes all of my strength, but I need to look at him properly. What does he have to be so sorry about? What has he done? He's trembling all over, poor lad, the tears running down his face. He covers his eyes with his hands. His whole body is racked with the sobs. I glance round at Anaïs, and see she is crying too. Fear sends little sharp spikes through my heart. What on earth is going on?

And then suddenly it comes to me. Suddenly I know – and yet how could I know? How could it be? Could this hope, now starting to leap in my heart, be real? I stare at his face … yes, is there is something? Is there a difference? A softness? Is it possible? Is it really possible?

'Donal …?' I whisper. 'Donal … is it you?'

For a minute he can't answer – just makes a gulping sound that shakes his whole body.

'Robert, is it …?' I try.

'Yes, Mother, it is … yes, it's me, Donal … it is … I'm so sorry …'

His words come out as a strangulated croak. They take a while to sink in, for the meaning of them to be real.

Then I hear my own words, as if they come from someone else. I howl them at him; I howl so loud my throat hurts.

'Is it really true? Can it be? You're Donal? My Donal? Are you come back to me after all these years? My Donal, oh my dearest boy!'

I reach my arms out to him and we embrace again. We hold each other. I cling to him, to my precious son, and we are both crying, and Anaïs too. And she comes and hugs us. The three of us, bathed in one another's tears, holding each other, as in some strange dance, a dance of sheer unbelievable joy.

'But, Donal,' I whisper at last, 'why did you say you're sorry, when you've brought me the greatest happiness imaginable? Why are you sorry when you've brought me this wonderful, wonderful miracle?'

He takes a deep, juddering breath. 'Yes, Mum, being here with you *is* a miracle, an answer to prayers I've been saying silently over and over again without even knowing it, these last thirty years and more – but … but, Mum, I have to tell you something …'

I stand back for a moment to look up at his face. There's something not right. I can feel it. I can tell. Fear clutches at me.

'What? What is it? Something … bad?'

I'm shaking all over.

'I'm sorry, so sorry, Mum … something sad, so sad …'

He sounds like he's choking.

'Tell me, Donal, you have to tell me.'

'Mum, I'm so sorry that I bring you a great sadness mixed with the happiness of our reunion.'

'What possible sadness can there be when you've made me so happy?'

Anaïs comes close to us both and speaks softly. 'Come, let's move to the sitting room. Let's go and sit down.'

So we all go in and sit down in the sitting room. I can't take

285

my eyes off him, my Donal. Him, who I've thought about, longed for, prayed for all this time for as long as I can remember. I'm afraid it's my mind playing tricks. Perhaps I'll wake suddenly and find it's all only a dream. But I pinch myself and the truth is still there. Donal is here with me, and I recognise him – I'd have known him anywhere. I see the baby in him. It's still there – it's not a dream. Donal has really come. He's found me. I will never, ever let him go again, never.

'But where is Barry?' I ask.

Donal goes very pale. He tells me that Barry had written to him two months ago. He describes how he'd been unsure whether to trust the contents of Barry's letter at first; he'd wondered if it was some sort of cruel hoax.

As he talks about their meeting in Durham I feel an icy cloud of fear enveloping me. This is not a story with a happy ending. I can sense that. But I listen intently to Donal's description of Barry's odd appearance, how they'd got on well, and had agreed to meet again in York shortly after. Barry had given Donal some money, and suggested they meet in one of his favourite places, high in the hills of Northumberland. A chance for them to spend a few days together, Barry had explained, to really get to know one another.

'Yes, he loved Northumberland. I think it was a relief from all the tension he felt in London,' I say tentatively.

'I went to the agreed remote meeting place,' Donal tells me. 'I'd been nervous, frantically excited to be seeing my brother again. Never having had any sort of family, it meant such a lot to me to think of having a twin brother. I'd hoped we would form a close and permanent relationship, and see each other regularly. I'd hoped too, that it would lead to discovering other members of my birth family, especially to finding *you, my mother.*'

At this point I interrupt his account to say how much I'd always hoped that he'd had a good and loving adoptive family. That would have been some comfort for me, I tell him, but through the investigator's research, we'd learned that this hadn't been the case.

'This news greatly upset me, darling Donal. I was heartbroken.'

Anaïs comes and sits next to me. She takes my hand in hers, holds it against her face and kisses it. Tears have begun to stream down her cheeks again. I sense some further news, *bad news*, which she's aware of – she *and* Donal – but I am not, is about to be imparted to me. Apprehension surges through me. My heart is beating fast, my breathing rapid and shallow.

While Anaïs holds me, Donal describes in detail his arrival at the car park lower down the rugged hill, of his laborious climb up the path to the appointed meeting place. His words come slowly, effortfully, as if he were reliving that strenuous climb. At last he came to the top, to the site of their meeting place. At first there was no sign of Barry. With every word, my terror of what is to come is growing.

Donal tells me he searched the whole area several times. Before giving up, he decided on one final attempt. This time, he spotted what at first had just looked like a jacket left in some heather, but as he neared it, he realised it was a *man's body*. He knew at once it was his brother; it was *Barry's body*.

I give a loud moan. I can't help it – a howl like that of a tortured animal, a desperate cry of sorrow. Anaïs hugs me tighter still. Donal comes and sits on the floor at my feet. He puts his arms around my knees and rests his head on my lap, tears flowing freely.

'I'm so sorry, Mum!' he sobs. 'If I'd got there sooner, maybe I could have helped him, called an ambulance, done something – anything. But it was too late. He was already dead; he was already cold.'

For a while I cannot speak; the pain, the horror is too great. I stroke my Donal's head and bend to kiss him. At last the words come. 'It's not your fault, Donal. There's no call to blame yourself, son. Barry was sick; I knew that. He was dependent on heroin and cocaine for nearly ten years, nearly all his adult life, in fact.'

'Marie, Donal was so shocked and so upset he couldn't think straight. He was convinced he would be blamed for Barry's death if the police knew he'd found Barry's body.'

Donal nods his head at Anaïs. 'I did something that may seem strange, Marie, may seem *wrong*. But I didn't know what else to do. I changed clothes with Barry, so it would be thought it was *me, Robert Carlton*, who was lying there dead. I so much wanted to find you. So I decided I'd come to London and live in Barry's flat for a few days. It appeared to be what Barry wanted me to do. He'd left detailed instructions and information for me to find in case he had died. He must have known how ill he was, and that him dying was a possibility.'

'Oh, he'd have been very organised about it all,' I say, shaking my head. 'He was like that.'

Then Donal shows me a letter he'd found in Barry's apartment from his renal consultant. It set out his need for a *kidney transplant*. He shows me the brochure about the private hospital in Newcastle too.

I realise immediately what one of Barry's main motives was in contacting his brother. Donal doesn't need to explain. I understand.

'I was terrified when I found Barry's body,' Donal tells me, 'and so desperately unhappy. Meeting Barry had been a great joy. A real proper brother! I'd been thrilled to find him – the first relative I'd set eyes on. Now suddenly, he'd been snatched away from me, for ever. I hated having to leave him up there on the cold hillside. It seemed so cruel, but I honestly didn't know what to do next?'

'Yes,' I said slowly, the words shaking me, 'I can't bear to think of him lying up there all alone in the bitter cold. That's a horrible thought.' I wipe the tears now overflowing from my eyes. Donal hugs me close on one side, and Anaïs on the other. We weep together.

***

But what to do next? That's the big question that now faces us all. At first, we all have different views. Donal, poor lad, is afraid that if it's discovered that he's 'stolen Barry's identity' and thereby gained access to his money, home and possessions, he'll have broken the law and will spend the rest of his life in prison. I'm convinced that won't happen. After all, he hasn't spent more than a fraction of what money could have been available to him. Besides, he had letters from Barry specifically telling him to help himself to anything that was his. Nevertheless, Donal wonders if maybe it's best for the world to continue to think he's Barry.

Little Nina, bless her, is already fond of Donal and though she's a bit confused that he looks so like her papa, she would probably just get used to calling him whatever she was told, once the relationship was explained.

The next steps matter a lot to Anaïs. She's suffered at Barry's hands; I know that. She doesn't want Donal to have to become some different version of Barry for the outside world. She wants him to be free to be *himself*, for everything to be out in the open.

I'm not blind. It's plain to me – as plain as anything – that Anaïs is already developing feelings for Donal, and he for her too. Maybe it's too soon, but I can understand her feelings. I love him already. It doesn't take long to realise what a lovely, sensitive, thoughtful, affectionate man he is. Anaïs wants him to remain *Donal*, for there to be no pretence. Maybe they're hoping to be together.

What about me? It's as if my heart is torn in two. I rejoice in being reunited with Donal. That part of my heart sings like a joyous bird in a tree on a summer's day. But I mourn desperately for Barry and the difficulties of his growing up, the sadness of his life, and for the tragedy of his death. For all his faults, he was my son and I loved him: baby, child and flawed adult. I loved him dearly.

The three of us discuss the situation over and over again.

'Donal, I don't feel that you and Barry can somehow *merge*, to become one and the same person. Yes, you were twins, and looked alike, but each of you had unique qualities and characteristics personal to yourself,' I say. 'If you're to be free to live your life honestly and openly, you have to be able to be *yourself*, and not to try to take on Barry's persona. You can't live a lie for the rest of your life. None of us can. That's what I believe.'

Marie and Donal nod their heads solemnly, considering this argument.

'Also,' I continue, 'it's just as important for me to have Barry's death acknowledged as it is to celebrate Donal's life and his return to the family fold. I need to *grieve* for Barry. I need to honour his person, and to rejoice in his life – however troubled it has been.'

'I absolutely agree with that,' says Donal, looking thoughtful.

'There needs to be a proper funeral, and memorial for Barry,' I continue, 'to acknowledge his qualities, and mark his passing. If that is to happen, we all know we have to make contact with the authorities in Newcastle *very soon* to make the arrangements, or else they might dispose of his body. They might assume that as "Robert Carlton" he's without any relatives. I dread to think that might have happened already.'

Donal looks horrified at this possibility. He clearly hadn't thought of that.

'That would be like wiping out the whole of my life, my identity, before meeting Barry,' he says.

***

I'm close to being overwhelmed by all that has happened, and by what needs to be done – immediately. As often at times of stress and doubt, I think of Erna Goldstein, and what she might have advised. I go to her room, where I always feel her spirit lingers. I speak to her and tell her of our predicament. I have always trusted in her wisdom.

***

Later that day, I call the whole family together again. Erna would have believed in consultation, in cooperation and agreement – I'm convinced of that. It's vital to find a way forward with which all of us feel comfortable. So we arrange for a further gathering, in two days' time, when all are free: Donal, Anaïs, Nina and myself, as well as Sylvia – who knew of my plight from when Barry and I were alone and desperate in London – and Elsie, who was there with me at the beginning of Barry and Donal's lives, and has witnessed my trauma of having to give one of them up. Like Sylvia, Elsie has always been my good friend and support. They're all my extended family.

We talk and talk, well into the night, with the coffee pot refilled several times. But in the end, we're all decided; we have agreed a plan of action.

Chapter 42

2004
Donal

It's two weeks since Marie and I met, and I've seen her twice more since, once with Anais, Nina, Sylvia and Elsie and once just the two of us. It feels almost as if I've known her for ever. This morning I wake early, as often my head is still full of the puzzles concerning my brother – his plans, personality and motivations. What sort of a man was he really? A bleak picture is emerging of a complex man apparently with little conscience, little kindness and little ability to genuinely love. If it weren't for the fact that I have been reunited my mother, Marie, I might have felt depressed, and desperately alone.

I sometimes wonder why on earth I ever responded to Barry's letter. In fact, why had I left my life in Newcastle behind, to be immersed in what sometimes felt like a nightmare? All right, I was hard-up and lonely, but my life had at least been relatively peaceful, simple and straightforward. What choices are open to me now?

One thing I've never regretted for a moment is now having Marie in my life, and I'm equally sure that I want to see more and more of my mother, and Anaïs and Nina as well – to really get to know them. I want *them* to know *me* – the *real* me. I want them to recognise that I'm different from Barry, in all sorts of ways.

It's still early, but impulsively, I dial Anaïs's phone number.

''Ello?'

Her voice is croaky with sleep, combined with that delightful French accent, even in a single word. I picture her face.

'Anaïs, it's me … er … Donal. I'm sorry it's so early. Did I wake you?'

'Oh … 'ello Donal. No, it's OK. I was just getting up – it's nice to hear you. Is everything all right?'

'Yes, yes, everything's good. I just wanted to say I had a really special time the other day, at Mum's. I enjoyed seeing you very much … and Nina, of course.'

There's a long pause. I can hear her breathing. 'I enjoyed our day too, and Nina did also. I'm always happy in Marie's company, and you seemed …' She pauses, apparently unsure how to continue.

I take a deep breath. 'What, Anaïs? What did I seem?'

'You seemed relaxed, affectionate … so very different to Barry … kind, warm, emotional … I don't know exactly, but you were very nice, you *are* very nice.'

'You're very nice too, Anaïs, very, very nice.'

'Oh, no need to say that, Donal.'

'I think there is a need, because it's true. Anyway, I'd really like to see you again, and soon. I wondered if Marie – and you and Nina – would like to come *here* for lunch, maybe next Saturday? Of course I can't promise as expert a meal as you made, but I'll do my best. Would you be able to come, Anaïs? Would you *like* to come?'

There's a long silence at the other end of the line. Have I made a mistake in asking her? Might she be uncomfortable contemplating a visit to me away from the security of her own home?

Does she have a new romantic involvement that might make her feel continuing to meet up with me is inappropriate? I hold my breath. I feel nervous as an adolescent arranging a first date.

'Yes, Donal. I would like to come very much,' she says at last.

I exhale, my heart beating hectically.

'I'm really keen to see you again. Nothing formal … just a simple lunch for the four of us … no need to dress up or anything, erm … just come as you are …'

Shut up you idiot, I think, sweating. *'Come as you are' indeed. Maybe she's in her nightdress or her underwear!'*

The still-present adolescent in me tries to repress an exciting image at that thought.

'Donal, you know … it will be a bit odd for me to have lunch in Barry's flat. I have never eaten a meal there before.'

How stupid of me not to think of that. She sounds nervous too, unsure of herself. I can hear her breathing.

'Would you like I bring dessert?' she asks.

'No need for dessert, I'll make something simple … but thank you for offering. Look, Anaïs, I'd just like us all to have a happy, peaceful time together. Maybe a chance for me to get to know you all better. Does that sound all right for you?'

'Yes, I would like that too, and Marie will enjoy it very much.'

***

As the week goes on, I spend time obsessively cleaning and tidying up the apartment. I try to see it through Marie and Anaïs's eyes. Would they see it as Barry's home – somewhere where he should be host, and not me? I remember Anaïs likes flowers. I'm sure Mum would too. On the Friday afternoon I walk to a small green-grocer and florist nearby. I choose a large bunch of deep blue irises and another of creamy white roses. I buy some small things to amuse Nina too: bubbles, some balloons, paper and crayons.

At the flat I arrange the flowers carefully in a simple, tall glass

294

vase I've found at the bottom of a kitchen cupboard. They look beautiful, the colour combination perfect. I imagine Mum and Anaïs seeing them for the first time, as they enter the sitting room.

As lunchtime on the Saturday approaches, I feel increasingly nervous and agitated. It's just as well I was kept busy preparing our meal: a quiche of tomatoes and mushrooms, fresh herbs and thin slices of smoked trout, topped with goat's cheese and a little parmesan. For dessert, I've followed a recipe cut out of the newspaper for a meringue base enclosing a mixture of fresh fruits, topped with a swirl of cream. I fret that I should have asked her what foods Nina likes, or more importantly, doesn't like.

They arrive punctually, for which I'm grateful. The quiche can't wait much longer, and nor can I. Mum smiles her lovely warm smile and hugs me close for several seconds.

'Hello, my dearest boy, my Donal. This is so good of you. What a treat,' she says, looking all about her. It appears Barry has never asked her to his flat before.

Then Anaïs enters and also gives me a hug. I'd nearly forgotten just how gorgeous she is. No, I hadn't. She smiles at me, her head to one side. Next comes Nina. She lifts her arms for me to lift her. I love the feel of her warm little body in my arms.

'Hello, Uncle Donal,' she says.

They look around at everything in the apartment with great interest. Anaïs exclaims in pleasure at the flowers, and Mum comments on the furniture, the floors, the bedroom, the kitchen and the roof garden. She especially likes the roof garden.

'Oh, it's lovely here! Look at all the trees. We could eat our lunch outside!'

'Better wait a couple of months for summer, Mum – it's still a bit chilly for sitting outside. Quite a lot warmer here than in the North East though …'

She smiles at me and takes my hands.

'Then we'll have to come back in the summertime, won't we?' she says.

We retreat inside again. I pour some wine, and some juice for Nina, who is engrossed in blowing bubbles.

Anaïs immediately admires the quiche. She tells me it's the most 'délicieux' quiche she's ever eaten, and asks for a second slice. The fruit meringue is pronounced 'expert' by Mum.

'Where did you ever learn to cook like this, Donal?' she asks.

'Entirely self-taught, Mum, this last fortnight. Before that it was non-stop fish and chips.'

They all laugh.

Nina eats everything without complaint, like the good little French girl she is.

'Donal, you keep this secret – you are cordon bleu! Have you been on a cooking course?' Anaïs says with a smile.

I don't tell her it's the first 'proper' meal I've ever cooked!

Afterwards, Anaïs helps me carry the dishes out to the kitchen, while Mum sits on the sofa. Nina is absorbed in her colouring now. I bring out a box of CDs and select a Saint-Saëns disc to put on the player.

'Some French music for you.'

I return to the sofa and sit next to Mum. She links her arm in mine and leans her head on my shoulder.

'You know, I've dreamt of this for so many years,' she says, 'to have you close, and safe.'

'You might get fed up with me in time,' I joke.

'Never, never, never.'

She leans against me and strokes my hand. We sit with the remains of our wine and we talk and talk. After a while I notice Nina getting a bit restless.

'Mum, Anaïs, it's such a nice day. Would you like to come out for a walk? Nina might enjoy it. I can show you something of this area – Primrose Hill, Regent's Park, and the zoo ...?'

'Oh yes, I like that very much. I don't really know this part of London,' Anaïs says, and Mum agrees.

***

We walk for about an hour, talking all the time. Mum clings firmly to my left arm for the entire walk. Anaïs slips her arm into my right one periodically, and Nina skips along chattering about everything she sees.

As we stand watching ducks and other birds drifting lazily on one of the ponds, on impulse I reach out and stroke Anaïs's hair. She does not pull it away. Mum smiles up at me. We head for the zoo and I tell them all how I like hearing the animals' noises. We decide to walk around the outside fence and save a proper visit for next time.

We play a game of listening and taking turns to guess what animal is making each noise. There's a roar.

'A lion?' suggests Mum.

'Hmm … an elephant perhaps?' says Anaïs.

'No … Sounds more like a big ape to me. A gorilla maybe?'

'Oh? You know him? Is he one of your cousins, Donal?' she says teasingly. Nina laughs and makes ape-like noises. Mum watches us, her head to one side.

Each minute that passes, I feel any stiffness, awkwardness between us gradually dissipating. Mum glances at me frequently, like she can't believe I'm really there. We spot a café in the park and head for it to warm up with coffees, and hot chocolate for Nina.

The afternoon is growing cooler, the shadows longer. The sun has sunk behind the trees.

'It's very beautiful here. I've so enjoyed our day together today, Donal,' says Mum. 'I only wish Barry could have shared it too.' She looks sad and pensive. I squeeze her hand.

'Anyway, my children, just look at Nina. She's nearly asleep on her feet. I think maybe it's time for us to take her home now.'

'All right, let's head back to my flat and pick up your things. Then I'll take you to the tube station.'

***

297

As their tube train rumbles towards us, we give each other more hugs. I want this time to last for ever. I help Mum into the carriage. Anaïs pauses and gazes up at my face.

'I really want to see you again soon, Anaïs,' I say quietly. 'I want to see you very, very soon.'

'I would like that too, Donal.'

'I'll ring you.'

'Yes. Ring me tomorrow,' she says as she extricates herself from my embrace.

I lift Nina on. The train doors shut. Mum and Anaïs stand inside, hands pressed against the glass of the door and watch me. Nina waves. Just as the train is moving out of my field of vision, Anaïs raises her hand towards me.

I watch them disappear into the tunnel, feeling very alone suddenly.

Chapter 43

2004
Donal

The following morning, there's a tentative knock on the door of the flat. I open it, and there stands Mrs Winkelman shifting nervously from foot to foot. She gives a start on seeing me, as if she hadn't really expected me to open the door to her.

'Esther – how nice to see you,' I say. 'Won't you come in?'

She hesitates on the spot. 'Well … er … Barry, you see, that was exactly why I've come. I … I wondered if *you* would like to come to *me* – to my flat I mean – for a cup of tea or coffee? Perhaps this afternoon or Wednesday morning – if you're not too busy, that is?'

'Well thank you, Esther, it would be lovely. How kind of you – this afternoon would suit me fine. I'd really enjoy that. What time would you like me to come?'

Mrs Winkelman's face breaks into a smile of delight and some surprise, as if she'd expected me to decline her invitation.

'Oh, well, that's very good … yes … good … um … shall we say about three-thirty this afternoon then?'

'Three-thirty would be fine – thank you, Esther, see you this afternoon. I look forward to it. Be careful on the stairs going down, won't you?'

***

Mrs Winkelman is very hospitable in her shy and self-effacing way. She leads me into her sitting room. Her flat is not unlike Barry's in its dimensions – a bit smaller, and without the sloping ceilings and roof garden. It's decorated and furnished in a much more traditional, old-fashioned style – a bit flowery and fussy. It feels warm and comfortable, and has a faint powdery 'old lady' smell, and a more fusty smell too, of times gone by. I remind myself she thinks I'm Barry.

'I think your apartment is rather lighter than mine, Barry,' she comments, seeing me looking about the room. 'I suppose it's partly having those big glass doors leading to the roof garden.'

I gaze at the heavy velvet curtains reaching from the ceiling to the floor.

Esther pours me a cup of slightly weak coffee and passes me a plate of oaty-looking biscuits.

'Have you made these yourself, Esther?'

She smiles and blushes slightly.

'Yes, actually, I have. I do hope they're all right? It's so nice to have a visitor to bake for – I don't have many visitors … and most people seem to be on diets these days. It's a recipe my mother used to make.'

'Well, probably I should be on a diet too, but these are *delicious*! I'm honoured that you made them for me. In fact, I'd love another, if that's allowed.'

'Oh goodness, Barry, you don't need to lose weight!' Esther passes the biscuit plate to me in delight. 'You're just right as you

are. Oh … oh … I'm sorry. I didn't mean to be personal …'
Esther blushes in confusion.

'Not at all, Esther. Thank you for the compliment. Far too many people fuss about their figures, don't you think?'

'Well, you'll have to take some home with you, I can't possibly eat them all myself …'

She folds her hands on her lap, and gives me a long, pensive look, her head to one side, as if trying to work out some mystery about me, something that was puzzling her.

'Barry?' she says, twiddling her fingers diffidently. 'I do hope you won't mind me saying this … but you seem to have … well … you seem to have *changed* in some way.'

'Oh?' I reply cautiously. 'The beard maybe?'

A chill envelops me suddenly, despite the rampant central heating.

'Yes … no it's not that, Barry. You've lived here for a while, and … I don't want to be rude … or over-personal … but … oh dear, Mother always criticised me for being too personal, and too nosy!'

'Mmm? Go on, Esther, ask away. I don't mind.'

'Well … you see, until very recently I was a bit concerned about you. Please don't be offended … but you didn't look awfully well, and you seemed rather withdrawn … rather depressed, I would say. In all the time you were here, I don't think you exchanged two words with me or any of the other neighbours, except maybe to greet Hector – you know, the jogger? – and he's such a cheery, hearty sort, he talks to everyone …'

She hesitates. 'I just wondered if anything had happened? I wondered if perhaps you had had some … sort of … *treatment*?

This question is so unexpected and I'm so taken aback by it that I roar with laughter, rather louder than I had intended.

Esther puts her bony hands up to her mouth and looks at me in alarm.

'Oh, I see! So you thought maybe I was *mad*, did you, Esther?'

'Oh no, no! No, of course not … I didn't say *that*, Barry …

I'm sorry, I really didn't mean to cause offence. Oh, I always say the wrong thing ...' she mumbles in confusion.

'No, don't worry. I'm not offended, not in the least. You're absolutely right – I've been a terrible grump since I moved here. I'm afraid things had all been very difficult a while – everything seemed to go wrong at once. I had problems at work, I wasn't very well, and I separated from my wife – so it wasn't a very happy time. I got pretty downhearted about it. It's observant of you to notice. But recently I'm making a conscious effort to put things right, and that's made me feel much better. I'm sorry if I appeared to be unfriendly before.'

I feel guilty about being so dishonest with her, but now is not the time to reveal the truth about my identity. She smiles at me in a sweet, shy way and pats my knee, as if I'm a schoolboy who has just bravely admitted to a misdemeanour.

Mr Lewis, my old drama teacher, would have been proud of me. He always did think I was a talented actor.

Chapter 44

2004
Donal

I can't settle this evening, my whole body tense with excitement; my head is full of images of Anaïs and her little daughter, and our times together. I hardly know her, I remind myself. Logic and good sense tell me to give her, and myself, time to think about the direction we appear to be heading, not to make assumptions, not to rush. But good sense gives way to the intensity of longing. I want to ring her *now*, this minute. I want to hear her voice again, but I know I shouldn't put pressure on her. I'm being ridiculous; like a love-sick schoolboy. I should act my age. *'Don't expect too much too soon,'* I mutter.

At that moment, the phone rings. I nearly jump out of my skin. My heart thunders.

'Hello?' I quaver.

'Donal? I just want to say thank you for the nice lunch, and the walk. It was such a lovely time. I liked being with you … very much. Marie was so happy. Nina also.'

'I enjoyed it too Anaïs. It was so … wonderful … so special. Can we meet again soon?'

'Yes. When would you like?'

'How about tomorrow? Shall I come to your house tomorrow?'

She laughs. 'Well, you could … but maybe you prefer I come to you?'

'Either way I'm happy, but what about Nina?'

'I'm free tomorrow, Donal … Nina will be in school and then having a sleepover with her friend Lola. Lola's mummy looking after her two days and nights. We take turns. Next time Lola comes to us.'

I take a deep breath. 'I see. Well, I'll love to see Nina again. She's such a sweet child. But … why don't you come to me this time, and I'll accompany you home … whenever you want.'

'OK, good. We can spend the day together, and I'll bring a simple picnic lunch.'

'Perfect. I'll provide the picnic wine.'

She gives a little laugh. 'OK then. See you tomorrow, Donal.'

'See you tomorrow, Anaïs …'

***

The day turns out to be fine and unseasonably mild. The sun's warmth is still gentle rather than strong, but sheltered from the breeze it's warm enough to be outside without coats or jackets. We decide to have our lunch on the roof garden. Anaïs is delighted with the view.

'Oh it's so beautiful! Like a park or a huge garden. It is magical. Such tall trees – oh, and look! There is a squirrel! Oh, Nina would love to see! Look, look, Donal! See how he runs round and round the trunk of the tree there! I think he is happy that spring is coming, don't you?'

I love her uninhibited enthusiasm. It's a joy to see that she shares my own pleasure in my temporary new home. Suddenly it feels like a real *home*, not just somewhere circumstances have decreed I should live.

We lean over the railing to watch as the squirrel disappears in a tangle of smaller trees and bushes. I spontaneously put my arm loosely round her shoulders. She glances at me, smiling, and does not resist.

After lunch we go inside to finish our wine. She tells me about her family in France, how she misses her mother who had died of cancer some years before, and how special Marie has become – like a second mother to her. I try hard to make sensitive and appropriate responses. I want to show my understanding of her sadness, and her appreciation of Marie – *my mother*. I would have loved to explore Anaïs's relationship with Marie, and her experience of her as a person, but it seems an area fraught with possible dangers, in view of Barry's difficult relationship both with his mother and his wife. Far easier to change to more neutral territory.

'Anaïs, would you like to go for a little walk along the canal while it's so fine? It's still getting dark quite early these days. Maybe we shouldn't leave it too late? Then I can take you back to the station, if you like.'

She looks a little surprised, but quickly agrees that she would enjoy a walk.

We amble along the towpath, looking at the houseboats, light-heartedly discussing what it would be like to live in a boat. Anaïs tells me she's never been to Camden Market, so we make our way there, fighting through the cosmopolitan crowds. Anaïs loves it – she comments with excitement on every stall: the jewellery, the clothes, the fragrant foods of every type. Spontaneously I ask her what her favourite colour is. 'It's turquoise! Why?' she says with a laugh.

'Oh, no reason. Just curiosity.'

We find a little pop-up café and order coffee. When I finish mine, I ask Anaïs to excuse me a moment, as if I need to find a gents' toilet. She nods amiably, stretching in the sunshine like a cat.

I rush off to find a stall I've noticed, with hand-made jewellery of semi-precious stones. The man shows me all he has in turquoise. He explains where each item comes from. He's travelled widely, he says, in Turkey and the Middle East, in China and South America, always searching for beautiful pieces of jewellery, but at a reasonable price. I choose a delicate bracelet of a series of turquoise stones set in antique silver. It's made in Turkey, the man tells me, and is neither too heavy and large, nor is it ostentatious. I can imagine it encircling Anaïs's wrist. The man puts it in a small plain box. I pay him and put it away in my pocket.

Anaïs smiles and stands up when I return to her. We walk slowly along the canal back to my apartment.

'That was lovely,' she says when we arrive at my flat. 'I love the market! I've heard about it, but never saw it before.'

'I'm glad you liked it. What do you want to do now? Shall I come to the tube station with you, or would you like something to eat first?'

'Neither,' she replies. 'I'm not hungry, and I don't want to go home yet. I would like to hear some music. You had that blues CD I saw last time. Will you play that?'

We sit on the sofa together.

'I got a little present for you, Anaïs.' I hand her the box.

She looks astonished. 'It's for me?'

I nod.

She opens it slowly, carefully, and then gasps.

'Oh … it's beautiful, beautiful. Donal … thank you.' Her eyes fill with tears. I wipe them away gently with my thumb and fasten the bracelet round her wrist. She smiles at me, shaking her head a little.

The music fills the room. Anaïs takes my hand and taps out the rhythm softly on my fingers. I look at her and she holds my gaze. Her body sways to the music. I raise her hand to my mouth and kiss it. She touches my hand to her cheek and closes her eyes.

'Anaïs …' I begin.

She puts a finger to my lips to shush me. She stands up and gently pulls me up too. I put my arms around her and pull her close to me. She does not resist. Her arms encircle my waist. We move slowly to the music. I feel her body softening and merging with mine. I kiss the top of her head, breathing in the fragrance of her hair. She raises her face. I kiss her very gently on the lips. I want her desperately, but is it too soon? Is it really what *she* wants too?

The music has ended. I extricate myself from our embrace, choose another disc and the music starts up again.

'I'll make us some coffee …' I say. She puts her head on one side and smiles at me. She stretches out on the sofa, while I make us both coffee. We don't drink it. We sit side by side, gazing at one another. Her eyes are dark, the pupils huge as saucers. I stroke back the hair that has fallen over her forehead. We both know we've reached a boundary, but neither of us wants to reverse, or even stay still. She takes my hand and kisses the fingers, one at a time. I trace the outline of her lips with my finger, and then kiss them. Anaïs stands up and, holding my hand, pulls me to the bedroom.

***

Moonlight seeps through a gap in the curtain and makes patterns on the wall beside the bed. We lie side by side, blissfully exhausted. She strokes my chest, softly, rhythmically. I run my fingers slowly along her arm and neck, spent, but thrilled by the depth of our feelings. She gazes at me in the shadowy gloom of the room, lit only by the light of the moon.

Suddenly she half sits up, propping herself on her elbow and looking into my eyes. She watches me in silence for several minutes.

'Donal,' she whispers at last, 'I want to know … is it all

right? Are these feelings all right, do you think, after all that has happened? You know I was married to your brother. It's not wrong is it, that I am … enjoying being with you? It's not as if I am … betraying Barry, is it?'

My heart lurches.

It is several minutes before I can speak. Her eyes are fixed on my face.

'Please believe me, I didn't consciously plan for us to sleep together today. Surely our feelings can't be wrong. Strange and tragic circumstances have brought us together, but I think I felt for you from the first time I saw you. Those feelings are spontaneous. I know it's harder for you. You were Barry's wife after all.'

'Yes, I was married to Barry for some years, it is true. At the beginning he loved me. In his way he loved me. But he was not gentle, not kind, not considerate, not thoughtful of my feelings. You are all these things. You are a very different man to Barry. I don't feel I am deceiving him. Our marriage was over long before you and I met.'

'Anaïs, you're a beautiful, warm, wonderful woman, and I think I've fallen in love with you.'

She lies down again, on her side, looking at me pensively as I speak.

'Do you know, one thing that first drew me to you, Anaïs, was that you called me *"Donal"* from the start. All my life people have called me Robert or variations of that name, because Robert was the name I was given legally by my adoptive parents, who gave me up when I was two years old. Then I was variously called Rob, Robert, Bobby, Bob in the children's homes I grew up in, until my wonderful foster parents, Len and Betty, called me Robbie. It was Barry who told me I'd been named *Donal* by our mother. When you started calling me Donal, it was as if you'd given me back my true identity.'

I stop to take a much-needed breath.

'I never knew I had a brother until Barry wrote to me, out

of the blue, and we met briefly in Durham and then York. I was really eager to meet up with him the third time, in the hills – to get to know him properly. I hoped perhaps through him to meet, and *know*, the rest of my family. But when I found him … and he was dead … it was terrible. I knew immediately he was dead, Anaïs. I was so sad, so upset – and so scared.

'I never planned any it – I just didn't know what to do when I found him dead.

'So when I changed clothes with him, I suppose at first I thought maybe I could just take his place in the family. I know it was stupid, illogical – it didn't make sense, but I so much wanted a family. I wanted my mother. I didn't mean to trick you, any of you. I didn't mean to deceive you. I'm sorry … but … I didn't expect to fall in love with you …'

She wraps her arms around my neck and rests her head on my shoulder. I stroke her hair.

'Will you go on calling me Donal, Anaïs?' I whisper.

She looks at me contemplatively for a long time. Her dark eyes fill with tears. She rests her head on my chest and strokes my shoulder.

'Yes, of course I will call you *Donal* … always, I will call you Donal, because that is the name you were always meant to have. It is the name your mother, Marie, called you when you were born.

'It is what she always called you when she spoke of you, which she did very, very often, and still does, because she has loved you – and longed for you – every day of her life, every single day since the sisters forced her to give you away …'

Anaïs sits up and looks at me. 'And, Donal, you should know that I too have fallen in love with *you*.'

She holds me, holds me tightly, while I weep.

Chapter 45

2004
Donal

Anaïs does not go back to Blackheath that night; she remains with me in my apartment, in my bed. Neither do we have much sleep; there is so much for her to share with me, and so much for me to share with her. We talk and talk.

Firstly, I tell her more about Barry's initial letter to me, requesting that I meet him; I actually show it to her. I tell her how taken aback I was to receive it, to hear of a brother of whose existence I knew nothing at all.

I explain about my initial reluctance to meet him, and my subsequent decision that I *would* meet this only relation that I knew of. I tell Anaïs of my excitement and thrill – as well as my *terror* – at the prospect of meeting him and getting to know him. She strokes my forehead sympathetically.

Next, I tell her the full story, the details of what happened the day I first went to meet Barry in Durham, and how odd he looked with his beard and his hat and his sunglasses.

'No!' Anaïs exclaims several times during the account. 'He pretended he had glaucoma?! Ah, so now I know why he grew that beard suddenly. We all wondered why he decide to grow one. I suppose he didn't want people to see you together, looking the same, hmm? Looking like twins.'

I remind Anaïs how the newspaper article had got some crucial details wrong: of course it was not *me*, '*Robert Carlton*', who had been found dead in the heather on the top of a remote hill in the Cheviots as the paper claimed – it was Anaïs's ex-husband, my brother: *Barry Tully*. She exhales and shakes her head to imagine the scene.

I go on to explain that when I found Barry dead, I was very shocked and deeply frightened, and totally unsure what to do next. Up there on that isolated, cold place, it was only after a while of fear, sorrow and confusion, that a tentative idea developed, and ultimately became a decision to change clothes, and temporarily change identities, with my brother. At first, I had been tempted simply by a desire to be close to Barry, to hold him and embrace him, even though I knew he was dead. Yes, I admit, then I was finally drawn predominantly by my longing for the contact with a real family, above all, *a mother*.

I describe for Anaïs my former life: the harshness and emptiness of my childhood, the lack of any warmth or love until Len and Betty took me to their home and their hearts, only to die before I was old enough or ready enough to live confidently in the world. She shakes her head in sympathy. She presses my head to her breast, and murmurs '*Mon pauvre, mon pauvre* Donal.' Her tears scald my cheeks.

***

Anaïs tells me how Barry had been possessive from the very start of their relationship. At first she had thought it was due to the depth, the intensity of his love for her. She was initially flattered.

As time went on he had become increasingly controlling, checking up on her every move, isolating her from her family and friends. To the outside world he appeared a devoted husband – but at home his obsession with her and his unpredictable mood swings became oppressive, and more and more threatening.

He kept his drugs habit concealed during the early years of their marriage, but gradually Anaïs began to suspect. When she asked him about her suspicions, he became uncontrollably angry, and violent towards her for the first time.

It was Marie who confronted Barry about his drug-taking, and his abuse towards his wife, and his impatience and anger, even with his infant daughter Nina. Furious with her son, Marie responded with threats of her own by telling Barry she would disinherit him if violence, or threatened violence, *ever* occurred again – thereby targeting one of the areas that she knew meant the most to him: *money*.

To Marie's sorrow, the marriage had been crumbling day by day. With her support, they separated – Anaïs and Nina moving to their small house, and what they hoped was a place of safety. Barry was not provided with keys. He sold his flat in Putney, and moved to one in north London, some distance away from Blackheath – the flat she and Donal now inhabited.

For the first year or two apart, Anaïs's trusting nature led her to hope that in time Barry would somehow be helped to come off drugs, regain his failing health, and see the error of his ways. She even hoped that, one day, perhaps a reconciliation might be possible.

She could not be so tolerant or forgiving of his threatening behaviour towards their child.

***

Eventually, physically and emotionally exhausted, Anaïs and I drift into sleep for a few hours. It's an unbelievable joy for me to wake in her arms, lying in her gentle embrace the following morning – to know our union has been real and not a dream.

Having breakfast together that morning is a new experience for me. Apart from the brief time with Tracy, the last time I've had company at breakfast was when I lived with Len and Betty.

While Anaïs showers, I rush round the corner to buy some fresh croissants. Seeing her in my dressing gown, pottering contentedly in the kitchen to make a pot of coffee is sheer delight for me. There's an intimacy in the simple activity of preparing breakfast together – almost greater than our lovemaking. It brings a lump to my throat. I feel intensely happy, ridiculously happy. I put my arms round her and hug her, breathing in the soft scent at the base of her neck.

'What?' she says, turning to face me with a smile, returning my embrace.

'You're wonderful.'

'You are wonderful too …'

Chapter 46

2004
Donal

My mother, Mum, Marie – how strange and how lovely it is to have someone to call Mum! I love saying all her names. She is such a wise, warm-hearted woman, such a brave woman too. I don't have to think about whether I love her. It's as if I always have. It's hardly two weeks since we met, but it feels much, much longer. A part of me feels I have always known her. Yet, if only we could have come together sooner, how wonderful that could have been. All those sad and difficult years gone by ... But, as she said, we shouldn't grieve for what hasn't been, we should be happy with what has happened now. She's right, but how different life could have been for both of us if we'd never been separated. I know how much she's suffered through missing me, her son – and I could certainly have done with her love and support – just her maternal *presence* over all those many harsh years.

How I wish she had *both* her sons, both restored to her as

she'd yearned for … but that's never to be, never again. We'll both miss Barry for ever more.

With Mum's guidance, by the end of our day of family discussion, we'd decided to engage a lawyer and to contact the police in Newcastle. We agreed I would be open and honest about all that has occurred. It feels somehow redemptive and liberating to know that everything is to be revealed; there will be no more secrets. But it also feels a risky and frightening path for me to follow. It scares me, but it's Mum who gives me strength.

We found a lawyer specialising in complex family enigmas and disputes. He quickly grasped the situation and was encouraging in his absolute agreement with our plan to reveal the full truth of Barry's and my identity, exactly what occurred at our planned meeting in the Cheviots, and what has happened since then.

Mum was relieved to learn that a full post-mortem has confirmed absolutely that Barry died of natural causes – kidney failure leading to a heart attack. There was no question of foul play. Mum was assured his death would have been sudden and quick, any suffering brief, for which we were all thankful. Barry's body is to be released for the family to arrange a funeral as they wish.

The police talked to me in strong terms about the seriousness of identity fraud, but they concluded that I was not motivated by financial gain, nor other sinister purpose. The excellent lawyer also explained that I had been extremely shocked and distressed to find Barry dead, and therefore could not be regarded as acting rationally. So, to my enormous relief, the police decided not to charge me.

All the family agreed that no one has suffered by my initial deceit in pretending to be my brother. In fact, Mum asserted that Barry had himself benefitted greatly from educational and financial advantages, and the generosity of Erna Goldstein for nearly forty years – advantages which I, as his twin brother, should strictly have shared. So, it is agreed that any financial gains I might have briefly acquired by adopting Barry's identity should be sorted out within the family.

315

The Crown Prosecution Service decided that, in the circumstances, nothing is to be gained by pursuing a prosecution. I am free to go, they said. We are all free to go and get on with our lives. A huge weight is lifted from my shoulders.

**

Barry's body is brought to London for the funeral. Mum wants him buried near her friend and his, Erna Goldstein, who had been so fond of Barry. I get the impression that Barry's feelings for Erna were the nearest he came to loving anyone, but I don't share that thought with Mum.

It's a sad little ceremony – Mum, Anaïs, Nina and me – and Mum's good friends Sylvia and Elsie, whom I'd met last week. My family's growing bigger by the day! So, that's it: six mourners. Not much to show for nearly forty years of life – but probably more than *I* would have attracted if I'd died before making contact with my family. Apart from dear Belle, bless her.

Once the funeral is over, it feels as though we can all look to the future. With everyone's agreement, I let it be known to my small circle of new friends and acquaintances, who know nothing of my background or Barry's – people like Oliver at the café, Hector the runner downstairs, and Esther my other downstairs neighbour – that I've decided to change my name from Barry to Donal. It was my original name, I tell them – the last untruth I ever want to tell.

I don't feel it's necessary to tell these recent contacts the *exact* truth about having taken my brother's name and identity, but neither do I want any further lies to persist. So I just explain that I'd been named Donal as a baby by my birth mother, but that my adoptive parents had given me a different name, as was their right. Now that I'm in close contact with my birth mother, it feels right to use my true original name. Nobody expresses suspicion, or even surprise, at this news. My explanation is

316

accepted without question, and gradually people become used to calling me Donal.

Mum and I arrange to get a duplicate birth certificate sent to me. Now Donal Tully really exists.– *I'm Donal, and he's me*! No one can argue with that. My newfound proof of identity enables me to replace my fake driving licence with a real, official one in my true name. I'm able to register with a GP and a dentist, even request a passport. As Robert Carlton I had never attempted to obtain any of these documents, other than one allowing me social security payments.

I'm suddenly aware of how very fragile my hold on existence had been. As the official documents build up, so too does my confidence, my sense of my own reality, my own identity.

Step by step we arrange other changes to my life. Much as I like Barry's apartment, I want a home that's mine, Donal's not Barry's. I want to be closer to Mum, and above all, I want to live with Anaïs and Nina. We agree there have been enough changes in Nina's young life for the time being, and that one stability we can arrange is for the three of us to live together in Anaïs and Nina's house in Blackheath. After a couple of years, we may consider moving somewhere different, but there is no urgency for that step.

Chapter 47

2005
Marie

Donal and I have long discussions together. We had so many years to catch up on. It's his suggestion to arrange a visit to Ma in Ireland as a priority, before it's too late. I show him a letter, left for me by Erna Goldstein just before her death, in which she urges me to make contact with my family, to arrange to visit them before it's too late. Not that I hadn't tried before, but Da ruled the roost at home, and had told Ma and all the family I'd emigrated and was out of contact. It was only after his death they discovered that was untrue and I'd written regular letters home, all secretly hidden away in Da's desk. Since then, Bridie and I have been in weekly contact. She, Ma and my brothers and sisters couldn't wait to see me and 'the boys'. Sadly, I had to tell them all of Barry's passing, but they all longed for the rest of us to visit. At eighty-seven Ma's too frail to make the journey to England.

***

So here we are – Donal, Anaïs, Nina and I – just arrived at the airport in Ireland. My brother Jack meets us and drives us the distance to the village I left as a girl of barely eighteen. I'm amazed at the wide new roads that have replaced the narrow, rough lanes, and the smart new houses that have grown up at the edge of the village. I notice the green is still there; the site of the fair all those years ago, the site of my 'downfall'. There's a bright, new children's playground on one side, and at the edge, colourful flower beds that hadn't been there before. The pub has a few more tables outside, but is otherwise unchanged. Jack drives out of the village and on to the farm. I'm astonished to see the little house has been extended and two new barns built across the yard. How grand it looks!

Sadly, my eldest brother Shaun had died in an accident with the tractor some years before. It's Jack who runs the farm now. Bridie had said all the family are dying to meet us. They're all there; Ma of course, and Bridie, Nuala, Grace and Ava, my 'little' sisters, now ageing ladies like myself! Also Jack's wife, my four brothers-in-law and my sister-in-law, Shaun's widow, and all the great horde of their children and grandchildren. Donal can't believe he's part of such a large tribe! No way can we match them in numbers, but our little family group is reinforced by Anaïs – now Donal's wife – who was eager to come with us, and Nina, of course.

There are hugs and tears galore, and plenty of good Irish craic. Nina is passed from her grandmother to her aunties and great-aunts, to be admired and kissed and chatted to. She impresses them all by changing from speaking French to English and back again at the drop of a hat.

Two long tables are fair groaning under all the food, and there's gallons of drink to ease the conversation along, not that we need it. Neighbours from miles around arrive to have a jar and cast their eyes on the family's 'English contingent'. Half the night is taken up with music and dancing, and the wee ones skipping about in the middle of it all 'til they're shooed off to

319

bed or drop asleep on the floor. I'd nearly forgotten how we Irish can enjoy a shindig.

Ma and I can hardly take our eyes off each other. She keeps a hold of my hand all the evening long, shaking her head in wonder from time to time, her sodden handkerchief clutched in one hand, the tears a steady stream down her cheeks.

The days that follow are taken up with catching up on family news that stretches over the previous thirty-five years or so, our throats sore from the endless talk.

'I wish I could have met Mrs Goldstein,' Ma says to me as we're preparing to leave. 'I'd have thanked her for taking in my precious daughter, sure I would, and poor baby Barry, bless him.'

'I thanked her enough times for both of us, Ma,' I tell her.

***

Just as we're setting off for home, Jack tells us to come and look what he's given Ma. It's a fine-looking computer.

'You'll never need be out of touch again,' he says. 'Skype. You'll be able to talk and *see each other*, just as if you're in the room together. We'll show you how to do it, Ma.'

Ma nods happily at the thought, but I must have looked anxious for a moment. I've never progressed beyond the little colour television Erna had given me years before – still working, but a bit fuzzy these days. I've never moved onto computers. Would we manage all the fancy new technology? Donal steps forward, smiling. He puts his arm around me and squeezes me.

'Don't worry, Mum, Jack and I have been talking about it. I've already ordered a bigger colour television for you, to replace your little one. *And* we'll get you all set up with a simple computer and all you need for Skype at home. I'll show you just what to do. It's easy when you know how, and Jack's been showing me.'

***

And so it is. I talk to Ma four or five times a week. There she is on my screen; we can see each other just like in the flesh. What a miracle technology is! Another visit to Ireland is planned for Christmas time too.

And Donal? That miracle doesn't need technology at all. He and I see one another every other day and I still can't get enough of him! Next month the four of us – Donal, Anaïs, Nina and I – are going to France to visit Anaïs's family, and have a holiday in the golden sunshine of the south.

The loss of Barry is a deep pain I'll have to live with for ever, I know that. He had so many positive qualities, but like most of us, he had his flaws too, and perhaps he allowed those to dominate sometimes. I hope he knew how much I loved him, and that I always will.

Acknowledgements

My huge thanks and appreciation go to my dedicated and meticulous editor, Cicely Aspinall, for her consistent expertise.

Grateful thanks, too, to Bill Goodall, my literary agent, whose support and calm wisdom helped steer me through some moments of panic.

Dear Reader,

We hope you enjoyed reading this book. If you did, we'd be so appreciative if you left a review. It really helps us and the author to bring more books like this to you.

Here at HQ Digital we are dedicated to publishing fiction that will keep you turning the pages into the early hours. Don't want to miss a thing? To find out more about our books, promotions, discover exclusive content and enter competitions you can keep in touch in the following ways:

JOIN OUR COMMUNITY:

Sign up to our new email newsletter: hyperurl.co/hqnewsletter

Read our new blog www.hqstories.co.uk

🐦 https://twitter.com/HQStories

f www.facebook.com/HQStories

BUDDING WRITER?

We're also looking for authors to join the HQ Digital family!
Find out more here:

https://www.hqstories.co.uk/want-to-write-for-us/

Thanks for reading, from the HQ Digital team

If you enjoyed *The Lost Twin*, then why not try another gripping and emotional novel from HQ Digital?